DEN OF
INIQUITY

ALSO BY J. A. JANCE

J. P. BEAUMONT MYSTERIES

Until Proven Guilty
Injustice for All
Trial by Fury
Taking the Fifth
Improbable Cause
A More Perfect Union
Dismissed with Prejudice
Minor in Possession
Payment in Kind
Without Due Process
Failure to Appear
Lying in Wait
Name Withheld
Breach of Duty
Birds of Prey

Partner in Crime: A J. P. Beaumont and
Joanna Brady Novel
Long Time Gone
Justice Denied
Fire and Ice: A J. P. Beaumont and Joanna
Brady Novel
Betrayal of Trust
Ring in the Dead (Novella)
Second Watch
Stand Down (Novella)
Dance of the Bones: A J. P. Beaumont and
Brandon Walker Novel
Still Dead (Novella)
Proof of Life
Sins of the Fathers
Nothing to Lose

JOANNA BRADY MYSTERIES

Desert Heat
Tombstone Courage
Shoot Don't Shoot
Dead to Rights
Skeleton Canyon
Rattlesnake Crossing
Outlaw Mountain
Devil's Claw
Paradise Lost
Partner in Crime: A J. P. Beaumont and
Joanna Brady Novel
Exit Wounds
Dead Wrong
Damage Control

Fire and Ice: A J. P. Beaumont and Joanna
Brady Novel
Judgment Call
The Old Blue Line (Novella)
Remains of Innocence
No Honor Among Thieves: An Ali
Reynolds and Joanna Brady Novella
Random Acts: A Joanna Brady and Ali
Reynolds Novella
Downfall
Field of Bones
Missing and Endangered
Blessing of the Lost Girls: A Brady and
Walker Family Novel

DEN OF INIQUITY

A J. P. BEAUMONT NOVEL

J. A. JANCE

WILLIAM MORROW

An Imprint of HarperCollins*Publishers*

DEN OF INIQUITY. Copyright © 2024 by J. A. Jance. All rights reserved. Printed in the United States of America. No part of this book may be used or reproduced in any manner whatsoever without written permission except in the case of brief quotations embodied in critical articles and reviews. For information, address HarperCollins Publishers, 195 Broadway, New York, NY 10007.

HarperCollins books may be purchased for educational, business, or sales promotional use. For information, please email the Special Markets Department at SPsales@harpercollins.com.

FIRST EDITION

Designed by Michele Cameron

Library of Congress Cataloging-in-Publication Data has been applied for.

ISBN 978-0-06-325258-5

24 25 26 27 28 LBC 5 4 3 2 1

In memory of Yolanda from my homeroom at Bisbee High

DEN OF
INIQUITY

PROLOGUE

Seattle, Washington
Thursday, November 22, 2018

THANKSGIVING DAY 2018 DAWNED DARK, COLD, RAINY, AND windy as hell in Seattle, Washington. That's hardly surprising. November in the Pacific Northwest is always dark and rainy. But on this day in particular, the steady downpour was accompanied by a raw wind blowing down from the north. A seemingly endless line of people stood outside a dilapidated brick warehouse on Seattle's somewhat seedy waterfront where there was zero shelter from the weather. They hunkered down there, hoping that once they stepped into the warehouse turned food bank they'd find a little warmth from the bone-chilling cold as well as a free Turkey Day dinner.

Inside an army of volunteers from various churches all over the city scurried around arranging tables and chairs, setting up serving lines, and putting out the food. By the time the doors opened promptly at ten A.M., the people waiting outside had been there for so long that a few of them were becoming belligerent.

That was not unexpected, and several of the heftier members of the volunteer crew had been drafted to provide security and maintain order. One of those was Darius Jackson, a member of the crew from the Mount Zion Baptist Church. He was six four and two hundred and eighty pounds. One look from him was generally enough to settle whatever trouble might be brewing among those waiting for their share of turkey, dressing, mashed potatoes, and gravy.

Not long ago, Darius would likely have been on the receiving end of one of those free dinners. Now thanks to his grandmother Matilda Jackson, he was out of jail, back on the straight and narrow, and working as a bouncer for a popular but sketchy bar on Rainier Avenue South. The place was owned by someone who was a friend of one of his grandmother's many friends and acquaintances. When Darius had agreed to accept the job offer, Granny had taken him to the woodshed and given him the lay of the land.

"It's a job," she told him, "and you need a job right now. I don't approve of drinking, but there aren't that many places that will give someone like you so much as a second chance to say nothing of a job. But just because you work in a place like that doesn't mean you've got a license to be drinking. You're living with me now instead of out on the streets or in some homeless camp. You come home with booze on your breath, you're out. Understand?"

"Yes, ma'am," he said. "Got it."

"And on Sunday mornings you'd best be dressed in your good clothes and have your butt on the pew right next to me when services start at Mount Zion."

"Got that, too," he replied.

That conversation had occurred months earlier, but Darius was still taking it to heart. He was working the same job and was still living in his grandmother's place just off Martin Luther King Way in the Rainier Valley. As a seventh grader, abandoned by his drug-addicted mother, living with Grandma Jackson had been mandatory rather than optional. The judge had given him a choice—go to juvie until he turned twenty-one or take probation and go live with his grandmother. He had chosen door number two. No matter how late he got off shift on Sunday mornings, she made sure he was present and accounted for at Mount Zion's morning services, but back when he was a kid and there under duress, he'd slept through a lot of it and paid scant attention to the rest. At the time all that crap about loving your neighbor as yourself just didn't grab him.

Unsurprisingly, once in high school, Darius had taken up with the wrong crowd, which had led him straight into the arms of the wrong kind of girl. Gypsy Tomkins had been bad news from the get-go. She was a wild child who was beautiful but tough as nails. Once she had Darius in her clutches, everything his grandmother had ever tried to teach him went out the window. Compared to him, Gypsy had been tiny—five two and barely a hundred pounds soaking wet—but from the time Darius was fifteen, he had been putty in her vividly manicured hands.

Eventually, since Gypsy's family was involved in the drug trade, Darius was, too. As for their personal relationship? It lasted for years but had become more and more volatile over time until recurring bouts of domestic violence between them became the order of the day. Gypsy always knew exactly which buttons to push to drive Darius over the edge. As soon as she succeeded, she'd call the cops on him—screaming into the phone that he was beating her or threatening to kill her. Once officers showed up, she would somehow manage to convince them that he was the one at fault. As a consequence, he was the one who usually got hauled off to jail. The next day, of course, when they'd let him out because Gypsy hadn't gone through with pressing charges, she'd laugh it off and act like it was all some kind of joke.

Darius knew this was messed up and wrong, but he loved her and could never quite bring himself to walk away. During their last screaming match, she had pulled a knife on him. He'd managed to get it away from her, but in the course of the struggle, she'd sliced open her hand and was still bleeding when she called 911. This time, though, when he went to jail, Gypsy did press charges. He ended up doing six months in the King County Jail for assault. When he got out, he learned that she had sworn out a protection order on him. He wasn't allowed inside the house even long enough to collect his stuff. Left with nothing but the clothes on his back and nowhere to live, he'd gone crawling back to Granny.

Once on the outside he'd soon learned that Gypsy had taken up with someone else during his absence. Two months later, Gypsy and her new boyfriend had been found shot to death in an alleyway in the Denny Regrade. Darius was her ex, so naturally the cops came around asking questions. His job as a bouncer—the one Granny had found for him—had saved his bacon, though, because at the time of Gypsy's death he'd been at work at a place with all kinds of surveillance cameras, and those had given Darius an airtight alibi. That didn't mean the cops didn't question him about it or check his hands for gunshot residue, but eventually there was nothing to link him to the double homicide, and he was cleared.

Darius knew it was only by the grace of God and Granny's job that he'd dodged being charged and possibly even convicted of the two murders. That was one of the reasons, maybe even the main one, that this time when he accompanied Granny to services at Mount Zion, he did pay attention. He found himself listening intently to what the reverend had to say. He let himself get caught up in both the Word and the music. Finally, one Sunday when people were invited to come forward to be saved, he got up and went, finding himself a whole new lease on life in the process. Which was why this year, when the call went out for Mount Zion's crew of volunteers for serving Thanksgiving Day dinner at the food bank, Darius had signed up.

It was well after dark when, while patrolling the line, Darius caught sight of an older woman leaning heavily on the end of her overloaded shopping cart. A few sprigs of white hair stuck out from under her hoodie. Swaying unsteadily on her feet, she looked as though she was about to keel over.

"Are you all right, ma'am?" he asked. "You don't have to wait in line. If you're not feeling well, I'll be glad to escort you inside."

"No, no," she said quickly. "I'm too tired to eat anything. If you'd just walk me back to my van, I'll be fine."

"Where is it?" he asked.

"Over there a block or two," she said, nodding toward the south.

"Are you sure? Do you think you can make it that far?"

"I believe so," she said, "but would you mind helping with the cart? I have some money. I can pay you."

"Paying me won't be necessary," he assured her. "I'm glad to help."

Darius went back to the head of the line and told one of the other volunteers that he was escorting someone back to her van. That was the last time anyone reported speaking to him. The next morning his lifeless body was found two blocks away lying next to an alleyway dumpster.

During the brief investigation that followed, footage from one of the warehouse's security cameras showed two people threading their way through the parking lot—a hulking Black male accompanied by a much shorter female. The woman, who appeared to be Caucasian and somewhat overweight, was leaning on a grocery cart so full of goods that it was almost as tall as she was. However, the grainy quality of the video made it impossible to make out any facial features. Law enforcement was never able to locate or identify the apparently homeless woman, and no sign of her shopping cart was ever found, either.

An autopsy performed by the King County Medical Examiner's Office determined that Darius had died of a fatal dose of fentanyl. His death was ruled to be accidental, and the case was closed. No further investigation was deemed necessary.

CHAPTER 1

Bellingham, Washington
Friday, February 14, 2020

VALENTINE'S DAY 2020 DAWNED CLEAR AND COLD IN BELLING-
ham, Washington. For most people in the area that was a welcome
change from several weeks of mixed rain and snow—definitely
not suitable for walking. But with the twenty-four-hour news cycle
consumed with the looming Covid pandemic, outside was exactly
where I wanted to be. So I called Hank Mitchell, my next-door
neighbor, and asked if he and his black-and-tan Chihuahua, Mr.
Bean, aka Beanie, would like to join my Irish wolfhound, Sarah,
and me for a walk along our street, Bayside Road. I'm sure passersby
find us an interesting foursome—two old guys accompanied by a
stately Irish wolfhound with a bouncy, noisy Chihuahua yapping
at her ankles.

The Mitchells' place is just down the hill from ours. When my
wife, Mel, and I first moved into the neighborhood, their house

had been a real eyesore. That was one of the reasons our house had been so affordable. Bayside Road, our street, is hilly. The blue tarp covering the leaky roof of the house next door had been fully visible from our living room windows. In the Pacific Northwest, tarp-covered houses are often vacant and generally regarded as teardowns. The problem is, this one was occupied by a whole slew of people with random vehicles coming and going at odd hours.

Mel happens to be the chief of police in Bellingham, Washington. From a law enforcement standpoint, that kind of activity is typical of drug houses inhabited by squatters up to no good. Before Mel had a chance to have anyone look into it, however, the residence became the subject of a police investigation when someone called in an anonymous tip asking for a welfare check on Lorraine Mitchell, the elderly woman who lived there.

By the time uniformed officers arrived on the scene, they found Lorraine, age ninety-four, deceased in her bed, apparently from natural causes. She had been gone for at least a week before the cops showed up. No one else was found at the residence, including Lorraine's supposed caretaker, and the place had been stripped clean of anything of value except for a derelict 1966 Shelby Mustang found rotting away in the garage. The vehicle probably would have been worth some money on the open market, but there's a good chance none of the lowlifes hanging around the place had bothered to steal it because they had no idea how to drive a standard transmission.

Within a matter of weeks, the tarp disappeared and decades of accumulated trash was carted away. The house was gutted down to the studs in preparation for a total rehab. And that's when and how I first met Hank, the new owner who, as it turned out, had a lifetime connection by marriage to Lorraine and had a personal interest in the place. He was a retired contractor. Rather than wielding a hammer himself, with Mr. Bean at his side, he was happy to serve as a sidewalk supervisor and observe the construction project from afar.

Hank is a couple of years younger than I am. When we first met, I was not yet a dog-person, so I wasn't exactly charmed by the obnoxious presence of Mr. Bean, but over time Hank and I became friends. While the remodel on their place continued, my life changed when an enormous Irish wolfhound named Lucy, my first dog ever, came into my life. She and Mr. Bean soon became fast friends. The same holds true of Sarah, Irish wolfhound number two. In the meantime, Hank's and my friendship has continued to flourish.

Growing up I had school pals, of course. In college I developed a network of drinking buddies, some of whom became holdovers in my new life once I became a cop. After that my friends were mostly LEOs, law enforcement officers of one stripe or another. When I went through rehab and sobered up, I became friends with any number of people in recovery, but Hank Mitchell is my first ever friend who also happens to be a next-door neighbor.

On our walks, by mutual agreement, we avoid discussing the news. It's all bad, anyway, so why bother? Instead, as we stroll along, we share the stories of our lives, and that's how I learned about Hank's somewhat challenging connection to our now deceased neighbor. It turned out Lorraine Mitchell had not only been Hank's father's first wife; she'd also been a very troublesome one.

As a teenager in the early forties, Lorraine Harding had been hot stuff at Bellingham High. Despite the fact that she had been two years older than Henry, the couple had been high school sweethearts. They married shortly after Henry graduated and days before he shipped out to serve his country during World War II. Lorraine didn't exactly sign up to be Rosie the Riveter in his absence, building up an unsavory reputation around town for playing the field while he was off serving his country. When word of her escapades got back to Daniel Mitchell, Hank's grandfather, a local attorney with a family reputation to uphold, the old man had been less than pleased.

Hank's father spent his time in the service in the Army Corps of Engineers. When he came home, he joined his uncle's construction business and built the place on Bayside expecting it to be his and Lorraine's forever home. Once he found out about her extramarital exploits, he tried to divorce her, but by then Lorraine had her eye fixed firmly on the prize, the Mitchell family's considerable fortune, and she refused to leave quietly, if at all.

Henry could easily have gotten a divorce by going to court and charging her with adultery, but in small-town Bellingham the resulting scandal would have been devastating. So his father, the attorney, worked out a deal. Since no children were involved, there was no question of child support. Instead, Lorraine was offered a generous amount of alimony. She was also allowed to stay in the house until such time as she should marry. At that time, the alimony would cease and the home on Bayside would revert either to her former husband or to his estate.

Henry Sr. remarried shortly after the divorce became final, and Hank, an only child, was the result of that second marriage. In the meantime, Lorraine, the cast-off first wife, remained a fly in the ointment for the remainder of Henry's life. She refused to remarry and didn't die. Instead, she engaged in one scandalous romantic entanglement after another, always making sure none of them ended up at the altar. As a consequence, she continued receiving alimony checks until Henry Sr.'s death in the early nineties.

Over the years, as the value of her monthly alimony checks had dwindled, Lorraine had been forced to supplement her income by working as a bartender. Once the checks stopped altogether, she began taking in lodgers to make ends meet, including the parade of very dodgy-looking lowlifes Mel and I had seen coming and going from her house.

At some point after Henry Sr.'s death, Hank, the son from that second marriage and a widower himself by then, became aware that Lorraine had stopped paying taxes on the property. To keep the house from going into foreclosure, he had brought the taxes up-to-date and kept them current with the idea that at some point he'd turn the property on Bayside Road into a retirement dream house for him and his relatively new wife, Ellen.

Their relationship is similar to Mel's and mine in that Hank's retired from the construction business now while Ellen is still employed full-time. That's another reason we don't discuss the news. With Covid bearing down, we were both worried about how that would impact both of our still-working wives—Mel is at Bellingham PD and Ellen is a 911 supervisor at What-Comm, Whatcom County's emergency communications center.

"What are you and Mel doing for Valentine's Day?" Hank asked.

"I scored a reservation at Dirty Dan's," I told him. In my opinion, Dirty Dan's is Fairhaven's premier fine dining establishment. "What about you?"

"Ellen's working tonight. We'll be doing our Valentine's celebration on Sunday, her next day off."

When we reached our driveway, Sarah and I peeled away and walked down to the house where I spotted an unfamiliar vehicle—an older-model Honda Accord—parked next to the garage. As we approached the car, the driver's door swung open and a long drink of water climbed out. It took a moment for me to recognize my grandson, Kyle Cartwright.

Because Kyle and his parents—my daughter Kelly and her husband, Jeremy—had spent the previous Christmas with Jeremy's folks in Southern California, the last time I had seen the boy—make that the young man—in the flesh had been during a family excursion to Cannon Beach the previous summer. He seemed to have shot up half a foot since then and was now a good two inches taller than I am.

"Hey, Kyle," I said, grabbing him into a hug. "What are you doing here?"

"Wanted to see you is all, I guess," he muttered noncommittally into my shoulder, accepting the hug but not exactly returning it.

His terse response didn't sound as though he was overjoyed to see me, and the lack of useful information in his reply got my attention, causing me to begin putting together the logistical aspects of this unexpected, early-afternoon visit.

At the moment it was just after two o'clock in the afternoon. My daughter's family lives in Ashland, a few miles north of the Oregon/California border. Their place is a good nine-hour drive from ours. As far as I knew, this was a school day, so not only was Kyle missing school, he would have had to leave home in the wee hours of the morning to turn up so far north at this time of day.

As he backed away from me, I glanced at his car. It seemed to be loaded to the gills. In the back seat, I caught sight of what looked like the top rim of a bass drum. Mel and I had given Kyle his first drum set as a Christmas present several years earlier while he was still in junior high. If he had left home with his drum set in tow, this was not a good sign. Something was definitely up.

At that point, Sarah stepped up to give him a brief sniff before honoring him with a welcoming wag of her tail. Kyle had no idea, but knowing the dog as I do, I understood Kyle had just been granted my Irish wolfhound's instant stamp of approval.

"It's cold out here," I suggested. "How about we go inside? Are you hungry?"

"Not really."

Whoever heard of an eighteen-year-old kid who wasn't hungry? I took that as another bad sign. Something serious was going on here, and I was determined to get to the bottom of it.

CHAPTER 2

Bellingham, Washington
Friday, February 14, 2020

I REMOVED SARAH'S LEASH AND LET HER LOOSE IN THE HOUSE.
Then I took off my jacket and hung it up. When I turned back
toward Kyle, I found he had walked through both the kitchen and
dining room and was standing in front of the west-facing windows,
staring out at Bellingham Bay. Cloud cover was rolling in, and the
water had gone from bright blue to gray.

"What is it, Kyle?" I asked, following him into the living room
and taking a seat. "What's wrong?"

"Everything," he said, suddenly bursting into tears. "I want to
come live with you and Grandma Mel, please."

Whoa, whoa, whoa! In those few words, he delivered way too
much information accompanied by zero useful context.

"Why?" I asked. "What's going on?"

He shuddered and sank down onto the sofa. "Mom and Dad are getting a divorce," he managed after a long pause.

Floored, I took a seat, too. Twenty years ago when I'd helped plan and oversee Jeremy and Kelly's quickie wedding, I'd had serious doubts about their potential for long-term marital bliss, but in the two decades since, I'd seen no signs of discord. When Mel and I were around them, everything seemed fine. There had been none of the usual sniping and bickering that often surfaces when a marriage is coming apart at the seams.

A thousand questions raced through my head, but I stifled them. Years of conducting interviews with witnesses and suspects in homicide cases has taught me the finer points about when to ask questions and when to keep quiet. This was one of the latter. I allowed the silence to linger for the better part of a minute before I finally spoke again.

"Do you want to tell me about it?"

Kyle looked up at me with eyes filled with anguish. "Dad's got a girlfriend," he managed. "Another girlfriend, that is, only this one's pregnant. Her name is Caroline Richards. When everything blew up, Mom quit her job with the Shakespeare Festival in Ashland and moved to Eugene. She's got a new job with the alumni association at the University of Oregon. She and Kayla have an apartment together. I was supposed to stay on with Dad in Ashland to finish out my senior year, but I don't want to, not with Caroline living there. If I can't stay here with you and Grandma Mel, I'll go live in a homeless camp somewhere. I saw plenty of those on the drive up."

Whoa again! Needing a moment to take it all in, I stood up. "I think I'll fix myself a cup of coffee. Care for one?"

"I'd rather have a Coke."

"Coming right up," I said.

The coffee machine had turned itself off while Sarah and I had been out walking. I put it through the warmup cycle, brought Kyle a Coke, and then went back to the kitchen counter to wait for my coffee to brew, mentally picking apart the bombshell that had just landed in my lap.

With regard to Jeremy's girlfriend, the word *another* was the most important. That meant the affair with Caroline wasn't his first extramarital offense. And I was all too aware that this wasn't his first out-of-wedlock pregnancy, either. I vividly remembered his and Kelly's hastily arranged shotgun wedding because I was the one who did most of the arranging. But if this current crisis had been going on long enough for Kelly to find a new job and move out of the house and into an apartment with Kyle's sister, why the hell hadn't Mel and I heard even so much as a peep about it?

And maybe this was nothing but history repeating itself. After all, at age seventeen Kelly had dropped out of high school, run away, and gotten knocked up by her boyfriend. Karen and I had divorced years earlier, but bottom line, our divorce had been the ultimate reason Kelly had left home. And now, with Kyle's life in shambles, he seemed to be doing the same thing—running away. Hopefully he hadn't left behind some girl who was also in a family way.

Mel and I had seen Kyle off and on over the years, but those were always holiday group events with everyone present and accounted for. The number of times the two of us had ever had a heart-to-heart about anything of substance was exactly zero. Discussing who won the latest Husky/Duck matchup counts as so much empty BS. It's verbal camouflage pretending to be a meaningful conversation. In other words, Kyle and I weren't total strangers, but we certainly weren't close.

As for taking in a grandchild on a permanent basis? Are you kidding? Mel and I had established a very comfortable, uncomplicated existence with just the two of us. Adding an eighteen-year-old male into the mix of our placid way of life was likely to upend everything. Why would we want to do that? Why would anybody? But then I remembered a guy named Alan Dale.

Back in my rowdier drinking days, I'd indulged in more than a few one-night stands, one of which had resulted in an unexpected pregnancy. The woman involved, Jasmine Day, never let on about the baby she named Naomi. Jasmine and Alan Dale, her future boyfriend and eventual husband, had raised the child together without my being any the wiser. As far as Alan was concerned, Naomi was his daughter. After Jasmine's death, Naomi had found her way to Seattle, but if she'd even known about me, she'd made no effort to find me. Instead, she hooked up with a guy her age and got pregnant. Somewhere during the pregnancy the boyfriend disappeared, leaving Naomi to believe she'd been abandoned. When the baby was born, Naomi did the same thing—she abandoned Athena, her drug-addicted newborn, in the neonatal nursery of the hospital.

Once Alan Dale got wind of what was going on, he had come riding to Athena's rescue by putting himself on the first available commercial flight to Seattle. It was Alan, not Naomi, who spent night after night in the nursery, rocking Athena through the agonies of drug withdrawal. Once she was finally released from the hospital, he was the one who took her home with him, while he began navigating the tangle of legal hurdles required to keep Athena from falling into the quagmire of foster care. He had come to me for help with that.

Unsurprisingly, sorting it out had taken longer than either of us anticipated. Eventually, however, we made it work, and Alan was able to take Athena back home to Jasper, Texas. In the meantime, my first wolfie, Lucy, had fallen in love with Athena, which is how I ended up losing her. Once Lucy met Athena, it was love at first sight. When Athena went home to Texas, so did Lucy.

If Alan Dale was man enough to tackle raising a newborn on his own, couldn't Mel and I tough it out with a high school senior? At least Kyle wasn't in diapers. According to the latest report from Alan, Athena was currently navigating the intricacies of potty training. We wouldn't be dealing with that, either. Besides, by the time fall came around, Kyle would most likely be heading off to college. Having given myself a stern talking-to and making certain mental adjustments, I headed back into the living room with my coffee in hand.

"Obviously I'll need to talk this over with Mel," I told him as I took a seat.

Kyle nodded. "I understand," he said.

"I doubt very much that you'll end up living in a homeless camp," I continued, "but if you want to stay here, you're going to have to clue me in about what's been going on at home. Do your folks even know where you are? Did you tell them where you were going? Did you leave them a note?"

Kyle shook his head. "I didn't tell them anything. I just left."

"You have to call them and let them know where you are."

"But they'll want me to come home," he objected.

"Which you clearly don't want to do," I replied. "I understand that, but I believe you had a birthday a few weeks ago. Didn't you?"

He nodded.

"So you're eighteen now. In Washington State, that means you're old enough to call the shots as far as where you choose to live. The fact that you came here and asked to stay with us tells me that you're smart enough to realize you're not quite ready to be entirely on your own. By now I'm sure your folks are worried sick. You should text them at least and let them know where you are."

"But what if they tell me I have to come home?"

"Then you explain that you're not ready—that you have some things you need to sort through first."

"You won't make me leave?"

"I'm not prepared to make you do anything. For right now, you're welcome to stay. As for being here on a permanent basis? As I said, Mel and I will have to talk that over before I can say yay or nay. Fair enough?"

Kyle nodded, then he pulled out his phone and began to type. I can text when it's absolutely necessary, but I'm no Quick Draw McGraw. I'm sometimes reduced to doing voice-to-text. Kyle, on the other hand, was able to text lightning fast by using both thumbs.

"There," he said, once he finished. "I told them both. Now they know where I am."

Within seconds, his phone began to buzz. He glanced at it. "That's my mom," he said. "Do I have to answer?"

"That's up to you," I told him.

He let the call go unanswered. As soon as his phone quit ringing, mine chimed in. "Mom?" Kyle asked.

I nodded.

"Are you going to answer?"

I nodded again.

"She'll be really mad," Kyle warned.

"I'm a big boy," I told him. "I think I can handle it."

Once I punched the button to answer, Kelly didn't wait around long enough for me to say hello.

"What the hell is going on up there?" she demanded.

"I could ask the same of you," I replied mildly. "What's going on at your end?"

"Put Kyle on the phone."

"He doesn't want to speak to you at the moment. I think he needs some space."

"Some space?" she echoed. "How much space does he need? For Pete's sake, he took off and drove four hundred fifty miles without a word to either his father or to me! He has some serious explaining to do, and you need to stay out of it."

"I'll let him know," I said.

"Dad—" she began.

"Look, Kelly," I interrupted. "I'm glad he told you where he is so you don't have to worry about him, but from what Kyle's been saying, it seems to me as though your whole family has been going through a bit of a rough patch. At the moment all the upheaval appears to have gotten the best of him. Maybe what he needs is some time to sort through everything that's been going on, so for right now, why don't you just let him be?"

"But, Dad—" Kelly objected.

"I hear you have a new job," I interjected, abruptly changing the subject. "How's that going, to say nothing of how's your new apartment? It sounds to me as though Kyle isn't the only one who needs some space."

She hung up on me then, which was a good thing because by then my phone was buzzing with a second incoming call, this one from Jeremy. I switched over to that one.

"Hello, Jeremy," I said cheerfully. "How's it going?"

"What do you mean how's it going? I want to talk to Kyle. He just now texted me and said he was there. Why didn't he take my call? I don't need to talk to you. Put my son on the line."

"I believe it's safe to say that Kyle's uncomfortable with having a new woman in the house," I said pointedly. "Under the circumstances, I can't say that I blame him. By the way, in case you're interested, I'm not eager to talk to you, either, so we're even on that score."

"I take it he told you about Caroline?"

"And about the approaching arrival of your new bundle of joy."

Jeremy paused for a moment before he replied. "If that's what this is all about, it's none of your business."

"Actually, it is my business, because Kyle showed up on my doorstep to talk to me about it," I responded. "From my point of view, he has good reason to be upset, so he's staying here for the weekend at least, and maybe longer. That has yet to be decided."

"Wait a minute," Jeremy began. "Where the hell do you get off?"

"I have to go now, Jeremy," I interrupted. "Talk to you later." With that, I ended the call.

"You hung up on him?" Kyle asked wonderingly.

"I did," I answered, putting the phone down on the side table. "Before I say anything more to anyone, I want to know more about what's really going on down there, and since you're the one who's here, I'd prefer to hear your version of the story before I hear either one of theirs. So tell me."

It wasn't pretty. Without Mel's or my knowledge, Jeremy had been carrying on with other women for years, while Kelly had been covering for him as far as our knowing about it was concerned. The fling before this one had involved a fellow teacher from school. One of Kyle's friends had seen the lovebirds together and had spilled the beans. I couldn't imagine anything much more humiliating than having your friends let you know that your father is screwing around on your mother. That affair had ended when the woman involved had left Ashland at the end of the previous school year to go somewhere else. As far as Kyle knew, no one had reported the situation to the school district and no official action had been taken against either of the two teachers.

Given that, it was easy to see why Kyle might be distrustful of the adults in his life. His father was a liar and a cheat and his mother had covered for him until Caroline's pregnancy made further covering impossible. In a world where all the grown-ups seemed to have lost their bearings, Kyle appeared to be the only one attempting to behave sensibly.

"Well," he said once finished with his sad tale. "What do you think?"

"What I think is that your parents have put you in a pretty tough situation," I replied. "For now you should probably unload your car and bring your stuff inside before it gets dark. You'll be staying in the guest room. While you're doing that, I'll try to figure out what we're having for dinner."

With Kyle busying himself with dragging his gear into the house, I called Dirty Dan's and managed to up our Valentine's dinner reservation from a two-top to a three. The fact that we're regular customers went a long way toward making that possible. Then I called Mel.

"Hey, what's up?"

"It's about dinner," I told her. "Dinner for two just became dinner for three, and I think our lives have become a lot more complicated."

"Why?" she wanted to know. "What's going on?"

So I told her. "Wow," she said when I finished. "That's a lot to take in. What did you tell him?"

"That we'd have to talk it over."

"I guess we will," she agreed. "But I wonder what's really going on. What he's told you so far doesn't sound like the whole story. It takes a hell of a lot to make a high school kid decide to change schools in the middle of the second semester of his senior year. When Dad got transferred my senior year, my parents left town, but I finished the year by staying with a friend."

HOURS LATER DURING our not-so-romantic but very expensive Valentine's dinner for three, Kyle recovered his appetite, making short work of his own eight-ounce prime rib and a good chunk of mine as well. In the meantime, Mel managed to elicit some useful information concerning the family dynamics down in Ashland. Jeremy's previous gal pal left town at the beginning of the summer. By December he had moved on to Caroline Richards, whom he had met through an online dating site—Alone in Jackson. That's where Ashland is located—in Jackson County.

At the time Caroline appeared on the scene, she was newly divorced and working as a waitress in a coffee shop in Medford. She had since moved to Ashland where she had settled into a similar job, one she had quit shortly after moving in with Jeremy.

"I get the feeling she thinks Dad is rich," Kyle admitted. "I'll bet that's what he told her. The thing is, the money from Texas belongs to Mom, not Dad."

That "money from Texas," as Kyle called it, is actually money from my father's long-lost family in Beaumont. They had been in the oil business for generations. Once my cousin tracked me down here in Washington, her mother—my late father's sister—made sure my kids received their fair share of the family fortune. Kelly had told me early on that she had used part of that initial influx of cash to pay off the mortgage on their home, but what Kyle said made it seem as though she had managed to keep some of it in her own name.

Good for her, I thought to myself during dinner when Kyle passed along that information. *Kelly may have been covering up for her jackass husband's serial infidelities, but she's been smart enough to keep her money separate from his.*

"Dad claims he's not the only one who's been fooling around," Kyle continued. "I don't know if that's true or not. I mean, since he lies about everything else, he's probably lying about that, too."

Wait, Jeremy's not the only one who's been unfaithful?

That was what was going through my head. Although I didn't say it aloud, I'm pretty sure Mel got the message because she changed the subject. "Let's talk about school for a moment."

"What about it?"

"It's your senior year," Mel said. "Are you sure you want to do this? Don't you want to graduate with your friends?"

"They all have families," he replied morosely. "I don't have a family anymore because mine's been blown apart. As for school? Once Covid hits, there probably won't be any school. They're talking about switching over to remote learning and doing everything online."

"If that happens, maybe we could arrange for you to do your remote Ashland classes from here in Bellingham," Mel suggested. "That way you could still graduate with your class."

"Why, so my parents could show up and pretend we're still one big happy family?" Kyle responded bitterly. "Thanks, but no thanks."

"If you stay with us, there will be rules," Mel warned him, "rules and expectations."

"That's all right," Kyle answered. "Rules and expectations sound like just what I need."

That may have been the most surprising moment of the whole evening—the one when I realized that maybe my grandson had more common sense than both his parents put together. It was also when I understood that, although I had yet to make up my mind on the whole issue, seemingly Mel Soames had already made up hers. In other words, she and I were about to become parents together for the very first time.

"We'll call your folks and talk things over in the morning," she said.

"Thanks," Kyle replied. "Maybe they'll listen to you. They sure as hell don't listen to me."

LATER, ONCE MEL and I were home and in bed, she turned to me and said, "That was unexpected."

Given the ground-shattering changes going on around us, the word *unexpected* barely covered it.

"What do you think?" I asked.

"We have to take him in," she said.

That was pretty unexpected, too. "Really?" I asked.

"What choice do we have?" she replied. "Where else is he going to go? He feels betrayed by both his parents. Initially he was fine with staying on in Ashland to finish the school year with his dad and Caroline, but now he's not. I wonder what changed?"

"Me, too," I said.

"Don't worry," she said. "Tomorrow's another day. We'll get all this sorted."

CHAPTER 3

Bellingham, Washington
Saturday, February 15, 2020

SARAH SPENT THE FIRST FIVE YEARS OF HER LIFE AS A MOMMY dog living in a bare-bones shed in a Palm Springs puppy mill. She'd had some socialization before she came to live with us but not much. She no longer freaks out at the sound of hair dryers or flushing toilets, but she doesn't really trust the doggy door. She makes her needs known to me by fixing me with an unblinking stare, which means either (a) it's time to eat or (b) it's time to go out. In the mornings, however, when the stare tactic is a nonstarter because I'm still asleep, she gives me the cold nose treatment in my armpit. That works.

Knowing we had a visitor lurking in the guest room, I made my own pit stop in our en suite and put on a robe before venturing out into the rest of the house. Sarah wasn't surprised when, on the way to the front door, I made my customary detour into the kitchen long enough to start the coffee machine on its morning calisthenics. Our home is of the water view variety. That means the front door, the one that leads into the living room, is the one that opens out into the fenced front yard. The back door is the one everyone uses to enter and leave the house.

Since the phone charger is on the kitchen counter next to the coffee machine, I picked my phone up and checked for emails and texts that might have come in overnight. The first text, a clearly furious one from Kelly, was written in all caps: I AM COMING TO GET HIM. I WILL BE THERE BY ELEVEN!

The previous evening, when Mel had assured me that we'd get it all sorted, I believe she anticipated some kind of reasonable discourse among a group of calm, sensible adults. Kelly's all-cap message made her sound a lot more like someone intent on a search-and-destroy mission rather than a civilized discussion. It made me feel as though what we were in for would be more like a cross between *Jerry Springer* and *Dr. Phil*.

The second text was from our housekeeper who comes every Saturday. Fortunately for all concerned, she wasn't coming today. With an irate Kelly on her way, that was a relief.

On weekends when Mel doesn't have to rise and shine at the crack of dawn, I usually let her sleep in. She was still in the bedroom sawing logs, and I saw no reason to go back and wake her up only to tell her that a very pissed-off Kelly was on her way. With that in mind, I stuffed the phone in my pocket and turned my attention to the coffee machine. By the time Kyle ventured out of the guest room, I was on my second cup of coffee and working my crosswords.

"Morning," I said.

He replied with a wary half grin.

"Coffee?" I asked.

"I guess."

"Help yourself. If you're using one of the big mugs, press the two-cup button. For a small cup use the other one. Cream and sugar?"

He nodded.

"Cream is in the fridge. Sugar is in the sugar bowl on the counter. If you want to stir your coffee, be sure to get a spoon out of the drawer. When people use the sugar bowl spoon to stir their coffee, it sends Mel around the bend."

"That's one of the rules?" Kyle asked.

"Yup," I told him. "Let's call it rule number one."

Our Magnifica coffee machine takes a while to grind the beans and brew the coffee, so it's not exactly an instantaneous process, but the wait means that each cup is freshly brewed. While Kyle's was in the making, I wondered what the hell we'd talk about. How does a seventysomething make casual conversation with a heartbroken teenager who is, more or less, a stranger? Chances are, Kyle was dealing with the same issue.

When he came into the living room, rather than settling on the sofa, he sank down onto the floor and sat cross-legged next to Sarah, who was curled up on her rug. She greeted him with a welcoming tail thump.

"How did you sleep?" I asked.

"Not very well."

That was hardly surprising. Neither had I.

"I got a text from your mom a little while ago," I told him.

"Oh?"

"She sounds mad as hell and says she's coming to get you. She'll be here by eleven."

Kyle looked alarmed. "But I thought you and Grandma Mel said I could stay."

"We said we needed to talk about it, and we did, but the bottom line on whether you go or stay is up to you. You get to decide. Mel and I are both on board if you want to stay, but the final decision will be yours."

"Mom's going to be mad."

Those words and the uncertainty with which they were uttered didn't sound like they came from someone prepared to regard himself as an adult.

"She already is," I advised him, "and that's hardly surprising. Moms are like that, and yours comes by it honestly. When my mother, your great-grandmother, got mad, believe me, she was something fierce."

"Really?"

"Really," I replied. "You see that framed photo at the far end of the mantel?"

Kyle nodded.

"Mind getting it down?"

He unfolded his long legs and stood up in one smooth movement without the slightest difficulty. I might have been able to get up and down that way once upon a time, but not anymore. My two fake knees just aren't up to it.

"This one?" Kyle asked, handing me a framed photo of a young man dressed in a World War II–era army uniform.

"That's the one," I said. "Does the guy in the photo look familiar?"

Kyle frowned. "He looks a lot like me."

It was true. That was the first thing that had struck me the day before when I first caught sight of him—how much Kyle looked like my father and like me, too, for that matter. DNA is weird that way. It picks and chooses and sometimes skips a generation or two.

"That's because he's my father," I told him, "your great-grandfather. He was only a few months older than you are now when he left home and joined the army. He and my mother were dating and about to get married when he died in a motorcycle accident. My mother learned she was pregnant after he was gone. Her parents wanted her to give me up for adoption but she refused. Over their objections, she kept me and raised me on her own without a bit of help from her folks or from my dad's family, either. As for her parents, she never spoke to either of them again."

"Never?"

"Never. That was at a time when single moms weren't as common as they are now. If she hadn't been fierce, she never would have managed."

"Do you think that's what'll happen with me and my mom—that she'll never speak to me again?"

"I doubt it, but if she's a chip off my mom's old block, you need to understand that, if you go head-to-head with her, that's always a possibility."

"You'd think my father would be old enough to not make the same mistake twice," Kyle muttered.

Obviously he was aware of the fact that his mother had been pregnant with Kayla well before his parents tied the knot.

"Yes, you'd think so," I agreed and let it go at that. After all, with my own newly discovered daughter, Naomi, in the picture, I didn't have any room to talk about out-of-wedlock offspring.

By the way, Naomi now works as a counselor in the rehab center where I originally sent her to get clean. Obviously the treatment worked.

At that moment and much to my relief, Mel turned up, rescuing me from what was fast becoming a difficult conversation. She waltzed into the room dressed, made-up, and looking for her own first cup of coffee. While she stopped off in the kitchen to press the coffee button, Kyle returned the photo to its place on the mantel and sat back down.

"What's up?" Mel asked as she joined us in the living room.

"My mom's coming to get me," Kyle said grimly. "She'll be here by eleven."

"What do you think about that? Do you want to go home with her?"

"I want to stay here."

"Then you'll have to tell her exactly that," Mel advised him, "but be prepared. There's a good chance your mother will be permanently pissed."

"I know," he said. "Gramps just told me the same thing."

"You can live with that?"

Kyle nodded.

The beep of an arriving text sounded, and Kyle pulled his phone out of his back pocket. He glanced at it briefly.

"It's Dad. They're ganging up on me. He says I should listen to Mom. Figures. That's what he usually does—puts it all on her, but at least he's not coming here."

My opinion of Jeremy Cartwright, already at an all-time low, plunged a few more points. He could have at least pretended to make the effort.

"But he's not coming here and dragging *her* along," Kyle added.

Obviously the "her" in question was Caroline Richards. With that said, Kyle stood up. "I think I'm going to go down by the beach and take a walk."

Referring to the rocky shoreline at the bottom of our bluff as a beach is a bit of a misnomer. Kyle disappeared into the guest room and emerged a moment later, pulling on a puffy jacket.

"Can Sarah come along?" he asked.

"Sure," I said, "but grab her leash first. If you go down to the bottom of the bluff, you'll be glad to have her tugging on the leash when you come back up."

Seconds later, he and Sarah took off. Once the door closed behind them, Mel turned to me. "Did you see his face when he mentioned Jeremy's girlfriend?"

"I did."

"I suspect she's at the bottom of what's going on," Mel offered.

"Probably," I said.

Mel shook her head. "Boy," she said, "it's weird that I never picked up on the fact that both Kelly and Jeremy were so unhappy. They've done a good job of covering it."

"Haven't they just," I agreed.

Mel finished her coffee and stood up. "I'd best get my rear in gear. With a growing boy in residence, I need to figure out what we're having for breakfast. I believe I feel an attack of pancakes coming on."

That wasn't necessarily good news. There's a reason we eat out as much as we do. Generally speaking, Mel's pancakes aren't something to write home about, but as she set about rattling pots and pans, I retreated to the bedroom to get dressed.

While doing so, I thought about what Mel had just said about having a growing boy in residence. I had worked my way through college as a Fuller Brush Man, selling my wares door-to-door. In the course of my sales career, I became quite adept at using the assumed close. I was taught to never ask a lady straight out if she wanted to buy a certain product. Instead I was directed to ask which color she would prefer or if she was going to pay by cash or check.

Mel Soames had just used one of those on me. We were having pancakes for breakfast because Kyle was coming to live with us. Kyle had made up his mind about that, more because it was what he needed rather than what he wanted. And in the process of Mel making up her mind, she'd made mine up as well.

I wasn't sure about why Mel had landed so firmly on Kyle's side of the equation, but she had, and I've been around Mel long enough not to argue the point. My mother may have been tough, but believe me—so is Mel. That's one of the things I love about her.

And so, as I stood in front of the bathroom mirror, shaving my somewhat grizzled face, I squared my shoulders and delivered another pep talk: "Welcome back to fatherhood, J.P. With any kind of luck, Kyle will be off to college in the fall."

THE PANCAKES WERE a bit thick, lumpy, and underdone in spots, but at least Mel tried. She was busy supervising Kyle's first time on KP duty when Kelly showed up. She marched in the back door without bothering to knock and came straight into the kitchen. That's when all hell broke loose.

"Get your stuff," she ordered her son. "We're leaving and we're leaving now!"

"I'm not going," Kyle replied mildly. "I'm staying here."

Kelly spun around and glared at me. "Is this your idea?" she demanded.

"Actually it's mine," Mel said, moving into the line of fire and physically inserting herself into the conversation. "There seems to be a good deal of uproar going on in your family at the moment. Kyle came here looking for a safe haven, and we've told him he's welcome to stay."

"He needs to come home."

"Which one?" Kyle asked.

That was a showstopper, and Kelly hesitated for a moment as if uncertain about how much of her current marital situation Kyle had shared with us. Mel quickly put her out of her misery by letting her know we were aware of what was going on.

"We already know that you've moved out of the house and are living in Eugene with Kayla, leaving Kyle in Ashland with Jeremy and his girlfriend."

"His *pregnant* girlfriend," Kyle specified.

At that point Kelly flushed furiously—the same thing she used to do when she was a little kid and got caught doing something she wasn't supposed to. Whatever it was, her bright red face was always a dead giveaway that she was guilty as sin.

Kelly took a deep breath. "Look," she said, addressing Kyle. "That was the arrangement we all agreed to when this first happened. We gave you a choice between coming to Eugene with Kayla and me or staying on in Ashland to finish out your senior year. You chose Ashland."

"Ashland isn't working," Kyle declared. "Besides, now that I'm eighteen, I get to have some say about where I live. I want to live here."

"What about finishing high school?" Kelly asked.

"There's a perfectly good high school here," Mel said. "We can get him enrolled on Monday."

Once again Kelly turned her fury on Mel. "You've got no business turning my own son against me."

"Nobody's turning me against you," Kyle interjected. "I can't live with Dad and Caroline anymore, and I don't want to live with you and Kayla, either."

"Why can't you live with them?" Kelly asked. "What changed?"

"None of your business," Kyle snarled back at her. With that he stormed off into the guest room, slamming the door behind him.

Kelly looked back at me as if all this was my fault. "I hope you're happy now."

In the old days I had always been first in line when it came to accepting blame because most of the time I deserved it. That was no longer the case.

"I don't think anybody in your family is happy right now, most especially not Kyle," I told her. "He came here asking for help, and Mel and I are prepared to give it to him."

"Screw you!" Kelly replied. With that, she turned and stomped out of the house. I already suspected Jeremy wouldn't show up to favor us with similar sentiments, and if he didn't, that would count as yet another black mark against him. At least Kelly had cared enough to come looking for her son and raise hell about it.

"That didn't go very well," Mel observed once Kelly took off, "but since this sounds like a done deal, we'd better go shopping."

"Shopping?" I echoed. "Why?"

"Because we're going to need lots more food around here, for one thing. For another we need to get another cable box so we can hook up the TV set in the guest room. I doubt Kyle will be interested in watching what we watch."

That's one of the things I love about Mel. She can sort out problems long before I know they exist.

CHAPTER 4

Bellingham, Washington
Saturday to Monday, February 15–17, 2020

AFTER A SURPRISINGLY EXTENSIVE SHOPPING SPREE, WE
spent the remainder of Saturday and all of Sunday getting Kyle
moved in and settled. After some discussion, we decided that, for
the time being, the best place for the drum set would be in the far
corner of the garage, tucked in among Mel's moving shelves of
Christmas decor. That's the part of the garage farthest from the
house itself and also from Hank and Ellen's place next door. If he
was going to be doing his drumming in the garage, and since it's
generally icy cold in February, I added a space heater to our Kyle-
related shopping list.

When we sold the condo in downtown Seattle, we had dragged
some pieces of furniture from there to here. I'd been unwilling to
part with two of the easy chairs from the family room, and they had

been literally gathering dust in the garage ever since. I was glad to haul them inside and put them to good use in the guest room. The sixty-inch flat-screen TV from the condo had also ended up in there, perched on an oversize dresser. It had been sitting that way for a couple of months. I hadn't exactly rushed out to get another cable box to hook it up, but now it was time.

I spent most of Monday in the uncompromising purgatory known as public education. Mel had made getting Kyle enrolled in school sound easy. It wasn't. Rather than simply walking him onto the campus and signing him up, we had to jump through all kinds of hoops. As an eighteen-year-old, he could enroll without parental permission, but we had to be able to prove that he really was eighteen and also that his residence would be inside district boundaries. The second matter was solved by a simple phone call to the chief of police, who just happens to be my wife. The first was much more challenging and involved several difficult conversations with Kelly and Jeremy. Since Kyle had been living with Jeremy, I tried him first. He quickly and unhelpfully informed me that Kelly always handled all the "paperwork junk" and that I should ask her. My call to Kelly didn't go much better.

In the old days, Kelly used to be something of a daddy's girl, but that counted for nothing when it came to laying hands on Kyle's birth certificate and school vaccination records. Right that moment, as far as Kelly was concerned, I was public enemy number one, and considering everything that was happening in her life, that was to be expected.

Her initial response to my request was to say that she had no idea where those documents might be, but I didn't buy that story for a minute. My daughter may be stubborn as all get-out, but she's always been levelheaded. I knew she would never go off and leave important paperwork behind in a house that was about to be occupied by her soon-to-be-former husband's new girlfriend.

I finally played my trump card. "Look, Kelly, I'm sure you remember how hard it was when you had to start from scratch with a GED instead of a high school diploma. I know you're pissed at me right now, and considering the circumstances, I can't say that I blame you, but we're talking about your son's future. Kyle either finishes his senior year here in Bellingham or he can kiss his high school diploma goodbye. So how do you suggest we go about fixing this?"

For a good ten to twenty seconds the line went dead silent. At first I thought she had hung up on me again. Finally I heard her sigh. "Okay," she said, caving. "I can make copies and send them. Where do they need to go?"

I gave her the registrar's email.

"What about his school transcripts?" she asked.

Kyle had previously managed to obtain those on his own. "They're already here," I told her.

"All right," Kelly said. "I'll have to leave work and go back to the apartment to get them. It'll take about half an hour."

Half an hour was a hell of a lot better than never. "Thanks," I said. "Appreciate it."

Even with the proper documents in hand, it took another two hours to get the job done, but eventually we prevailed. With Kyle successfully enrolled as a Bellingham Bayhawk as opposed to an Ashland Grizzly, we drove home with everything we needed: a class schedule, all required textbooks, an ASB—Associated Student Body—card, and even a parking permit. That's something I never had when I was in high school—a parking permit. Back then, unlike Kyle, I didn't have my own car.

Once back at the house it was time to deal with the television issue. In the old days, if you wanted a new TV set, you bought one, dragged it home, plugged it in, slapped a pair of rabbit ears on top, and you were in business. That's not the case now. So after all the rigamarole of getting Kyle signed up for school, we came home and went to work getting the cable box and TV set hooked up and working. We also connected to and initialized all preferred streaming services, both his and ours. Since Mel had agreed to bring home takeout, at least I didn't have to worry about dinner.

Kyle was a cheerful enough worker but not a talkative one. We had been dealing with various electronics issues for some time when suddenly, out of the blue, he muttered, "She came on to one of my friends—to Gabe."

Mrs. Reeder, my senior English teacher at Ballard High, was a killer when it came to faulty pronoun references. Pronouns aren't designed to stand on their own two feet. They're supposed to refer back to the nearest noun. In this case, there wasn't one, so I wasn't sure which "she" we were discussing, and I hadn't the foggiest notion about who Gabe might be.

"Gabe who?" I asked.

"Gabe Lawson. He plays bass guitar in our band—the Rockets."

"And who came on to him?"

"Dad's girlfriend, Caroline. I mean, Gabe's just a kid. He's only a sophomore. They were getting it on, right there in our house. The band was down in the basement hanging out. I came upstairs and caught them in plain sight, right there in the kitchen."

"Caught them doing what?"

J. A. JANCE

"They were all over each other. Her top was pulled up, showing off her belly, and her hand was inside his pants, feeling him up."

My face must have registered shock. "Really?"

Kyle nodded. It was clear that he was still terribly upset by what he'd witnessed, but with that in mind, his sudden exit from Ashland made a lot more sense.

"When was this?"

"A couple of days ago," he answered. "Wednesday afternoon after school."

"Did you think they were only making out or were they going to have sex?"

"Making out, I guess," Kyle muttered uncomfortably, "but if I hadn't shown up right then . . ."

I couldn't help wondering if my old-fashioned terminology translated understandably into the current vernacular.

"Anyway," he continued finally. "I didn't know what to do, so I stood there like I was frozen. Gabe saw me and pushed her away. When Caroline spotted me, she was angry. 'What are you staring at?' she demanded, like I was in the wrong, and she wasn't."

"What happened to Gabe?"

"He took off. He didn't even go back down to the basement to say goodbye to the other guys."

"Did you tell your dad about what had happened?"

Kyle shook his head. "I didn't bother. As far as he's concerned, Caroline can do no wrong. Anyway, it would have been my word against hers. He probably wouldn't have believed me even if I had, and I doubt Gabe would've backed me up. He was too embarrassed."

There it was. The old he said/she said dichotomy. "You may be right about that," I conceded. "People might not have believed you."

"I mean, like, you hear of this kind of thing happening with older men and young girls," Kyle continued, "but I didn't know it could happen to boys, too."

"Believe me," I said. "It happens."

As a former cop, I know the statistics. In the course of their lifetimes, three out of ten girls will fall victim to a sexual assault of some kind. For boys it's more like one out of ten. If Gabe was under sixteen, the kind of behavior Kyle was talking about constituted sexual assault.

"Exactly how old is Gabe?" I asked.

Kyle shrugged. "I'm not sure. Fifteen, maybe. He doesn't have his driver's license yet."

"And Caroline?"

He shrugged again. "Twenty-five maybe? She's a lot younger than Dad."

"From what you've told me, it sounds as though Caroline might be a sexual predator, someone who preys on younger men. Those sorts of offenders seldom limit themselves to a single victim. Is this the first time she made any overtures to one of your friends?"

"As far as I know," he said. "If she did, nobody ever mentioned it, at least not to me."

"But they wouldn't, now would they?"

Kyle thought about that for a moment. "Probably not," he finally agreed. "But she's always, like, you know, flirting with the guys when they're at the house, and that's where we usually practice— down in the basement." He paused before adding regretfully, "At least that's where we used to practice."

"And that's why you left—because of what happened to Gabe?"

Kyle sighed. "I thought if I was gone, he wouldn't be hanging around the house anymore, and that would make it harder for her to lay her hands on him."

"What happened next, after you saw them together?"

"When I went to bed that night, I couldn't sleep. I stayed awake worrying about it, thinking it was all my fault. And I kept wondering what I'd do if she came after me. That's when I decided that the best thing for me to do was leave, but at first I didn't have any idea about where I'd go. The next day at school I finally hit on the idea of coming here. I left in the middle of the night on Thursday while Dad and Caroline were asleep. I wanted to be sure I was across the state line before they woke up and called the cops."

He needn't have worried too much on that score. Ashland cops might have taken an immediate missing persons report on an eighteen-year-old runaway, but it was unlikely—if a report had even been called in, that is. As a local educator, Jeremy Cartwright might not have wanted to call outside attention to his somewhat unconventional living arrangements.

"Good thinking," I said aloud.

"Are you going to tell Grandma Mel about all this?"

"Yes, I am."

"Do you have to?"

"Yes, I do. This is her house, too, and she needs to know the whole story. She'd already figured out there had to have been something seriously out of whack at home for you to up and leave the way you did. That's why she agreed right off that we should let you stay."

"I thought that was you."

"No," I told him, "it was definitely Mel, and believe me, we're both lucky as hell to have her in our corner."

CHAPTER 5

Bellingham, Washington
Tuesday, February 18, 2020

I WASN'T AROUND ALL THOSE YEARS AGO WHEN KELLY AND Scott first headed off to kindergarten. I had a free pass back then because I was at work and Karen, their mother, was at home. But on that Tuesday morning, as Kyle was about to set off to finish his senior year at a brand-new school, I felt a sense of unease that was probably closely akin to what Karen felt back when that first-day-of-school shoe was on her foot as opposed to mine.

Kyle didn't say anything aloud, but he, too, was clearly a bundle of nerves. I offered him food. He declined. I wanted to tell him I knew how he felt, but of course I didn't. I went all through school—grade school and high school both—with the same bunch of kids. Here he was starting over from scratch eleven and a half years in. If people asked him about why he had suddenly moved away from his family to live with his grandparents, what was he supposed to say?

If I were in his shoes, I wouldn't have wanted to tell them the truth, and I doubted he was going to, either.

That day when Sarah and I met up with Hank and Mr. Bean for our afternoon walk, Hank was curious.

"I missed walking with you yesterday," he said, "but I noticed a lot of comings and goings around your place over the weekend. It looked like you had plenty of company."

"Turns out we did and still do," I told him. "There are some upsetting marital issues going on with our kids down in Ashland. Our grandson, Kyle, is going to be staying with us for the next little while."

"Oh, boy," Hank said. "How old is he?"

"Eighteen. He's now enrolled as a senior at Bellingham High."

"Good luck with that," Hank muttered. "I'm glad he's yours and Mel's problem instead of Ellen's and mine. I already did my time in that barrel, and I wouldn't want to relive it for all the tea in China."

"He seems to be a good enough kid."

"I hope so," Hank agreed dubiously, "but get back to me about that in a month or so and let me know how it's going."

"I will," I answered.

The night before, while Mel and I were getting ready for bed, I had brought her up-to-date about the Gabe/Caroline situation. She was as troubled about it as I had been.

"So that's the real reason Kyle left home, to keep Gabe out of harm's way as far as Caroline is concerned?" she asked.

"That's what it sounds like," I said. "But the way people like that work, it was probably only a matter of time before she tried putting the moves on Kyle as well."

"Could be," Mel agreed, "but the idea of his leaving in the middle of the last semester of his senior year to protect his friend makes Kyle Cartwright a hero in my book."

"Mine, too," I said.

With that she had rolled over and fallen asleep. So did I.

AS SOON AS Kyle left for school, I turned my hand to tracking down whatever information there was to be found on Caroline Richards, Jeremy Cartwright's not-so-true-blue girlfriend.

Cops aren't allowed to use police resources to look into any kind of private matter. Mel could have come up with all kinds of information on Caroline with only a few clicks on her office computer, but that would have been illegal and any resulting information would have been entirely off-limits. At this point Caroline was definitely a family issue, but as a likely sexual predator she might eventually become a criminal one. As for private investigators? They're free to gather information wherever they happen to find it.

For starters I put in a call to my favorite nerd, Todd Hatcher. Mel and I had first met him while we were working for the Special Homicide Investigation Team, aka S.H.I.T. Officially, he's a forensic economist. Unofficially, he's a fount of information. He's an absolute wizard at tracking down mountains of details on anything or anybody, and having him in my pocket makes my work as a PI immeasurably easier.

According to his voicemail, he was currently at a conference and would return calls as soon as possible. I left a message. "As soon as possible" turned out to be several hours later. He called back just as Sarah and I returned from our afternoon walk.

"What's up?" Todd asked.

"It's a family issue," I told him. "I need to know anything you can find out about someone named Caroline Richards, formerly of Medford, Oregon, and now living in Ashland."

"Can you give me any other info?" Todd asked. "Having a date of birth would be helpful."

Talking about cases is easy. Talking about cases involving family members is not.

"She's my soon-to-be-former son-in-law's current girlfriend," I told him, "and her first and last names are all I know. I suspect she may be somewhat on the sketchy side, but I'd like to know that for sure."

"I don't blame you," Todd said. "I'll look into this, but I won't be able to get to it until later this evening."

"That's great," I told him. "No rush."

When Kyle came home from school, I asked him how it went. "Okay, I guess."

I would soon learn that was typical Kyle. He wasn't a big talker to begin with and the current complications in his life were wearing him down. In hopes of raising his spirits we ordered pizza for dinner. After that, he once again disappeared into his room and wasn't around when Todd called back later in the evening.

"When you said you thought Caroline Richards was sketchy," he said, "you certainly called that shot. I was able to locate a Caroline Louise Richards all right, one whose date of birth is the same as the one on Ashland Caroline's driver's license. The problem is, that first Caroline Richards was born in 1996 in Salem, Oregon, and died a year later of natural causes—some kind of heart ailment."

"So who she really is and where she's from is anybody's guess?" I asked.

"Looks that way," Todd said. "How'd your son-in-law hook up with her?"

"I'll give you two guesses," I replied. "A dating app."

"Which one?"

"I believe it's called Alone in Jackson. Why?"

"I'll take a look at that one and see if her profile is still there. If it is, that might give us some clues. And since I've located her driver's license, once I'm back home on Friday, I'll be able to run her photo through some of my facial recognition databases to see what turns up. Clearly she's gone to a lot of trouble to conceal her true identity, and it would be helpful to know why."

"What?" Mel asked when the call ended. She had been privy to my side of the conversation but not to Todd's.

"The real Caroline Richards was a year old when she died in Salem, Oregon, in 1997."

"So now Caroline is not only a possible sexual predator, she's also an identify thief?"

"Apparently."

"People don't go to the trouble of changing their identity for no reason."

"My thoughts exactly," I agreed. "It's usually because they've done something wrong and don't want to be caught."

"Are you going to tell Kyle about this?"

"Not for the time being. The poor kid's got enough on his plate right now. Let's wait and see what else Todd can dig up."

A few minutes later a text alert came in on my phone. Todd had sent me a copy of Caroline's driver's license photo. She was good-looking, all right, with fine features and a thick mane of blond hair. It takes something for someone to look that good in a driver's license photo. In the old days, I would have referred to her as a blond bomb-shell. I was beginning to understand how Jeremy might've fallen for her, especially if the rest of her body measured up to her facial features.

I passed my phone to Mel. She took a look and whistled. "She's gorgeous."

"Isn't she just," I muttered, "but as my mother used to say, 'Pretty is as pretty does.'"

Later, after we were in bed, Mel snuggled up to me and asked, "So how's this second gig at parenthood going for you?"

"So far," I told her, "it's not exactly smooth sailing."

A week earlier, Kyle had stayed awake all night, worrying about Caroline Richards. That night it was my turn to lie awake worrying about the same thing. What kind of a mess had Jeremy Cartwright gotten himself into? Because now the rest of us had been dragged into it, too.

CHAPTER 6

THE NEXT AFTERNOON FOUND ME PERUSING THE FROZEN FOOD section of our local Safeway. Since Mel had an after-work meeting that evening, I wanted to buy a microwavable meal that would allow someone with limited cooking skills to provide a reasonable facsimile of a family dinner. That's when my phone rang with an unrecognized 206 number. Despite the fact that I suspected it to be a spam call, I went ahead and answered.

"Hey, Beau," someone said. "Ben Weston here. How're you doing?"

Ben Weston is actually Benjamin Harrison Weston Jr., someone I first encountered when he was a five-year-old kid who was the only survivor of a horrific home invasion in which both his parents, his older brother, and his brother's best friend had all been murdered. Ben had been playing hide-and-seek with the older boys and had fallen asleep in a closet when the killers entered the home. That was how he had escaped being killed along with everyone else. Shortly before that incident, a local radio station had initiated the Teddy Bear Patrol, providing stuffed bears in the vehicles of first responders. That crime scene was the first time in my career as a Seattle homicide cop that I had deployed the Teddy Bear Patrol stuffed bear stowed in the trunk of my unmarked. Sadly enough, that wasn't the only time I needed one.

After the deaths of his parents, little Benny had been raised by his aunt and uncle. His father had been a Seattle cop, and as an adult, Ben Jr. had followed in those footsteps. The last time I'd had any dealings with him had been several years earlier. At the time he'd been working undercover for Seattle PD.

"Ben!" I exclaimed. "Delighted to hear from you. How are you doing these days?"

"Not too shabby," he said. "I joined the detective division, and I'm working Homicide these days. Scotty's desk is the next one over. He says hello, by the way."

Like Ben, my son, Scott, had also followed in his father's footsteps. When he joined Seattle PD, he was initially assigned to the Tech unit, but he, too, had recently moved over to investigations.

"Tell him hello back," I said. "What's going on with you?"

"Well, my son's a junior in high school, and my daughter's about to graduate from eighth grade. They're both honors students."

I was stunned. "Congratulations," I managed lamely.

I had no idea that Ben was even married to say nothing of having kids that old. Time flies when you're not paying attention.

"How's Bellingham treating you?" he asked.

"Not bad," I said.

Someone tapped me on the shoulder. I turned and found a woman with a shopping cart standing behind me with her eyes shooting daggers in my direction. Obviously she needed to get past me to reach that section of frozen entrees.

"Do you mind?" she demanded.

"Sorry," I muttered, stepping aside.

"What was that?" Ben asked.

"I was talking to someone else," I told him. "You were saying?"

"I hear you're working as a PI now."

"Yes, I am," I replied. "Is there something I can do for you?"

"Actually, there is. I need a favor."

Remembering that shattered and newly orphaned little boy clutching his teddy bear, there was nothing in my power that I wouldn't do for him.

"Sure thing," I said. "Name it."

"After my folks passed, there was this lady at church named Matilda Jackson. She was my Sunday school teacher, and she always looked out for me. I didn't find out until much later that she and my mother had been good friends. She always asked about how I was doing and if there was anything I needed. Now she's the one who needs help. It's about her grandson. He's a lot younger than I am, so he isn't someone I know personally."

"Is the grandson in trouble?" I asked.

"He's dead," Ben responded. "That's why she needs help."

This wasn't something to be discussed in the frozen food aisle. "I'm actually in a grocery store right now," I explained. "How about if you text me her contact info, and I'll be in touch?"

"Whatever the charges are . . ." Ben began.

"Don't worry about any charges," I told him. "As far as you're concerned there won't be any. As I said, just send me her info."

"Will do," Ben replied. "Thanks. I really appreciate it."

Putting away my phone, I continued shopping. On my way

through the store, in addition to my microwavable entrees, I picked up several boxes of macaroni and cheese. Back in my bachelor days, that was the one thing I for sure knew how to cook.

THAT EVENING KYLE and I dined on Hungry-Man frozen dinners. He ate all of his and half of mine. I was beginning to get a better idea of what it means to feed a growing boy. Once he headed for his room, I picked up my phone. Ben had sent me a text that contained Matilda Jackson's name and phone number and nothing else. Whatever her issue was, I was going to have to find out about it on my own, without any help from Ben.

"Matilda Jackson?" I asked when a woman answered.

"Yes, who's this?"

"My name is Beaumont," I said. "J. P. Beaumont. Ben Weston gave me your number."

"Oh, my goodness," she said. "You're the detective who gave Benny that teddy bear on the day his parents were murdered. He still has it, you know. He told me he keeps it in a desk drawer in his office in case he needs it again."

I had no idea Ben had hung on to his teddy bear, but knowing what horrors await homicide cops on a daily basis, maybe having a teddy bear stowed in a nearby desk drawer isn't such a bad idea.

"Guilty as charged," I told her. "Ben mentioned that you might be in need of a private investigator."

Matilda sighed. "I certainly am," she said. "It's about my grandson. His name was Darius. He died of a drug overdose in November of 2018. I want to know who killed him."

"Mrs. Jackson— It is Mrs., correct?"

"Yes, Mrs. But you can call me Matilda."

"Matilda, as I said, I'm a private investigator now. I'm no longer a homicide detective. If someone murdered your grandson, this is something the police should handle."

"Except they won't," she replied. "They claim he died of an accidental overdose—fentanyl. As soon as the medical examiner declared his death to be accidental, Seattle PD closed the case and refused to lift a finger."

"But you believe Darius was murdered?"

"I *know* he was murdered," Matilda declared. "When he went to volunteer at the food bank that day, he hadn't used in months. Why would he spend the day handing out free turkey dinners to homeless people and then walk away from the food bank and overdose in a dark alley? Answer me that!"

I happen to know a little about those kinds of situations. When drug addicts clean up their acts and go for a time without using, if they go back to it, they're putting their lives in mortal danger. Amounts of their drug of choice that they could formerly use with impunity are now powerful enough to kill them because they no longer have their former level of built-up resistance working for them. I thought about all that but I didn't say any of it aloud to Matilda. Clearly she had enough to worry about without my piling on.

"This happened on Thanksgiving Day?"

"Yes, and he was in high spirits when he left the house."

"He was living with you at the time?"

"Yes, but he knew good and well that if he ever started using again, I'd throw him out and he'd be back on the streets so fast that it would make his head spin. The thing is, he never came home."

"You reported him missing?"

"I thought maybe he'd decided to spend the night with his girl-friend, so I wasn't really worried. I was just mad that he hadn't bothered to let me know his plans. The next morning when he still wasn't home and wasn't answering his phone, I started thinking about calling in a missing persons report, but before I got around to it, two detectives turned up and told me that Darius was dead. The driver of a garbage truck spotted him in the alley earlier that morning and called it in. They found both his phone and his wallet. They also ran his prints, but they still wanted me to come in and positively identify him."

"His prints were in AFIS?" I asked.

Matilda took a steadying breath. "My grandson had a few run-ins with the law and spent some time in jail, if that's what you're asking, Mr. Beaumont, and there were certainly times he deserved to be there, but he didn't deserve to die. He was starting over. He was working. He was going to meetings for his addiction issues, and he was also going to church. He had even started seeing someone he met there—a young widow. He was looking forward to living a normal life, but now he's dead, and the only person who gives a damn about him is me."

That struck a chord. How many people think their kids and grandkids are doing fine when they're not? You can count me as one of those. In spades.

"I'm so sorry to hear about this, Mrs. Jackson, but as I told you earlier, I'm no longer a police officer . . ."

"That's the whole point. Benny explained to me that the cops won't look into the case because Darius's manner of death has been determined to be accidental. As far as Seattle PD is concerned, the case is closed. I need someone who isn't a police officer to reopen it."

God knows I wanted to say no, but that wasn't really an option. Benjamin Harrison Weston had asked me to look into the situation as a personal favor to him, and look into it I would.

"I'm going to need a lot more information than I have so far," I said at last. "Where do you live?"

"I used to live in the south end of Seattle. A few months after Darius passed, I had a stroke. After that, I couldn't handle the stairs anymore, so I sold the house to someone who's all wound up about gentrifying the neighborhood. I moved in with my sister down here in Renton. She's a widow, too, so we look after each other and share expenses. Besides, her house doesn't have any stairs—except for the ones on the front porch. Thankfully some people from church installed a wheelchair ramp for us."

"Where in Renton?" I asked.

She gave me an address.

"I'm calling from Bellingham. That's where I live these days. Would it be possible for me to see you tomorrow, maybe some time in the early afternoon?"

"That would be fine," Matilda said. "I have a doctor's appointment in the morning, but I should be home by twelve thirty or one."

"In the meantime, I need Darius's date of birth and date of death."

"He was born September 18, 1992," Matilda answered. "He died on November 22, 2018."

After the call ended, I continued to think about Darius's birth date. He would have been twenty-six when he died—eight years older than Kyle. At that age he should have been a young man at the beginning of the prime of his life rather than dead in a grimy Seattle alleyway. I was sitting there thinking about that when Mel turned up.

"Hey," she said. "How are things on the home front?"

"Okay," I said.

"What did the two of you have to eat?"

"Frozen dinners," I admitted. "I heated them up in the micro-wave."

She laughed at that. "Hardly cooking 101," she said. "Where's Kyle?"

"He took Sarah for a walk after dinner and then disappeared into his room. He's not exactly the talkative type."

"I don't blame him. He's got a lot to process right now."

"So do I . . . have a lot to process, that is," I told her. "I've caught a case."

"A paying case or another freebie?" she asked.

"The latter," I said. "It's a cold case Benjamin Weston asked me to look into."

"Your 'teddy bear' boy?" Mel asked.

The incident in question had occurred years before Mel and I met, but she knows me too well.

"The very one," I said.

"How about if I pour myself a glass of wine?" she asked. "Then you can tell me all about it."

CHAPTER 7

Renton, Washington
Thursday, February 20, 2020

AT ONE P.M. THE NEXT AFTERNOON, I PULLED UP IN FRONT OF A
small bungalow on NE Tenth Street in Renton, one of Seattle's near
neighbors to the south. What set this house apart from its neighbors
was the clearly newly installed wheelchair ramp leading up to the
front porch. A red Dodge minivan with a handicapped license plate
sat in the driveway.

I walked up the sidewalk and used the steps to access the front
door. When I rang the bell, an older Black woman, maybe in her
late sixties or early seventies, opened the door.

"May I help you?" she asked.

"My name's J. P. Beaumont. I'm here to see Matilda Jackson."

"Glad to meet you, Mr. Beaumont," she said, offering her hand.
"I'm Margaret Dawson, Matty's sister. She's inside. Won't you
come in?"

The house I stepped into, built in the fifties or sixties, was decades away from today's current passion for open-concept designs. The living room was tiny. By far the largest piece of furniture in the room was one of those self-rising recliners with a wheelchair parked nearby. The woman seated there so closely resembled the one who had answered the door that the two of them might have been twins.

"Mrs. Jackson?" I inquired. "I'm J. P. Beaumont."

"Welcome," Matilda said. "Thank you so much for coming. Do have a seat."

She pointed me in the direction of a love seat while Margaret hovered in a doorway that most likely led to the kitchen.

"Can I get you something?" she asked.

"No, thanks. I'm good."

"All right," Margaret said. "I'll leave you to it."

The recliner had been in a laid-back position. Now Matilda pressed the button and raised the back until she was seated upright before she spoke again.

"I really appreciate your coming," she said. "Bellingham's a long way from here."

"Not that far," I told her. "It's a little over ninety miles. At this time of day there wasn't much traffic."

Between the time I had first spoken to Matilda and now I had done some online research and learned that in 2018 a total of 403 overdose deaths had been recorded in King County, approximately a third of which were attributed to fentanyl. In hospital settings, the drug has important medical uses, but out on the streets, it's a killer. In terms of how Darius Jackson died, he was far from alone.

I pulled out my notebook. In private, I'm proficient with my iPad, but out in public, I find the old tech of pen and paper often makes the people I'm speaking to feel more at ease.

"Tell me about your grandson," I said for openers.

"Darius was right-handed," Matilda said.

That was a strikingly odd reply. In answer to that question most people will reply with a description of someone being kind, or the sort of person who would give you the shirt off his back, or a hard worker, or a good neighbor.

"And why is that so important?" I asked.

"Because I finally got my hands on the autopsy report," Matilda answered. "The drawing shows that the needle mark was on the inside of his right wrist. If Darius was shooting himself up, he would have used his right hand to do it, not his left."

That got my attention. It was something so basic that even a rudimentary investigation should have disclosed that striking discrepancy.

"Did you point that detail out to any of the detectives on the case?"

"What detectives?" Matilda asked. "Two of them showed up that first morning and told me he was gone—that he'd been found dead. At the time, I hadn't even gotten around to reporting him missing. I still thought he had spent the night with Gina."

"Gina was his girlfriend?" I asked.

Matilda nodded. "Her name is Gina Riding. Her real name's Virginia, but she goes by Gina. She's a young widow with three little boys. She and Darius met at Bible Study and really hit it off. Darius was crazy about her, and he adored her kids. In fact, he had told me in the October before he died that he was making payments on a diamond engagement ring he was planning on giving her for Christmas."

"But he died on Thanksgiving."

"Yes," Matilda agreed regretfully. "Gina was even more devastated by his death than I was."

Had there been any kind of investigation at the time of the incident, Gina would have been at the top of the detectives' lists of potential interviewees as well as potential suspects. Now she was at the top of mine.

"Do you have contact information for her?"

Matilda replied by reaching over to a cluttered side table and collecting a small notebook of her own. As she thumbed through it, I could tell that her left hand had been more seriously impacted by the stroke than her right one had.

"Here it is," she said, after which she rattled off both a phone number and an email address. "She's a nurse who works nights at Harborview, so you're better off sending her a text or an email. That way you won't risk waking her up when she's trying to sleep."

As I mentioned earlier, fentanyl has medicinal uses and is often found in hospital settings. It was feasible that a nurse might have been able to access doses of the drug without having to go looking for it out on the street.

"How was Darius and Gina's relationship at the time of his death? Had there been any quarrels or disagreements between them?"

Matilda shook her head. "Absolutely not," she declared; then, giving me a piercing look, she added, "Are you saying you think Gina might have had something to do with this? If so, you're a damn fool!"

"Sorry," I said, "just trying to cover the bases. Any unhappy exes in the picture?"

"None," Matilda said. "Like I said, Gina's a widow. Her husband was killed by a hit-and-run driver. As for Darius's so-called wife? Gypsy's dead and gone, and so is her boyfriend."

It didn't sound like there was any love lost there, but I decided to return to the subject of Darius's ex-wife later.

"In the days leading up to Darius's death, did you notice anything off about his behavior? Was he out of sorts or upset about anything?"

"No."

"Did he seem depressed to you?"

"Not at all, and if you're building up to suggesting that maybe he committed suicide, then I guess we're done here."

"I'm trying to establish his state of mind," I assured her. "Now, going back to those officers who gave you the death notice," I continued. "You had no idea that anything might be amiss in Darius's life before they showed up?"

"Nope," Matilda answered, "except for his not answering his phone. And if those guys were detectives, they're the only ones I saw. After I made the identification, the next thing that happened was a week or so later when someone from the medical examiner's office stopped by to give me Darius's personal effects. That was it."

"No one else ever came around to speak to you?"

Matilda shook her head. "Not at the time, and at first I didn't fault them for that. For one thing, I had a stroke, and that kept me out of commission for the better part of a year. I was in the hospital a month and in rehab for another two months after that. It took me a long time to learn to speak again and to get used to living in that thing." She gestured in the direction of the wheelchair.

"When Margaret offered to let me move in with her, it was an answer to a prayer. It was only after I got settled in here that I finally felt strong enough to start asking questions about what had happened to Darius and why. I couldn't accept the idea that he had started using again. That's when I finally reached out to Seattle PD."

"When was that exactly?" I asked.

"About six months ago now. I saw Benny at church. I knew he was with Seattle PD by then, so I called and talked to him about it. He told me that once a death has been ruled accidental, it's almost impossible to reopen an investigation from inside the system—that the cops' hands would all be tied. But he suggested that I still try reaching out to one of the detectives. He gave me the name and number for a Detective Sandra Sechrest and I gave her a call. She's the one who said I should ask the M.E. for a copy of the autopsy."

She reached over, plucked an envelope out of the mess on her table, and handed it to me. The return address read: King County Medical Examiner's Office. I unfolded the paper, revealing the all-too-familiar line drawings. There were only two injuries noted on the drawing. One was blunt force trauma to the left side of the victim's head, a wound that could have been consistent with someone falling to the ground. The other was the site of the needle mark on the interior of the victim's right wrist.

The M.E.'s determination was clear. Cause of death: Fentanyl overdose. Manner of death: Accidental. That was when I knew for sure that Matilda was right and that most likely Darius Jackson really had been murdered. No drug user on the planet would use his nondominant hand to shoot himself up. Why risk wasting a perfectly good hit by using the wrong hand?

Matilda waited patiently until I had finished examining the paperwork, returned it to the envelope, and handed it back to her.

"When I called Benny back and told him about the right hand/left hand business, that's when he said I should speak to you—that you were a former Seattle PD homicide detective and that you'd know what to do."

I understood all too well that both Sandra Sechrest and Ben Weston were on the money as far as restarting an investigation into a death that has already been ruled accidental. Getting an M.E. to change that kind of ruling is an almost Herculean task.

"So that's what I'm looking for, Mr. Beaumont," Matilda concluded, "answers. I'm an old woman and not in the best of health, but before I pass, I want to know what really happened to Darius and who did it."

"All right," I said finally. "In that case, what we have to do is start from the beginning with you telling me everything there is to know about Darius Jackson in addition to the fact that he was right-handed."

She sighed. "My husband, Leroy, was a good man—a long-haul trucker. With him driving trucks and me working as a waitress, we were doing fine. We'd even managed to buy a place of our own down in the Rainier Valley. At the time we made the purchase, he insisted on buying mortgage insurance, and it's a good thing, too. When our daughter, Breanna, was twelve, Leroy was off on a trip in California. He drove off the road and crashed somewhere around L.A. They thought he'd fallen asleep at the wheel. Turned out he'd had a heart attack and died. So I ended up with the house paid for and with some group insurance from his company, too. I thought Breanna and I would be fine, but we weren't.

"Bree had always been a daddy's girl. For some strange reason, she got it into her head that her father's death was all my fault because he'd had to work so hard to support me. After that things were never the same between us. She ran away the first time when she was in seventh grade and left permanently to live at a friend's house when she was a freshman in high school. That may be when she started doing drugs or she may have started even earlier. She was sixteen when she had Darius. If she knew who his father was, she never mentioned his name, and she never married him, either. She wrote 'father unknown' on his birth certificate and gave him her last name.

"I knew she and her baby were mixed up with bad people," Matilda continued, "but there was nothing I could do about it. All I could do was pray that they'd be safe. Then, when Darius was in seventh grade, he got to running with a rough crowd and ended up being involved in an armed robbery. Darius was charged along with the others, even though, as he told me later, he was just along for the ride and didn't know what was going to happen.

"The judge must have believed him, too, because, instead of sending him to juvie, she offered him probation. But once his case-worker outlined Bree's unsuitable lifestyle—the two of them had been living in her car at the time—it was either come live with me or go to the slammer."

"That's when you took him in?"

Matilda nodded. "That's when I took him in the first time. He may have been a bad boy, but he was my grandson. Still, even though I did my best, he'd already started down the wrong path, and things got a lot worse after his mom died."

"What of?"

Matilda shrugged. "What else? An overdose."

"And when was that?"

"A year or so after he came to live with me. He was still in eighth grade at the time." Matilda paused and wiped a single tear from her eye. "So much bad stuff. It's hard to come back from something like that."

"Yes, it is," I agreed.

"Once Darius got to high school, he was totally out of control, even before he met that she-devil, Gypsy. After that it was all down-hill."

"Tell me about her."

Matilda sighed. "Her name was Gypsy Tomkins. Her daddy was the local drug dealer so she had money to burn. As far as the kids at school were concerned, she was practically royalty. She was a beauty all right, but wild as they come and dangerous, too. If she was wearing boots, you could count on her having a knife hidden inside one of them. Why she picked Darius out of the crowd and turned him into her personal property, I'll never know, but she did. I saw through that little bitch, pardon the expression, the moment I met her, but Darius never did. He was nothing but a lovesick puppy in her hands.

"Everybody thinks that in domestic violence cases it's always the man," Matilda continued, "but not with Gypsy. I heard from some of Darius's friends that she liked to flirt with other guys in front of him, just to make him jealous. The two of them fought constantly, and when those fights turned violent, by the time cops showed up, who do you think they blamed? Not pretty little Miss Priss, that's for sure. Their last fight, she pulled a knife on him. He managed to get the knife away from her, but she ended up with a cut on her hand. According to the cops, he was the one at fault."

"That's when he went to jail?" I asked.

Matilda nodded. "He did six months for assault. Once Darius got out he learned that, in the meantime, she'd gone to court and taken out a restraining order. He couldn't even go home for his things."

"How long did he live with you?"

"For close to a year before he died. A friend of mine helped him get a job, and I could tell that he had cleaned up his act. He was working steady and going to church."

"Where he met Gina," I supplied.

Matilda nodded.

"What happened to Gypsy?"

"She and her boyfriend both were murdered, shot to death in an alley in downtown Seattle a few months after Darius got out of jail on her bogus assault charge. It was most likely a drug deal gone bad, but naturally the cops came looking for Darius, thinking he was responsible. At the time, he was working as a bouncer at a place called Jojo's. It's an unsavory dive in a bad neighborhood, so they have security cameras everywhere. They had video of Darius on the job during the time Gypsy was killed. Even so, the cops still had him take a lie detector test, which he passed with flying colors."

"They cleared him?"

Matilda nodded again. "More or less, but as far as I know, that case is still unsolved, and so is Darius's."

"Getting back to his case," I said, "was there any indication of a robbery gone bad?"

"No," Matilda replied. "Nothing was taken."

"You're sure of that?"

"Absolutely. This is what they gave me when they brought me his personal effects." She reached down beside her chair and produced another envelope, a brown manila one this time, which she passed over to me. It was preprinted with the local M.E.'s return address, and the flap was held down by the attached metal clip.

"May I?" I asked.

She nodded. I opened the envelope and shook out the contents: a cheap Timex watch—no longer ticking—a long-dead iPhone, a worn brown wallet, and some pocket change.

Of all the items, the phone seemed to be the most promising. If it could be unlocked and brought back to life, it might reveal all kinds of information about Darius's last days on earth. Among the coins I found something I recognized—a one-year chip from Narcotics Anonymous.

"How long had Darius been out of jail before he died?" I asked.

"A little under a year," Matilda said. "Why?"

I handed her the chip. "Having that chip means he'd been drug free for at least a year, so he must have started with Narcotics Anonymous while he was still incarcerated."

Matilda nodded. "That's what he told me. He was very proud of that."

"You saw no evidence that he had slipped?"

She shook her head. "None."

"And you didn't find anything related to drug use in his room after his death?"

"Nothing at all."

I opened the wallet and thumbed through it. Among the contents were a driver's license, a bank debit card, a Costco card, a Safeway loyalty card, and a single photograph of a smiling young woman.

Holding it up, I asked, "Gina?"

Matilda nodded. "Yes, that's Gina."

In the back of the wallet, concealed under an interior flap, I found two crisp one-hundred-dollar bills. "Did you know these were here?"

"No, and I have no idea where they would have come from. His paychecks from Jojo's were on direct deposit. As far as I knew, he never in his life had two hundred-dollar bills to rub together at the same time, unless . . ."

As her unfinished sentence faded away into nothing, a worried expression passed over Matilda's face. For the first time in the course of our conversation, she seemed uncertain. It didn't take long for me to figure out why. Just because Darius wasn't using drugs didn't mean he wasn't selling them.

"Do you mind if I take this?" I asked, returning everything to the envelope.

"Take whatever you need, but bring it back when you're done with it. Except for the money. Knowing where it might have come from, I don't care if I ever see it again."

After that, Matilda gave me contact information for Darius's boss at Jojo's along with the names for several of the guys who had been part of Mount Zion's Thanksgiving Day volunteer crew, all of which gave me some leads to follow. However, when I left her residence, it seemed as though my visit had done the exact opposite of what I had intended. Rather than improving Matilda Jackson's frame of mind, I feared I had left her feeling infinitely worse.

I wasn't happy about that—not in the least.

CHAPTER 8

Bellingham, Washington
Thursday, February 20, 2020

AS I LEFT RENTON AND HEADED HOME THROUGH TRAFFIC, IT was late enough in the day that southbound 405 was already bumper-to-bumper for miles. I was northbound, and traffic there wasn't nearly as bad. I was approaching Everett when my phone rang. I was surprised to see Kelly's name showing in caller ID. It was coming up on a week since our big blowup over Kyle. Other than the tense series of calls regarding school records on Monday, I hadn't heard a word from her.

This is going to be fun, I thought. "Hey there," I said aloud, doing my best to sound jovial. "How's my favorite daughter?"

Once upon a time, back when, as far as I knew, I'd had only one daughter, that had been a running joke between us. Now with Naomi in the picture, I realized that I'd just stepped in it. I was busy wondering how I'd go about fixing that blunder, when Kelly stunned me with her opening line.

"I'm sorry, Dad," she said. "Sorry about everything. How's Kyle doing? Did you get him enrolled?"

"This is only his third day," I told her. "I've been working a case in Seattle, so I won't find out how things went today until I get back to Bellingham, but all things considered, he seems to be okay. And there's no need for you to apologize. It sounds as though the whole family has been through hell."

I heard her draw a deep breath. "You know, this isn't the first time Jeremy has cheated on me," she said finally.

Of course, that was something I'd already learned from Kyle, but I was glad to hear it from Kelly.

"I'm so sorry," I said. "Mel and I had no idea anything was amiss."

"I know," Kelly replied. "When it comes to being an enabler, I'm at the head of the class. I've covered for him for years."

That was heartbreaking to hear. "I always thought you and Jeremy were happy."

"I was at first," she said, "and I thought he was, too. You never said it aloud, but I knew at the time how much you disapproved of our getting married. But once I caught him cheating, I didn't want to admit it to anyone—most especially to you—and have to tell you that you were right and I was wrong. I was afraid of disappointing you."

"I'm disappointed as hell in Jeremy," I said, "but I've never been disappointed in you. Even with small kids at home, you picked yourself up, went back to school. You got your GED, and earned both a bachelor's and a master's. First you started your own company and then, after selling that, you've gone on to hold demanding jobs. Getting people to cough up charitable contributions isn't easy."

"It's easier than getting a divorce," she put in.

"Yes," I agreed. "I suppose it is."

"Anyway," she continued, "when I decided to move out, I really did give Kyle a chance to decide what he wanted to do—whether he would move in with Kayla and me in Eugene or stay on in Ashland with his dad. Considering it's his senior year, when he chose to stay, I thought that was a reasonable decision. I don't understand why he changed his mind all of a sudden or why he decided to go running to you, either. Why didn't he come straight to Eugene?"

I couldn't answer that question without betraying Kyle's confidence. I may have been his grandfather, but in asking me to look into his family situation, I was functioning as a private investigator. That meant that whatever passed between us was confidential information. Rather than answering her question, I deflected it instead. "Sometimes, teenage boys are as much of a mystery to themselves as they are to their mothers."

"I suppose that's true," Kelly said. "But do you think he's going to be okay? Really?"

That was the Kelly Beaumont Cartwright I had always known and loved, the sensible girl who cared for her children more than life itself.

"I think he'll be fine," I said. "He's a likable, responsible kid with a good head on his shoulders. What he needed was some distance from the situation."

"You mean distance from me."

"No, I mean distance from everything. Being away may let him gain perspective on what's happened. Right now it all seems like the end of the world, or at least the end of the world as he knew it. Eventually he'll be able to figure out that's not the case."

"But what if all the schools end up getting shut down because of Covid?" Kelly asked.

I may have been on a self-imposed news blackout, but Mel wasn't. She, too, had raised concerns that school shutdowns were most likely coming sooner than later.

"I'm telling you the same thing I told Mel," I said to Kelly. "We'll cope, and Kyle will cope. I said we'd look after him, and we will, come what may, but Mel and I are both going to have to upgrade our cooking skills."

"I miss him," Kelly said sadly.

"I'm sure you do," I agreed, "but try to think about it this way. Kyle's eighteen. Even with all the family upheaval, chances are he'd be leaving home to go to college in the fall. How about trying to think of this short stay at our place as his getting an early start on that?"

"You mean look on this as an opportunity for him rather than a failure on my part?"

In that moment I wanted desperately to take my grieving daughter in my arms, hold her close, and tell her that, no matter what, everything was going to be okay.

"Look," I said, "it strikes me that your whole family is trying to make the best of a very bad bargain, including Jeremy, I suppose. He may have been a crappy husband all this time, but he's always struck me as a good dad, and that catch-colt baby of his is going to need a father."

"What kind of baby?" Kelly asked.

"A catch-colt," I explained. "It's something my mother used to call me—her little catch-colt. When I was little, I thought it meant I was part horse. It wasn't until years later that she told me it was an old-fashioned term for an out-of-wedlock baby. All it really meant was that she and my father weren't married at the time I was born."

"So, illegitimate then," Kelly said.

As a catch-colt myself and with both an out-of-wedlock daughter and granddaughter, the word *illegitimate* when used in regard to children rubs me the wrong way. If I were Kyle's age, I might even say it "triggers" me.

"No, Kelly," I said. "The parents may be screwed up six ways to Sunday, but I don't think babies are ever illegitimate—they're all just fine."

In that moment it occurred to me that eventually the same statement would apply to Caroline and Jeremy's baby as well—that he or she would be perfect, too, but I was smart enough to not say that out loud. Instead, I changed the subject.

"So tell me how you and Kayla are doing? How's the new job?"

You'll notice I also had brains enough not to ask anything about whether or not Kelly had a new man in her life. Maybe there's something to be said for getting older and wiser.

The remainder of the conversation had to do with what would happen to both Kyle and Kayla in the event schools did shut down in the face of the coming pandemic. I tried to reassure Kelly that one way or the other we'd all get through it, but I doubt she was convinced. Come to think of it, I'm not sure I was, either.

I ARRIVED HOME in Fairhaven in time for dinner. Mel had brought home a heat-and-serve meatloaf. Kyle had made macaroni and cheese. It wasn't gourmet, but it was food, and no one left the table hungry. After dinner, Kyle took charge of the cleanup, which, according to Mel's "rules and regulations," was going to be one of his primary duties.

Once he finished and disappeared into his room, Mel and I settled in the living room for some privacy. I brought her up-to-date on my long conversation with Matilda Jackson, including showing her the contents of the envelope that had contained Darius's personal effects. She went through them one by one. When it came time to examine the hundred-dollar bills, she held one of them up to the lamplight.

"There's no security strip," she announced. "So these bills are either very old or very well done counterfeit. There's no way to tell how they happened to be in Darius's possession?"

"When I found them, I could tell from Matilda's immediate reaction that she was afraid he might have been dealing drugs. Considering Darius's history, that's a reasonable assumption." Then, after a momentary pause, I asked, "How long ago did the US mint start printing bills with security strips?"

Without a word, Mel picked up her iPad and typed in a few words. Moments later she provided the answer. "It says here that happened in 1990."

Putting down the iPad, Mel picked up one of the bills and ran her finger over it. "This doesn't feel that old," she objected. "And it doesn't feel used, either."

"So who goes around buying drugs with thirty-year-old cash?" I asked.

"Or maybe it's counterfeit," Mel suggested, "but if that's the case, whoever printed it did a hell of a good job."

I thought that was the end of the conversation, but it wasn't. We were in bed and I had almost dozed off when Mel said one more thing, and that final comment turned out to be the most important one.

"Drug users don't ever shoot up with their nondominant hand," she told me. "That never happens."

She fell fast asleep after that. I didn't. Maybe someone else had given Darius that fatal dose of fentanyl, but finding out who was responsible for that wouldn't fix everything. Darius Jackson may have stopped using, but if it turned out he was selling drugs, learning that was bound to break whatever was left of Matilda Jackson's heart.

CHAPTER 9

Bellingham, Washington
Friday, February 21, 2020

IT PAINS ME TO ADMIT IT NOW, BUT BACK WHEN I WAS A COP, I had very little respect for private investigators. I regarded most of them as annoying pains in the ass. They always seemed to be sticking their noses into places where they didn't belong. And, from where I stood, their primary job was getting the goods on philandering spouses to improve whatever was due to their clients in the course of upcoming divorce proceedings.

Now that I'm a PI myself, the shoe is on the other foot, and I see things differently. Private investigators often function as courts of last resort for people for whom the justice system has devolved into an injustice system. Although I didn't have an official private investigator license when I volunteered for The Last Chance, I was doing similar work there, gathering leads and tracking down evidence in cold case homicides that had been left unsolved for decades. In my work with TLC I had helped bring down a number of killers who had gotten away with murder for decades and who figured for sure that they were home free. Much to my surprise, however, I also discovered that there's a flip side to cold cases. My work for TLC has also helped exonerate two people who had spent years in prison for crimes they didn't commit.

Having a PI license gives me the opportunity to investigate cases, but it doesn't oblige me to charge for my services, and mostly I don't. I've helped identify long unidentified human remains and located a missing person or two without a single divorce lawyer in sight. In the face of Jeremy and Kelly's contentious marital situation, my divorce-free practice record might be about to change, but working to sort out what had happened to Darius Jackson on behalf of his grandmother made me feel as though I was still on the side of the angels.

And that's what I did on Friday—I went to work on the Jackson case. Once Mel left for work and Kyle set off for school, I settled in with my notebook and started following up on the leads Matilda had given me. Ironically enough, I began by placing a call to my old stomping grounds, Seattle PD's Homicide unit, where, instead of requesting to speak to my son or to Ben Weston, I asked for Sandra Sechrest.

"Detective Sechrest," she said when her phone stopped ringing.

"Good morning," I said. "My name's Beaumont, J. P. Beaumont."

I had been away from Seattle PD for so long that I didn't expect my name to ring any bells, but it did.

"Any relation to Scotty?" she asked.

Karen and I had always called our son Scotty as a child, but once he started working for Seattle PD, I had deliberately banished that nickname from both my lips and my consciousness. I figured that

77

inside law enforcement circles, someone named Scotty might not be taken seriously. Turns out, I needn't have bothered with that kind of self-censorship. Ben Weston wasn't the only member of the Homicide squad who called my son that, and chances were, everybody else did, too.

"He's my son," I said.

"Good to know," Detective Sechrest replied. "So what can I do for you today, Mr. Beaumont?"

"I'm working as a PI these days," I explained. "My client, Matilda Jackson, has asked me to look into the death of her grandson, Darius Jackson."

"Is this an open case?"

"No," I replied, "it's actually closed. Darius died of a fentanyl overdose on Thanksgiving Day in 2018. The M.E. ruled it as accidental."

"Oh, that's right," she said. "I vaguely remember speaking to a female relative about that case several months ago. As I told her on the phone, once a death has been ruled accidental, the case is closed and we're no longer able to investigate it."

"Yes," I assured her. "I understand all that, but on your advice Mrs. Jackson went ahead and ordered the autopsy report. According to the autopsy, the needle mark was in Darius's right wrist. The problem with that is he was right-handed."

"Really?" she asked. "Knowing that might make a difference, but I doubt it's enough to reopen the case."

"Probably not," I agreed, "but I'd still like to look into it. So I was wondering, is evidence from closed cases still stored in that warehouse south of CenturyLink Field?"

"As far as I know."

"I'd like to stop by and take a look at what's there," I told her, "but it would be helpful to have a case number. Would you mind looking it up?"

"Sure thing," she said. "Hang on."

She put down the phone, and I heard computer keys clacking in the background. Moments later she said, "Hey, Scotty, your dad's on the phone. Want to talk to him?"

"Not right now," he said from some distance. "Tell him we'll talk later."

That was a relief because I suddenly realized that Scott and Cherisse were most likely completely in the dark about what was going on with Kelly and Jeremy. The last thing I wanted to do was have to deliver that troublesome information over the phone while Scott was at work.

Detective Sechrest came back on the line. "Got it," she said. "Here's the number."

I jotted it down in my notebook. Visiting the warehouse would call for another drive up and down the I-5 corridor, but doing that in the midst of Seattle's notoriously bad traffic made no sense. So that went on my to-do list for the following week. Darius had already been dead for going on two years. Obviously this wasn't going to be a rush kind of job.

My next call was to Jojo's, the bar where Darius had been working at the time of his death. "Does the owner happen to be in?" I asked when someone picked up the phone.

"Hang on. I'll check."

It took a while before someone answered. I was surprised when the person who came on the line was female. "Patrice here," she said.

"Are you the owner?"

"Yes, I am. How can I help you?"

"My name's J. P. Beaumont. I'm a private investigator doing some work for Matilda Jackson."

"Looking into Darius's death, I hope?" she asked.

"Exactly," I replied. "His grandmother doesn't believe he was using at the time of his death."

"Neither do I," Patrice said. "Darius didn't drink and didn't use. He was in recovery and serious about it. Sometimes it takes one to know one," she added. "That's why, when my mother told me about him, I went ahead and hired him."

"Your mother and Mrs. Jackson are friends?"

"Not just friends," she said with a laugh. "They're forever friends, from kindergarten on. Neither one of them would be caught dead in a place like this. I ended up owning it after my husband died. We were both involved in drugs at the time. After he OD'd I decided to get clean. Most of the people who work here are in recovery from one thing or another, and if I find out they're using again, I send them down the road."

That was unexpected. Years ago there was a booze-free bar in Seattle. It disappeared decades back for unknown reasons, but finding a bar in the Rainier Valley—one popular enough to need bouncers—that required all their employees to be clean and sober came as a surprise to me.

"How long did he work for you?"

"Not quite a year, and he was totally dependable," Patrice replied. "Never missed a shift. Always showed up on time. And he was big enough and tough-enough-looking that most people didn't even think about messing with him."

Except, I thought, *someone who happened to have a syringe loaded with fentanyl.*

"Any complaints about him in the days or weeks leading up to his death?"

"None that I know of. I know he had a girlfriend. She wasn't someone who stopped by Jojo's, and I didn't learn until his funeral that they were about to become engaged."

"You attended the funeral?"

"We all did," Patrice said. "I had to shut the place down that day because everyone who worked here wanted to go to the service. Some of my guys served as pallbearers."

I've frequented a lot of bars in my time, but this was one my mother would have called "a white horse of a different color."

"What about customers?" I asked. "Did Darius have beefs with any of them?"

"Nothing that ever came to my attention."

"All right," I said, preparing to end the call. "If you think of anything that might be of use, here's my number."

I gave it to her, and I could hear the scratching of a pen or pencil on paper.

"What do you think happened to him?" Patrice asked.

If I'd still been a sworn officer, I wouldn't have been able to answer that question. As a PI, I could. "I believe Darius Jackson was murdered," I replied without hesitation.

"So do I," Patrice declared. "Since the cops aren't going to lift a finger to find out what happened to him, I hope to hell you do."

"That makes two of us," I told her, "and Matilda Jackson makes three."

Once off the phone with Patrice, I worked my way through the list of friends Matilda had given me and came up empty. Most of the numbers were out of date. Some were simply disconnected or had been reassigned to someone else. Unfortunately, gone are the days when I could have picked up my phone, dialed information, and simply asked for assistance.

Finally, before Kyle came home from school but hopefully late enough not to awaken someone who had to work nights, I dialed Gina Riding's number. A woman answered after the second ring. "Hello."

I started to introduce myself but was interrupted by some kind of a ruckus on the other end of the line.

"Boys, settle down!" she ordered. "I'm on the phone." The background racket fell silent. "Sorry about that," she resumed. "What were you saying?"

"My name is J. P. Beaumont . . ." I began.

"Right," she said, before I could go any further. "You're the private investigator. Matilda left me a message that you'd most likely be calling. I hope you'll be able to do something about Darius."

"I hope so, too, and I'm so sorry for your loss," I agreed. "I understand you two were in a serious relationship."

"Thank you," she said, "and yes, it was a serious relationship. I would have married the man in a heartbeat, and my boys were crazy about him. I didn't know it at the time, but he was planning to give me an engagement ring at Christmas. He still did, in a way. He was making payments on it. His boss from work found out where he was buying it. She paid it off and gave it to me after the funeral."

I was touched. *Score another point for Patrice Moser!* I thought.

"It didn't seem right to wear it on my finger," Gina continued, "so I wear it on a chain around my neck. I think about him every day. At the time he died, I didn't believe for a minute that he had died of an accidental overdose. I work in the ER. I know about fentanyl overdoses and how common they are. But I knew in my heart Darius wouldn't have done that. I tried to talk to the cops about it, but I was only the girlfriend. No one was interested in my opinion. Matilda might have been able to get more traction, but after that stroke, she wasn't able to do much of anything."

"You saw the autopsy report?"

"I did but only because Matilda showed it to me. There was some blunt force trauma to the left side of his head—consistent with a fall—and that single needle mark on the inside of his right wrist. You're aware that Darius was right-handed?"

"Matilda told me. But I'm interested to learn if you know about anyone who might have wished to harm him—a friend or acquaintance with whom he'd had a falling-out."

"I can't think of anyone," Gina said. "He had broken off all connections with the people he used to know back when he was with Gypsy. He went to work, he went to church, and he went to NA meetings. That's it. The rest of his spare time was spent with me and the boys."

"But what about some other individual from back in the bad old days, someone besides Gypsy and her boyfriend? Did he ever mention having problems with anybody else?"

"I can't think of anyone at all," Gina replied.

"This is a cell phone, isn't it?" I asked.

"Yes."

"So now you have my number. If you think of anything that might be helpful, please give me a call."

"Before you go, Mr. Beaumont, do you mind if I ask you a question?"

"Fire away."

"I don't know how much you charge for your services. If Matilda is paying for this, I know she's not made of money. I can't chip in much, but I'd like to help."

"Don't give that another thought," I assured her. "My fees are being handled by someone who wishes to remain anonymous."

When the phone call ended, I sat there for several minutes in silence thinking about why I was doing this—for Matilda and for Gina and her boys, yes, but also for that other little boy. I can still see Ben's tear-soaked face clear as day, staring up at me, trying to make sense of what had just happened, all the while clutching the only thing he owned—that single teddy bear.

Eventually I had found the people responsible for the murder of Ben Weston's family and had brought them to justice, but that hadn't been enough, not nearly. Helping Matilda Jackson and Gina Riding navigate their loved one's death was something I could do right now that might help wipe out some of that deficit.

CHAPTER 10

Bellingham, Washington
Saturday, February 22, 2020

IN THE OLD DAYS, KELLY AND SCOTTY TOOK THEIR
Saturday morning Frosted Flakes with a side of Scooby-Doo.
Maybe that was true for Naomi, too, although I didn't know her
back then. For Mel's and my second Saturday morning with Kyle
in residence, cartoons were nowhere in evidence.

Mel and I both grew up during an age when Saturdays were designated for housecleaning. That tradition holds true in our house
to this day, but with us, it's usually every Saturday. On Kyle's first
day, she had called in sick. With only two of us, we keep things
reasonably neat, but we're not offended by a dust bunny or two.
And since neither of us is exactly skilled in the art of domestic
science, we have help.

Alice Patterson is a feisty little fiftysomething who drives a
school bus during the week and cleans other people's houses on

weekends. I'm not sure when she cleans her own. She doesn't have any use for the vacuum system we installed when we remodeled the house. Instead, she shows up on Saturday mornings with her trusty Dyson at the ready while lugging a five-gallon plastic container loaded with her approved cleaning solutions along with a whole collection of dustcloths and -rags.

During breakfast, Mel leveled a look at Kyle and said, "How's your room?"

"Fine, I guess. Why?"

"Because Alice, our housekeeper, comes today," Mel explained. "Sheets, pillowcases, and towels need to be in the laundry room before she gets here, and anything that might interfere with her dusting, vacuuming, or cleaning needs to be put away."

I've always gotten a kick out of Mel's propensity for cleaning the house before the cleaning lady arrives, but in this case it was necessary. After breakfast she walked Kyle to the guest room and performed a preliminary inspection—which he failed. Mel grew up with a US Army colonel for a father, so she comes with fairly stringent standards, and Kelly's and Jeremy's expectations regarding room cleanliness were obviously lower than Mel's. It took half an hour of remedial work on Kyle's part before Mel pronounced the room as "Alice ready."

Once released from cleaning duty, Kyle headed out to the garage where he began whaling away on his drums. I didn't blame him. After school the day before, while the two of us were walking Sarah together, I had asked him if he'd met anyone at school who interested him.

"Why bother trying to make new friends?" he had asked hopelessly. "They're going to shut down school in a couple of weeks anyway."

He was right about that, of course. Breaking into a new social circle in high school isn't easy under the best of circumstances, and these were anything but normal. He was brokenhearted, lonely, and living with a pair of old people he barely knew. With that in mind, I figured beating the living hell out of that drum set was good for what ailed him. As for disturbing the neighbors? I didn't worry too much about that. Once spring comes around, weekend mornings all over Fairhaven are punctuated by the noise of lawn mowers followed by a barrage of leaf blowers come fall. Compared to the noisy racket from those, the steady beat on his drums barely counted as a disturbance.

As chief of police, Mel is regarded as an important player in terms of city government. As a result, she's part of several citywide networking organizations. I was deep in my crosswords when she looked up and remarked, "This isn't going to be good."

"What's that?"

"I talked with people from the school district last night. Our shutdown will most likely hit sooner than later, probably by the first or second week in March. The big delay right now is trying to figure out how to switch over from in-person to online learning."

"A complete shutdown?" I asked. "Are you sure? And is that even a good idea? For years the experts have been telling us that too much screen time is bad for kids. Now they want them to use screen time instead of going to school?"

"Evidently," Mel said.

"And is this whole Covid thing going to be as bad as everyone is making it out to be? Have we had even so much as a single case here in Bellingham?"

Mel and I don't share the same mental health regimen. She tolerates my aversion to news these days, but she doesn't necessarily approve of it.

"You can bury your head in your news blackout all you want," she answered, "but believe me, cases will be coming to Bellingham. I've been watching the numbers, Beau. People, especially older people, are dying of Covid all over the world, and so far nobody knows how to treat it. So, yes, it's going to be bad—very bad. They're saying as bad as or even worse than the Spanish flu in the early part of the last century."

"But how exactly is this school shutdown going to work?" I asked. "It's Kyle's senior year, for Pete's sake."

"It'll be mandatory for everybody, seniors included," she said. "We'll just have to figure out how to live with it."

I went back to my crossword, but my heart wasn't in it. I was thinking about how things had been back in my senior year of high school. At that point in my life I'd never met any of my grandparents, but being eighteen years old and having to be locked up for an unknown period of time with only a couple of elderly folks for company didn't sound like my idea of a good time. Would Kyle have been better off staying in Ashland or moving to Eugene with his mom? Maybe. Probably. Was it too late now for him to change his mind?

Just then a call came in from Todd Hatcher.

"Sorry, I know I said I'd get back to you on this last night, but that didn't happen."

"That's all right. What do you have for me?" I asked.

"Things are getting more and more interesting," he replied. "I ran Caroline Richards's driver's license photo through a number of law enforcement facial rec databases. The first hit I got was to an eighteen-year-old named Lindsey Baylor. Seven years ago, she was arrested in Seattle and charged with prostitution. She was bailed out by her mother, Phyllis Baylor, and the charges were later dropped. But here's the problem. As near as I can tell, those initial IDs dating from 2003, both hers and her mother's, were as fake as the one belonging to your son-in-law's new main squeeze, Caroline. Between that first arrest and her emergence as Caroline Richards late last year, there's no sign of her."

"You're saying those other IDs first surfaced back in 2003?" I asked.

"That September is when Phyllis used a Washington State driver's license ID to sign her daughter up for the free/reduced-cost lunch program at Bow Lake Elementary School in SeaTac. Their address at the time was at a place on Pacific Highway South called the TaxiWay Motel, which has since been demolished. I found a much later address for them in a mobile home park located in Federal Way. Like her daughter, Phyllis had numerous arrests for prostitution, dating from early on up until 2015."

"Sounds like prostitution was the family business," I suggested. "If her first arrest was at age eighteen, my guess is that the daughter started working the streets earlier than that. So where's Phyllis now?"

"Deceased. Died of natural causes—hep C—in October of 2016. Her last arrest was in early 2015. After that she may have been too ill to work. She was alone and homeless at the time of her death. The King County Sheriff's Office attempted to locate her daughter or some other relative to take charge of her remains, but those efforts were unsuccessful. Eventually Phyllis was laid to rest in Mount Olivet Cemetery in Renton, along with 215 other homeless individuals. I'm thinking both mother and child may have been in Witness Protection."

That story—where a mother and a young child or two all turn up with fake IDs—sounded all too familiar to me, because I'd heard it before, and always in connection with Witness Protection.

WITSEC is shorthand for the US Marshals Witness Protection Security Program. The only things most people know about Witness Protection is what they see on TV or in the movies. In those fictional stories, prosecutors often assure terrified individuals that they won't need to worry about testifying against some dangerous bad guy because they'll be placed in Witness Protection.

Sounds good, right? Viewers who don't know better probably imagine that the Witness Protection program comes complete with a modest two-bedroom/one-bath bungalow surrounded by a picket fence. The reality is often far different. In my experience many of the so-called protectees are dropped off at run-down apartment buildings or fleabag hotels in not-so-nice parts of strange towns. For women in those kinds of situations, especially ones with little kids and no marketable skills, working the streets ends up being their only option. In my work as a cop it's something I saw all too often.

As soon as Todd mentioned Witness Protection, I was sure he was on the right track, and for the first time, I found myself feeling the smallest smidgeon of sympathy for Caroline Richards, aka Lindsey Baylor. She had to have been younger than five when she'd been saddled with that brand-new but phony name. And if she had grown up with a destitute and likely drug-abusing mother, she would have endured a difficult and chaotic childhood. No wonder she had glommed on to Jeremy Cartwright. She no doubt saw him as a meal ticket, someone who would offer her some stability. But who was she really, and what kind of criminal situation from the past had put both mother and child in that situation? Those were questions with no easy answers.

"I'll keep looking," Todd said, bringing me back to the conversation at hand, "but don't hold your breath. Getting a facial rec hit on something from 2003 and from a completely unknown location isn't very likely."

THAT EVENING KYLE surprised us by offering to cook dinner, and he delivered a respectable batch of spaghetti. I doubt Gordon Ramsay would have called it elevated, but it was certainly edible and better than anything I could have conjured up.

"Who taught you to cook?" Mel asked after taking a tentative bite.

"My mom," he said. "Dad can't cook for beans, and neither can Caroline. I'm the one who had to do most of the cooking."

"Their loss is our gain then," Mel said with a smile, "but you'll end up having to give Grandpa and me a few lessons."

He grinned back at her. "I'll try," he said.

As a cop I was accustomed to not discussing active investigations, but I'm not a cop any longer. Still, since my family was all bound up in this one, it seemed reasonable that if I wanted Kyle to be straight with me, I needed to be the same with him.

"By the way," I said, "her real name isn't Caroline Richards."

Both Mel and Kyle looked at me in disbelief. "It's not?" Kyle managed.

I gave them a brief overview of what Todd and I had surmised about Caroline Richards's history, leaving them both gobsmacked.

"You really think she grew up in Witness Protection starting when she was just a little kid?" Kyle asked when I finished.

"That's only a guess on our part," I admitted, "but the trail of multiple IDs strongly suggests that might be the case."

"What do you think her mother did?" Kyle asked.

"I'm not sure if it's something she did or if it's something someone else did that she knew about. One way or another, Phyllis ended up with a target on her back, and her daughter ended up having to go along for the ride."

"That sounds awful," Kyle said. "It almost makes me feel sorry for her. Is there any way to find out what really happened?"

"If the US Marshals are involved, probably not," I explained. "Information on people in Witness Protection is never made public. Once someone walks through that door, there's usually no going back, not without putting yourself in mortal danger."

"Even after this long?" Kyle asked. "I mean, in 2003, I had barely been born."

"Any number of bad guys out there are a lot like elephants," I told him. "Once you cross them, they never forget."

CHAPTER 11

Bellingham, Washington
Saturday, February 22, 2020

THE NEED TO STRATEGIZE ABOUT MEALS ON A DAILY BASIS
wasn't the only change brought about after adding Kyle to the
mix of Mel's and my way of life. Our bedroom boasts a completely
acceptable master bath, which includes a double vanity and an
amazing shower. In reality, the en suite bath is mostly Mel's do-
main. In the past, for everything other than showers, I had used
the powder room. With Kyle present, I no longer felt comfortable
hotfooting it between our bedroom and the powder room in my
skivvies.

We'd also learned that private conversations often needed to
happen in our bedroom. Which is why Mel waited until we were
on our way to bed before putting in her two cents' worth on our
dinnertime discussion regarding Phyllis and Lindsey Baylor.

"I'm really curious about what happened there," she said. "What kind of a case would have been important enough to put someone like Phyllis into Witness Protection?"

"Maybe something drug related?" I suggested. "Or, more likely, cartel related, but good luck prying any information about that out of the US Marshals."

"Maybe you don't have to," Mel said.

"What do you mean?"

"Forensic genealogy has caught up with a lot of bad guys in the last few years," Mel suggested, "but maybe it's caught up with the US Marshals Service, too. Maybe it's time you gave Lulu Benson a call."

Have I mentioned that there are times when Mel Soames is nothing short of brilliant?

Lucille Benson, aka Little Lulu because she's barely four ten, is a recent addition to TLC's collection of volunteer cold case investigators. The Last Chance was created years ago by a woman named Hedda Brinker. Frustrated by the fact that her daughter's homicide had gone unsolved for decades, she decided to use her winnings from a huge Powerball jackpot to create an all-volunteer cold case squad to tackle abandoned cold cases for the benefit of other grieving families.

When it came time to set TLC in motion, she had called on a guy named Ralph Ames to handle all the organizational details and to make sure any residual funds were reinvested to cover ongoing expenses. Ralph is also the guy who brought me to TLC in the aftermath of my forced retirement due to the dismantling of the Special Homicide Investigation Team. Ralph first came into my life when I met and married my second wife, Anne Corley. Anne died on the day of our wedding, but Ralph and I have remained friends ever since.

Like me, Ralph is getting up there in terms of age, and he's recently handed over the reins for overseeing TLC to his son, Rafe, who, not surprisingly, is also an attorney and who happens to live in Denver, the location of TLC's headquarters. By way of introducing Rafe to all the folks involved—a group made up of retired detectives, prosecutors, and forensic folk—earlier that year we had all, spouses included, trekked to Denver's Brown Palace for a meet and greet where Mel and Lulu had hit it off like gangbusters.

Lulu and I are about the same age, and we both grew up with *Little Lulu* comics, which were the only comic books my mother allowed in our apartment. While my friends read *Superman* and *Batman*, I was stuck with *Little Lulu*. Mel is fifteen years younger than I am and never saw one of those comic books, but when we told her about Little Lulu's pal, Tubby, and his clubhouse plainly marked "NO GIRLS ALLOWED," she got the picture.

Lucille Benson had entered the "boys only" world of law enforcement much earlier than Mel. After graduating cum laude from the University of Nebraska with double majors in Chemistry and Microbiology, she had gone to work in Nebraska State Patrol's Crime Lab. Her first day on the job, she was taken to task by the director for wearing a miniskirt to work, something he said would serve as a distraction to her fellow criminalists—all of whom happened to be male. The next day she had shown up in a pair of cut-down overalls and tiny work boots. Turned out that costume was deemed to be a distraction as well. Shortly thereafter, everyone working in the lab, male and female alike, were directed to wear knee-length lab coats. Once that happened, whatever was worn underneath was no longer an issue.

Relating that story made Lulu and Mel instant pals. Mel, too, had her own set of law enforcement hazing stories from a somewhat later generation, giving the two women a good deal in common. Despite Lulu's somewhat problematic introduction to the crime lab, she had hung in there. By the time she retired some forty years later, she'd been the director for the previous ten. In retirement, rather than reading books or traveling or gardening, Lulu had set her sights on tracking down her family tree. Eventually she had succeeded in tracing her roots on both sides of her family as far back as the sixteenth century in the UK. One of her distant ancestors had actually been on board the *Mayflower*.

But then 2018 came along when cops in California used DNA and forensic genealogy to finally bring down the Golden State killer. Suddenly something that had been little more than a retirement hobby for Lulu Benson morphed into a crime-fighting tool. Just like that, she was ready to take everything she had learned about genealogy and go back to work.

TLC didn't come looking for her. She went looking for them. She had introduced herself to Rafe Ames about the time he was taking charge and made him an offer he couldn't refuse. She'd be willing to join forces with TLC and bring several other retired criminalists along for the ride if TLC would spring for a full-fledged laboratory equipped with the latest in DNA profiling equipment.

Most of the cold cases that come to TLC as a last resort are there because the homicides in question had occurred in jurisdictions with limited funds and even more limited investigative resources. Not only is DNA testing expensive, it takes time—lots of it. Wait times on active cases may seem frustratingly slow, but for cold cases, they're downright interminable.

Knowing Hedda Brinker would approve, Rafe agreed to spend a big chunk of her Powerball fortune to purchase an appropriate lab location. He then set about filling it with the latest and greatest

DNA processing equipment. Most of the people at TLC are volunteers, but to have a properly certified lab whose results would stand up in court, it was necessary to actually hire qualified personnel to work there. That was a far more complicated task than anyone had anticipated. Months later, it still wasn't up and running—which meant Lulu wasn't, either. It occurred to me that if she was sitting around twiddling her thumbs, maybe she wouldn't mind taking on a side gig, even if it wasn't exactly TLC's cup of tea.

"Great idea, Mel," I said, giving her a good night kiss as she settled down beside me in bed. "I'll give Lulu a call first thing Monday morning."

CHAPTER 12

Bellingham, Washington
Monday, February 24, 2020

BY WEEK TWO OF OUR NEW FAMILY'S BACK-TO-SCHOOL ADVEN-ture, we were starting to get the hang of things. Kyle was okay with cold cereal and toast for breakfast, and that suited me just fine because I'm generally good with toast and coffee. Once he left, I picked up the phone and dialed Lulu.

"How are things?" I asked.

"I'm bored to tears," she replied.

"Still no movement on getting the lab up and running?"

"Not so as you'd notice. The whole purpose of having our own lab is being able to cut through the red tape. The problem is, there's a mountain of red tape to get through before we can get the lab certified and operational. What's up with you and Mel?"

"Well," I said. "That's what I wanted to talk to you about."

It took some time to explain our sudden return to the world of parenthood and the background that led to it.

"So you're asking for my assistance in tracking down the real identities of two people who may have been placed in WITSEC in the early two thousands?"

"Correct."

"If we succeed, that's not going to win us any points with the US Marshals Service."

"No, it won't."

"Well," Lulu observed, "if the case was big enough that the Marshals were pulled into it, you can bet it was large enough to have garnered a good deal of media coverage, such as it was back then. My guess would be something to do with either cartels or organized crime. What we really need is some idea of how many cases like that were active back in 2002 or 2003. Do you have any DNA?"

"That would be a hard no. When Kyle left home, he didn't exactly come away with his father's pregnant girlfriend's toothbrush stowed in his backpack. Said girlfriend is easily a good eight-and-a-half-hour drive from here. Given the circumstances, I don't think a visit from me would be very welcome at this point."

"Does the girlfriend smoke?"

"She's expecting a baby, so I doubt it," I answered.

"Lots of people smoke while they're pregnant," Lula countered, "but they don't go around talking about it. Does your son-in-law smoke?"

"He never used to," I replied, "but that might have changed. Why?"

"When it comes to getting DNA samples from people who don't want to share them, a potential suspect's garbage can can be your best friend," she told me, "and cigarette butts make for a very useful kind of garbage. How old is your grandson?"

"Just turned eighteen."

"Even though he's no longer living in the area, I'm sure he still has friends there. Check with him to see if Caroline smokes or has a favorite kind of soda or other beverage, then see if he can enlist one of his friends to stage a raid on their trash can, looking for items she's likely to have touched. It would be best if whoever does that uses latex gloves, but it's not essential. And since we don't need something that will hold up in court, there's no need to worry about maintaining a chain of evidence."

"But how does Kyle explain this whole caper to a friend?"

"His father and Caroline met on a dating site, right?"

"Correct," I said.

"How many times have you heard about people hooking up with people on dating sites who turn out to be something other than what they're pretending? Have him say he's just trying to look into her background. That should work.

"If you and Kyle can come up with a sample attributable to the woman in question, I'll be responsible for getting the profile. Then, if we can find a blood relative of Caroline's, no matter how distant, I'll go about working up family trees, which may help us sort out the geography involved. At that point, we start tracking down cases—most likely ones involving the feds—from back in 2002 and 2003 that also originate from that general area."

"That should keep us off the streets for a while," I observed.

"Yes, it will," she agreed with a chuckle, "but at some point, someone from that family tree is going to intersect with a name from one of those cases. Then we'll be in business. How are you fixed for search capability?"

"Not so hot personally," I admitted, "but I have a friend who's a whiz at it, and he has access to sites I've never even heard of."

"Great," Lulu replied. "Sounds like just the kind of guy we're going to need."

THAT AFTERNOON, ONCE Kyle came home and before Mel did, I broached the subject of trying to obtain samples of Caroline's DNA to learn her true identity through the use of forensic genealogy.

"Should we tell Dad about this?" he asked.

"Not until we know for sure," I told him. "The first problem is getting a sample of her DNA. Does she happen to smoke?"

"She shouldn't, but she does," he replied. "How did you know that?"

"Lucky guess," I answered. "Cigarettes only or something else?"

"Nothing else that I know of."

That was also good news. I didn't want to be caught shipping the remains of a joint across state lines through the US Postal Service.

"What about your father?"

"He doesn't smoke, and I don't think he knows she's doing it. She only does it behind his back."

"Sounds like she does a lot of things behind his back," I observed. "So here's the deal. Do you know which day of the week is trash day at the house in Ashland?"

"Wednesdays," he said. "I had to make sure the cans were hauled out to the curb every Tuesday night. Why?"

"Who's your best friend down there?" I asked.

"Ricky," he said at once. "Rick Malden. We've been friends since first grade. He's the lead singer in the Rockets. Why?"

"How good of a friend is he?" I wondered. "The kind who would be willing to raid your family's trash can to see if he can find any cigarette butts hiding there, especially cigarette butts with lipstick on them?"

"Probably, but what we're asking him to do sounds pretty weird. What am I supposed to tell him about why we need her cigarette butts?"

"Does Rick know about the stunt Caroline pulled with your other friend?" I asked.

"With Gabe you mean?"

"Yes, does Rick know about that?"

Kyle nodded. "When Gabe up and quit the band, Rick couldn't figure out how come, so I told him."

"Tell him that's why you're worried and why you want to find out more about Caroline. And tell him that since we're looking for DNA, it would be best if he wore gloves while he's searching through the trash, and anything he finds should go in a plastic bag."

"Like a sandwich bag?"

"Yes."

"Okay," Kyle said. "I'll ask him and see what he says."

A while later, when Kyle was out in the yard, playing fetch with Sarah, I noticed that he was texting on his phone between throws. A little while later, when he came in, he gave me a thumbs-up.

"Rick says he'll be glad to," he told me, "and he'll do it tomorrow night."

Mel was home by then. "Rick will be glad to do what?" she asked.

"Kyle's friend Rick is going to raid Jeremy's trash can tomorrow evening and see if he can come up with some possible evidence containing a sample of Caroline's DNA so we can ship it off to Lulu Benson."

"Good-o," Mel said. "I'm glad you took my advice."

So was I.

CHAPTER 13

Bellingham, Washington
Tuesday, February 25, 2020

DETERMINED TO GET A LOOK AT DARIUS'S EVIDENCE BOX, ONCE Mel and Kyle were out of the house on Tuesday morning, Sarah and I headed for Seattle. On the way, I placed a call to Todd Hatcher.

"Good morning," he said cheerfully.

"Any luck tracking down Caroline Richards's history?" I asked.

"Not so far," he told me.

"Well," I said, "if we can lay hands on a sample of her DNA, we may try going the forensic genealogy route."

"Given the circumstances, you can't very well turn up on her doorstep and ask for a cheek swab," he commented.

"No, I can't," I agreed. "We're having to be a bit more underhanded than that. One of Kyle's friends is going to raid their trash can tonight looking for cigarette butts. I've been led to believe she's the only person in the residence who smokes."

J. A. JANCE

"Good luck with that," Todd said, "but I suspect this isn't a social call. What else can I do you for?"

"If Caroline and her mother were put into Witness Protection in 2002 or 2003, presumably they were connected, one way or another, to some operation—maybe a federal one, maybe not. Do you know any experts I might be able to contact for details concerning what was going on back then?"

"I might, but I'll need to have some idea as far as the locale is concerned."

"And I won't have any information regarding that until we see if the DNA data points us in a specific direction."

"Okey dokey," he said. "Let me know."

Todd sounded like he was getting ready to hang up. "One more thing," I said quickly, "only this is on another subject altogether."

"What's that?"

"I know how many drug overdose deaths there were in King County in 2018, but can you give me a breakdown of how many of those were determined to be accidental?"

"I'd guess most of them," he replied. "People who manufacture illegal drugs don't exactly operate under FDA supervision or follow recommended dosage guidelines. So the dim bulb out on the street who thinks he's buying a recreational hit may end up with a dose that's a whole lot more powerful."

"As in lethal?" I asked.

"Exactly, but here's the problem," Todd continued. "To sort out which of those deaths were designated as accidental rather than suicide or homicide, I'd have to go through all the individual death certificates. That's too big a job for me to tackle right now. Sorry."

I drove on feeling more than a little disheartened. I was sure Todd was correct in his assumption that the vast majority of the fentanyl deaths really were entirely accidental. Most of the victims wouldn't have taken that final dose of Jackpot, fentanyl's street name, with the intention of ending their own lives. Once the word *accidental* is written on a death certificate, any law enforcement agency involved would be entirely justified in declaring the investigations closed. Period. Ditto for deaths designated as suicides. But how many of those supposed suicides and accidental deaths weren't either one but were actually unsolved homicides? Were there other deaths besides Darius Jackson's that might fit that bill?

Seattle PD's Evidence unit is now located in Seattle's SODO neighborhood. That acronym used to mean South of the Kingdome, which was then a cutesy way of referring to the area that actually worked. Once the Kingdome was blown to smithereens, the moniker didn't change but the meaning did. Now it's short for South of Downtown, which isn't nearly as evocative. It's also a neighborhood that has devolved into Seattle's homeless camp central.

Once there, knowing there was no way I could pass Sarah off as a service dog, I took her for a quick walk and then locked her in the back seat of my S 550 with the windows on both sides of the car cracked partway open. It was cold but not freezing, and I was sure she'd welcome the fresh air.

The last time I had come to the Evidence unit I had been on a mission to figure out what had really happened to my old nemesis, Maxwell Cole. That time I'd had a free pass for admittance from my former partner and now assistant chief of police, Ron Peters. This time I was on my own.

The fortysomething woman behind the counter wore a Seattle PD uniform with a name tag identifying her as Officer M. Harriman.

"Good morning," I told her. "My name's J. P. Beaumont. I'm a private investigator, and I'd like to look at an evidence box for a man named Darius Jackson. He died of an overdose on Thanksgiving night, 2018, and his manner of death was designated as accidental."

"Beaumont," Officer Harriman repeated with a thoughtful frown. It was as though that was the only information from my introduction that had actually registered. "Any relation to Scotty?" she asked.

Scotty again. Obviously my participation at Seattle PD had been erased from the departmental memory banks and had been replaced by someone else's.

"He's my son," I said.

But sharing Scott's name worked well enough for me to gain entry. With a welcoming smile, Officer Harriman handed me a clipboard with a form attached as well as an accompanying ballpoint pen.

"Please fill this out," she said.

I sat down and set about completing the form, thankful that Detective Sechrest had provided me with the case number. When I handed the clipboard back, Officer Harriman gave it a quick once-over.

"A closed case then," she said. "That shouldn't be a problem. I'll have the evidence box brought to a private room where you'll be able to go through it at your leisure. You can take photos as needed, but please don't remove any items. As I'm sure you know, there are video cameras posted in each room."

"Thanks," I told her. "I know the drill."

A few minutes later, I found myself in a small room with a single table, a single chair, and a virtually empty evidence box. I went through all the contents. There was everything you'd expect, including the clothing Darius was wearing at the time of his death. A copy of the death certificate laid out the extent of his injuries, which included blunt force trauma to the side of his head, most likely as a result of a fall, and the needle track—a single needle track—on the inside of his right wrist. I examined the crime-scene photos. They showed Darius lying on his side in a trash-strewn alleyway under the Alaskan Way Viaduct, which, like the King-dome, is also now a thing of the past. Those were the last sounds Darius would have heard before he died—the rumble of traffic on that roadway overhead.

At the very bottom of the evidence box I found two separate items—a DVD and a sheaf of paperwork from the Washington State Patrol Crime Lab indicating that residue from inside the syringe indicated the presence of liquid fentanyl. Fingerprints and DNA found on the outside of the syringe were identified as belonging to Darius Jackson. In addition, the exterior of the syringe contained trace DNA from an unknown female. That DNA had been entered into CODIS with no resulting match. Because I still have friends in the crime lab, I made a note of the case number.

As for the DVD? I had to go back out to the front office and ask for assistance. Officer Harriman took possession of the DVD and then inserted it into a player that sent the resulting video to a computer and monitor located in my viewing room. It turned out to be the food bank's security footage from Thanksgiving night. It showed two figures: a tall male—Darius, most likely—and a somewhat wobbly female leaning on the handle of an overloaded grocery cart, threading their way through the parking lot.

The woman was far shorter than her male companion with the top of her head several inches shy of Darius's shoulder. She wore a hoodie. The video was too grainy to make out any features, but a few wisps of light-colored hair seemed to have escaped from under the covering on her head.

I replayed the clip several times over, watching from the moment they emerged from the food bank's main entrance until they disappeared on the far side of the parking lot as they walked out of camera range. There was nothing in the behavior of either one of them that indicated anything amiss. There was no sign of their being in distress. They appeared to be walking and talking in a completely normal fashion.

Once finished with my survey of the evidence, I thanked Officer Harriman for her assistance and headed for the Washington State Patrol Crime Lab, which, as it happens, is only a few short blocks away. Gretchen Walther, who is now in charge of the DNA lab there, is an old pal of mine, and she's helped me out more than once both before and after I turned in my S.H.I.T. badge in favor of becoming a private investigator.

GRETCHEN GREETED ME with a hug and a smile. "To what do I owe the honor?" she asked. "Obviously you're here asking for help with something."

"What are you, some kind of mind reader?"

"You don't have to be clairvoyant when you're dealing with a one-trick pony," she replied. "The only time you ever show up around here is when you're looking for a favor. What now?"

"I'm working on behalf of a woman named Matilda Jackson whose grandson, Darius, died of a fentanyl overdose on Thanksgiving night, 2018. His death was ruled an accident, but she believes he was murdered, and so do I."

"You're trying to reopen the case?"

I nodded.

"Good luck with that," Gretchen said, "but how can I help?"

"In going through the evidence box, I found that a female DNA profile was obtained from a syringe located at the scene, and I'm wondering what you can tell me about it."

I handed her my notebook, pointing to the place where I had written down the state patrol's assigned case number. She studied it for a moment, then typed something into her computer.

"Here it is," she said. "What do you want to know?"

I said, "A note in the evidence book indicated that the profile was entered into CODIS, but that you didn't get a hit."

"We didn't," Gretchen told me, "but someone else did."

That remark put me on full alert. "Who?" I demanded. "When?"

"The same female profile—still unidentified—was found in connection with another drug overdose victim, one from over near Spokane. The guy's name was Jake Spaulding, age thirty-four. On July 10, 2019, he was found dead in a vehicle parked outside a local bar in Liberty Lake, Washington."

"Case number?" I asked.

She read it off to me.

"Manner of death?"

"Undetermined."

"Cause of death?"

"Inhaling vaporized fentanyl," Gretchen replied. "A vape pen with his fingerprints on it was found inside the vehicle. As for the female DNA profile? That was found on a car door handle rather than on the vape pen itself."

"Do you know what happened to the case once they had that information?"

"Our job is to process the evidence," she reminded me. "What investigators do with it after that is none of our business, but as far as I know the case remains unresolved at this time."

"Was there a detective assigned to the Liberty Lake case?"

"Yes, sir."

"Do you have a name?"

"Detective Ronald Wang," she answered, consulting her computer screen. "And I suppose you'd like to have his number?"

"Absolutely."

"What are you thinking about all this?" Gretchen asked, once I had added Detective Wang's name and number to my notebook.

"I suspect we could be looking at a female drug dealer who is somehow managing to operate under the radar. And since we've linked her to at least two separate overdose deaths, I'm wondering how many more of those are still out there that we have yet to discover."

"All right," Gretchen replied. "Keep me posted. If there's anything more we can do on this end, let me know."

"Believe me, I will," I told her. I started to leave, but then one more thought occurred to me. "What about this? If someone from TLC asked for a copy of that female DNA profile, would you be able to release it?"

"TLC," she repeated. "Isn't that the cold case organization you work with?"

"Yes, The Last Chance."

"I don't see why not," Gretchen said with a shrug.

"Stay tuned then," I told her. "And don't be surprised if you get a call from Lulu Benson asking for exactly that—a copy of the profile. She's recently joined TLC."

Gretchen's face lit up. "Lulu Benson. Are you kidding? You mean as in the Lucille Benson from the Nebraska State Crime Lab in Omaha?"

I have to admit that I was surprised by Gretchen's instant recognition of the name. "That's the one," I replied. "Do you know her?"

"Not personally, but I'd like to," Gretchen replied. "She's a legend in her own time. There's not a woman who works in this lab, me included, who doesn't want to be just like Lulu Benson when she grows up."

That's when I realized that, although we were decades away from the time when miniskirts weren't allowed in crime labs, the world of women in law enforcement in general and forensics in particular remains a small, tightly knit circle.

CHAPTER 14

Bellingham, Washington
Wednesday, February 26, 2020

THE NEXT MORNING MEL WAS ALREADY OFF TO WORK WHEN Kyle showed up for breakfast. He gave me a grin and a double thumbs-up.

"Mission accomplished," he said. "Rick did the trash raid last night and scored a dozen or so cigarette butts. I told him to mail them to me here. He said he won't be able to get to the post office until after school today."

"Good-o," I said.

"He says they're getting ready to shut schools down in Ashland, too," he added. "It'll probably happen in both places about the same time—sometime in the next couple of weeks. I guess everyone's trying to figure out how to go about putting things online."

"Like band, for instance?" I asked. "How's your dad going to manage that?"

Kyle shrugged. "That's his problem."

"What about you, Kyle? Are you sure you want to be locked up with a couple of old fogies like Mel and me for the duration of all this, or would you rather wait out Covid in Eugene with your mom and sister?"

"Are you trying to get rid of me?" he asked.

"No, I'm trying to find out what you want. Mel and I are good either way."

"I'd rather be here," he said.

"All right then," I told him. "I'm glad that's settled. Like it or not, online schooling here we come."

Once he left the house, I dialed up Lulu.

"You called that shot," I said. "We're expecting a shipment of Caroline Richards's cigarette butts to arrive here sometime later this week. What's your best address?"

She gave it to me, and I jotted it down. "So now how about tackling another case?" I asked.

"You've got another one for me?"

"As a matter of fact, I do," I told her. Then I filled her in on the Darius Jackson situation.

"I know your type, J. P. Beaumont," she said with a sigh. "Give you an inch and you think you're a ruler. Now you've got me working three separate cases—Caroline's and two separate overdose cases."

"Two for right now," I told her. "But there may be more."

"Keep me posted then," she said. "I'm glad to be of service. And as soon as I get off the phone, I'll give Gretchen Walther a call."

"She'll be over the moon," I told her. "Turns out the storied Lucille Benson is one of her idols."

"Give me a break," Lulu said dismissively. "People tend to give me way too much credit for something that's nothing other than longevity."

Longevity, I thought, *combined with a whole lot of smarts.*

CHAPTER 15

Bellingham, Washington
Thursday, February 27, 2020

THE CALL THAT CAME IN FROM AN UNIDENTIFIED NUMBER
shortly after noon on Thursday was completely out of the blue,
but it was a game changer.

"Mr. Beaumont?" an unfamiliar female voice asked.

"Yes," I answered. "Who's this?"

"My name is Yolanda Aguirre. I'm a forensic economist based in
Seattle. An acquaintance of mine, Todd Hatcher, suggested I give
you a call."

That was a relief. I was afraid it was someone asking me for a
donation to their pet charity.

"Todd's a good friend of mine," I said. "How can I help you, Ms.
Aguirre?"

"I believe we have a mutual interest," she replied. "I'm working
on a grant from the Washington Department of Social Services to

study the long-term economic and psychological effects of drug overdose deaths on surviving family members. He said you were interested in knowing how overdose deaths broke down in terms of manner of death rulings. I may be able to shed some light on that."

My heart skipped a beat. "You've actually studied the individual cases?" I asked.

"And interviewed a good number of the surviving family members," she told me.

I could barely believe my ears. God love Todd Hatcher! If someone else had already gone to the trouble of combing through that long catalog of death certificates, I wouldn't have to.

"I'm doing a five-year study, starting in 2013," Yolanda continued. "I've finished interviews through 2016, and I'm working on 2017."

I struggled to contain my excitement. "And you're interviewing affected family members?" I asked, just to confirm what I thought I'd heard.

"Wherever possible," she replied. "In some cases, especially in terms of homeless victims, I was unable to locate any surviving family members at all. And wherever migrant families are involved, they're generally unwilling to speak. Some of the refuseniks thought I was actually a cop of some kind masquerading as someone else, probably Border Patrol. But a surprisingly large number of the ones I did interview were more than willing to speak primarily because they really wanted to talk to someone about their dead loved one when everyone else seemed to have forgotten. When their parent, child, brother, or grandson died of a drug overdose—by and large the victims are male—the death may have registered as an overdose statistic in the M.E.'s office, but that was it. No one was ever held responsible for what had happened. The lives of those individual families had been forever changed, but nobody else seemed to give a rat's ass."

I thought about Matilda Jackson. That was what she had wanted when I had gone to see her—an opportunity to talk about her dead grandson to someone who would actually listen.

"As for law enforcement?" Yolanda continued. "As soon as there's a suicide or accident ruling on an autopsy report and the death certificate, it's like the cops have King's X. They close the books on the case and walk away."

The term "King's X" was something I remembered from playing tag during recess back in grade school. I had initially assumed Yolanda to be fairly young. Now I revised that estimate upward by several decades.

"That's been my experience, too," I offered. "I suspect that the term 'accidental overdose' is a bureaucratic black hole used to cover a multitude of sins. In fact, I'm currently working on just such a case from 2018, one in which the family believes the victim was murdered."

"I know," Yolanda said. "Todd mentioned that might be the situation. I've encountered a few of those, too. That's why I called."

"Is there a chance I'd be able to read through any of those interviews?"

"I promised the families anonymity, so I'd need to redact the last names before handing them over."

"That's fine. If I see something that doesn't look right, maybe you could go back to the families and get permission from them to bring me into the picture. Whereabouts are you located?"

"I'm on the backside of Queen Anne Hill in Seattle. Why?"

"I'm in Bellingham," I told her. "Maybe I could drive down and take a look at those interviews."

"That won't be necessary," she said. "I recorded the interviews and had my intern, Elena Moreno, transcribe them. As I said, I can have her redact the surnames and send you the pdfs. Would that work?"

"That would be amazing," I said.

I gave her my email information.

"Okay," she said. "I'll have Elena get on this right away."

A BATCH OF unseasonably warm air had blown in off the Pacific. With the thermometer on the back porch registering a balmy fifty-five, Sarah and I set off on our walk. Naturally we ran into Hank Mitchell and Mr. Bean along the way.

"How's that grandson of yours working out?" Hank asked.

"We're doing all right so far," I told him. "As for how things will be once the shutdown comes and he's home round the clock? That's anybody's guess."

"I take it he's something of a musician," Hank observed.

"Right," I said. "A drummer. I hope his playing isn't bothering you."

"Not at all," Hank replied. "I used to be something of a drummer myself back in the day. Fancied I'd be the next Gene Krupa when I grew up. That didn't happen, of course. Ended up building houses instead."

Was there a hint of regret in his voice when he said that? Maybe.

"We all have roads not taken," I said.

"Isn't that the truth," he agreed. "I still have that first drum set, though," he added. "I gave it to a grandson, but he gave it back when he joined the military. When we moved here, Ellen wanted me to unload it, but I told her as long as she still has all her quilting stuff, I'm keeping my drums. Maybe someday a great-grandson will love them as much as I do."

Up until that moment, I hadn't known Hank was a drummer and his wife was a quilter. They were our next-door neighbors, yes, but there was a lot I didn't know about them.

"Have you ever thought about taking up drumming again?" I asked.

"Are you kidding?" he returned. "At my age?"

"How old will you be if you don't?"

"There is that," he agreed, and we both kept on walking.

Back at the house, I was sitting at the kitchen counter staring at Darius's resurrected cell phone. It was no longer dead. One of the CSIs at Mel's department had managed to produce the right charger. The device was on, but it was still locked.

That was when Kyle walked past, heading for the fridge to grab a soda. "What's up?" he asked.

"This phone belongs to a guy who died of a drug overdose a couple of years ago," I told him. "I need to unlock it, but I don't know the password. It has six characters, but I know if I screw it up too many times, it'll lock me out permanently."

"What's the password on your phone?" Kyle asked.

"My birthday," I said. "What's yours?"

"My birthday," he answered. "If you know the guy's birthday, why don't you try that?"

After locating Darius's birth date in my notebook, I typed in 09-18-92. Once I did that, the phone opened right up.

"Voilà!" I told Kyle. "You're a genius."

"No, I'm not," he said, grinning back at me. "I'm a teenager."

I SPENT THE remainder of Thursday afternoon going through Darius's list of recent calls. There was nothing out of the ordinary. The people he had spoken to in either direction were all in his contacts list—Matilda, Gina Rising, his boss, Patrice Moser. There were numerous calls and texts to and from a guy named Norm, no last name. Scanning through the collection of texts it was clear that he had been Darius's NA sponsor. If Darius had slipped in the days leading up to his death, Norm for sure would know about it.

I tried Norm's number, but the call went to voicemail. I left a message. "My name is J. P. Beaumont. I'm a private investigator looking into Darius Jackson's death on behalf of his grandmother. I'd appreciate it if you'd give me a call back." I left my number but I didn't hold my breath about getting a call back.

For dinner that night, Mel brought home a bag of freshly made tamales and flour tortillas purchased from the mother of one of Bellingham's finest, a new recruit recently graduated from the police academy. The tamales along with servings of canned refried beans topped with melted cheese made for a perfectly acceptable Mexican dinner.

"Word came down shortly before I left the office," Mel told us as we ate. "The school shutdown will start the second week of March. Given that, Kyle, are you sure you want to stay here with us?"

Kyle favored her with an exasperated look. "Don't you guys ever talk?" he asked.

"What do you mean?"

"Gramps already asked me the same thing, and I told him I want to stay here."

"Fair enough then," she told him, "but don't forget, Alice Patterson comes on Saturday, so your room needs to be ready. That means your dirty clothes need to be washed, dried, and put away before she gets here. Got it?"

"Yes, ma'am," Kyle said.

Good answer, I thought. It sounded to me like he was catching on pretty fast.

CHAPTER 16

Bellingham, Washington
Friday, February 28, 2020

WHEN I LOOKED AT MY EMAIL ACCOUNT THE NEXT MORNING,
I had 136 new messages. At first I thought I had been the victim of a
massive spam attack, but it turned out they were all from Yolanda
Aguirre's assistant, Elena Moreno—one email per interview. Wanting to dig into them, I bypassed my daily crosswords in favor of
going to work. And that's how I spent the whole of Friday—reading
through those files. For dinner that night, Mel brought home Sub-
way sandwiches. I ate mine and then went straight back to reading.

Each separate interview followed the same format, and they were
incredibly thorough. In another life, Yolanda would have made an
excellent detective. In every case, she began by expressing her
condolences on the loss of each loved one and thanking the partic-
ipants for agreeing to talk to her.

The files contained the deceased individual's redacted last name, their date of birth, and date of death. Wherever possible, they also included information on next of kin as well as the identification of the person being interviewed—mother, sister, brother, and so on. Yolanda phrased her questions in a way that made it clear that she was interested in the family dynamics in play both prior to and after the death of their loved one. She charted each victim's drug usage and police interactions—including case file numbers—preceding the fatal overdoses. Yolanda also included in meticulous detail each family's interactions—or lack thereof—with law enforcement in the aftermath of each death. The final section of each interview covered the ongoing struggles of the bereaved family members, including, in many instances, the custodial outcomes for any surviving minor children. Several files in, I realized that every one was a step-by-step depiction of a family tragedy—of early promise and aspirations wiped out sooner or later by the scourge of drug abuse.

Some of the interviewees replied reluctantly, limiting their answers to as few words as possible, but for others Yolanda's interest in what had befallen them seemed to have breached a dam, allowing a flood of emotions to spill out. Like Matilda Jackson, rather than simply revealing the bare bones of the story, they wanted to tell all of it.

Several of those hit close to home. Over and over families related tales of trying to encourage their sons or daughters or brothers to get help, of holding interventions, of begging and pleading for the addict to make changes in their lives. Naturally those generally didn't work. Help imposed on someone who doesn't want it is so much wasted breath and, in many cases, so much wasted money and effort as well. Until addicts are ready to make those changes for themselves, stints in rehab are less than useless.

In other words, reading through the interviews was tough going

for yours truly. It reminded me about that little kid, cheerfully digging his way out of a room filled with horse turds. When someone
asked him why he was so happy, he replied, "With all this horse
shit, there's bound to be a pony in here somewhere."

I had worked my way up to file 18, and that's where I found my
pony. His first name was Raymond. His body had been found on
June 9, 2013, near the railroad tracks in Seattle's Golden Gardens
neighborhood. Because the body was found next to the track, the
initial assumption was that he'd been hit by a passing train. A subsequent autopsy revealed that he had died of a fentanyl overdose.
The autopsy also revealed that he suffered from a TBI—a traumatic
brain injury.

At first the family history as related by Ray's daughter Leann
sounded like the proverbial American dream. When Ray graduated
from Shoreline High School at the north end of the Seattle metropolitan area, he had done so as valedictorian of the class of 1979
where he had also been voted most likely to succeed. After being a
star athlete throughout his high school years, once Ray enrolled at
the University of Washington, he became a redshirt addition to the
U Dub's Huskies football team where he played tackle all four years.

After graduating with a degree in Civil Engineering, he married
his high school sweetheart, Meredith, and went to work for an engineering firm that specialized in airport facilities. His first project
involved working on an addition to SeaTac's already massive parking
garage.

Together, he and Meredith had three kids. They bought an older
home in the Green Lake area and everything seemed to be hunky-
dory. Then, in 1997, he made the fateful decision of taking his son,
Andrew, to a Seattle Mariner's home game as a father-son outing
to celebrate the boy's tenth birthday. After leaving the Kingdome,

they had been walking back to their vehicle when a passing motorist suffered a medical emergency and plowed into them. Ray managed to shove his son out of harm's way, but he himself suffered life-changing injuries, including multiple broken bones and a massive concussion. After that, he was never the same.

Unable to return to work and plagued by chronic pain, he ended up on opioid painkillers where he eventually became addicted. Not only that, his personality changed almost overnight. Before the accident, Ray had been a friendly, easygoing guy. Now he seemed to have a hair-trigger temper, and Meredith was his usual target. Leann, one of Ray's daughters, was the family spokesperson in this case, and reading her version of the story in Yolanda's interview was heartbreaking.

Leann: It was like a stranger had moved into our house. Dad wasn't our dad anymore. He was angry all the time, and the smallest thing could set him off. If we kids did the least little thing wrong, he would be furious. Mom told us that it wasn't his fault, that he was sick and couldn't help it, but that didn't make it any easier to live with. And because she was always trying to intercede for us, she usually ended up being his target and taking the brunt of his anger.

Yolanda: He was violent?

Leann: Absolutely. He was a big guy. When we were little she used to call him her Gentle Ben; after the accident, he was downright dangerous. One time he picked Mom up and threw her across the living room like she was a rag doll. Luckily she landed on the sofa.

That was the first time she called the cops on him. We kids were terrified. We thought he was going to kill her. They took him to jail, but he was only there overnight because she refused to press charges. She never did press charges, even though the same kind of thing happened time and again.

By then it was clear that he was hooked on drugs. We kids were the ones who told Mom that he needed to move out, that it was either him or us. We said if he didn't leave, we would all go to Shoreline and live with Grandma and Grandpa.

At that point Mom rented an apartment for Dad in Ballard so he could live there. The problem is, the apartment was still within walking distance of the house, so although he wasn't actually living with us, he was still there almost every day and even angrier than he had been before.

My sister, Marlise, left home and joined the military as soon as she graduated from high school. When Dad ended up getting evicted from his apartment, Mom let him come back home. It was like she was addicted to him and couldn't abandon him.

Once Andrew left for WSU, he was gone for good, too. By then the ongoing drama was too much for me, and I went to live with Mom's parents in Shoreline for my last two years of high school.

That passage hit me hard. Kyle Cartwright wasn't the only kid on the planet who, as a last resort, had been forced to turn to his grandparents for help.

Yolanda: But the domestic violence continued?
Leann: It seemed to be better for a while. Maybe, without us kids there, things weren't quite as stressful. But as far as I was concerned, out of sight was out of mind. But then in 2013, things heated up again, and Mom started having to call 911.

Law enforcement responded several times. It's a miracle he didn't kill her. Then one day Dad left the house without telling Mom where he was going and never came back. His body was found two days later in Golden Gardens.

Yolanda: He was still living with your mom at the time he disappeared?

Leann: For years, he lived down in the basement and she lived upstairs. When he didn't come home, Mom was frantic. She called me in hysterics and begged me to come help. I had recently graduated with my master's in nursing. Since I didn't have a job, I came home, and it's a good thing, too.

Mom had always been the strongest person I knew. She had spent years doing everything within her power to help him, but once they found his body, she was a complete basket case. After all those years of looking after him, she just couldn't cope anymore. I've never seen anyone so broken. Marlise is career navy and wasn't able to get leave, and Andrew had hired on to a new job, so I stepped up. I'm the one who had to deal with everything—the cops, the M.E., the positive ID, and the funeral arrangements.

That one struck me, too. Here were three kids, not unlike Kyle, who had grown up under challenging circumstances as far as their parental units were concerned. Not only had they all survived, they had thrived. They were self-sufficient, responsible adults. Maybe the same thing would be true for my grandson as well.

Yolanda: You were there when detectives came to make the notification?

Leann: Yes, I was. Mom insisted that the whole thing had to be a mistake and that Dad couldn't be dead, but of course he was. They found his ID in his wallet, and that was one of the reasons they said it was unlikely it was a robbery. Nothing was taken, not even the two hundred-dollar bills they found in his wallet.

I almost jumped out of my skin! *Holy crap! Are you frigging kidding me? Two hundred-dollar bills?*

I wasn't aware I was talking to myself, but I was, enough so that I disturbed Sarah. She raised her head off her rug and gave me a look as if to reassure herself that I was all right. But I wasn't, not at all. I was beside myself, because I really had found that damned pony!

I had started that day with two overdose cases linked by DNA. Now one of those was linked to yet a third case by the presence of Darius Jackson's two hundred-dollar bills. Yes, I was definitely on the right track, and no matter how many more files Yolanda Aguirre sent me, I was going to read every one of them word for word.

Eventually I settled down and got back to reading. Yolanda's subsequent questions led Leann through the immediate aftermath of her father's death.

Leann: Mom never recovered. She believed that if she had somehow taken better care of my father, he wouldn't have died. That wasn't true. You can't save someone who isn't interested in saving himself, but she never got over losing him. She committed suicide five years ago. Her suicide note said, "It's all my fault."

Yolanda: I'm so sorry. What a tragedy. How are you, your sister, and your brother doing?

Leann: Marlise will be retiring from the navy in a couple of years. She's trying to figure out what she's going to do with the rest of her life. Andrew is married with two kids. He lives in Greeley, Colorado, where he's a high school special ed teacher.

Yolanda: And you?

Leann: I'm still single. I'm a nurse and work at the U Dub Hospital. In my spare time, I volunteer on a suicide prevention hotline. It's the best I can do.

That was the end of the interview. I didn't have to see Leann's face to understand the hurt and lingering heartbreak in those last few words. Leann's mother had tried and failed to save her father, and Leann had failed to save her mother, and seven years later, Leann was still trying to save everyone else.

At that point, she was still Leann Nolastname as far as I was concerned. We had never met, but from that moment she became one of my clients. She still believed that her father had died due to an accidental overdose. I, on the other hand, was pretty sure Raymond had been murdered, and one of these days I hoped I would somehow bring his killer to justice not only for him, but also for his kids. All three of them deserved it, but most especially Leann. Her mother had borne the brunt of her husband's physical violence, but Leann was the one still carrying the weight of the emotional fallout his death had left behind.

CHAPTER 17

Bellingham, Washington
Saturday, February 29, 2020

I STAYED UP UNTIL THE WEE HOURS FRIDAY NIGHT AND SATURDAY
morning reading Yolanda Aguirre's interview files. I went to bed
only when my eyes were too tired to read any more. When Sarah
nosed me awake Saturday, she was probably surprised when I walked
straight past the coffee machine twice, coming and going, without
even pausing. Once she was back inside, I fell into bed and slept until
several hours later when Mel shook me awake.

"Time to rise and shine," she told me. "Alice is almost ready to
work on our room, and she can't do that when you're still sleeping."

I quickly pulled on some clothing. When I exited the bedroom, I
found Alice Patterson waiting in the hallway right outside. She was
standing there looking annoyed with one hand resting on her hip
while the other held her trusty Dyson at the ready.

"It's about time," I heard her mutter under her breath as I walked past.

"Sorry," I murmured, but I doubt my apology was accepted. Alice is your basic worker-bee with little or no patience for people who are slugabeds.

I made my coffee and headed into the living room where Mel was perusing something on her iPad.

"I held her off as long as I could," she explained. "The problem is, Alice usually starts with our bedroom, and she doesn't like having to change her routine. How late were you up?"

"I'm not sure," I answered. "I got caught up in reading those overdose family interviews and time got away from me."

"Find anything?" she asked.

"I certainly did," I told her and spent the next fifteen minutes and my first cup of coffee bringing her up to speed. It wasn't until I was ready for cup number two when I noticed the two of us were alone—no Kyle and no Sarah, either.

"Where is everybody?" I asked.

"Sarah's still leery of the vacuum cleaner," Mel explained, "so Kyle took her for a walk. I figure an extra walk or two is good for both of them."

"Speaking of Kyle, how did his room inspection go?"

"He passed with flying colors."

Intent on staying out of Alice's way, I settled down in the living room. Worn out by reading files, I decided to try following up on the Jake Spaulding case. Gretchen had given me the direct number to Detective Ron Wang, the original Liberty Lake detective working the case. When I dialed it, however, the person who picked up wasn't Detective Wang.

The woman who answered identified herself as Detective Byrd, "That's Byrd with a *y* rather than an *i*," she informed me.

"My name is J. P. Beaumont," I told her. "I'm a private investigator looking into a series of fatal fentanyl overdoses. My understanding is that Detective Wang is working one of those, a case that may be related to one I'm working. Could I speak to him, please?"

"Ron pulled the plug a couple of months back," Detective Byrd said. "He and his wife bought some horse property somewhere over near SeeQuiUm."

Ouch. The state of Washington is divided into two distinct parts, separated by the Cascade Mountain Range. The Westside, dominated by the Seattle metropolitan area, generally leans to the left. The Eastside leans right, and what each side doesn't know about the other could fill volumes. For instance, until that phone call to Detective Byrd, I'd never knowingly had any dealings with someone from Liberty Lake, and, other than knowing it's somewhere in eastern Washington, I couldn't tell you right off the bat exactly where it's located.

Clearly, Detective Byrd was equally ignorant about this side of the mountains. The town of Sequim is located in Clallam County on the Olympic Peninsula. The problem is, only western Washington outsiders pronounce it SeeQuiUm. It's supposed to be pronounced like *swim* with a *K* added into the mix—in other words, *skwim*, like *squish*.

So I thought about who I was and what I needed. Then I thought about what sounded like a much younger woman on the other end of the line and wondered how much interest she'd have in helping me with a case she likely knew nothing about. I suspected that wouldn't result in a positive outcome for either one of us.

"You wouldn't happen to know how I could get in touch with him, would you?" I asked.

Detective Byrd held the phone away from her mouth. "Hey, does anybody here have Ronnie's cell number?"

"Who's asking?"

"A private eye from Seattle who's looking into one of Ron's old cases."

In Seattle, there wouldn't be a chance in hell that someone would actually pass along that kind of information over the phone, but Liberty Lake must still have had something of a small-town vibe to it.

"Sure," I heard someone else say in the background. "I've got his number right here."

When Detective Byrd repeated it for me, I fed it into my phone. "Thanks," I said. "I really appreciate it."

A moment later, when I dialed the number, my phone helpfully told me that I was calling Liberty Lake, Washington, even though I knew good and well I wasn't.

"Hello," a wary male voice answered.

"Ronald Wang?"

"Who's asking?"

"My name's J. P. Beaumont, formerly with the attorney general's Special Homicide Investigation Team."

"S.H.I.T. you mean?" he asked.

Somehow that was the only name for that agency that ever resonated with anyone. Special Homicide Investigation Team never rang any bells. S.H.I.T. did back then and obviously still does.

"Exactly," I replied. "S.H.I.T., but now I'm a private investigator and looking into a fentanyl overdose case that might or might not be related to the unsolved death of Jake Spaulding."

That's all I said, and then I waited. I know from personal experience how much homicide cops hate to walk away from the job, leaving an unresolved case on the table. No matter how much time passes, those cases stay with us for the remainder of our lives. Luckily for me, Ron Wang was true to type.

"That son of a bitch?" he said after a long moment. "Whoever booted Jake Spaulding off the planet did everybody else a huge favor, but what do you want to know?"

Biased maybe? If this was the guy in charge of investigating Jake Spaulding's death, maybe it wasn't so surprising that the case remained unresolved.

"What can you tell me about him?" I asked.

"His folks have lived in the Liberty Lake area all their lives, and believe me, Darlene and Tom Spaulding are terrific people—churchgoing, salt-of-the-earth people. They're the backbone of the local high school sports booster club. They volunteer for the local Meals on Wheels. No way did that poor couple deserve to be saddled with a worthless son like Jake."

"So what happened?"

"He was a top-drawer football player and passable at baseball, but he was one of those kids who peaked early. After his senior year in high school, it was all downhill from there. All through school he was reported to be a bully who liked to pick fights, but because he was a standout at sports, everybody gave him a pass. He picked up his first DUI at age eighteen, the summer after he graduated. He had a full-ride athletic scholarship to WSU, but he fell in with the wrong crowd and flunked out by the end of his freshman year. After that, he moved to Seattle and started working construction. He married and had a couple of kids. According to his wife's family, his wife, Lisa, was a sweetheart who thought she could somehow fix him."

"I'm guessing that didn't happen."

"Hardly," Ron replied. "His drinking got worse over time, and so did the violence. He beat the crap out of her on a regular basis, but she never pressed charges."

"Big surprise there."

"In 2010, they were living in Seattle when he damn near killed her. Kicked her in the small of the back so hard that it left her a paraplegic. While she was hospitalized for that, she suffered a stroke and still has difficulty speaking. That time there was no question about charges being filed. When he was arrested, Lisa was still in the hospital hovering between life and death. Originally he was charged with attempted homicide. Since she didn't die, he ended up with a plea deal—ninety-three months flat time for assault in the first degree."

"Flat time means he served out his whole sentence?"

"Yup," Ron said, "every single day of it."

"And once he was out of the slammer, he went straight back to his parents' place in Liberty Lake?" I asked.

"You bet he did, because that's the kind of folks Tom and Darlene Spaulding are. They believe in the power of forgiveness. When their son got out of prison and had nowhere else to go, they let him come home. A week later he was dead."

"One week?"

"One week to the day. As far as I'm concerned, that's more freedom than he deserved," Ron declared. "Beth and I caught the case, but I was lead."

"Beth?" I asked.

"That's my former partner, Detective Byrd. Her name's Elizabeth, but she goes by Beth. I think most people in town were of the opinion that Jake Spaulding finally got exactly what he deserved, but we worked it like we would have any other case. The fact that he had overdosed on vaporized fentanyl was odd. According to everyone we talked to, booze was his drug of choice, but maybe that changed while he was locked up. The Washington State Corrections System isn't exactly a drug-free zone."

I certainly know that to be true.

"The night he died, he'd been drinking at a joint called the Hitching Post, just off the freeway on the far east side of town. It's probably the scuzziest bar around, and there's known to be a good deal of drug activity in that area. When the daytime bartender came to open up at six A.M. the next morning, he found Spaulding dead in his car in the parking lot. He was sitting in the driver's seat of his vehicle with his window wide open. By the way, the vehicle involved, an old Crown Vic, belonged to Tom Spaulding, his dad. Jake hadn't been out of prison long enough to have wheels of his own.

"When Beth and I arrived on the scene we saw no sign of any violence, and our first thought was that maybe Spaulding had died of natural causes. We were able to locate and interview most of the people who had been at the Hitching Post the night before—both the bartender on duty as well as the customers. No one reported seeing or hearing anything out of the ordinary—no fights, no arguments, nothing like that."

"Any video surveillance?" I asked.

"Are you kidding? We noticed there were cameras located inside the building and outside as well, but when I asked the bartender about viewing the footage, the guy laughed his head off. He said he'd worked there for more than five years, and that the surveillance system had been broken the whole time."

"Too bad," I said.

"When we went to Tom and Darlene and asked if they knew

of anyone who may have wanted to kill their son, they told us to watch the video of Jake's sentencing hearing, so we did. Lisa was there, but since she couldn't speak on her own back then and still can't, as far as I know, her older brother, Dave, spoke on her behalf. He was so angry it looked like the man was going to explode. He said the plea deal was a pile of crap. Considering the extent of Lisa's injuries, I happen to agree with him on that score—the plea deal was a joke. Dave also said, and I quote, 'If you ever get out of prison, you'd better watch your back, buddy, because I'm coming for you.'"

"Which turned him into suspect number one?" I asked.

"It certainly did. The problem is, Dave was fishing in Alaska when Jake died. He voluntarily gave us unlimited access to his electronic devices. He also agreed to a polygraph test, which he passed with flying colors. Dave had no involvement whatsoever in Jake's death, and we were able to clear him almost immediately.

"Once that female DNA profile turned up, we asked Lisa's female friends and relations to submit DNA samples. They all complied with no questions asked. Since most of them live in the Seattle area, it was easy to verify their alibis, and we cleared them as well. We wondered if maybe the female involved could have been Jake's dealer, but we were unable to identify any potential suspects.

"That's about the time the Spokane County Medical Examiner's report came in pegging Spaulding's death as undetermined, so naturally that case didn't get the same kind of attention as the next case, which happened only a few weeks later and turned out to be an actual homicide from the get-go. By the time I retired, the Spaulding case had gone cold. Beth and the new guy may have done some work on it after I left, but I doubt it."

"New guy?" I asked.

"The department generally has only two investigators on staff, and they handle everything, from soup to nuts. A couple of guys were under consideration for the job when I left, but I'm not sure who they promoted to take my place."

"One more question," I said. "Was any money found on the body?"

Ron hesitated. "Why do you want to know?" he asked at last.

"Well," I insisted, "was there?"

"As a matter of fact there was," Ron replied. "We discovered a couple of twenties and a five or two in his wallet, but there were also two crisp one-hundred-dollar bills. His folks were really mys- tified about those. Jake was fresh out of prison and wasn't working. As far as they knew, he was dead broke, so where did the money come from?"

Bingo! Two one-hundred-dollar bills! With that I knew for sure that there was a connection here. The presence of those two pieces of currency meant that although the woman matching our DNA profile might not be responsible for all three deaths, she was sure as hell connected to all three victims.

After that I spent the next twenty minutes bringing Ron Wang up to speed as far as what I was working on and giving him an overview of everything I had learned so far about both Raymond with the redacted last name and Darius Jackson.

"Sounds like you've got a serial killer on your hands," Ron ob- served when I finished, "and possibly a female one at that. Consider- ing the three victims' criminal histories, maybe she's some kind of domestic violence vigilante."

That's why every case needs new eyes and new perspectives. I felt as though I'd been whacked upside the head. A domestic violence vigilante? Of course! That made perfect sense. I had been so busy looking at the details of each case that I had failed to look at the big picture. My mother would have said that I wasn't seeing the forest for the trees.

Domestic violence was a common denominator in all three cases. Each of the victims had a long history of DV-related arrests that had seldom resulted in their doing any kind of serious jail time. And although Jake Spaulding may have died in Liberty Lake, his domestic violence crimes had been committed in Seattle.

I'm well aware that female vigilantes can be tough to pick out of a crowd. After all, I married one, didn't I? Anne Corley had been the kind of beauty no one would ever have pegged as a possible serial killer, but she was. Maybe that homeless woman at the food bank who had asked Darius for help with her grocery cart of goods hadn't been nearly as helpless or harmless as she seemed.

"A vigilante," I said finally, repeating Ron's word back to him. "You may have just hit the nail on the head!"

"What are you going to do now?" Ron asked.

"I'm going to go back to reading through the rest of Yolanda Aguirre's overdose interviews to see if I can identify any other possible victims."

For the second day in a row, I skipped my crosswords entirely. Now that I was firmly on the trail of a killer, the crosswords would have to wait.

CHAPTER 18

Bellingham, Washington
Saturday, February 29, 2020

COP SHOWS ON TV ARE ALL HIGH-SPEED CHASES, SIRENS, AND shoot-outs. The reality is far less exciting, and to that end I spent the remainder of Saturday reading. This time, with Ron Wang's comments in mind, I made a note of each file number wherever a history of domestic violence surfaced in the case transcript. None of those rose to the level of an obvious connection, but it seemed to me that at least seven of them merited further investigation, and I intended to ask Yolanda if she would try putting me in touch with members of those individual families.

While I sat with my nose buried in my iPad, Mel announced that she was going to make chicken curry for dinner. She and I eat a good deal of Thai food takeout, so that seemed like a reasonable idea. Our kitchen is more or less for show—high on looks and low on function. After locating a recipe online, she made an extensive shopping list of all necessary ingredients that we didn't have in stock and headed for the store.

For the remainder of the day, I kept on reading while she was busy in the kitchen. Meanwhile Kyle spent most of the day out in the garage with the heater on, hammering away on his drums. Over the years I had heard the term "garage band" tossed around. For the first time ever, those words were now part of my reality.

When he came into the house later, he presented me with an open brown manila envelope that was addressed to him. "I picked up the mail from the street," he announced. "It's the cigarette butts from Rick."

The Ziploc bag inside held a total of twenty or so cigarette butts, most of them with a smear of lipstick on them. For our purposes, the presence of lipstick was a good sign.

"Thanks," I said. "I'll drop these off at FedEx first thing on Monday."

By the time Mel announced dinner was ready, I was surprised to see that we would be eating at the dining room table. We generally eat at the island in the kitchen, but in this case, every flat surface in the kitchen, including the island, was littered with some kind of food prep debris. Looking at the mess, I didn't envy Kyle his evening KP duties.

The curry wasn't exactly a roaring success. The sauce was so hot—spicy hot—that when I took my first bite, tears actually shot out of my eyes and dripped onto my napkin. Through the course of the meal, I think each of us went through two or three glasses of milk. As for the chicken itself? It was, as Gordon Ramsay would say, "RAW!" We had to zap our individual servings in the microwave for five minutes or so to cook the chicken enough that we didn't risk food poisoning.

But Mel had made the effort, after all, and both Kyle and I manned up and ate without complaint.

"I ran into our neighbor, Mr. Mitchell, while Sarah and I were out walking," he said casually, partway through the meal.

I was grateful for that bit of polite conversation for two very different reasons. For one, it wasn't a commentary on the quality of the food, which would have been problematic regardless of what he said. For another, the fact that he had referred to Hank Mitchell as "our" neighbor made me feel as though Kyle was starting to feel at home.

"I'm not sure about that little dog of his, but Hank seems like a nice guy," Kyle observed.

Wait, I thought. *Mr. Mitchell had already morphed into Hank?*

"I couldn't agree more," I said. "And Mr. Bean may grow on you. He has on me."

"Did you know Hank used to be a drummer?"

"I believe he may have mentioned that somewhere along the way."

Kyle took a bite of curry, washed it down with another swallow of milk, and added, "Did you ever hear of a guy named Gene Krupa?"

I nodded. "He was an old-time drummer and bandleader. My mom was a big fan. His band played in Seattle once when I was a kid. My mother actually hired a babysitter to look after me so she could go see him. It was a big deal for her. She hung on to the program from that night. I found it when I was cleaning out her place after she died."

"Really?"

"Really."

"And did you know Gene Krupa is the guy who actually invented the original drum set, like the one I have in the garage?"

"That's news to me," I said, and Mel nodded in agreement.

"Hank actually has one of Krupa's original sets," Kyle continued. "He also has a record—a seventy-something . . . of Gene Krupa's band."

"A seventy-eight maybe?" I inserted.

That's when it occurred to me that Kyle had most likely never seen a vinyl record of any kind, thirty-three-and-a-thirds and forty-fives included, to say nothing of a record player.

"That's it," Kyle said. "A seventy-eight. He said if I drop by their house sometime, he'll play it for me."

For the first time since Kyle had been with us, he sounded excited about something. That did my heart good, but the idea that the poor kid was having to pal around with a pair of old geezers was still a bit heart-wrenching.

Although neither Kyle nor I had said anything bad about the meal Mel had prepared, she was under no illusions about the quality of what had been served. After dinner, she opted for some time in her soaking tub. Mel holds herself to very high standards in everything she does, and it didn't surprise me at all that she needed some alone time to suds off her disappointment.

In the meantime, the kitchen was such a mess that I took pity on Kyle and helped with the cleanup. I was working away on scrubbing the stovetop where something had boiled over when I asked, "Have you heard anything from your folks?"

Yes, it was a nosy question, but it was also a conversation starter.

"Mom called," he answered. "She wanted to know how school was. I told her it was fine. I guess Dad can't be bothered. I'm sure he's got other things on his mind."

I heard the depth of betrayal in his voice, and I couldn't help but feel sorry for him. "I guess that's about par for the course," I suggested.

"I guess it is."

A bit of time passed before he spoke again. "Care to see a movie tonight?"

At first, I thought he was asking if I wanted to go to a movie. Two years of working at the Bagdad Theater in Ballard while I was in high school pretty much cured me of going to movies and of all things related to either popcorn or bubble gum. On those occasions when I do venture out to a movie, instead of paying attention to what's on the screen, I'm always worrying about what's on the sticky floors.

"I'm not much of a movie buff," I admitted.

"Have you ever seen *The Martian*?"

I instantly had visions of some kind of animated Disney movie filled with little green men. "Not that I remember," I said.

"It's an old movie, sci-fi, and one of my favorites," Kyle explained. "I brought my DVDs with me. If you're interested, we could watch it together on the TV in the family room."

An "old movie" for me would be something like *Gone with the Wind*, and I'm not big on sci-fi, either. But Kyle and I weren't just on opposite sides of a generation gap—it was more like a generation chasm—and this unexpected offer of social interaction with my grandson was one I could hardly refuse.

"Sure," I said. "Why not?"

As far as the movie goes, I ended up being pleasantly surprised. There wasn't a little green man in sight. It was a gripping story about an astronaut who is inadvertently left behind on Mars and of his struggle to survive long enough for someone to come back to get him. I enjoyed every minute of it.

Mel emerged from the bathroom shortly after the movie started. Wrapped in a bathrobe and with her hair smelling of something flowery, she poured her evening glass of merlot and curled up beside me on the couch.

"What's this?" she asked, nodding toward the screen.

"It's called *The Martian*," I explained. "It's one of Kyle's favorites."

The three of us watched the film together. It felt comfortable and surprisingly normal, almost as though we were an ordinary family. Considering the circumstances, that was the best any of us could have hoped for.

It was only after the movie ended and we were getting ready for bed that Mel asked if I was making any progress on either of my current cases. I told her about the arrival of Caroline's cigarette butts and then recounted my conversation with Ron Wang as it related to Darius Jackson's case and to one of Yolanda Aguirre's as well.

"A vigilante?" she mused thoughtfully. "I suppose that's possible, but it's also pretty worrisome. If Spaulding died within days of being let out on parole, how did his killer know he was back on the streets almost as soon as it happened?"

"Good question."

"Makes it sound as though there might be some kind of law enforcement component to all this," she added. "What if you're looking for a cop who's gone rogue and decided to take the law into his or her own hands?"

What if indeed?

That was certainly a disturbing possibility. And since all three cases had connections to Seattle, what if said rogue cop ended up being someone connected to Seattle PD? That wouldn't be the best way for this newly minted private investigator to win friends and influence people at my old department. I'd end up being permanently labeled persona non grata among my old cohorts, and it wouldn't do my son, Scotty, any favors, either, as far as his departmental reputation was concerned.

Mel went to sleep almost as soon as her head hit the pillow. I didn't, because now I had something other than Kyle and Kelly to worry about. There was a good chance that by solving Benjamin Weston's problem, I'd be inadvertently creating a whole new set of issues for my son. Which reminds me of an old adage that all too often turns out to be true—the one that says no good deed goes unpunished.

CHAPTER 19

Bellingham, Washington
Sunday, March 1, 2020

ON SUNDAY MORNING KYLE WAS IN THE MOOD FOR BACON and eggs. The problem is, we had eggs but no bacon.

"Fixing bacon at home is too messy," Mel informed him. "Cleaning up the stove after frying bacon isn't worth the trouble."

Kyle rolled his eyes. "You mean you've never heard of Costco bacon?"

Mel and I exchanged puzzled looks and both shook our heads. The truth is, at that point in my life, I hadn't set foot inside a Costco warehouse. With only two of us to feed, Mel and I don't have much reason to buy groceries in bulk.

"What's Costco bacon?" she asked.

"It comes in a package already partially cooked," Kyle explained. "You put the bacon between two paper plates with a paper towel or napkin over and under the bacon. Then you put it in the microwave for a minute or so. That way the bacon is cooked without any kind of mess because the grease all ends up on the paper towels."

"Sounds interesting," Mel said. "There's a Costco here in town, but we've never been. We don't have a membership card. We don't buy that much food."

"I have a card," Kyle returned. "It's my dad's, but who do you think did all the grocery shopping down in Ashland? It sure as hell wasn't Dad or Caroline."

Instead of bacon and eggs, we ended up having Honey Nut Cheerios for breakfast. After the previous night's curry, no one was up for another batch of Mel's lumpy pancakes.

Once breakfast was done, I went back to my library of overdose interviews. The last ones brought me up to the middle of 2016. In the process I flagged another six for additional scrutiny. To do so, with the last names redacted, that meant going back to Yolanda for assistance.

Cops have days off, but those don't necessarily fall on weekends. Ditto for private investigators. Since I had already spent half of my Sunday reading files, apparently I didn't get weekends off, either. So although I didn't mind putting in the hours, I wasn't sure about forensic economists. Rather than interrupting Yolanda's day with a phone call, I sent her an email.

Dear Yolanda,

Please forgive me for interrupting your weekend with a work email. I've now read through all 136 files that were previously sent. I've found one case that is clearly connected to Darius Jackson's. I've also discovered a separate case, one that was not in your files, that is also related.

In finishing the files I located several more cases—a dozen or so—that may or may not be related and that, in my opinion, should be studied further. As you know, all last names have been redacted from my files. If I were to send you the file numbers, would you be willing to contact the families to see if any of them would consent to speaking with me?

Thanks.
JP

With that done, and knowing a cold front with possible snow was due to come in overnight, I grabbed Sarah's leash and headed out for a walk. They say dogs are good for your health. I'll second that. I know I walk far more now that I have a dog in my life than I ever did without one.

Ellen Mitchell works long hours at the call center, and I have no doubt that Hank gets lonely rattling around their house on his own for so many hours each day. I also suspect that he has a lot less to keep himself occupied than I do, so it's possible that he keeps an eye out for any occasional walkers passing by just to have some human interaction. At any rate, even though this wasn't Sarah's and my usual walking time, as we approached the Mitchells' driveway, Hank came hotfooting it up the hill with Mr. Bean at his heels.

"Mind if we join you?" he asked.

"Not at all."

The hike up the hill had left him slightly out of breath, so it was a minute or so before he had anything more to say.

"Ran into your grandson the other day," he said finally. "Seems like a really good kid—polite, well-mannered."

"Thanks," I said. "That's how he strikes me, too, as a good kid."

"Odd for him to change schools that way, right in the middle of his senior year."

Obviously Hank was fishing for information, and I wasn't prepared to breach Kyle's confidence. Why he had left Ashland was his story to tell rather than mine.

"He made the decision," I said, noncommittally, "but he seems to be handling it all right."

"But how's it possible he'd never heard of Gene Krupa?" Hank demanded. "What a crying shame. You'd think, considering his interest in drums, that his band teacher would have had the good sense to at least mention that world-famous drummer."

It occurred to me that maybe Kyle's band teacher, who also happened to be his father, had never heard of Gene Krupa, either. That's what I thought but didn't say aloud.

"Did you know Krupa is the guy who invented drum sets as they are now?" Hank continued.

"Only because Kyle told me," I said.

"That's why I've held on to mine. It's a Gene Krupa original. My dad paid a pretty penny for it back in the day. It's a genuine antique—a collector's piece, if you will, but it still works. And speaking of antiques, I was wondering if I could ask a favor of you."

"What's that?" I asked.

"Remember that old car I had towed out of the garage before we tore it down to rehab the house?"

"It was an old Mustang, right?"

"Right," Hank said, "a 1966 Shelby Mustang."

"Shelbys were a big deal back in the day."

"They still are," Hank said. "I told Ellen that I'd had it towed to a junkyard, but that was a little white lie. Instead, I took it to an auto restoration outfit down in Seattle. I'm calling it a late-blooming midlife crisis. It cost me a bundle to have it brought back to life, but it's done now and ready to be picked up. You go back and forth to Seattle a lot more often than I do. I was wondering if I could ask you for a lift to go pick it up the next time you head in that direction. I could ask Ellen to drive me there, but I want to surprise her and have it parked out front when she gets off shift."

I love surprises.

"You bet," I said. "I'll probably end up driving down there sometime this coming week, but I don't know exactly when."

"Let me know," he said. "I'll be ever so grateful."

Once the walk was over and as I headed back toward our place, a call came in from Yolanda Aguirre.

"Are you telling me that now there are three connected cases?" she asked when I answered.

"I am indeed," I told her, so I went on to bring her up to speed on everything I had learned and how DNA and the combination of pairs of hundred-dollar bills had linked two other cases to her file 18.

"And now you believe all three are homicides?" she asked.

"Yes, I do."

"Just a sec," she said. A keyboard clicked in the background before she spoke again. "File 18. I remember that one. I interviewed the daughter because the mother had committed suicide. Can I contact her and let her know you're trying to reopen the case?"

"Not yet," I answered. "That would be premature at this point because we still don't have enough to reopen the case. I don't like making promises I may not be able to keep."

"Then what do I tell the families?" Yolanda asked.

"Just let them know that a private investigator who is looking into a number of overdose deaths would like to speak to them about what happened to their loved one. Give them my email address. After that, we'll have to sit around and wait to see if any of them contact me."

"That seems fair," she agreed. "That puts the ball in their court."

SEEING AS HOW I was now up-to-date as far as anything more I could do on either of my current cases, I gave myself the rest of the day off. While I'd been out walking, the "what's for dinner" problem had been handled, and the pizza delivery guy showed up exactly on cue. We spent the evening watching *America's Funniest Videos* and Masterpiece on PBS. I never expected to like a show entitled *Call the Midwife*, but it's grown on me over time.

CHAPTER 20

BY THE TIME I CLAMBERED OUT OF BED THE NEXT MORNING, BOTH
Mel and Kyle were long gone. Mel had left a note next to the coffee
machine saying that she'd bring home Kentucky Fried Chicken for
dinner. A check in the fridge revealed that the remains of her fire-
breathing curry from Saturday night had somehow vanished. I was
smart enough not to ask where it had gone, but I suspect it made an
ignominious exit down the kitchen garbage disposal.

With the house to myself, and knowing there was plenty of time
to meet the FedEx pickup deadline for Bellingham, I gave myself
the morning off, lounging around in a robe rather than getting
dressed. I also caught up on my backlog of unworked crossword
puzzles. I remember reading somewhere that doing crosswords on a
daily basis is good for keeping aging brain cells alive and functioning.

So far, despite our steady diet of fast food, I seem to be doing all right in that department.

The previous week the weather had been so warm that it had felt as though spring had sprung. Today winter was back with a vengeance. It was windy, wet, and cold, with occasional snow showers mixed with rain blowing in off the Pacific. At the bottom of our bluff, the heaving waters of Bellingham Bay were a forbidding gunmetal gray as far as the eye could see.

"No walk today, old girl," I told Sarah.

I don't know if she understood me, but she responded with a brief thump of her lanky tail.

It was close to noon and I was thinking about getting dressed when an email from someone named Greta Halliday showed up on my iPad.

My name is Greta Halliday. I just had a call from Yolanda Aguirre, saying that a private investigator named J. P. Beaumont is looking into the death of my late brother, Loren Gregson, on the off chance that he might have been murdered. I know Ms. Aguirre is involved in some kind of study of drug overdose deaths in the Seattle area. She interviewed my mother, Alma Gregson, about this a while ago. She wanted to interview me as well, but at that time I declined to participate.

When Loren died in 2015, his death was deemed to be accidental, but Mother always felt as though there was something unresolved about it. She passed away two months ago, shortly after the first of the year, leaving me in charge of handling her final affairs.

I was ten years old when Loren was born, and we were never

close, but if there really are unanswered questions concerning his death, I'll be happy to be of whatever assistance I can. Please feel free to contact me at any time at the numbers listed below. According to Ms. Aguirre, my mother's interview is file number 87.

I was glad to know she was willing to talk to me, but rather than reach for my phone, I wanted to reread file 87 and have all my ducks in a row.

At the time Loren died, my mother was heartbroken and insisted that he must have been murdered. My brother had a history of mental health issues and resisted taking medications of any kind. Based on that, my mother claimed that he never would have self-administered a lethal dose of fentanyl either by accident or as an attempted suicide.

As I said, my brother and I weren't close, and I have to say that the idea Loren might have been murdered seems unlikely to me, but with my mother gone, settling the question of his death once and for all is the one thing I can still do for her. Please feel free to reach out to me at your convenience.

Sincerely,
Greta Halliday

Abandoning the whole idea of getting dressed, I turned to my iPad. File 87 was dated September 4, 2018. I had read it before, but now I knew that the redacted name had been Gregson. He had been found in Seattle's Fremont District on the morning of Monday,

155

January 12, 2015. A woman out walking her dog in the grassy area between North Canal Street and the Ship Canal had spotted his body lying partly concealed in a clump of blackberry bushes.

Law enforcement was summoned to the scene. The medical examiner determined that the death had occurred sometime overnight on Saturday, January 10. Documents found at the scene—a state-issued ID card as opposed to a driver's license—identified the victim as Loren R. Gregson, age thirty-eight. His manner of death was deemed to be accidental. Cause of death? A fentanyl overdose combined with exposure.

Loren was the youngest of three children born to Alma and Harold Gregson. Although he hadn't spent much time in jail, his interactions with law enforcement consisted mostly of arrests for being drunk and disorderly and disturbing the peace. There were also several domestic violence arrests stemming from disputes with his widowed mother, Alma. The last one of those had occurred in 2014. Unlike previous incidents, on that occasion, his mother had gone ahead and pressed charges, resulting in his spending sixty days in the King County Jail. Upon release, he was met with a no-contact order on the part of his mother. Since he had still been living at home at the time of his arrest, he suddenly found himself homeless.

In today's vernacular, Loren Gregson represented a serious case of failure to launch. He had dropped out of school as a high school sophomore. He worked occasionally at various menial jobs, but mostly he lived off his mother. With that much background it was time for the meat of Yolanda's interview.

Yolanda: Once again, I'm so sorry for your loss, but please tell me about your son.

Alma: Loren was always a challenging child. It wasn't his fault, though. He was one of those change-of-life babies. I was forty-three when I found out I was pregnant. I thought I was old enough to be beyond all that nonsense and had gone off the pill on my doctor's orders because he was concerned about their long-term side effects.

When I found out I was expecting, Harold, my husband, was thrilled at the news. I was worried. I had heard that babies with older mothers tended to have ongoing issues, and that was certainly true for Loren. He was angry almost from the day he was born. He was never cuddly or happy like my older two children were, and from kindergarten on, school was a nightmare.

Part of that was due to dyslexia. He was diagnosed fairly early. The schools did the best they could. They gave him tools that would have helped him to learn to read, but he wasn't interested in doing the work. He couldn't be bothered.

After dropping out of high school, he went to work for his father. Harold and a partner had a boat repair shop down on Lake Union, a few blocks down the hill from our home in Fremont. It was close enough that they could walk back and forth from home to work. That lasted for several years, but after Harold died and the partner took over, Loren didn't like working for him. That's when he quit. He took various jobs here and there, but they never lasted long. And because he couldn't read, his choices were limited.

Yolanda: I understand the two of you had some domestic violence issues.

Alma: That's true. Loren always had a temper. Something as simple as asking him to take out the trash could be enough to set him off. He hit me a couple of times, and yes, I did have to call 911 on occasion, but once he cooled off everything was always fine.

Yolanda: So you never pressed charges?

Alma: Only that once, and that was all Greta's fault.

Yolanda: And Greta is?

Alma: My daughter. She was ten years old when Loren was born, and the two of them never got on very well. Fought like cats and dogs. She always claimed that I spoiled Loren too much—that he was handed things she and James, my other son, had to work for. Not only that, Greta has a very high opinion of herself, and she's always been full of business.

One night when Loren was having one of his spells, she happened to turn up at the house unannounced. I had some bruises on my arms and my nose was bleeding just a little, but she called 911 anyway. She's the one who insisted that I file charges against him and apply for a restraining order. What she did was nothing short of blackmail. Greta told me that if I didn't do as she said, she'd wash her hands of me and that I'd be totally on my own except for Loren.

I had macular degeneration by then, you see, and could no longer drive. I had to count on Greta to get me out to the grocery store or to the doctor or even to the beauty shop. I needed her help too much to disregard what she said, so I went along with the program, and that's how I ended up living here. Greta suggested it because it's only for people fifty-five and over, and Loren was too young.

Yolanda: Wait, about getting groceries and taking you to the doctor? Couldn't Loren have done the driving?

Alma: He never got his license. He couldn't read well enough to pass the test.

Yolanda: Was the no-contact order still in effect at the time Loren died?

Alma: Of course. We didn't dare disregard it, because I didn't want Loren going back to jail, but I didn't want him living on the streets, either. I had promised Harold on his deathbed that I would look after Loren, and I did. When Loren was let out of jail, I had one of Harold's friends track him down. I rented a room for him in a house with several students from Seattle Pacific University. It was down near the Fremont Bridge. That way he had a roof over his head, but he wasn't too far away, either.

One of Harold's old friends runs the Fremont Inn, a joint where Loren and his dad used to go for lunch. I set up an account there so Loren could stop by and have a bite to eat and something to drink. Once a week, I'd call up the owner and put the bill on my credit card. After Loren died, when Greta found out about that—about my renting a room for him and paying his food tab—she was absolutely livid. I didn't think it was any of her business.

I stopped reading momentarily because all of a sudden my homicide investigative sensors had switched into high gear. Loren's death had been ruled accidental. Had there been any kind of investigation, questions should have been asked about anyone with ongoing issues with the victim. Clearly his sister, Greta, had a decades-long beef with him, and she would most likely have been a primary person of interest.

One of the customary lines of inquiry in homicide investigations is to follow the money. How much of Greta's insisting that Alma file domestic violence charges against Loren and obtain the protection order had been out of concern for Alma's well-being, and how much of it had to do with protecting Greta's future financial interests? The fact that she had been outraged that Alma had continued to pay Loren's bills suggested that maybe her anger could have had more to do with preserving her mother's money than it did with keeping her from physical harm.

And then there was the matter of the email I had received from Greta earlier that day. In 2018 when Yolanda had been conducting her familial interviews, Greta had refused to participate. Now here she was volunteering to meet with me. Why? More than once in my career as a homicide cop, I've had perpetrators attempt to insert themselves into investigations to find out what was going on. And why did they do that? To find out how close we were to discovering their personal involvement in the crime. Was that what was happening here?

Yolanda: How are things between you and Greta now?
Alma: Prickly. I never imagined myself in assisted living, and I don't really like it, but they have vans to take people where they need to go, so I don't have to rely on Greta for a ride anymore now that she's barely speaking to me. That's the thing that breaks my heart. When I lost Loren, I didn't just lose one child. In actual fact I lost all three of them.
Yolanda: I'm so sorry.
Alma: Me, too.
Yolanda: If you don't mind, I'd like to return to the time Loren died. He passed away on Saturday night but wasn't found until Monday. Were you aware that something was wrong and that he'd gone missing?
Alma: Oh, I knew he was missing all right. I always called the Fremont Inn first thing on Monday morning to pay Loren's bill

for the previous week. George, the owner, told me the last time Loren showed up was on Saturday. He never stopped by on Sunday at all. As soon as I heard that, I knew something was wrong.

Right away, I tried to call and report him as missing, but when the 911 operator asked me when was the last time I'd seen him and I told her several months ago, she practically laughed her head off, especially when she found out that he was missing from a bar rather than from home. So when those two detectives showed up on Monday afternoon to tell me that he was gone, I wasn't surprised in the least.

Yolanda: What kind of interaction did you have with law enforcement back then?

Alma: Not very much. The next time I saw anyone was when someone from the M.E.'s office turned up to drop off his personal effects—the things they found at the scene—his phone, his wallet, and his father's Elks Club ring. Those are the only remnants I have of him. I keep them in my jewelry case. As for everything else? There wasn't much. His roommates brought me a garbage bag filled with what they'd emptied out of his room. I don't know why they bothered. The only things he owned were some secondhand clothes that he'd picked up from Goodwill.

Yolanda: Was your son known to use drugs?

Alma: Absolutely not. He drank beer and had the occasional shot of tequila, but hard drugs? No way. He had mental health issues all his life, and he hated taking medications of any kind. I tried to tell people that at the time—that the idea of his dying of a self-injected drug overdose was a total joke—but nobody was interested in hearing what I had to say. After all, I was only his mother. What did I know?

Yolanda: Any final thoughts?

Alma: Only one. No matter how Loren died, I still hold Greta responsible. If she hadn't stuck her nose into things that were none of her business and forced me to get that so-called protection order, none of this would have happened.

That was the end of the interview, but with those last words, Alma Gregson had lit a fire under me. One way or the other, she had held her daughter responsible for Loren's death. I now believed, as Alma had, that her son had possibly been murdered, although, at the time, everyone else, including Greta Halliday, had been happy to go along with the theory of an accidental death.

But something had changed on that score. Greta hadn't been willing to be interviewed by Yolanda Aguirre earlier, but now she was willing to talk to me. How come? Was it possible that my poking around in the case was cause for concern on her part? For most people an M.E.'s death certificate designations of manner of death—undetermined, accident, or homicide—are nothing but so many words on paper. But that's not true for perpetrators—the person or persons actually responsible. For them a change in designation from accident or unresolved to homicide can make all the difference, with the ultimate possibility of their spending the remainder of their lives in prison. Was that what was fueling Greta Halliday's sudden change of heart?

Suspicions are one thing; proof is another. As of now, I didn't have nearly enough evidence to justify reopening any of the cases. The only way forward would be following the money on Loren's death, but that would have to wait for a while—at least long enough for me to pack up and deliver Caroline Richards's cigarette butts to the FedEx office. I wanted them on their way to Lulu Benson in Omaha without any further delay.

CHAPTER 21

Sammamish, Washington
Tuesday, March 3, 2020

TEN O'CLOCK THE NEXT MORNING FOUND HANK MITCHELL, Sarah, and me driving down I-5 through a mixture of sleet and rain. Mr. Bean was at home, spending the day with their cleaning lady, so Sarah had the back seat all to herself. She took full advantage of the situation by stretching out full length from one door to the other.

After my trip to FedEx the previous afternoon, I had called Greta Halliday. Turns out she's a real estate agent who had been working an open house at the time. Since Tuesday was her day off, we'd made an appointment for one P.M. My next call had been to Hank, letting him know that the lift he needed to retrieve his restored Shelby would be somewhat sooner than either of us had expected.

He had said the car restoration outfit was in Seattle. That wasn't entirely true. To people from outside the area, the word *Seattle* includes the entire metropolitan area. In actual fact, the address I keyed into my phone's GPS was in Woodinville, a suburb located on the far northeast side of Lake Washington and a good twelve or thirteen miles from Seattle proper. That address was fine with me, however, since Greta and her husband lived in Sammamish, which is also on the Eastside.

LEAVING SARAH IN the car, I accompanied Hank into the garage to take a gander at his restored Shelby. It was gorgeous—a sight to be seen! It looked as though it was fresh out of the factory and sitting on an original showroom floor. It was blue with gray racing stripes. Blue happens to be my favorite color.

"Love the color," I murmured.

Hank nodded. "Sapphire Blue and Silver Mist," he said, "the original factory colors."

He opened the driver's door and took a seat. I bent down to examine the interior. It was mostly black with gray leather seats and a matching steering wheel that were the same color as the racing stripes on the exterior.

"Nice," I said.

"And take a look at this," Hank added, patting the gearshift. "It comes with original equipment antitheft protection—a standard transmission."

I was still chuckling about that as I drove away, heading south. Since traffic had been nonexistent, I had some extra time on my hands before my appointment with Greta Halliday, so I stopped off at Burgermaster along the way and ordered a pair of burgers—a plain one for Sarah and a loaded one for me. I didn't envy the carhops who cheerfully delivered our food despite the miserable weather, but the burgers were great.

As soon as we turned east on I-90, I saw a sign on the roadway warning that Snoqualmie Pass was closed at the summit due to accidents. Fortunately for us, we weren't going that far. After dinner the previous evening I had done some research on Greta and her husband, Connor. They were clearly your basic power couple. He was a Microsoft exec, while she was listed as the top-selling agent in her real estate office. The two of them were front and center at local art scene events and charity galas. She had left her humble beginnings in Seattle's Fremont neighborhood far behind. No wonder she was so dismissive of her underperforming and now deceased brother.

So why, if Greta was that well-off, had she been so angry to learn that Alma had been continuing to provide financial support to Loren despite the presence of that no-contact order? Or was she simply pissed over her mother's continuing enabling? As the King of Siam would say, "Is a puzzlement."

E. Sammamish Parkway runs north and south along the east side of Lake Sammamish. The steep driveway leading down to the Hallidays' lakefront home would have been a nail-biter if the snow had actually been sticking, but this was snow mixed with rain, and right then the rain was still winning. When I parked in front of their three-car garage, Sarah sat up and looked around. I had a leash and could have taken her for a brief walk, but she's still a California dog at heart, and she made her feelings clear by shaking her head, doing three full body turns, and then lying back down. In dog language, that's known as *Thanks, but no thanks.*

People who can afford sprawling water-view homes in the Seattle area all have one thing in common—they're loaded. So when I rang the bell, the woman who came to the door wasn't what I expected. Dressed in a pair of old sweats and grimy tennis shoes, and with her blond hair pulled back in a noticeably damp ponytail, Greta didn't look anything at all like the social butterfly I'd seen in photos of her at various galas.

"Mr. Beaumont, I presume?" Greta Halliday asked, holding out her hand and delivering a surprisingly firm handshake. "Come on in. Please pardon the outfit," she added, "I just came inside from working on the boat."

She led me into a living room with what would have been a gorgeous view of the lake. Today, however, the only view available was an expanse of gray on gray.

"A little cold to be out working on a boat," I commented by way of making polite conversation.

"Oh, I wasn't outside," she said, gesturing me toward an easy chair facing a wall of floor-to-ceiling lake-view windows. "When we bought this place three years ago, it came complete with an empty boathouse, so I bought something to put inside it for my husband's fiftieth birthday—a 1956 twenty-six-foot Chris-Craft Flybridge Sedan. We've renamed her the *Midlife Crisis*."

That comment made me smile. The Hallidays' midlife crisis vehicle was ten years older than Hank's.

"So far it's been more of a project boat than a pleasure one," she went on. "We've had to replace engines, repaint and revarnish inside and out, and put in a new Garmin GPS. We're currently having all the upholstery redone. My job is polishing the chrome, and believe me there's a lot of that. Thank God for gel manicures, otherwise my nails would be a mess. But by the time summer comes around this year, after two years of work, she should be ready to do a star turn around Lake Sammamish."

Greta Halliday was a boat owner who actually polished her own chrome? The woman was becoming more unexpected with every word she uttered.

"Didn't your father own a boat repair shop?" I asked.

"Yes," she said. "It was called the Lake Union Boat Shed. That's how come I knew that if I was going to buy a boat for Connor, it needed to be a classic. That's also where I learned to polish chrome. James and I—James is my older brother—worked in Dad's boathouse from sixth grade on. He paid us, of course, and encouraged us to save every penny. That's how Jimmy and I both worked our way through college—working for our dad on weekends and during summer vacations. I've never understood why the hell they didn't do Loren the same favor."

I was surprised that she was the first one to mention her late brother's name.

"I understand he was a lot younger than you," I ventured.

"That's true," she answered. "Ten years younger than me and twelve years younger than James. By the time he came along our parents were totally different people from who they'd been when Jimmy and I were little. For one thing, my mother almost died in childbirth when Loren was born. She was in the delivery room for more than an hour before they finally did an emergency C-section.

"Loren was always mean, from the time he was a toddler. I've long suspected that he might have had some frontal lobe damage that could have been attributed to that difficult delivery situation. And then, once he got to school, there was a lot of bullying because of his dyslexia, but Mom always handled him with kid gloves. He was an annoying, spoiled brat as far as I was concerned, but she treated him like he was made of spun gold."

So far this was sounding like a case of plain old, ordinary sibling rivalry. Had it somehow turned deadly along the way? But letting Greta tell the story her way seemed to be working, so I stifled the questions I'd been planning to ask and listened instead.

"Loren worked in Dad's boat shop the same way James and I did. In fact, after he dropped out of high school, that's the only place he ever held a steady job, but he wasn't much of a worker. I remember Dad complaining that he was lazy and undependable. When Dad had to retire due to health issues, he sold out to his partner who didn't waste any time giving Loren his walking papers. From then on Loren became my mother's problem. Once a mama's boy, always a mama's boy."

I noticed that version of the story was slightly different from the one Alma had told Yolanda. According to Alma, Loren had quit. According to Greta, he'd been fired.

"When Dad died, he left my mother in pretty good financial shape, but that was for her on her own. Since Loren didn't work and was dependent on her for everything, he was a big drain on her finances, but that was the least of her problems.

"Even as a kid, Loren had a hair-trigger temper. I suspected he was mistreating her because I saw bruising on her arms a couple of times, but she always brushed it off—claimed she'd tripped on the staircase or banged her arm on a car door. But that day in 2014 when I walked in on them unexpectedly, he had blackened both her eyes and left her with a bloody nose and with her upper lip bleeding. When I called 911 to report it, he kept screaming at me to put down the phone. Mom was yelling the same thing. But then he lunged at me, trying to take the phone away from me. That's when I put him down."

"Put him down?" I repeated.

"I'm a woman who works in real estate," Greta replied. "I never go anywhere without a Taser in my pocket and a loaded handgun in my purse. After I tased him, he was out for a few seconds. By the time the Taser wore off, I had him at gunpoint. When the cops showed up, it took a few minutes for them to sort out that Loren was the one who needed to be taken into custody. After that I did some sleuthing and found out about all the other times cops had been called to the house—all the times he'd been arrested without my mother pressing charges. That's when I insisted on the no-contact order. I more or less strong-armed Mom into selling the house and moving into an assisted-living facility where he couldn't move back in with her."

"It sounds like your mother was in denial."

"You think?" Greta asked with a sad smile. "But then, when Loren turned up dead, Mom blamed me one hundred percent. Connor and I were actually in Hawaii when it happened, but as far as Mom was concerned, it was all my fault. And I suppose that's why I agreed to talk to you—because I want to know the truth about what really happened, not so much for my mother's sake but for mine. So what's this all about?"

Once again, I was caught up in an interview that wasn't unfolding anywhere near the way I had anticipated. So I backed off and pulled the standard interrogation technique of asking a question to which, thanks to Yolanda Aguirre, I already knew the answer.

"How many times was Loren taken into custody for domestic violence against your mother?" I asked.

Greta nodded. "Seven in all, but if I hadn't caught him red-handed that last time, I never would have known about any of them. And since she never pressed charges, he was always out of jail and back at her house the very next day. Why do you ask?"

"Before I answer that question, let me ask another. As far as you know, was your brother involved with drugs?"

"To my knowledge, Loren's only drug of choice was booze. As I said, we were never close. If he was on drugs, the only person who might have known about it would have been my mother. At the time he died, she wasn't speaking to me, but she told my brother James that the cops had it all wrong. She insisted his death was no accident. She thought he'd been murdered."

"Turns out, I've unearthed several cases with circumstances surprisingly similar to Loren's," I told her. "A number of weeks ago, I was contacted by a grandmother whose grandson, Darius, had died, supposedly of an accidental overdose. She thought the cops had it wrong, too. He'd been involved in drugs in the past, but, as far as she knew, Darius was clean and sober at the time of his death, and it seems he may well be the victim of a homicide. With Yolanda Aguirre's help, I've now located two other cases with links to Darius's. I suspect that your brother may be number four."

"Are you kidding?" Greta demanded.

"Not in the least. In two cases the death was ruled accidental. In another, manner of death was left as undetermined, but one way or the other, the investigations either stopped completely or else went cold. One of the common denominators in each case is that all of the dead victims—all of them male—had a history of domestic violence arrests, arrests, yes, but few convictions."

"Just like Loren," Greta murmured.

"Exactly," I agreed.

"You said 'one of the common denominators.' Are there others?"

"First," I said, "tell me about your brother's personal effects. In your mother's interview with Ms. Aguirre, she mentioned having received them. Did you by any chance see them, or did your mother ever share any information about them with you?"

"No," Greta replied. "At the time he died, we weren't on speaking terms. James was here for the funeral. She might have shared something about them with him. If so, he never mentioned it to me."

"But considering the close relationship your mother had with Loren, do you think she would have gotten rid of them?"

"Not at all," Greta replied. "She would have hung on to them for dear life."

"After she passed away, what happened to her belongings?"

"They all came here," Greta answered with a shrug. "The facilities manager at the assisted-living place had everything packed up for me. I took her clothing directly to Goodwill. Everything else is still in boxes, out in the garage. Going through those is on my to-do list, but I haven't been up to facing that, at least not yet. Did you know my mother was in the process of writing me out of her will when she passed away?"

"I had no idea," I replied.

Greta took a deep breath. "That hurt," she said. "The estate didn't amount to much. It primarily consisted of the proceeds from selling her house. The cost of assisted living was eating into those at a rapid clip. Had she lived another year or so, Connor and I and James, too, would have had to pitch in to pay the freight. So taking me out of the will was sheer meanness on her part—one final slap in the face. It was one last time where Loren would have won and I would have lost, but because the new will hadn't been witnessed and signed, it wasn't considered valid."

So much for following the money to find my killer. That strategy wasn't going to work here—not at all.

"How many boxes?" I asked.

"Out in the garage, you mean?"

I nodded.

"Not that many," Greta replied. "Six or seven in all, but the problem is, for me, they're packed with a lifetime's worth of emotional baggage."

"I'm sure that's true," I agreed, "but they might also contain information that would help me convince law enforcement to re-open not only your brother's case, but the others as well. I know this is a tough call, but would you allow me to sort through them for you?"

"No," she said after a moment's thought. "I'm a big girl. We'll do it together."

"Right now?" I asked.

"Right now," she agreed.

So out to the garage we went. As I mentioned earlier, the garage had been built to hold three vehicles. One stall contained a bright red Maserati GranTurismo. Next to that was a sleek black Mercedes sedan, an S 400 that was a good decade newer than my S 550. Seeing the two parked vehicles made me wonder what her husband had driven to work. As for Alma Gregson's pitiful collection of boxes? All six of them sat forlornly piled against the front wall of the empty stall. It was shocking to see how little was left behind after a whole lifetime of living.

Greta quickly located a box cutter and began slicing through the strips of packing tape that had sealed the boxes shut. One contained nothing but books, including six copies of *Strenuous Life*, Roosevelt High School's yearbook. The six years covered the time both Alma and her husband, Harold, had been in attendance. Among the books was a well-thumbed Holy Bible with the name Alma Adams written in cracked and barely legible gold leaf on the faded leather cover. The remainder of the books included a slew of *Reader's Digest Condensed Books*. It had been years since I had run across any of those. There were also three baby books—one for James, one for Greta, and one for Loren. Greta glanced at those and quickly set them aside.

Several of the boxes contained a plethora of various knickknacks, each of which had been carefully wrapped in old newspapers. It was an oddball collection of quirky things people hang on to for no particular reason—a wooden Scandinavian horse, painted in bright orange and blue; a set of silver teaspoons from various countries; a massive crystal ashtray; a number of clay pots. But the one item that really caught my eye was a glass bottle with a ship inside it, except the ship in question turned out to be a miniature but clearly classic Chris-Craft.

"That was my dad's," Greta murmured when she saw it. "I had forgotten about it completely. Connor will want to display it somewhere on the *Midlife Crisis*."

The next box contained all kinds of personal items—as though someone had swept through a bathroom and gathered up everything from medicine chest, counter, and drawers. A worn toothbrush, toothpaste, mouthwash, a hairbrush, a comb, hair spray, deodorant, shampoo, conditioner, makeup, and medications had all been tossed inside the box helter-skelter. In other words, that one turned out to be a bust, too.

By then I was losing heart because we kept coming up empty, and we were down to the last two boxes. But the next-to-last box was where we hit the jackpot. The topmost item, perched on everything else, was a polished wooden box. Someone has used a wood-burning kit to draw a heart on top of the lid—a heart with two names written inside: Alma and Harold.

Greta picked up the box and allowed her fingers to absently trace their way around the heart.

"I had forgotten about this, too," she said. "Daddy made the jewelry box in woodshop his senior year at Roosevelt. He gave it to my mom for Valentine's Day that year."

The moment she lifted the lid we both caught sight of what was inside—a still-sealed plastic bag with the words KING COUNTY MEDICAL EXAMINER printed on the red label. After the bag had been handed to Alma Gregson, she had kept it without ever opening it. Through the clear plastic I could see that it contained three items—an old wallet, a dead cell phone, and an Elks ring.

I shot Greta a questioning look. "May I?" I asked.

She nodded. "Please," she said.

With her approval, I tore open the seal and allowed the contents to slip out of the plastic and back onto the lid of the open box.

"Do you happen to have any latex gloves handy?" I asked.

"Not handy," Greta answered. "I have a whole box of them, but it's down in the boat shed. It'll take a minute or two for me to go get it."

It wasn't long before she returned carrying an open box of gloves. Pulling out a pair, I slipped them on before ever touching the wallet. There wasn't much inside it: a Washington State official identification card in Loren's name, a Social Security card, and a photo of Loren as a kid—age six or seven at most—standing in front of a middle-aged couple I assumed to be Harold and Alma Gregson. That's when I finally spread open the bill container at the back of the wallet, and there they were, as big as life—two hundred-dollar bills neatly tucked inside.

Greta saw the bills almost as soon as I did. "Where the hell did those come from?" she demanded.

She reached out to take them, but I quickly moved the wallet out of her reach.

"These came from whoever killed him," I said. "These two hundred-dollar bills happen to be a serial killer's calling card."

All color drained from Greta's face. "You're saying Loren really was murdered then?"

"You'd better believe it," I told her. "Now I need to get someone from Seattle PD to believe it, too. May I take these?"

"Sure," she said. "You can have the wallet and the phone, but I want to keep Daddy's ring. I'm the one who gave it to him, and it pissed the hell out of me that Loren got it, instead of me."

That's the weird thing about sibling rivalry. Just because one or the other of them dies, the problem doesn't automatically go away.

CHAPTER 22

Seattle, Washington
Tuesday, March 3, 2020

BY THE TIME GRETA AND I FINISHED, SARAH HAD BEEN LEFT
alone for far longer than I intended, but at least the rain had
stopped. When I opened the car door, Sarah scrambled her long-
legged body into the front seat. That's Sarah-speak for *I need to go,*
and I need to go now!

Walking my dog right outside the Hallidays' lakefront home
didn't seem like the proper thing to do, so I drove far enough up the
driveway to be around the curve and out of sight before I stopped to
let her out. Back in the old days, for evidence reasons, I used to carry
a container of latex gloves around in my glove box for evidence-
collection purposes. Now I carry a roll of doggie poop bags. To my
immense relief one of those wasn't necessary this time around.

Sarah's pee pause gave me a few minutes to consider my next
step. A quick check of my email revealed that no one other than

Greta Halliday had responded to the requests for additional interviews, so there was no sense in my waiting around for another case to surface. I needed to move forward with the ones I had, and that called for another trip to the Homicide unit at Seattle PD, because Seattle is where three of my four dead bodies had been found.

I could have jumped the line by going straight to my friend and former partner, Ron Peters, who is now the longtime assistant chief of police at SPD, but pulling rank was bound to piss off all the people whose help I would need to reopen any or all of my cases. Insulting those lower-totem-pole folks seemed like a plan to fail. No, in this instance I needed to go through channels, across desks, and up the chain of command, carefully crossing all t's and dotting all i's along the way. As for my starting point? That would be the only Seattle PD officer connected to the Darius Jackson case, Detective Sandra Sechrest.

In establishing any kind of working relationship, I prefer my initial encounters to be face-to-face. With that in mind, and with Sarah once again stretched out full length on the back seat, we headed for downtown Seattle on I-90. On the way, I called both Mel and Kyle, leaving messages to let them know that this was taking longer than expected and that they were on their own as far as figuring out plans for dinner.

During my years at Seattle PD, I worked out of the fifth floor of the Public Safety Building, known throughout the city for having the slowest elevator in town. That's all gone now, not only the elevator, but also the building itself. It went bye-bye years ago and was replaced by the new Seattle Police Department Headquarters a few blocks away at Fifth and Cherry. I had been to the new building several times during my years with the Special Homicide Investigation Team, but not often enough to know my way around.

In the lobby I was asked who I was and why I was there. "My name's J. P. Beaumont," I told the clerk. "I'm here to see Detective Sandra Sechrest."

"Any relation to Scotty?" the clerk asked.

Here we go again!

"He's my son," I told her.

"You must be very proud of him then," she said, beaming at me as she handed over my visitor badge. "He's a real go-getter."

I made my way to the elevator and rode up to the seventh floor where I was met by a uniformed desk sergeant who acted as gate-keeper to a well-appointed office space that bore no resemblance to the Homicide squad's old digs in the Public Safety Building, where Captain Larry Powell's glass-lined office, the Fish Bowl, had dominated the interior landscape.

The desk sergeant greeted me and inquired about my business.

"I'm here to see Detective Sechrest," I told him.

"Regarding?"

"Regarding some cold cases, three to be exact."

That got his attention. He picked up his phone. "Detective Sechrest? There's a J. P. Beaumont here at the desk. Says he has three cold cases for you."

The woman who showed up a few minutes later was a petite red-head who reminded me for all the world of someone I had met in Arizona years earlier, the sheriff of Cochise County, Joanna Brady.

"Glad to meet you," Sandra Sechrest said, holding out her hand, "and call me Sandy, please, but three cases? I thought you were working on Darius Jackson."

"I am," I told her, "but now I've found some other cases, and I sus-pect all of them are connected—two occurred here in Seattle while a third happened in Liberty Lake over in eastern Washington."

"Whoa," she said. Then, turning back to the desk sergeant, she asked, "Is anyone using the conference room at the moment?"

"Nope," he said. "It's free and clear."

Sandra turned back to me. "Let's talk in there, then, shall we?"

She led the way. Inside the room, she waited until I was seated before leveling a green-eyed stare in my direction. "Okay," she said, "tell me."

So I did, from the beginning, starting with Matilda Jackson right on through my afternoon meeting with Greta Halliday, including how Yolanda Aguirre's study into long-term ramifications of over-dose deaths in families of the deceased had allowed me to zero in on victims whose death rulings of suicide or accident I considered to be erroneous.

Sandra Sechrest was a fast study. "Do you think there might be others beyond the four you've already identified?" she asked when I finished.

"I do," I said, with a nod. "There are close to a dozen additional files that may or may not be connected, ones where I need to conduct further interviews. And there are also additional files that have yet to be reviewed. The problem is, those initial interviews by Yolanda Aguirre were conducted with the understanding that they were confidential, so I'm having to wait to see if any of those other interviewees will reach out to me to provide additional information."

"Where do we stand right now?" Sandra asked.

Her use of the word *we* made me think that, as far as Sandra Sechrest was concerned, we were already in this together. That's when I pulled the evidence bag containing Loren Gregson's personal effects out of my pocket and laid it on the table in front of her.

"I suggest we start here," I said. "I used gloves when I handled the wallet, but I'd like to have that swabbed for DNA. Ditto for the two hundred-dollar bills I found inside."

"You know the drill," she said. "I can't submit evidence for testing without having an active case number. None of your cases are active. They're linked, yes, but at this point I still doubt you have enough to get the M.E. to change manner of death rulings here, or even to get traction in Liberty Lake. But for our purposes, the fact that all the Seattle cases are considered closed may be a godsend."

"How so?"

"Because you can go take a look at the existing evidence boxes, the same way you did with the Jackson case. You know as well as I do that a lot of the investigation happens in the first forty-eight hours after a body is discovered. Depending on what else the M.E. had on her plate at the time, the autopsy itself might have been delayed for that long or even longer."

"And you're thinking a lot of that evidence may not have been examined very closely?"

"Exactly," Sandra Sechrest said, "and guess what? I can provide all the case numbers."

"That would be greatly appreciated," I said.

"Give me those names again."

So I did.

"Okay," she said, rising to her feet. "Hang on. I'll be right back."

She had no more than left the room when there was a tap on the door. When it opened, a frowning Scott Beaumont stepped inside. "I was coming on shift, and the clerk downstairs told me you were here. What's up?"

I was momentarily stumped as to where to start. "Working a closed case," I said. "It's something Ben Weston asked me to look into."

"Darius Jackson?"

Obviously he and Ben had discussed the situation. "Yup," I said. "That's the one."

"Making any progress?"

"Maybe," I said. "I've uncovered some other cases with similar circumstances. Detective Sechrest is helping me look into them."

"Good-o," Scott said. "Glad to hear it. If there's anything I can do . . ."

The way he said it made me think he was about to head to his desk, but I needed to discuss a few other things with him before he left.

"Have you heard anything from Kelly?" I asked.

Scott frowned. "No, why? Is something wrong?"

Actually a whole lot of things were wrong, and I had been sitting on them. I gave him a very short version of the current family situation, leaving out the puzzling part about Caroline Richards having grown up as part of Witness Protection. Unsurprisingly, Scott was outraged.

"So Kyle is staying with you and Mel, Kelly and Kayla are living in an apartment in Eugene, and Jeremy is shacked up with his pregnant girlfriend in the house Kelly paid off with her inheritance?"

"That's about the size of it," I agreed.

"If I had known all this was going on, I would have driven down to Ashland and cleaned his clock."

"I expect that's part of the reason Kelly didn't tell either one of us," I said, "but don't go off half-cocked. When I saw Kelly, she was holding it together, but only just barely. You can let her know that I told you about what's going on, but don't go inserting yourself into the drama. She's dealing with enough right now, and your going to fist-city with Jeremy won't help matters."

Scott was about to take issue with that when Detective Sechrest showed back up with a piece of Post-it paper in her hand.

"Here they are . . ." she began. "Hey, Scotty. Sorry to interrupt. I was getting your dad some case numbers." She handed them over. "Let me know if there's anything else I can do."

"Thanks," I said. "Will do."

Once she exited, Scott was still there. "I can hardly believe all this crap," he muttered. "I never really warmed up to Jeremy, but I always thought the two of them had the perfect life."

I patted him on the shoulder. "You're not the only one," I said. "My mother always used to say, 'What you don't know can't hurt you,' but for the record, I think she was wrong about that, because it sure as hell can."

CHAPTER 23

Bellingham, Washington
Tuesday, March 3, 2020

BY THE TIME I LEFT SEATTLE PD, A FEW MINUTES BEFORE
five P.M., it was raining pitchforks and hammer handles. I was
soaked to the skin before I made it back to the parking garage.
When it came time to pay the piper there, I was left with a severe
case of sticker shock. When did parking in downtown Seattle get
to be so expensive?

In the not-too-recent past, if I'd found myself in Seattle at that
hour of the day, I would have called Mel and let her know I'd be
spending the night in our condo at Belltown Terrace. Since that
ship had sailed, I now had no option other than heading home to
Bellingham.

Dogs don't count as second express lane travelers, so there was
no way for me to use that lane as I headed north. At the closed

express lane entrance at Cherry and Fifth, however, I learned there was a multicar pileup north of Forty-Fifth. In other words, all northbound traffic was going to be a nightmare, and the pouring rain made it even worse. It took me close to two hours to make it from downtown Seattle to Everett. I was on the north side of that and partway through Marysville when my phone rang with Unknown Caller listed in caller ID. I started to let the call go to voicemail, but then, thinking whoever it was might be one of Yolanda Aguirre's interviewees, I went ahead and picked up.

"J. P. Beaumont here," I said.

"This is Detective Elizabeth Byrd, with Liberty Lake PD," the caller informed me. "My former partner, Ron Wang, gave me your number. Would now be a convenient time to talk?"

In good weather and decent traffic, driving time from Marysville to our home in Fairhaven takes an hour give or take. This time the GPS was saying I'd arrive at my destination in an hour and a half, a little after nine P.M. As far as talking on the phone was concerned, I had all the time in the world.

"I'm driving north on I-5," I told her. "Talking now is fine. Shoot."

"Ron gave me a call earlier today. He said that after speaking to you, he thought he remembered that somewhere in the Jake Spaulding file, one of the witnesses had mentioned something about seeing a homeless woman hanging around the Hitching Post on the night in question.

"Today I went back through the file, and Ron was right. One of the witnesses is a guy named Matt Barr. When asked if anything out of the ordinary had happened that night, he complained that a homeless woman with a loaded grocery cart had been hanging around the bar's front entrance when he parked his truck. Somehow the woman lost control of her cart, and it rolled off the side-walk and nailed the front bumper of his truck. There wasn't that much damage, but he was pissed about it."

Another homeless lady? I thought, as a wave of gooseflesh ran up my legs.

"Were you able to locate her?" I asked.

"We tried, but no dice," Detective Byrd answered. "If she was hanging around the parking lot that night, there's a possibility that she might have seen what went on. Officers didn't see any sign of her when they were out doing the neighborhood canvass, and by the time the crime lab got back to us with that female DNA profile from the door handle, she had disappeared into thin air."

"Did the witness give any kind of description of her?" I asked.

"White female, maybe five one, and heavyset. He said he'd put her weight at around a hundred fifty pounds. Matt also indicated that she had short, curly white hair. She was wearing ragtag cloth-ing and a pair of ratty tennis shoes."

I was excited. Maybe now we were getting somewhere. In the grainy food bank video, the female walking with Darius Jackson had appeared to be white with light-colored hair. This description was certainly a match to that, and I told Detective Byrd as much.

"Would it be possible for you to put me in touch with your witness?" I asked.

"Possibly," she answered. "It might be better if I gave him your number."

"Absolutely," I said. "Feel free. Tell him he can call me any time."

Amazingly enough, half an hour or so later, just as I was passing the first Mount Vernon exit, my phone rang again with another unknown number, but this one indicated the location was Liberty Lake. Matt Barr maybe?

"Hello," I answered.

"Is this the private eye Detective Byrd told me about?"

I did my best not to grit my teeth. The term "private eye" offends me. It reminds me of all those old-time Mickey Spillane paperback books with dead blondes on the covers. I'm an investigator, not an eye, but there was no need of my mentioning that pet peeve to my caller.

"Yes, it is," I answered. "My name is J. P. Beaumont. And yes, Mr. Barr, I'm definitely interested in speaking to you. I'm taking another look at Jake Spaulding's death and was wondering if you could tell me anything more about the homeless woman you saw outside the Hitching Post on the night Mr. Spaulding died."

"Other than the fact that the old bat's overloaded shopping cart messed up the front bumper of my brand-new pickup truck? Pissed the hell out of me. She didn't even bother saying she was sorry."

"What else can you tell me about her?"

"Not much more than I told the cops at the time. Five one or two, overweight, older—late fifties or early sixties, short, curly white hair. She was dressed in sweats and wearing a hoodie, which was surprising given it was almost the middle of July and hot as hell. Grubby tennis shoes. That's about it."

"You didn't notice any distinguishing features?"

"Well," he allowed, "now that you mention it, there was one thing. When she came to retrieve her damned shopping cart, she reached out to grab the handle. At that point, her shirt sleeve pulled up some. That's when I noticed she was wearing an Apple Watch. I remember thinking, *What the hell? If she's homeless, how the hell did she come by that?* They don't exactly hand those out for free at the local food bank. And where does she charge it? Mine runs out of juice after twenty hours or so and has to be recharged."

"Where indeed!" I muttered aloud, but what I was really doing was stifling a vocal cheer.

We had now identified a group of four separate overdose deaths linked together by a history of domestic violence and two hundred-dollar bills. In addition, a homeless female pushing a shopping cart had been connected to two of them, but Matt Barr's telling detail—that Apple Watch—was both new and incredibly significant. That's something that would set her apart from most homeless people—something that made her memorable. More than that, if we ever caught up with her, that watch would leave behind a trail of digital breadcrumbs almost as revealing as those from a cell phone. It would tell us where she had been and when. Having that might also give us access to her contacts as well as her text, email, and call history.

"You've provided me with some really important information, Mr. Barr, and I can't thank you enough," I said, trying hard to rein in my exuberance. "I really appreciate your getting in touch. It could mean a lot."

"You're welcome," Matt said. Then, after a moment he added, "I didn't really know the guy personally—Spaulding, I mean. Supposedly he'd just gotten out of prison after serving time for something or other. I've been told he'd had quite the reputation around here for being a bully back when he was younger, but when I saw him in the bar, he didn't seem to be causing trouble or doing anything out of line, so maybe the time he spent in the slammer did him some good. Maybe he learned his lesson."

"It's possible," I said to Mr. Barr, but inside my head I was muttering, *But not bloody likely.*

If Jake Spaulding had had a chance to live a little longer, I expect that eventually he would have gone right back to being the same kind of jerk he'd always been. In my experience, most of the time, once a bully, always a bully. That's usually not something being sent to prison will fix.

CHAPTER 24

Seattle, Washington
Tuesday to Wednesday, March 3–4, 2020

IT WAS LATE WHEN I GOT HOME TUESDAY NIGHT, BUT I WAS IN high spirits. The conversations with Detective Byrd and Matt Barr had made me feel as though I was making enormous forward progress, but it was clear from talking to them and to Detective Sechrest as well that a trip back to Seattle PD's Evidence unit was definitely in order, and that needed to happen sooner rather than later.

However, my good mood pretty much evaporated once I found a grim-faced Mel glued to the TV set where a newscaster was saying that multiple Covid deaths had been reported at a nursing home in Kirkland, another of Seattle's Eastside suburbs. I paused long enough to feed Sarah and make myself a peanut butter and jelly sandwich before joining Mel on the sofa.

"You look upset," I ventured.

"I am upset," she said. "Very. People are dying of something that spreads like wildfire and that no one knows how to treat. Schools and restaurants and businesses are going to be shut down, but I can't close the doors on the department. Public safety still matters, and crime isn't going to magically go away just because there's a pandemic in progress. Some of my people may be able to work from home, but most won't. There are going to be mask mandates. I've spent the whole day trying to source masks for the department. It's been frustrating as hell."

Believe me, Mel Soames is not a complainer. She's your basic perpetual optimist, someone who sees solutions where others see only problems. In all the years I've known her, those were more negative words than I had ever heard her utter at one time. But I also knew that telling her everything was going to be okay was a sure path to disaster. Either she'd think I was patronizing her or, even worse, "mansplaining." In this situation, my best course of action was to simply agree with everything she said.

"You're right," I said. "It's going to be tough."

Turns out, not minimizing the problem was the right strategy. Sarah, sensing something amiss, finished snarfing down her food and then came over to the couch where she laid her massive head on Mel's lap. Both those things seemed to help snap Mel out of her funk. She switched off the TV. Then, absently petting the dog with one hand and glancing at her watch, she commented, "You're home late. How was your day?"

It was a long story, and bringing her up-to-date took time.

"With those new case numbers, I'm assuming your next step is to examine the evidence boxes," she said.

I nodded. "With the pandemic bearing down on us, no telling how long before the Evidence unit will be on lockdown, too. But commuting ninety miles back and forth doesn't sound like a good idea. If you can take Sarah to work with you tomorrow, I'll head back to Seattle. That way, if need be, I can get a hotel room and stay over."

"I wish we still had the condo," Mel said wistfully. "I hate to think about your checking into a hotel with lots of other people, travelers especially, when you don't know where they've been. Not only that, according to everything I've read and heard, older people are the ones most susceptible to Covid."

In our marriage, the fifteen-year age difference between Mel and me doesn't usually rear its ugly head, but it just had. I could have been offended, but in that moment, we both needed to lighten the load, so I went for humor.

"That's what you get for tying the knot with an old duffer," I told her. "So here's the deal. If you'll take Sarah with you, I'll head back to Seattle first thing in the morning. If I can get everything I need done in one day, I will, and I promise not to stay over unless it's absolutely necessary. Fair enough?"

She smiled and nodded. "Fair enough," she agreed.

Sensing that the tension had left the room, Sarah abandoned Mel's lap in favor of curling up on her rug.

"How did Kyle fare today?" I asked.

"All right," Mel said. "When I came home, he was sitting at the island doing homework, although he told me he didn't think there was much point. He said the teachers are all in a flap about switching over to online learning next week, and they're all acting weird."

"Next week?" I echoed. "That soon?"

Mel nodded. "Next Wednesday, the eleventh."

"So it's coming for sure."

"For sure," she repeated, "and we're all going to have to do the best we can."

Knowing I'd need to get an early start the next day, we decided it was time to hit the hay. I let Sarah out for one last walk, then we all headed for the bedroom.

THE NEXT MORNING Kyle, eating breakfast at the kitchen island, was surprised when all three of us—Mel, Sarah, and I—emerged from the bedroom at the same time. I had packed an overnight bag to take along, just in case. The TV set was off, and I, for one, was very grateful about that.

Over coffee we explained the logistics for the day, and Kyle volunteered to help. "Would you like me to come by your office after school and take Sarah for a walk?" he asked.

"That would be a huge help," Mel said. "Come to think of it, there's something else you could do."

She reached into her pocket, fished out her wallet, and extracted her Visa card. "Once you finish walking her, how about if you go by Costco and stock up on all the things you like to eat. If the restaurants are going to be closed, there's going to be a lot of panicky shopping, and it'll be crowded, but since Grandpa and I are so dependent on takeout, I don't want any of us to starve to death."

"Will do," Kyle said, pocketing the credit card. "And I'm guessing this is for groceries only," he added with a grin. "I'm not allowed to pick up a new computer while I'm at it?"

"In your dreams," Mel replied, but she was smiling, too.

It seemed as though a night's sleep had done all of us a world of good. However, to avoid my having to visit any restaurants, Mel insisted on packing a lunch for me—an amount of food equal to several lunches in fact. I hit the road laden with a bag containing four PB&J sandwiches, a bag of sour-cream-and-onion potato chips, and a bunch of bananas. If we'd owned an old-fashioned thermos,

I'm sure Mel would have insisted that I fill that with coffee before leaving the house.

"Not to worry," I told her. "The Evidence unit is part of Seattle PD. I'm sure I'll be able to scrounge up coffee as needed."

Out in the garage, Sarah seemed a little confused when I ordered her into the back seat of Mel's Interceptor rather than into my Mercedes, but once she realized that her rug was already there and waiting, she complied at once. By the time I shut the car door, she was curled up and settled in.

When it came time for Mel to climb into the driver's seat, she gave me a quick kiss. "Be safe," she said.

In the years I had known her, I had seldom seen Mel scared or even so much as spooked. In that moment, I could see in her eyes how frightened she was, not just for me, but for Kyle, for her department, her country, and maybe even for the whole world. I wanted to tell her, *You need to stop watching so much news*, but there wasn't any point.

"I will be," I said. "I promise."

Heading south, I was grateful it was overcast but not raining. Had it been clear, the moisture from the previous day's rainstorms might have left a coating of black ice on the roadway. The marine layer meant the road was wet but not slick. I had started late enough that, by the time I reached Everett, the worst of Seattle's inbound morning traffic was beginning to subside. I made straight for SODO without passing Go and without paying two hundred dollars.

OFFICER HARRIMAN RECOGNIZED me on sight. "You again?" she asked.

"Just call me the bad penny."

"What do you need this time?"

On the drive down, I'd made up my mind that I needed to revisit the Darius Jackson file along with the other two.

"I need the same file you gave me last time—the one on Darius Jackson—and a couple more besides," I told her, handing over Sandra Sechrest's Post-it note. "I'll also need to be able to view any DVDs that may be included."

Thankfully, I didn't have to go through the whole rigamarole of showing my ID. Officer Harriman handed me a clipboard and told me to sign in while she dispatched someone else to fetch the evidence files. But then she eyed the bag Mel had packed for me. "What's in that?" she asked.

"My lunch," I explained.

"No food or beverages are allowed in evidence rooms. You'll need to stow it in one of the lockers over there," she said, pointing to a bank of lockers, most of which had keys in the doors.

"Not many visitors here today," she added, "so take your pick."

The clerk who brought the evidence boxes from wherever they were kept escorted me into a different room and then gave me a quick lesson on how to operate the video equipment. I'm sure Scotty Beaumont wouldn't have had the least bit of trouble with it, but his dear old dad required some assistance. After the food bank video was locked and loaded, it took a few practice tries for me to master the art of frame-by-frame viewing, along with using the keyboard to increase and decrease the size of the images I was examining.

And that's how I studied the video footage of Darius Jackson and the unidentified homeless woman as they left the entrance of the food bank and walked through the darkness toward the street on Thanksgiving night. They moved in sync with him on the right and her on the left and closer to the camera.

One frame at a time, almost one step at a time, I followed their movements. Then, as they reached the sidewalk and turned left, I saw what I was looking for—a tiny pinprick of light gleaming on the woman's left wrist. At regular speed it had been invisible, and it appeared only during the step or two it took for her to turn the corner, but the movements involved must have inadvertently caused the sleeve of her coat to ride up slightly on her arm, enough so that the camera lens captured what I was now sure was a momentary flash of light from the glowing face of an Apple Watch.

My emotional response was much the same as Matt Barr's had been. What the hell was a homeless woman doing with an Apple Watch? Where had she gotten it and how did she charge it? Did she have a solar panel hidden in that cart of hers so she could recharge the watch as needed? No, there was only one answer to the Apple Watch question. This woman wasn't homeless at all. She was masquerading as someone who was.

"Gotcha!" I exclaimed aloud to the image on the screen. "I may not know who the hell you are at the moment, but you'd better believe I'm coming for you."

The next box I had requested was the one for Loren Gregson. Once the dog-walker called in to report finding a dead body in a blackberry patch, uniformed officers had been first to respond. Shortly thereafter, Seattle PD detectives had been summoned, and there I spotted a familiar name. Detective Sandra Sechrest had been one of the original investigators on the scene. No wonder she'd been willing to give me the case numbers. Not only had she spoken to Matilda Jackson, she'd also been required to walk away from the Gregson case once the M.E. made the autopsy call.

The detectives had initiated a neighborhood canvass to see if anything out of line had been reported from the night before. That turned up nothing. The detectives had collected surveillance footage from three separate businesses in the area—a mini-mart, a restaurant, and a bar: the Fremont Inn, the very one Loren Gregson's mother had mentioned. The footage had then been transferred to DVDs, which were placed in the evidence box, but no notation in the accompanying murder book indicated that any of the video material had ever been analyzed. My best guess was that once the accidental death ruling came in, the investigation into Loren Gregson's death had ground to a halt. At that point, further examination of any evidence would have been deemed unnecessary.

The M.E. had reported the time of death as being sometime overnight on Saturday, January 10. During wintertime Seattle, nights are long indeed. It made sense that someone committing a crime would aim to do so late at night, thus lessening the risk of having possible witnesses out and about. I decided arbitrarily that I'd focus my attention on the footage time-stamped between the hours of eleven P.M. and five A.M., but that was a hell of a lot of footage to review, especially since I was doing the job solo.

Not only that, there was no way to make use of the fast-forward button. Depending on the speed of movement, vehicles especially and even pedestrians passed in and out of camera range in mere seconds. That meant every scrap of video had to be examined in real time. So that's what I did, minute by minute and hour by hour. Knowing that late-night trouble often occurs in bars, I examined the bar's interior video first—reviewing the evening of January tenth both outside and inside the Fremont Inn starting at seven P.M.

Having seen Loren's various mug shots, I had a reasonably good idea of who I was looking for. The resolution on the bar's interior surveillance system was excellent, allowing me to view the goings-on from several different angles. That took even more time. While the time stamp on the video moved from seven to nine thirty, noon my time came and went. By then my eyes were killing me and so was my back. I was about to give up, but when I hit the 9:30 P.M. time stamp, that's when my perseverance paid off.

There Loren was, big as life. It turned out he was a little more portly than I would have expected. He marched in through the entrance as though he owned the place, bellied up to the bar, and immediately placed an order without bothering to consult a menu. His first and second drinks were both delivered shot-glass style with a clear liquid inside both—either vodka or tequila, I surmised. Those had both gone down the hatch before his meal showed up. It was a platter of bar food that looked like a chiliburger although I couldn't tell for sure. His food was accompanied by two more shots. Right about 10:45, he pushed his plate away, signaled for his bill and signed his mother's tab, and then staggered out of the bar in far worse shape than when he'd first entered.

At that point, I switched over to the Fremont Inn's exterior footage. Here the resolution wasn't nearly as clear, but I was able to see long piles of plowed snow lining the sidewalk. I queued the video to 10:45 P.M. Only a few frames in, Loren Gregson appeared, exiting the bar and stepping out onto the sidewalk. He paused long enough to tug his sagging pants back into position. Then, after looking around for a moment, he pulled his jacket tighter around him and staggered away, westbound toward the Ship Canal rather than away from it.

Considering the weather that night, he certainly wasn't dressed for a long walk outdoors. I watched as he set off down the sidewalk. Then, stepping out of camera range, he disappeared from view. That was a sobering moment. I sat there realizing that I had just watched a badly impaired man stroll out of sight and into the darkness, totally oblivious to the reality that he was walking straight into the arms of the grim reaper. For several seconds I stared at the monitor and dealing with the reality that I was now one of the last people on earth to see Loren Gregson alive.

But then something else caught my eye as another figure entered camera range, coming from the north. It was swathed in what appeared to be a light-colored blanket of some kind, one that was draped around the person's shoulders and fell all the way to the ground where it scraped along the sidewalk. Straining to get a closer look at this ghostlike visage, I caught sight of the hoodie underneath the blanket that completely obscured the person's face from the surveilling camera's lens.

A wave of excitement swept through me as I realized exactly what I was seeing. I had just watched Loren Gregson wander off into the night. Now here was his stone-cold killer, clearly stalking her prey. That was her, I was sure of it. She hadn't been waiting for him inside the Fremont Inn, but outside it. I suspected that she had been somewhere nearby, wrapped in the blanket and huddled against a building and virtually invisible. Passersby might have walked around her or even stepped over her without actually seeing her. Because that's what most people do about homeless people—they ignore them.

I stopped the footage in the last frame before she would have walked out of range. Her left wrist was facing me, but both of her hands and arms were hidden from view under the blanket. If she was wearing the Apple Watch that night, there was no way for me to catch sight of it. Nor was there a chance of spotting any distinguishing facial features.

I was beside myself with a weird mix of conflicting emotions consisting of equal parts excitement and frustration. I was sure this was the killer—it had to be—but I had no way of identifying her.

Who was she? Where had she come from? How had she gotten there? Was her grocery cart hidden somewhere nearby but out of sight? And even though my whole being said I was right, everything I had so far was completely circumstantial. Down deep I knew that I still didn't have enough to get Seattle PD to move off the dime on any of these cases.

At that moment, I needed a break in the very worst way, so I abandoned the evidence room and went looking for one of my PB&Js. I collected my lunch bag from the locker and headed for the break room, which was totally deserted. I went straight to the Keurig setup where there was a selection of coffees and an honor jar asking for a dollar a pop. Figuring I was in for the day, I dropped in a fiver and collected my first cup of java. It wasn't up to what I'm used to from our freshly ground beans at home, but beggars can't be choosers.

I settled down at one of the tables and unwrapped my sandwich. Not wanting to be disturbed, I had turned my phone off while I had been in the evidence room. When I turned it back on, the phone practically blew up. I suddenly had eighty-eight emails I hadn't had earlier. All of those came from Yolanda Aguirre's intern, so now I was in possession of that many new files in need of examination. And then there were three text messages from Lulu Benson. The first one had come in at ten A.M.: Please give me a call. The one at eleven thirty was a bit more terse: Call me. Message number three had come in at 1:15. It was in all caps: ARE YOU GOING TO CALL ME BACK OR WHAT?

Thinking she might now be in possession of Caroline Richards's DNA profile, I dialed her number.

"It's about damned time you called," she muttered irritably.

"You've got the profile already?" I asked.

"Not only a profile, dummy," she snapped back. "I've got a name for you. Now, are you going to shut up and listen or not?"

Not wanting to tangle with Lulu Benson, I shut up, and she continued, "The DNA profile obtained from Caroline Richards led to a woman who was born in Princeton, New Jersey, on April 12, 1977. Her birth name was Patricia Ann Bledsoe. She was the daughter of a Princeton philosophy professor named Arnold Bledsoe and a stay-at-home mom named Lila Anderson Bledsoe. Her sister, Marisa Bledsoe Young, who was three years younger than Patricia, aka Phyllis Baylor, entered her own DNA into NamUs and also in GED-match two years ago in an effort to locate her long-lost sister as well as Patricia's daughter, Serena, aka Lindsey Baylor, both of whom disappeared without a trace in 2002."

NamUs is a national database of missing persons. Individuals as well as law enforcement are able to post entries including names, dental records, and DNA profiles. They're also able to do their own online searches. A similar organization in the private sector is the nonprofit DNA Doe Project, which focuses on human remains that may have gone unidentified for decades.

I was so astonished by Lulu's revelations that I could barely speak, but eventually I did. "That's how you found her?" I asked. "Through NamUs."

"I didn't do it personally," she replied, "but once my DNA tech had the profile, I had her run it. That way it goes through the proper channels. Marisa currently lives in Fountain Hills, Arizona, which is somewhere near Scottsdale. Would you like her phone number?"

"Are you kidding? Absolutely!"

Lulu gave me a number with a 480 area code. "You should probably call her right away," she added. "Notification of the match may turn up in her email any minute now if it hasn't already."

"Will do," I said.

My mother was always a big proponent of "think before you speak." In this case, I certainly could have used some more thinking time before opening my big mouth, but I didn't want to risk it. I wanted to get to Marisa Young before someone from NamUs did.

Downing one last sip of coffee for luck, I keyed her number into my phone and waited for it to ring. If Marisa had been born in 1980, she was about forty. At this hour of the day, chances are she'd be at work, but I crossed my fingers and hoped to hell she'd answer.

CHAPTER 25

"HELLO."

"Marisa Young?" I asked.

"Yes, who's calling?"

"My name is J. P. Beaumont. I'm a private investigator, and I'm calling in regard to your missing persons post on NamUs."

I heard a small gasp before she spoke again. "Is this about Patricia and Serena?" the woman demanded. "Have you found them?"

That was when I realized I had blundered into an emotional minefield. Yes, we had located Marisa's sister and niece. That was the good news. The bad news was that my call was also a death notice. No doubt the woman had resigned herself to the idea that both her missing loved ones had been dead for years, but now I was about to make that a certainty, at least as far as her sister was concerned.

"Yes, we have," I told her, "but I'm terribly sorry to have to inform you that your sister passed away several years ago. She died of natural causes in 2016 and was buried in the Mount Olivet Cemetery in Renton, Washington."

"Where the hell is Renton, Washington?" Marisa wanted to know.

"It's in the Seattle area."

"What on earth was Patricia doing in Seattle?" Marisa demanded. "That's all the way across the country from Plainfield, New Jersey. That's where she was the last time I saw her. And how could she die of natural causes at age thirty-nine? That seems really young unless she died of some kind of cancer."

In that moment, the woman on the phone sounded more angry than grief-stricken, and I couldn't fault her for that. She had spent years hoping for some kind of tearful reunion with her missing family members. This was anything but.

"I'm afraid your sister had a long history of drug abuse," I told her. "She died of hepatitis C."

Marisa took a moment to process that information. "Well, at least she wasn't murdered," she said at last. "I suppose that's what I was expecting—that she would be found as nothing more than unidentified human remains. What about Serena? Is she dead, too?"

This time I was the one who took a breath. This was where the conversation would become much more complicated.

"No," I said, "your niece is still alive. At the moment, she's living in Ashland, Oregon, under the name of Caroline Richards. She's had a number of other aliases over the years, but that's her current one. I'm afraid she and her mother lived a pretty rough life once they came to Seattle. Your sister managed to scrabble out a living for them, but . . ."

"Was Patricia working the streets as a sex worker?" Marisa wanted to know.

In many circles, the word *prostitute* is slowly but surely going out of favor, but Marisa was clearly prepared to hear the truth, and I gave it to her straight.

"Yes, she was," I answered. "For at least some of that time, she and her daughter were homeless. At the time of Patricia's death, the two of them may have been estranged. It's possible Serena may not even be aware that her mother is deceased."

"Estranged," Marisa repeated. "Are you telling me Serena ran away?"

"It seems likely."

"How old would she have been when that happened?"

"I'm not entirely sure," I answered. "In her midteens, maybe."

"Like mother like daughter then," Marisa murmured with a sigh. "That's about how old Patricia was when she took off for the second time and never came back. My parents never recovered from losing her, but tell me about Serena. Is there any chance you can put me in touch with her?"

"Before I answer that question," I told her, "I need to let you know how I came to be involved in all this."

"Didn't you say you're a private investigator?"

"Yes, I am."

"So who hired you?"

"I'm actually working on behalf of my grandson, Kyle Cartwright. He's eighteen and came to live with my wife and me a few weeks ago because his parents—my daughter and her husband—are divorcing, and his dad has moved his much younger pregnant girlfriend into the house."

"And Serena's the pregnant girlfriend?" Marisa asked faintly.

I gave Marisa Young several points for being perceptive. "Yes, she is."

That one seemed to stop the conversation cold. "This all sounds very complicated," Marisa said at last.

"It is, so before we go into all those details, please tell me what you can about your sister, and then I'll share what I've learned so far."

"Do you know anything about our parents?" she asked.

"Not very much," I replied. "I believe your father was an academic of some kind."

"Yes, a professor of philosophy at Princeton. Believe me, he was a very straitlaced individual, and so was my mother. In that regard, they were a matched pair. As for Tricia? She was a rebel from the get-go. She was a firecracker who went toe-to-toe with them at every opportunity. She was always a beauty, but she routinely got into trouble at school. She started getting into fights with both boys and girls while she was still in grade school. She began smoking, drinking, and hanging out with much older kids when she was twelve, and that only got worse over time. By the time she was in high school, she had graduated to hard drugs. The thing is, she and I were still really close back then. I knew all about everything Tricia was up to because I was the one who helped her sneak in and out of the house late at night.

"She was fourteen when she ran away from home the first time. The cops found her within a day and brought her back. When she took off the next time, a year or so later, she never came home. The folks were devastated, but Tricia and I stayed in touch through one of my friends by leaving numbers where I could call her.

"I knew she was living in Newark and working underage as a pole dancer, but she begged me not to tell our parents about that.

When Tricia started going steady with a guy named Sal del Veccio, she told me all about him. She said she had met him at the club. I suppose he started out as one of her customers, but she said he was rich, and she thought he was her Prince Charming.

"That's about the time Mom took sick and was diagnosed with breast cancer. She didn't believe in having mammograms, so it was already stage four by the time the cancer was found. The next three years were hellish for her, for Dad, and for me, too. I was still in high school at the time. I begged Tricia to come home and see Mom before she died, but she wouldn't. And she didn't come to Mom's funeral, either. For one thing, she was pregnant by then, and she thought showing up in that condition would make matters worse. Knowing my dad, she most likely wasn't wrong about that, but through it all, Tricia and I stayed connected.

"After Tricia turned up pregnant, she and Sal got married. At first everything seemed fine. According to her, Sal's family was well-to-do, and Sal had a good job—enough so that they were able to buy a nice home in a good neighborhood. From what she told me, Tricia seemed happier than I had ever known her to be. She told me once that sometimes she felt like a princess living in a fairy tale, but then it all went bad."

"How so?"

"I had no idea that Sal's father was connected to the Mafia, but he was, and fairly high up, too. Around that time, in the late nineties and early two thousands, there was some kind of changing of the guard in the mob with a lot of infighting. There were a number of murders related to all that. Sal's father ended up being implicated in one of them. Tricia told me he was in jail awaiting trial.

"Then, shortly before Serena turned four, Tricia called our friend and asked me to call her back. When I did, she was in tears. She told me that her father-in-law was considering taking a plea deal. She said that if that happened, she and Sal would have to disappear. That's exactly what she said to me, 'We'll have to disappear and I'll never be able to see or talk to you again.'

"I was desperate to see her before that happened. Finally she relented and agreed that I could come visit. The very next day I drove up to their house in Plainfield. I wanted to give Serena something special for her birthday, so I took along the pink teddy bear Mom and Dad had given me when I was about her age.

"Once I saw her, I couldn't believe how cute Serena was. She looked exactly like Tricia had looked in pictures of the two of us together when I was still a baby. When I handed over the teddy bear, Serena gave me a huge smile, then she hugged the teddy close to her body and held on to it like she wasn't ever going to let it go. I wish I had an actual photograph of that moment, but all I have is the image that's engraved on my heart.

"When I asked Tricia about what was really going on, she shook her head and said she couldn't talk about it. I left the house an hour or so later and cried all the way back home because I was afraid that was the last time I'd see her, and I was right. There were no more phone calls after that, but at least I got to hug her and say goodbye. That's more than my father got."

"Did you tell him about that final visit?"

"My mother had died a few months earlier, and knowing the reality of Tricia's situation would have crushed him. Still, I believed that she and Sal had done exactly what she had said they were going to do—that they'd disappeared to somewhere far away and were living happily ever after. For a long time, I hoped that sooner or later, they'd all turn up. Five years ago that all changed, and I stopped hoping."

"How come?"

"In 2015 someone doing construction on an abandoned farm a few miles outside of Plainfield stumbled across human remains. They were eventually identified as those of Salvatore del Veccio, Tricia's husband. I thought they'd find Tricia's and Serena's bodies somewhere nearby, but they didn't.

"That's when I started looking into what had happened to Sal's father, Bernardo del Veccio. I found out that, as the prime suspect in a mob-related homicide, he had taken a plea and testified against his coconspirators. They were all given life without parole. Bernardo's sentence was twenty-five to life. After the trials ended, he was transported to the New Jersey State Prison in Trenton where, within weeks of his arrival, he was murdered, stabbed to death in the showers."

"So his reduced sentence turned into a life sentence after all," I observed, "and a very short one at that. Were the same people who killed the father responsible for Sal's death, too? And if so, why?"

"I don't know," Marisa responded. "Maybe he was involved with the Mafia, too, or maybe Sal knew too much. I've never been able to sort that out, but once Sal's body turned up and Tricia's and Serena's didn't, I began hoping that maybe somehow, somewhere, the two of them had survived. That's when I really started looking for them. I couldn't very well file a missing persons report on Tricia because, as far as anyone knew, she'd already been reported missing years earlier. Once someone told me about NamUs and the DNA Doe Project, I went ahead and posted them as missing on both those sites. I also submitted my DNA to GEDmatch in hopes of finding a match."

"What about your father?" I asked. "Is he still around?"

"Sadly no," Marisa replied. "He never recovered from losing my mom and from everything we all went through before she died. I believe he suffered from PTSD and started self-medicating with alcohol. He died in a one-car rollover accident two years after Mom's passing. The M.E. ruled his death as accidental, which was good for me financially due to the double indemnity clauses on both his life insurance policies. I was his only surviving beneficiary. After he died, people told me over and over that his death was accidental. I never bought that story. I believe he did it on purpose. With Mom and Tricia gone, he was done. He didn't want to go on living, so he quit."

After hearing that, it all made sense. Todd Hatcher is a smart guy, and everything he had surmised about Phyllis Baylor and her daughter being taken into WITSEC had been absolutely on the money.

"I think I can tell you exactly what happened to your sister and her daughter," I told Marisa Young. "Considering everything you've just told me about Bernardo and Sal del Veccio, I'm pretty sure your sister and her daughter disappeared into the US Marshals Witness Protection Program."

CHAPTER 26

Seattle, Washington
Wednesday, March 4, 2020

IT WASN'T AN EASY CONVERSATION. I TOLD MARISA ALL OF IT
without pulling any punches, including letting her know about
the string of aliases her niece had used and about how her trying
to put the make on one of Kyle's fifteen-year-old buddies had been
the catalyst that had prompted my grandson's decision to run away.

As I did so, however, I couldn't help but feel somewhat sorry
for two young women previously known as Tricia and Serena del
Veccio. Both had been plucked out of what sounded like an upper-
middle-class existence, banished to the far side of the continent, and
dumped into Seattle's seamy underbelly. With no education to speak
of and no training, in order to support her daughter, Tricia had been
forced to make do with what she'd had available—her good looks,
for as long as those lasted. Had she known about her father-in-law's
connections to the mob, his subsequent murder, or her husband's

murder? And what *about* her husband? I had a sneaking suspicion that Sal had been connected to his father's underworld dealings, but had Tricia been aware of any of that?

Rather than spending years in prison serving judge- and jury-imposed sentences, both men had been murdered, most likely by Bernardo's unsavory former associates. Meanwhile, Sal's widow and daughter had been handed lifetime sentences of their own. The US Marshals' misguided attempt to protect them had, instead, hurled mother and daughter into a marginal existence from which Caroline Richards seemed to be making an equally misguided effort to escape. Unfortunately for all concerned, Jeremy Cartwright had been her ticket out. There were a lot of things not to like about the young woman, but I had to give her credit for being a survivor.

"So what do we do now?" Marisa asked when I finished.

"What about the cops back in Princeton?" I asked. "After Tricia ran away that second time, did they do any active investigating?"

"I doubt it. I got the feeling that since she'd done it before, they didn't pay much attention when it happened again. If my parents had been on their backs about it, they might have done more, but once my mom got sick, everything else went by the wayside."

"The authorities never collected DNA from either you or your parents?"

"Not that I remember."

"So you'll be the only one notified about the NamUs DNA match?"

"As far as I know," Marisa said before adding, "So what should I do about Serena, call her or what?"

That's when I wished Mel were involved in the conversation. In situations like this she would have instinctively known exactly how to proceed. I was at a loss. A glance at my watch told me it was 3:15 in the afternoon. Marisa and I had been on the phone for the better part of an hour and a half, and the charge on my phone was in the red zone.

"My phone's almost out of power," I told her. "Let me run out to the car and get a charger. Then I'll get back to you."

On my way out to the parking lot, I thought about Jeremy and wondered how much of this he knew. Probably zero. If Marisa called and dumped all this on Caroline when he was home, it wouldn't go over well for anyone. With the last of my phone power, I dialed Kyle.

"Where are you?" I asked.

"Costco," he answered. "The place is a zoo. What's up?"

"What time does your dad usually get home from school?"

"Around four or so, but it could be later," he answered. "Right now teachers are working almost around the clock trying to get ready for the big switcheroo over to online learning. Why, do you need to talk to him?"

"No," I replied. "I need to talk to Caroline in private."

"Caroline! How come? Have you found out something?"

"I've found out a lot," I told him, "but I can't tell you about it right now. I want to try to reach her before your father gets home. Do you happen to have her cell phone number?"

"Sure."

He gave it to me.

"Thanks, Kyle," I told him. "Happy shopping. Buy lots of good stuff, and I'll bring you up-to-date as soon as I can."

With the charger in hand, I returned to the evidence room and plugged in my phone before dialing the next number.

Caroline must have seen the Bellingham location and assumed

the call to be from Kyle. "Hello, Kyle," she said when she answered. "What's going on?"

"This isn't Kyle," I replied. "It's J. P. Beaumont, Kyle's grandfather. Kyle gave me your number."

"Why are you calling me?" she demanded. "You shouldn't be. I've got nothing to say to you. I'm going to hang up now."

"Please," I said. "Before you do, let me ask you this: Once a long time ago, did somebody give you a pink teddy bear?"

I heard a sharp intake of breath. "Mindy?" she asked. "How the hell do you know about her?"

"I know the person who gave you that teddy bear back when you and your mother were still living in Plainfield, New Jersey. Her name is Marisa Young. She's your mother's younger sister—your aunt. She gave you the teddy bear in honor of your fourth birthday, and she's been searching for you and your mother for years. She'd love to speak to you."

The stark silence on the other end of the line made me think Caroline had hung up on me after all, but that wasn't the case. Finally she spoke again. "Is this for real or is this a bunch of bullshit?"

"It's for real, all right," I said. "I know all about how you and your mother ended up in Seattle. I'm happy to tell you everything I know, but it's a long story."

"Jeremy's due home any minute. I can't talk about this in front of him. Can I call you back in a little while? I'll tell him I need to go to the store or something. I can call once I'm out of the house."

"Fine," I said. "I'll be waiting."

I sent Marisa a text letting her know I was waiting for a call back from her niece. Then I turned my attention back to Loren Gregson. I decided to examine the mini-mart footage next. On a hunch,

J. A. JANCE

I started that study several hours earlier than the one in the bar. This time I wasn't just looking for Loren's image. I wanted to see if there was any sign of a homeless woman with a loaded grocery cart. She was a lot more likely to be hanging around a mini-mart than a restaurant.

When my phone rang a few minutes later, I thought the caller would be Caroline. It wasn't.

"Hey," Mel said. "Just checking in. How's it going?"

For starters, I told her about watching Loren Gregson eat his final meal before leaving the bar and walking to his death with no idea that a killer was lurking behind him in the darkness.

"That had to be tough to see," Mel said.

"It was," I agreed. "Knowing what was about to happen and being totally helpless to prevent it was awful. But just seeing that his killer was there doesn't come close to having enough to reopen the case. The only way that's going to happen is if I can actually ID her."

"You'll get there," Mel assured me. "Look at how much you've managed to pull together in just a matter of days."

"And that's not all," I added. "I'm also making progress on Caroline Richards."

After that I gave Mel a brief recap of my conversations with first Marisa and finally with Caroline.

"Wow," Mel said. "It sounds like the only reason she didn't hang up on you was due to that powerful teddy bear connection. Who knew you'd end up working two separate cases with teddy bears front and center in both of them?"

I hadn't thought of that, but of course Mel was right. Benjamin Weston's teddy bear had set me on the path to solving Darius Jackson's overdose death, and Caroline's teddy bear, Mindy, was likely to be the key to Marisa's yearslong search for her missing niece.

"Not just teddy bears," I said with a laugh. "Old teddy bears."

"And in trying to sort out Caroline Richards's backstory, you've been able to locate Marisa Young's relatives who've been missing for years. You're bringing them back into her life."

"I won't know that for sure until if and when Caroline returns my call," I said. "At this point I don't know if she'll be willing to reconnect with Marisa or even speak to her. I also don't know if Caroline is aware that her mother is deceased."

"That's going to be a fun conversation," Mel said, "and not one I'd be keen on making."

"Me, either," I agreed, "but while I'm waiting, I've queued up the footage from the mini-mart starting late in the afternoon of January 10, 2015. Going through that in real time and looking for a homeless woman with a loaded grocery cart will take hours."

"Actually," Mel said, "that's exactly why I called. There's no sense in your driving all the way home tonight only to turn around and drive right back to Seattle in the morning. Why don't I call the Westin and book you a room for the night?"

I would have come to the same conclusion eventually, but it would have taken me a lot longer. And I wouldn't have picked a hotel nearly as posh as the Westin.

"Good idea," I said.

"I'll text you the reservation info," Mel said. "Gotta run."

I turned back to my keyboard and monitor, located the time stamp for four P.M., and started from there.

We usually have a big snowstorm in the Seattle area about the time kids are supposed to go back to school after Christmas vacation, and 2015 was no exception. There had still been snow next to the gutters and lining nearby sidewalks when I'd been studying the footage from the Fremont Inn. The mini-mart had gas pumps as well as a large parking lot. Snow cleared from those areas was piled four feet deep next to the trash bins located at the back of the building. The weather looked cold and miserable, and not many people were visible, coming or going. And since days are short in wintertime Seattle, by the time the footage time stamp registered 4:15 P.M., it was almost dark.

JUST AS I was about to give up on getting a call back from Caroline, my phone rang.

"Hello."

"What am I supposed to call you?" Caroline Richards wanted to know.

Since I was possibly her boyfriend's soon-to-be-former father-in-law, I could see how sorting that out might be tricky.

"Beau or J.P.," I answered. "Either one works."

"I told Jeremy I'm going out to get a massage," she said. "And I am, because once the shutdown hits, no telling when I'll be able to have another. But I can talk on my way there, so what do you have to say?"

It wasn't exactly a cordial way to launch a conversation, but it was better than not talking at all.

"What do you know about your father?" I asked.

"Not much. My mother told me that when she got knocked up, her parents kicked her out and her boyfriend took off and left her. Even so, she wanted to keep me, and she did, although she wasn't ever what you might call mother-of-the-year material."

"Your parents' story is actually a bit more complicated than that," I told her, "and I believe that your mother most likely did the best she could under very difficult circumstances. But first, tell me about that teddy bear. I suspect that's the only reason you agreed to talk to me."

"It is," Caroline conceded. "Believe it or not, I still have it. Jeremy's never seen it because I keep it in my bottom dresser drawer. It's the only thing I have left from my childhood. My mother didn't keep report cards or school photos or anything like that, but I managed to hang on to Mindy."

"If you ever do get around to speaking to your aunt Marisa, she'll be thrilled to know that. It was something her parents—your grandparents—gave her when she was a little girl. By the way, the only time she ever saw you in person was the day she gave you that teddy bear."

"My mother never mentioned having a sister," Caroline objected. "She told me she was an only child."

"Then she lied about that," I said. "Your DNA says otherwise, and DNA doesn't lie."

"So what happened? If this Marisa person loved me enough to give me the teddy bear, where's she been all my life? Why don't I know anything about her?"

"The truth is," I said quietly, "nothing your mom told you about your history was true. She wasn't kicked out of the house because she got pregnant. She ran away when she was only fifteen and earned a living as a stripper. She met a guy named Salvatore del Veccio at the club where she was working. I believe they married, although I have yet to verify that.

"I've also learned that your father's family, and especially his father, Bernardo, had serious ties to the mob. When he was arrested and charged with a mob-related homicide, he warned his son, your father, that he was taking a plea deal and was going to testify against some of his former associates. Bernardo advised his son to take his family and disappear. I believe that's when the US Marshals Service swooped in and took you and your mother into Witness Protection."

"Me and my mother but not my father?"

"Apparently the Marshals got to you and your mom in time to get you out of town. Your father didn't make it. His remains were found years later, and his death was ruled as a homicide. I don't know if the case was ever solved. As for Bernardo? He was murdered shortly after going to prison. Once your father's remains were located and identified around five years ago, Marisa fully expected that you and your mother would be found dead in the same location. When you weren't, she began looking for you, and she's been searching ever since."

"But how did she find me?"

"I'm afraid that's my fault," I admitted. "I'm a private investigator now, but I used to be a cop. I'm also a grandfather. When Kyle showed up at our house, let's say he was more than slightly upset. He told Mel and me about you, and not in the most flattering of terms. That's why I ran a background check on you—to find out who you were. The background check turned up a string of aliases for both you and your mother. The Caroline Richards identity is relatively recent, but the first time Phyllis and Lindsey Baylor surfaced was when you were in kindergarten. That's when I started wondering about Witness Protection."

"I remember that night," Caroline said suddenly. "I woke up because someone was pounding on the front door. Then I heard people yelling. When I came out of my bedroom, there was this bunch of strange men with guns standing around in the living room, and one of them was yelling at my mom. 'You have to go, and you have to go now,' he said. 'You can bring along two suitcases, and that's it!'

"I didn't know what was happening, and I was scared to death. Mom packed suitcases, and they hustled us out of the house. Mom had her purse, and I had Mindy. They took us to an airport and put us on a plane—to what turned out to be Seattle. I cried for what seemed like hours. I remember some guy in the row of seats in front of us turning around and growling at my mother, 'Can't you get that kid to shut up?' She couldn't."

And that, I thought, *was the beginning of a whole new nightmare.*

"They must have given my mother some amount of money because we were all right for a while," Caroline continued, "but once that ran out and she had to go to work . . . well, I guess you know how that turned out. It wasn't good. In fact, it was hell. But you still haven't told me how you figured all this out."

"You smoke," I answered.

"Yes, I do, but . . ."

"Kyle asked one of his friends to raid your garbage cans. We got a DNA profile off one of the cigarette butts he dug out of your trash. Once we had your profile, someone ran it through NamUs. That's a national missing persons database. Marisa had already posted her own profile there in hopes of finding you, and it worked."

"What about my mother?" Caroline asked. "Have you found her, too?"

My heart gave a lurch. She still didn't know that her mother was dead, and now I was the one who had to deliver the news.

"I'm sorry to have to tell you, but your mother passed away in 2016."

"Of what, an overdose?"

"No," I replied. "Natural causes. Hep C."

"Not surprised," Caroline returned with a singular lack of emotion. "Those last few years were awful. She was using all the time. We had no money. I finally told her that she was supposed to be the mother, and that I couldn't take care of her anymore. We had

219

a huge fight, a real screaming match. I said I was leaving, and that I hoped I'd never see her again. I saw her one more time when she bailed me out of jail, but that's it."

"I can tell you where she's buried if . . ."

"No," Caroline said quickly. "I don't want to know or need to know. When I said I was done with her, I meant it, and I still do."

There was nothing I could say in response to that. Serena del Veccio and Lindsey Baylor had been betrayed by everyone. No wonder this young woman had found it necessary to escape into being someone else entirely, namely Caroline Richards. Who could blame her?

"So what am I supposed to do about this so-called aunt of mine, Aunt Marisa?" Caroline asked at last.

"That's up to you," I told her. "I can tell you that she was beyond thrilled to know that you're still alive. I know she'd love to talk to you at least, and she'd like to meet you in person. I'll text you her number, and then you can decide if you want to contact her or not."

"What about Jeremy?" Caroline asked. "Are you going to tell him?"

"I started looking into your background on Kyle's behalf. He's my client. I'll be reporting my findings to him. He may or may not choose to share the information with his father, although they're not exactly on the best of terms at the moment. So my guess is that what you tell Jeremy is in your court, right along with whether or not you contact Marisa."

"All right," she said. "I'll think about it. As for Kyle? Tell him I'm sorry."

I didn't ask sorry for what. There were all kinds of things for her to be sorry about in this scenario, and I had no idea which of those that brief apology was meant to address.

CHAPTER 27

Seattle, Washington
Wednesday to Thursday, March 4–5, 2020

ONCE OFF THE PHONE WITH CAROLINE, I CALLED MARISA BACK and gave her an update. I think she sounded disappointed that I had left the ball about further contact in Caroline's court, but I felt that was the right call. With Jeremy still in the dark about all this, any communication between them had to be done at times when Caroline was able to speak freely.

I had expected to go straight back to viewing the mini-mart footage, but Officer Harriman tapped on the door. "Time's up," she said. "Shutting down for the day. Will you be back tomorrow?"

"That's the plan," I told her.

"All right then," she said. "You can leave all your crap in here. I'll lock it up so no one disturbs it. That way I won't have to have someone put it away tonight and then drag it out again in the morning."

"Sounds good," I said. "Thanks."

I headed for the barn—in this case the Westin in downtown Seattle, and that was a good thing. After spending hours studying video footage and talking on the phone, my eyes were worn out and so was my butt. Chairs in evidence rooms aren't designed for putting in a full day's work. Not only that, driving ninety miles to get home would have been tough. While I'd been locked away in a windowless room that was smaller than Mel's walk-in closet, the weather had taken a turn for the worse.

I checked in, went up to my room, and ordered a carafe of coffee from room service. My crosswords were calling me, but I decided it was time to give Kyle a call and let him know how things stood.

When he answered the phone, he sounded excited. "Hey, Gramps," he said. "Did you know that Hank's car is a freaking Shelby?"

Color me surprised. Shelbys were new when I was Kyle's age. How the hell would an eighteen-year-old Gen Zer (If that's what they're called these days!) even know about Shelbys? I made the mistake of saying as much.

"How do you know about Shelbys?" I asked.

"Didn't you see the movie?" he asked.

I was caught flat-footed. "What movie?"

Kyle sighed. *Ford v Ferrari*," he answered, sounding aggrieved.

"Never heard of it," I said.

"It's a terrific movie," he told me, "and I've got the DVD. We should watch it together sometime once you're back home."

Having been pleasantly surprised by *The Martian*, I went ahead and agreed with him. "Yes," I said, "by all means, let's. Maybe we could invite Hank to join us."

"That would be great!" Kyle agreed enthusiastically, surprising me for the second time in less than a minute.

"On another subject," I said, "would you like an update on your case?"

"My case?"

"I'm a private investigator. You're the client who asked me to look into the background of one Caroline Richards, and I'm prepared to fill you in on what I've learned so far."

"Please do," he said, and so I did.

"Does my dad know about any of this?" Kyle asked when I finished.

"Not so far," I replied, "unless Caroline clued him in after we got off the phone this afternoon."

"So I probably shouldn't tell him?"

"I wouldn't if I were you," I cautioned. "This is something that needs to be sorted out between the two of them—your dad and Caroline."

"Okay, then," Kyle agreed. "I'll keep my mouth shut."

My room service coffee arrived right then, so I signed off with Kyle to go answer the door. Once I took my first sip, I realized I owed Todd Hatcher a call as well. He needed to know where his trail of aliases had led me and that, for the moment at least, I no longer required his services. When I called, I reached his voice-mail, so I left a brief message to that effect, and let it go at that. Next I called Lulu Benson and brought her up-to-date as well.

My mother was big on my saying please and thank you, and following her advice on that score has served me well during my years as a homicide cop. When someone helps me, I make it a point to thank them.

Tired of talking, I ordered dinner from room service to go with the rest of my coffee. After dinner I climbed into bed and finally got around to tackling my backed-up supply of crossword puzzles.

Somewhere along the way, I drifted off. When Mel called me at ten o'clock to tell me good night, I was already fast asleep. I suspect I may have growled at her a little. Being awakened out of a sound sleep so someone can tell you good night can be annoying.

BY NINE O'CLOCK Thursday morning I was back at the Evidence unit. Officer Harriman's greeting wasn't entirely welcoming. "I think you forgot about your damned bananas," she muttered. "They're starting to stink."

She was right. When I opened the door to the locker, they were way beyond what my mother would have turned into banana bread, so I unloaded them into the nearest trash bin, which happened to be in the men's room off the lobby. Then I followed Officer Harriman back down the hallway where she unlocked the door to my evidence room closet. I wasn't looking forward to spending another day staring at a computer screen, but that was what I had signed on for.

Since Officer Harriman had allowed me to leave the evidence room intact, I was able to go right back to where I'd left off, which was examining the mini-mart parking lot. I could have picked up the action at 5:07 P.M.—Loren hadn't shown up at the Fremont Inn until hours later, and there was no telling when his killer might have arrived in the neighborhood—but for the sake of completeness, I backed up the footage to the twelve P.M. time stamp.

This time studying the video was a two-pronged process. Even though the woman I'd seen following Loren Gregson to his death hadn't been pushing a loaded grocery cart, that's what I looked for again, at least in the foreground—a stray grocery cart. One of Darius's fellow food bank volunteers had mentioned to me that he had been assisting that supposedly homeless woman back to her van, so I looked at vans, too—ones coming and going in the mini-mart parking lot as well as those passing by on the street.

It was painstaking, mind-numbing work. Two hours in I was only up to 2:35 P.M. on the time stamp, but I was done for, and so were my eyes, so I took a break. I happened to know that there was a Krispy Kreme in the neighborhood. Wanting to worm my way back into Officer Harriman's good graces, at lunchtime I went looking for it. I bought a box containing a dozen glazed doughnuts—two for me to eat for lunch and ten more to leave in the break room at the Evidence unit. Yes, I'm well aware that cops and doughnuts are a cliché, but the reason they are is that they happen to go together, sort of like love and marriage, as it were.

On the way back I drove past another longtime favorite—Pecos Pit Barbecue. Since I'd only brought along one change of clothes, I had already determined I was going home to Bellingham that night come hell or high water, so why not come home a hero? Mel adores Pecos Pit, so I stopped by and stood in line at a building that had started out decades earlier as a gas station. Most of the hungry customers were on their lunch breaks. I was the only one ordering an entire family dinner, which consisted of a batch of some-assembly-required barbecued beef sandwiches, keeping the buns separate from the meat. Then, armed with tubs of beef, coleslaw, and baked beans, I texted both Mel and Kyle, letting them know that I'd be home in time for dinner and that I was personally in charge of that evening's takeout.

To say Officer Harriman was thrilled when I dropped off my peace offering on my way past would be an understatement. Once in my evidence room closet, I went back to work. Three more hours in and shortly after six P.M. on the video time stamp and three P.M. in real time, I called it quits. If I wanted to beat the worst of the traffic, I was probably already too late.

Officer Harriman glanced at her watch. "You're heading out early today," she observed.

"I live in Bellingham, so I've got a ninety-mile drive ahead of me."

"Will you be back tomorrow?"

I now had more than 150 emails in my inbox, most of them interview transcripts from Yolanda's assistant. I had already decided that I'd spend the next three days at home sorting my way through those.

"I won't be back until sometime next week," I said as I signed out on the clipboard. "I've got some other things to catch up on, and I'll be working from there over the weekend."

"Whoever he is, he must be loaded," Officer Harriman said.

"Who?" I asked.

"Your client, of course," she said. "With all the hours you're putting in, you must be costing him a fortune."

I didn't bother telling her I was working for free.

"Yup," I said. "People get what they pay for."

"Well, you take care now," she added with a smile. "Afternoon traffic around here can be a real bitch."

Thank God for Krispy Kreme!

OFFICER HARRIMAN WAS right on both counts—traffic was a mess, and I was putting in way too many hours on this project. What had started out as a favor for Benjamin Weston was now a sprawling case with four known victims and possibly others as well. The scope of it should have required the creation of a whole task force, but so far it was a task force of one. If I was ever able to identify the female suspect, I was pretty sure I'd be able to get someone at Seattle PD to reopen the case, even if I had to pull in a favor from Ron Peters, but for right now, if it was to be, it was up to me.

Despite heading out early, I didn't arrive home much before dinnertime where my Pecos Pit Barbecue was received with even more enthusiasm than Officer Harriman had shown for her Krispy Kreme doughnuts. Over dinner I gave Kyle and Mel both a detailed update on my progress with the unmasking of Caroline Richards.

"Sounds like she's had a pretty difficult life," Mel commented. "After what she's been through, it's hard not to feel sorry for her. No wonder she's somewhat troubled."

"And she wanted you to tell me she's sorry?" Kyle asked. "What's that all about? What's she sorry for?"

"Who knows?" I said. "For messing up your life, maybe, or for making a pass at your friend? Take your pick."

"Do you think she'll contact her aunt?"

"No idea," I said. "I hope so, but there's no way to tell. So that's what's been going on with me. What's been happening with everyone else?"

"You know," Mel said dismissively. "Same old, same old."

I took that to mean there was likely something going on at work that she didn't want to talk about in front of Kyle. Whatever it was would have to be discussed between us later and in private.

"What about you?" I asked, turning to Kyle.

"You'll never guess," Kyle said.

"What?"

"Hank is going to teach me how to drive a stick shift! Isn't that great?"

I almost choked on my last bite of barbecued beef sandwich.

I had some idea of how much a restored 1966 Shelby Mustang would be worth, and putting a teenaged driver behind the wheel of one of those sounded like a recipe for disaster. In other words I didn't think it was great at all, and since Kyle was probably still listed as an inexperienced driver on his parents' car insurance policy, I doubted Kelly and Jeremy would be thrilled by that news, either.

"In the Shelby?" I managed. "You've got to be kidding!"

"I'm not," Kyle replied. "He said we'll go somewhere out in the boonies for me to learn. I don't think any of the other kids my age know how to drive a standard transmission."

I was about to say something to the effect that there's no way in hell that's going to happen, but Mel beat me to the punch.

"That's right," she said with a smile. "When it comes to joyriding teenagers, standard transmission vehicles come with built-in immunity."

That was enough to make me laugh. It also got me off my high horse. If Hank Mitchell was dumb enough to let Kyle drive his freshly restored automotive heirloom, who was I to stand in his way?

Kyle, completely oblivious, continued in the same vein and with the same amount of enthusiasm.

"I told him about the movie—*Ford v Ferrari*. Turns out he's never heard of it, either. I know his wife is working tonight. Could we maybe invite him over to watch it?"

And that's how, after spending hour upon hour staring at video footage in the evidence room, I unexpectedly ended up watching a movie that night. Truth be told, I enjoyed the hell out of it, and I think Hank did, too.

I'm beginning to think Kyle Cartwright has pretty good taste in movies.

CHAPTER 28

Bellingham, Washington
Thursday to Friday, March 5–6, 2020

ONCE MEL AND I REPAIRED TO THE BEDROOM THURSDAY NIGHT, we stayed up late talking about any number of things besides Hank Mitchell's ill-advised decision to teach Kyle how to handle a stick shift on board his very expensive and recently restored Shelby.

Mel's major concern had to do with two sets of disgruntled parents who had turned up at her office earlier in the day. They had come to discuss their daughters, both of whom were seniors at Bellingham High and who were both involved in chorus. According to the girls, their teacher, a Mr. George Pritchard, had been fondling their breasts under the pretext of teaching them how to breathe properly. They had taken their complaints to the school counselor two weeks earlier, but when nothing happened, they went to their parents. Now the hot potato had landed on Mel's desk.

"What did you do about it?" I asked.

"Incidents like that are serious stuff," Mel said. "Naturally I dispatched a pair of detectives to the high school. When they spoke to the counselor, someone must have let her know that the hammer was about to fall, because she had spoken to the principal earlier this morning, and together they had called our nonemergency number to make a report. According to the counselor, she's been so overwhelmed with shutdown preparation that she hadn't gotten around to doing it sooner."

"Right," I said. "Of course she's been far too preoccupied."

"As of noon today, Mr. Pritchard is on leave. According to the parents, the girls are both prepared to press charges, but before that happens, I want to know exactly what we're up against, because those two girls may be only the tip of the iceberg. There may be lots more victims, and he may have committed far more egregious acts than just fondling breasts.

"Shortly before I left the office, I got a judge to sign off on a search warrant for Pritchard's home and all his electronic devices. That was executed this evening, but as far as the electronics are concerned, we're going to have to get our tech team to break into them because they're all password protected. And how we'll track down and speak to other possible victims once the shutdown is in effect is anybody's guess."

"Good luck with that," I told her.

Being a police chief is no walk in the park. Mel usually falls asleep long before I do, but that night she was still tossing and turning when I dozed off, and she was already up and out before I opened my eyes the next morning.

WHEN I ARRIVED in the kitchen around ten on Friday morning, it was late enough that the coffee machine had turned itself off.

While I was waiting for the coffee to brew, Sarah came over to the counter, sat down in front of me, and gave me "the look"—the one that means *Where the hell have you been and don't you know it's past my breakfast time?*

Which was a lie, of course. In case no one has mentioned this previously, dogs do tell lies. The reason I knew for sure that Sarah was lying was due to the note Mel had left on the counter saying that she had fed Sarah before leaving the house.

"Oh, no, you don't," I told Sarah. "Don't you go giving me that old song and dance. I'm not falling for it."

I doubt she understood my spoken words, but the negative shake of my head that accompanied them got my point across. She tucked her tail between her legs and headed for the other room.

I'd kept my nose so close to the grindstone for so many days that I figured I deserved some time off, so without even opening my email box, which now had 163 messages in it, I went straight to my crosswords. I hadn't made a dent in the backlog of those before falling asleep at the Westin, and I was determined to catch up.

My phone rang half an hour later with Marisa Young's name in caller ID. Remember the old days when you had no idea who was calling until *after* you said hello?

"Good morning, Marisa," I said. "What's up?"

"Serena called," she said excitedly. "Or Caroline. I still don't know what I should call her."

"That's something the two of you will need to sort out in the future," I said. "What did she have to say?"

"We talked for a long time. She said she'd like to meet me, so I'm flying into Portland tomorrow, and she'll drive up from Ashland. I've booked a pair of rooms at River Place."

"Does Jeremy know about any of this?" I wanted to know.

"I doubt it," Marisa replied. "She told him that I'm an old school chum of hers who's coming to town briefly and that Saturday is the only day the two of us can get together."

That statement caused a small lurch in the pit of my stomach. Both knowingly and unknowingly, the woman we knew as Caroline Richards had been living a lie for years, and she'd had enough practice to be good at it. Now, even though the jig was up and people were onto her, she hadn't stopped lying. That told me that Caroline Richards was a scammer at heart. That didn't bode well for Jeremy Cartwright and not for Marisa Young, either. She had a tremendous amount of emotion invested in finding her long-lost niece, and I worried that she was going to be disappointed.

"I'm so excited," Marisa went on. "I can't wait to see her and have her back in my life."

"What you lost all those years ago was an innocent child," I cautioned. "What you're getting back is a grown woman who has spent the past ten years surviving on the streets on little more than her wits. Don't get your hopes too high."

"Oh, I won't," Marisa assured me. "We'll be fine. I wanted to thank you. I still can't believe you found her."

"You're welcome," I said. "Glad to be of service."

But as I hung up, I couldn't help but worry that the wheels I had set in motion might not turn out well for anybody.

By then, my crossword mood had totally evaporated. After the phone call, I went to the kitchen where I made myself another cup of coffee and a piece of toast. Then I returned to the living room. Settled into my recliner, I opened my email account and prepared to face the music. I now had 186 new messages. To my dismay only a small number of those were spam. The rest were all for me. Most of the emails were from Yolanda's intern, but three were from Yolanda herself. I suspected those might have something to do with the case files I had flagged earlier.

The sheer magnitude of the problem was disheartening. That's when I remembered Benjamin Weston and Sandra Sechrest. Ben had skin in the game because of his relationship to Matilda Jackson. And Sandra had been willing to give me the case numbers that had made my Evidence unit experience infinitely easier. Maybe Seattle PD itself wasn't ready to reopen any of my overdose cases, but there was no rule that said cops couldn't look into something on their own time, especially if they knew the kind of progress I'd already managed to make on my own. And if I had some help with scanning through those lengthy interviews, maybe we could speed up the process.

So that was the next thing I did—I began assembling my very own multicase task force. Picking up my phone, I located Ben Weston's number in my contacts list, and pressed send.

"Hey, Beau," Ben said when he answered. "How's it going?"

"How many homeless people do you know who go around wearing Apple Watches?" I asked.

"That would be zero."

"Correct," I replied. "So what would you say if I told you that, in viewing the footage of Darius Jackson leaving the food bank, I noticed that the woman he was accompanying, the supposedly homeless one pushing that overloaded grocery cart, was actually wearing an Apple Watch?"

"How the hell did you find that out?" he demanded.

"By going to the Evidence unit, putting my butt in a chair, and viewing hours of surveillance footage one frame at a time," I told him. "While I was doing so, I saw a flash of light on her left wrist that I believe came from an Apple Watch."

"What makes you think that?" Ben asked.

"Because in looking into a number of those overdose fatalities, I found another one that's most likely related to Darius's. That victim actually died in eastern Washington, but shortly before his death, a homeless woman was spotted in that vicinity. During the subsequent investigation, a witness mentioned having seen a homeless woman wearing an Apple Watch. When I went back and studied the Darius surveillance video, that's when I spotted that suspicious glow on her arm."

"Whoa," Ben said. "That sounds like more than a coincidence."

"Way more," I agreed. "Not only that, I'm convinced she might be involved in more than just those two cases. I'm worried I'm only scratching the surface."

That's when I explained about how, with help from Gretchen at the crime lab and by examining Yolanda Aguirre's five-year study of overdose deaths, I had managed to establish several common denominators that now linked four separate cases, three of which had happened in Seattle—the pairs of hundred-dollar bills, the domestic violence arrests, the homeless woman equipped with an Apple Watch, and the unidentified female DNA profile.

"How can I help?" Ben asked when I finished.

"What I've found so far all came from studying that initial set of interviews. But here's the deal," I said. "There are now several more interviews that have raised enough red flags for me to want to look into them as well. This morning I received a whole new set of interviews, which need to be scanned to see if any similarities turn up."

"That's all you need, then," Ben asked, "another pair of eyes doing initial run-throughs on that new batch of interviews?"

"Exactly."

"Count me in," Ben said. "Send along as many as you like. I have the next three days off. I'll be glad to dive into them."

"What about Detective Sechrest?" I asked.

"Sandy? She's good people. Why?"

"When I was headed for the Evidence unit, she gave me the case numbers I needed and made my life infinitely easier. I knew going in that at some point she had spoken with Matilda Jackson, but I had no idea she and her partner had been summoned to the crime scene for one of my other victims, Loren Gregson. Do you think she might be interested in helping out?"

"Maybe," Ben said. "Let me give her a call. I'll let you know. In the meantime feel free to start sending files to me. I'll get right on them."

After getting off the phone, I forwarded a dozen or so interview transcripts to Ben. About that time Sarah meandered over to me and laid her massive head on my knee. I have now learned enough about dog-speak to know that she was ready to go for a walk. Guilt ridden from having neglected her for the last couple of days, I complied. We went for a walk.

We'd made it to the top of the driveway and turned down Bayside when my phone rang.

"J.P.?" a female voice asked.

I didn't recognize it right off. "Yes," I said. "Who's this?"

"Sandra," she replied. "Sandy Sechrest. I'm guessing you've found out that I was called to Loren Gregson's death scene."

"I did notice that. Why didn't you mention it when you gave me the case number?"

"Because I didn't want to skew your investigation one way or the other, but it pissed the hell out of me when they shut down that investigation. It just didn't look right. Gregson's apartment was only a couple of blocks away. Given that, why the hell would he sit down under a blackberry bush in the dead of winter to shoot himself up? Why not go home to do that?"

"Why not indeed?" I agreed.

"So how can I help? Ben said something about a bunch of files in need of reviewing."

I took her through the case, starting with Yolanda Aguirre's five-year study of overdose deaths. By now I was feeling like a broken record, but if she was going to help sort through files, she needed to know all the pertinent details.

"Okay," Sandy said when I finished. "That's what I'm looking for—victims with a history of domestic violence arrests and/or convictions and ones found to be carrying inexplicable pairs of hundred-dollar bills. In addition to a homeless woman, especially one wearing an Apple Watch, who may have been seen in the vicinity of the crime scenes."

"That's the ticket," I said.

"You said that the Liberty Lake victim . . ." Sandy began.

"Jake Spaulding," I supplied.

"Spaulding died within a week of his being released from prison. That would suggest his killer was either a family member or someone close enough to the family to know about his upcoming release."

"As far as I can tell, those have all been ruled out," I told her.

"Have you considered someone with a law enforcement background?" Sandy asked.

"You mean like a cop gone rogue?"

"Not necessarily," she replied. "What about a first responder of some kind, like a medic or even a 911 operator? When it comes to domestic violence situations, they may not be on the scene, but they're still in the thick of it. They're the ones who deal with women screaming while kids are crying in the background. They're also the ones who know how many of those assholes do the same thing over and over and walk away every time because the victims are too scared to press charges. It's frustrating as hell."

"Am I by any chance hearing the voice of experience speaking?" I asked.

"What was your first clue?" Sandy responded with a laugh. "I spent two and a half years working in a call center before I decided to join the force. I got tired of listening to those jerks torment their families and wanted to be the one hauling their asses off to jail. The first time I slapped cuffs on a guy like that, I felt like a million bucks. He got off, too, of course, but it turns out wearing a badge was the right thing for me to do.

"But what I said earlier about 911 operators is true. They may not see those domestic violence offenders face-to-face, but they probably deal with more of them on a daily basis than regular patrol officers do, and take it from me, the fact that most of those guys get away with what they've done really does get old."

I thought about that. For me, 911 operators have always been heroes. I could imagine a renegade cop, but a renegade 911 operator? No way!

"When those dispatchers are sitting at their computers summoning assistance," Sandy continued, "they have all kinds of pertinent information at their disposal. For instance, they can look at a physical address and know exactly how many domestic violence calls have been made from that residence in the past and how many times officers have responded. Believe me, when an abuser gets away with beating the crap out of a spouse, or a parent, or a sibling time and again, those operators tend to take it personally. They're not supposed to but they do. I know I did."

"Enough to go on a killing spree?" I asked.

"Maybe," Sandy said. "I'd hate to think that could happen, but it might. Come to think of it, they're also on the front line when it comes to the fentanyl crisis. Someone finds a dead body, the first thing they do is call 911."

I was stunned. The idea of a 911 operator somehow going off the rails and morphing into a serial killer made me feel like a little kid who's just been told for the first time that Santa Claus and the Easter Bunny aren't real.

"So I'm all in," Sandy continued. "When do you want me to start?"

"How about now?" I replied. "Give me your email address, and I'll send over some transcripts. Yolanda's study covers all of King County, but the cases we've identified so far all originated inside the Seattle city limits."

"So focus on Seattle cases then?" she asked.

"I think that makes sense."

"Okay. My daughter has a swim meet this afternoon, but maybe I can knock out a couple of those before it's time to go to that."

While I had been caught up in the phone call, Sarah had been operating on automatic pilot. When we reached our customary turnaround, she had done so without any direction from me. Now as the call ended, we were almost back at the house, but I was still lost in thought.

I was wondering about how much information the 911 operators had available to them on their work computers and how much of that one of them might have been able to carry out of the call center on a thumb drive. And then I thought about all the supposedly secure and password-protected information Todd Hatcher had available to him at the touch of his keyboard. He wasn't the only one with unauthorized access to a lot of supposedly private information.

In that moment I wondered if our Apple Watch–wearing homeless lady wasn't every bit as tech-savvy as Todd Hatcher, only a hell of a lot more dangerous.

CHAPTER 29

Bellingham, Washington
Friday, March 6, 2020

KNOWING I HAD BEN AND SANDY BACKING ME UP ON GOING through the interview transcripts, it was easier to face up to the ones Yolanda had sent me overnight—the ones where people had agreed to second interviews.

But before I did so, I thought about the logistics involved. Yolanda's study covered all of King County. So far all our cases had originated inside Seattle's city limits. With that in mind, it made sense to limit our examinations to deaths that were Seattle-centric. Before I opened any of Yolanda's emails, I sent one of my own to Ben and Sandy as well as to Elena Moreno, letting them know that from now on we would focus on Seattle cases only. To my way of thinking, narrowing the scope of our investigation would automatically reduce the workload.

My mother died of breast cancer when I was in my early twenties. Now that I'm so much older, I'm surprised by how often the words she said to me way back then resurface in my head. Only a few minutes after telling my mini task force that we could probably ignore cases occurring outside Seattle's city limits, I remembered Mom telling me time and again that "pride goeth before the fall." I took a hit on that score as soon as I started reading through Yolanda Aguirre's next interview, file number 143.

That one was with a woman named Felicity, the widow of one Xavier Jesus. Xavier, age thirty-six, had died of a fentanyl overdose—delivered by means of a vape pen—on August 14, 2016, in Kent, Washington. Yolanda gave me Felicity's phone number, indicating that she was eager to speak with me.

Prior to calling Xavier's widow, I quickly reviewed her initial interview. Her husband's body had been found next to the railroad tracks in Kent's warehouse district, where he had worked as a forklift operator. Kent may be inside King County, but it's well outside Seattle's city limits.

When I had initially flagged the file, I had done so because of the commonality of the crime scenes between the two incidents. Although miles apart, both bodies had been found in close proximity to railroad tracks. Now I saw that, like Jake Spaulding's, Xavier's fatal fentanyl overdose had been administered by means of a vape pipe. And the similarities didn't end there.

According to what Felicity had told Yolanda, there had been several instances of increasingly violent physical confrontations between her and her husband in the months prior to his death, during some of which law enforcement had been summoned. Xavier had been taken into custody on three separate occasions,

241

but as the mother of three young children, Felicity had never gone through with pressing charges against him, although she had filed for a divorce the week prior to her husband's death.

Although Felicity admitted that her husband had often become violent when he was drinking, she had insisted that he had never, to her knowledge, been a drug user of any kind—no marijuana, no cocaine, no crack, and most definitely no fentanyl. That was not unlike Matilda Jackson's claim that Darius Jackson hadn't been using at the time of his death.

In addition, Felicity claimed that Xavier loved his kids and would never, ever have committed suicide and certainly not by using a vape pen filled with fentanyl. That was the only reason Felicity had agreed to speak to Yolanda in the first place—she was convinced that Kent PD and the King County Medical Examiner had gotten her husband's manner of death all wrong. The vape pen detail hadn't leaped out at me while I was bingeing my way through files the previous weekend, but now, knowing Jake Spaulding had also died of an overdose delivered via a vape pen, the connection was stunning.

At that point I picked up my phone and dialed her number. "Ms. Delgado?" I asked when she answered.

"Yes, who's this?"

"My name's J. P. Beaumont."

"You're the man Yolanda Aguirre said might be calling about Xavier?"

"Yes, I am. I'm looking into several overdose deaths that may have been mishandled. I'm wondering if that might also be true in your husband's case."

"Thank God," she murmured fervently. "Maybe someone will finally believe me."

"I'm hoping someone will believe me, too," I told her. "I'm finding that the cases in question have several things in common."

"Like what?"

"Prior to their deaths, all the victims were involved in numerous domestic violence situations in which calls were made to 911."

"I definitely made some of those," Felicity admitted. "When I called, though, I simply wanted Xavier out of the house long enough to sober up. I never wanted him arrested because I didn't want him to lose his job. But like I told the cops, my husband may have been a drunk, but he never used drugs. And he wouldn't have killed himself, either."

"Why not?" I asked.

"Xavier hardly ever went to Mass, but he was raised Catholic, and he would never, ever have committed suicide. Even though I had filed for a divorce, he wouldn't have done that."

"So you had filed?"

"Yes," she said. "I had to. The last time we got in a fight, he hit me so hard, he broke my nose. My daughter was seven at the time, and she called 911. That's when I made up my mind. I couldn't let my kids grow up seeing their father act that way. That very day I went to court and got a protection order. The day after that I filed for a divorce.

"I was scared to death. I didn't have a job or any money. I ended up having to go to the food bank just so I could feed my kids. I was starting to think that if he showed up at the house, maybe I'd take him back, but that's when the cops came by and told me he was dead—that they'd found his body by the railroad tracks. Later, when they told me he'd committed suicide, I tried to tell them they were wrong—that Xavier would never do such a thing—but nobody listened to me."

"So what did you do?"

"I got a job working nights as a cashier at a Circle K. My mom comes over and sleeps at the house so someone is there with the kids while I'm at work. I don't make very much. I'm able to pay the rent and buy food, but there's never anything left over for extras.

"At the time Xavier died, school was about to start. The kids needed clothes and school supplies, and I had no idea how I was going to pay for any of it because he had taken off without leaving me any money. That's when someone from the M.E.'s office came by to drop off Xavier's personal effects, including his wallet. There was money in that."

My heart skipped a beat. "How much money?"

"Almost three hundred dollars."

"You didn't mention that in your interview with Yolanda Aguirre," I suggested.

"No, I didn't," she agreed. "I was too ashamed."

"Ashamed? Why?"

I heard her sigh. "I decided to use that money—Xavier's money— to buy the kids' school stuff, so I went shopping at Target. I knew exactly how much money I had and was careful not to go over that amount. But when I got to the check stand, the clerk held up one of the hundred-dollar bills . . ."

"Hundreds?" I asked.

"Yes, there were two hundred-dollar bills and some smaller ones in the wallet. They added up to $288."

"What happened then?" I asked.

"The clerk said she couldn't take the money because it didn't have a security strip, and she thought it was counterfeit. She said I'd need to pay by credit card."

"What did you do?"

"What could I do?" Felicity replied. "I didn't have a credit card, so I took the money, left everything I had picked out either in the basket or on the check stand counter, and walked away. I cried all the way home. How could Xavier have gotten involved in passing out counterfeit money? Did I even know him?"

"Do you still have those two hundreds?"

"Of course I do," she said. "I didn't dare spend them. I was afraid someone would end up accusing me of trying to pass counterfeit money."

"It's not counterfeit," I told her. "It's legal tender, but it's old. Still, please don't spend it. I'm reasonably sure your husband was murdered, and that whoever is responsible has killed four other people as well, because in all those cases two mysterious hundred-dollar bills were found among the victims' personal effects."

"Four other cases?" Felicity repeated. "Really? Does that mean Xavier was murdered by a serial killer?"

As a general rule, it takes three victims for someone to graduate to serial killer status. Xavier Delgado's death meant we were now two over that grim milestone.

"Yes," I agreed. "I believe your husband was quite possibly the victim of a serial killer."

The next words out of Felicity's mouth took me aback. "Thank you," she whispered brokenly. "Thank you so much!"

I was truly mystified. "Why would you thank me?"

"Because of my mother-in-law," she said, "my kids' nana. She's a good Catholic. She believes that suicide is a mortal sin and that anyone who commits a mortal sin without repentance goes to hell. She's convinced that Xavier committed suicide because I had filed for a divorce. The last time she spoke to me was at his funeral."

I heard the genuine relief in her voice, but I needed to put the brakes on what she might say to anyone else.

"Please, Ms. Delgado," I pleaded, "I can tell how important this is to you, but whatever you do, don't discuss any of what I've told you with anyone else, including your mother-in-law. As far as law enforcement is concerned, your husband's case is closed, and so far so are the others. I'm doing my best to get them reopened, but if word of what I'm doing gets back to the killer, that person might be able to get away."

"Will you call me when you know for sure?" Felicity asked. "You promise?"

"Cross my heart," I replied. "You may not be the first person I call, but I promise I'll be in touch."

"Thank you," Felicity breathed. "Thank you so much."

"You're welcome," I told her.

After ending the call, what do you think I did next? I fired off a group email to Ben Weston, Sandra Sechrest, Yolanda's hardworking intern, and Yolanda herself.

Hey, guys, when I'm wrong, I'm wrong. Please disregard my previous message. I've just now located another possibly related case. Number five is an overdose death designated suicide that originated in Kent, which is well outside the Seattle city limits.

I'm a great believer in the idea that where there's smoke there's fire. With five cases that I'm now reasonably sure are connected, I suspect there are probably more—no telling how many. So let's not take our foot off the gas pedal. I want to get whoever did this and hold them accountable.

As I pressed send, a thought occurred to me about pressing gas pedals. My aging Mercedes has a gas pedal, but what about all those electric cars out on the road these days? If they don't have gas pedals, what do they have? Accelerators maybe? Will gas pedals end up going the way of the buggy whip, right along with standard transmissions?

Yes, indeed, I told myself. *J.P., old boy, you really are getting up there!*

CHAPTER 30

Bellingham, Washington
Friday, March 6, 2020

WITH THE GAS PEDAL ANALOGY STILL FRONT AND CENTER IN MY
brain, I tried calling the nonemergency number for Kent PD. Good
luck with that. I soon found myself wandering in that vale of tears
known as "Your Call Is Very Important to Us." Sure it is! Once there
I was advised to press number one for this, number two for that,
and numbers three, four, and five for something else. Since none
of the suggested options included investigations, I pressed zero for
the operator only to be told that no one was available to take my
call at this time. "If this is an emergency, please hang up and dial
911. Otherwise, leave a message, and we'll get back to you as soon
as possible."

Right! I already knew that a return call on a message wasn't
bloody likely, either, so I didn't bother. Instead, I asked Siri to dial
911 in Kent, Washington.

When the operator came on the line and wanted to know the nature of my emergency, I got straight to the point.

"My name's J. P. Beaumont. I'm working a homicide out of Liberty Lake, Washington, and I need to speak to someone in the Investigations unit at the Kent Police Department."

"Sir," the operator replied, "for nonemergency calls, you should call the nonemergency number."

The way I was feeling by then, it was about to turn into an emergency because I was close to smashing my cell phone to pieces.

"I already tried that," I growled back at him. "When it comes to pressing buttons, Investigations isn't on the list. Could you please either connect me or give me their direct number so I can dial it myself?"

I hadn't exactly claimed to be a police officer as opposed to a PI, but I was indeed working a homicide case from Liberty Lake, and I must have sounded legit enough because he gave me the number. Playing faux cop may have worked with the 911 operator, but I had no intention of pulling that same stunt with a full-fledged detective. As for who would be on the other end of my call? No idea. I had certainly lucked out with Detective Byrd in Liberty Lake, but I figured my chances of getting a good detective as opposed to a dud were about fifty/fifty.

A male voice answered the call. "Detective Boyce Miller here."

"My name is J. P. Beaumont," I told him, "formerly with the AG's Special Homicide Investigation Team."

"Oh, that old S.H.I.T. squad?" Miller replied with a chuckle.

See what I mean? Every cop in the state remembers that unfortunate moniker. They can't help it.

"That's the one," I replied. "I got let go along with everyone else when it was disbanded. Now I'm working as a private investigator."

"What can I do you for?" Miller asked. That's when I knew for sure he wasn't a dud.

"I've been pursuing a number of King County drug overdose deaths that may have been erroneously classified as accidents or suicides when they should have been labeled homicides. I've learned that one of yours bears a surprising resemblance to a case over in Liberty Lake where the victim's death was ruled as undetermined. The case is assigned to a Liberty Lake PD detective named Elizabeth Byrd—that's Byrd with a *y* not an *i*."

"Which of our cases?" Detective Miller asked. "We're generally more into drive-by shootings than drug overdoses."

"Xavier Jesus Delgado," I replied.

"I remember that one," Miller said, "the guy found down by the railroad tracks. Overdosed on inhaled fentanyl, as I recall. And you're in luck. My partner and I actually responded to that one. What do you want to know?"

"Is it true the overdose was administered via a vape pen?" I asked.

"Yup, you've got that right. The pen was found at the scene with drug residue still inside the refillable cartridge. You can't exactly go out and buy vape cartridges already loaded with fentanyl. For those you more or less have to roll your own."

There's nothing like a little black humor between cops to break the ice, and we both chuckled over that one.

"Anyway," Miller continued, "Marty and I started with the victim's inner circle, including Xavier's wife, Felicity, who had recently filed for a divorce. She swore on a stack of bibles that there was no way her husband would have been using drugs. We were just getting started with the investigation when the M.E.'s suicide ruling came in. That's when we boxed up the evidence and shut 'er down. So what does this have to do with Liberty Lake?"

"The victim there is a guy named Jake Spaulding. He also died of a fentanyl overdose delivered by means of a vape pen. He'd had multiple arrests for domestic violence as did Mr. Delgado. Unlike your victim, Spaulding was eventually arrested and sent to prison. He died shortly after being released on parole. And like your guy, at the time of his death, he was carrying some cash, which included two hundred-dollar bills."

I heard a noise on the other end of the line that sounded distinctly as though Miller had taken both feet off his desk and put them on the floor. My mentioning of those two hundreds had caught his full attention.

"As soon as we found the money, we knew Delgado's death wasn't a robbery gone bad," Miller said. "He was still wearing his watch, and he had close to three hundred bucks in his wallet, including two hundred-dollar bills."

"Did you happen to take a close look at any of that cash?" I asked.

"Other than noticing Benjamin Franklin was on a couple of them, no. Why?"

"Because those two Benjamin Franklins are so old that they're missing their security strips. When Felicity tried to spend them later, the clerk at Target wouldn't accept them because she thought they were counterfeit."

"When did they start putting in—"

"Security strips were added to hundred-dollar bills in 1990," I answered, without waiting for him to complete the question. "So the money must have been printed before then, but I doubt they've been out in circulation because the bills appear to be pristine."

"Somebody's been sitting on them all this time, and now they're leaving them on the bodies of homicide victims?" Miller asked.

"Evidently," I told him. "We've now found two each among the

251

personal effects of victims in five different fatal overdose cases—three were determined to be accidental, one was labeled a suicide, and the last was left as undetermined. That's the only one still open at this time, but just barely. Until now it's been stone cold."

"That's really weird," Miller said. "So is the money the killer's calling card of some kind—sort of like a signature?"

"Maybe," I replied. "Once we determine who that person is, I'll be happy to ask that question. In the meantime, I've been trying to pull together enough evidence to convince Seattle PD to reopen the three closed cases that occurred inside their jurisdiction."

"You've certainly convinced me about ours," Detective Miller told me. "How can I help?"

"Tell me about the vape pen. Do you still have it?"

"I'm sure it's still in the evidence box," he answered. "Why?"

"As many now convicted killers have learned to their dismay, law enforcement is often able to trace batches of garbage bags and blue tarps back to their manufacturer and eventually to the point of sale. Now we've got two different vape pens and it would be nice to know the make and model. Do you happen to remember if yours had a serial number on it—either on the pen itself or else on the cartridge?"

"I don't remember," Miller said, "but I can sure as hell check. Our evidence storage is located off-site. Give me your number. I'll go have a look and give you a call back."

Kyle had wandered into the house while I was on the phone. It was only a little past noon. "What are you doing home so early?" I asked when the call ended.

"We had an early dismissal today. Don't you remember?" he asked.

I hadn't been involved in school affairs long enough to know there was any such thing as an early dismissal day. I don't remember ever having had any of those at Ballard High. Since starting next Wednesday school would be shut down for the foreseeable future, having an early dismissal day the week before seemed a bit silly, but I zipped my lip, once again recalling my mother's oft-repeated advice to "think before you speak."

"What's all this talk about vape pens?" Kyle wanted to know.

Two of the cases in question were now active investigations, and I should have kept mum, but he had overheard enough that there was no sense in shutting him out, so I went ahead and explained.

"It's about some cold case homicides I'm working on," I told him. "There are several instances where drug overdose deaths were declared to be accidents or suicides when I believe they should have been treated as homicides. In at least two of those crimes, vape pens were used to administer the drugs."

"Wow," Kyle said. "I thought you were retired. I didn't know you were still investigating murders."

That made me laugh. "It's hard to teach an old dog new tricks," I told him, but by then I was already dialing Detective Byrd's number in Liberty Lake.

"What's up?" she asked, once I identified myself.

I spent the next several minutes telling her about the Delgado case, ending with, "So I hope you still have your vape pen."

"As a matter of fact I do. In fact, it's right here on my desk at the moment, still in the evidence box. Why?"

"Does it happen to have a serial number?"

"Hold on," she said. She came back on the line a moment later. "I'm looking at it now. I can see a spot where there probably used to be a serial number, but it looks as though someone has gone to the trouble of grinding it off. That's pretty interesting. I'll get this over to the State Patrol Crime Lab in Spokane first thing tomorrow. They have the technology to retrieve serial numbers that have been ground off weapons, so they should be able to do the same thing with this."

"Thanks, Beth," I told her. "Let me know what you find out, and I'll do the same on this end."

Detective Miller called back ten minutes later. "I can see where the serial number is supposed to be," he began.

"But it's been ground off, right?" I asked.

"Right."

"Same thing over in Liberty Lake. Detective Byrd is going to submit hers to the crime lab in Spokane tomorrow morning to see if they can retrieve it. Spaulding's death was ruled undetermined, so she doesn't have to wait around for the case to be reopened."

"I don't, either," Detective Miller told me. "I checked with the chief on my way past. Five questionable deaths with two hundred-dollar bills left as calling cards were enough to convince him. Delgado's death may still be a suicide as far as the M.E. is concerned, but it's been reopened here at the Kent Police Department. Marty, my partner, actually lives in Seattle. I'll have him drop the pen off at the crime lab on his way home tonight so they can check it out."

"Great," I said. "Keep me posted."

"Will do," he said. "You do the same."

I put the phone down with a real sense of exhilaration. The three related Seattle cases still remained closed, but two of the other ones were back on track. With any kind of luck, maybe the others would fall into place as well.

Kyle was over by the kitchen island making himself a bologna sandwich. Mel has never approved of our having bologna around, but when Kyle had come dragging it home from Costco, she had made an exception to that rule.

"Making any progress?" Kyle asked.

"As a matter of fact I am," I assured him. "On these cases and on yours as well."

"Really?" he wanted to know. "What's going on with mine?"

So I told him about the call from Marisa and about her plan to meet up with Caroline Richards in Portland on Saturday. Kyle listened in silence, but by the time I finished, he was frowning.

"If Caroline's finally getting a chance to meet up with her family, that should be good news, but you don't sound very happy about it."

"Because I'm not," I admitted. "Rather than tell your father the truth, Caroline told your dad that she's meeting up with an old school chum instead of with her mother's sister."

"So she's lying to him," Kyle surmised.

"She's *still* lying to him," I corrected. "And if that's the case, what's to keep her from lying to Marisa as well? I have a bad feeling that your father's going to be hurt real bad before all this is over, and I hope Marisa Young doesn't end up in the same boat."

Kyle finished polishing off the last of his sandwich and then gave me a quizzical look. "Any idea what's for dinner?" he asked.

That wasn't too surprising. After all, he's still a growing boy, but slick as can be, I dodged the what's-for-dinner bullet. "I'm meeting Mel for a late lunch," I told him, "and I'll see what she has to say."

"Please," Kyle said, "but whatever you do, don't let her make any more curry."

"Trust me on that," I said, "I'll do my best."

CHAPTER 31

Bellingham, Washington
Friday, March 6, 2020

BEFORE MEETING MEL FOR LUNCH, I TURNED TO MY EMAIL account; sixty-four more interview transcriptions had arrived from Elena, along with a separate one stating that those were all the ones she had at present. Ben Weston and Sandra Sechrest were continuing to make good progress going through the case files I was sending them. Between them they had flagged five more files for further study, but Yolanda had yet to notify me if any of those people had consented to additional interviews.

I met up with Mel at our favorite daytime hangout, Jack and Jill's, an old-fashioned diner two blocks from Mel's office. Today marked three weeks since Kyle had unexpectedly shown up in our lives. Sitting in a booth together, just the two of us, seemed special somehow—almost like a date. And having a homey meal that required no advance planning on either of our parts was like going on vacation. It also gave us a chance to talk, one-on-one.

For Mel, the breast-fondling situation at the high school was boiling over. When her detectives had done a canvass of current students involved in the school's music program, eleven more female students had come forward with inappropriate touching complaints.

"George Pritchard has been at Bellingham High for the past five years, so there are probably additional victims who have either graduated, transferred to another school, or dropped out. I also had one of my investigators contact the school district in Sacramento where Pritchard taught prior to coming here. It would appear that he left there under some kind of cloud, but so far no one's willing to share any details. The district didn't out and out fire him, but they also didn't discourage him from leaving."

"No wonder no one's talking," I said. "Instead of dealing with the problem straight out, they sent a guy who should have been unmasked as a sex offender along to some other unsuspecting school district where he's had access to a whole new set of victims."

"Right," Mel said bitterly. "And now he's my problem instead of theirs. I'll be talking to the county attorney this afternoon to see if he's willing to swear out an arrest warrant. The thing is, Pritchard has a wife and two school-age kids who most likely have no idea about who he really is, so putting him in jail will be hell on them, too."

I nodded my head in agreement. That's something I had come to realize over the years. Whenever I arrested a killer, the victims' families were always adversely affected by whatever crime had been committed, but there were often plenty of injured innocent bystanders among the offenders' loved ones as well. It was about then that I realized that same dynamic was currently at work in my own family. Jeremy Cartwright was the one who was screwing around on his wife, but Kelly, Kayla, and Kyle were all suffering the consequences.

"I don't remember stuff like this happening back when I was a kid," I muttered.

"I'm pretty sure pedophiles have always been with us," Mel said. "The big difference is that back in your day, girls—and boys, too—were far more reticent about coming forward."

Put in my place but realizing she was right, I sat back and took the front tip off a piece of Jill's incomparable lemon meringue pie.

"Thanks for reminding me that I'm a grouchy old man," I said.

"Grouchy on occasion, yes," Mel told me, "but pretty darned nice most of the time."

BUOYED BY THAT last remark, I was on my way home from lunch when a call came in from Lulu Benson.

"I've got a familial hit on that unidentified female profile your friend Gretchen Walther sent over."

"Boy, lady," I said. "You're batting a thousand. How close a match?"

"Second cousin. Your unidentified female DNA belongs to this woman's mother's first cousin."

"Where is she from?"

"Lexington, Kentucky."

"That's a hell of a long way from Seattle," I commented.

"Yes, it is," Lulu agreed. "She posted her DNA on GEDmatch, looking for her mother's long-lost cousin. Do you want her name and number or not?"

I hesitated for a moment. By rights, this had to do with Detective Elizabeth Byrd's open homicide investigation, and I should probably have turned it over to her to begin with, but it was my longtime connection to Gretchen Walther that had made the hit possible.

"Of course I want her number," I replied.

Lulu laughed. "Somehow I thought you would," she said.

Thirty seconds later I was introducing myself to Harriet Bonham of Lexington, Kentucky, someone with a very interesting tale to tell. Once I got her on the phone and introduced myself, she was happy to share the story of the man who ended up becoming the celebrated black sheep of her family.

"William Landon was my mother's favorite cousin," she said. "I grew up hearing stories about him, about how Mom and Billy used to play together when they were kids—climbing trees, building forts, swimming in the lake on my grandfather's farm. Mom was born in 1927. Billy was a year older. She always talked about how smart he was and how handsome. After his older brother Frank died in childhood, his folks expected that eventually Billy would step up and take over running the family farm, but he wasn't interested in farming. He left home and joined the army as soon as he turned eighteen."

"Just in time for the tail end of World War II?" I asked.

"He wasn't overseas for all that long, but Mom said he was a different person when he came home, and they were never close again. He moved to Cincinnati, got married, and had a couple of kids. By the midfifties he was driving an armored car for Brinks. In 1956 there was a robbery. Three men were involved, and Billy was one of them. He took off before the cops figured out it was an inside job. The other two guys ended up going to prison. Billy vanished without a trace."

"And got away with the money," I suggested.

"How did you know that?"

"Lucky guess," I said.

"How did you make the connection back to me?" Harriet wanted to know.

"We got a hit from unidentified DNA found at the scene of a crime," I told her. Two separate ones, in fact, but there was no need to go into that.

"What kind of crime?" Harriet asked. "Billy was born in 1926. That would make him close to a hundred years old by now. How's it even possible that he's still going around committing crimes?"

"I'm sorry," I told her. "That information is a part of an ongoing police investigation, and I'm unable to comment at this time."

There was a short silence between us before the reality dawned on her. "It must be one of his children then," she surmised, "or maybe even one of his grandchildren. He abandoned a wife and kids when he left Ohio. She got a divorce and eventually remarried, and Billy must have done the same thing—starting over someplace else and ending up with a whole new family."

That was my guess, too, but I didn't say so. Instead I asked another question. "How much money did he make off with?"

"Four hundred thousand," she said. "When I started doing research on my own, that's what the newspaper articles said. I wasn't even born when it happened, so everything I know about William Landon is secondhand. Every once in a while as a kid, I'd overhear my mother talking with one of her sisters or cousins about Billy, the black sheep of the family. Whenever I tried to ask my mother about him, though, she'd shut me down. It wasn't until after Mom died that I started looking into what happened. That's when I connected William Landon with her beloved Cousin Billy. Once I finally got around to googling William Landon's name, that was the first link that turned up—one to a newspaper article about the Brinks robbery."

She kept talking but for a time I wasn't really paying attention, I was too busy thinking. *Four hundred thousand dollars would have added up to a hell of a lot of hundred-dollar bills!*

"And that got me to wondering," Harriet was saying when I tuned back in on the conversation. "How did he manage to disappear so completely that the cops were never able to find him? Where did he go? What happened to him? Was he dead or alive?

"I watch a lot of true crime on TV," she continued. "That's where I heard about how long-forgotten cold cases are now being solved when relatives of a suspect post their DNA on ancestry databases. According to what I read, GEDmatch is one of the few of those that actually cooperates with law enforcement. That's why I chose them. I wanted to find out what happened to him after he left Ohio."

"Thank you for that," I told her, and I meant it, too. "I can't tell you how much you've helped us already. Apparently we're dealing with far more than a single cold case—it's actually several. Once those are solved, Ms. Bonham, I promise that I'll get back to you with the whole story."

"You will?"

"Mark my words."

"And I helped? Really?"

"More than you know," I replied.

With that I ended the call, but I didn't put down the phone. Instead, I located my friend Ron Peters's cell phone number and punched it. That 1956 armored car robbery had to be the source of the hundred-dollar bills that linked all five cases together, and that made me confident that I finally had enough information to compel

Seattle PD to reopen those three mislabeled cases. I believed Ron Peters was the guy who could get the job done.

"Hey, Beau," he said genially when he answered. "It's been a while. How are things and what are you up to?"

"When you find out why I'm calling," I told him, "you're not going to be happy, because I'm about to become a real pain in your ass."

"When haven't you been a pain in my ass?" he replied with a laugh. "Tell me about it."

So I did. Once I got off the phone with him, I called everybody else, too—Ben Weston and Sandy Sechrest at Seattle PD, Elizabeth Byrd in Liberty Lake, Boyce Miller in Kent, Yolanda Aguirre, and even Gretchen Walther from the crime lab. Once all hell broke loose on this, I wanted all of us to be on the same page.

CHAPTER 32

I STAGGERED OUT OF THE BEDROOM ON SATURDAY MORNING, let Sarah out, and then went to the kitchen to start the coffee. When I found a note from Kyle next to the coffee machine, it was all I could do to keep from grinding my teeth in annoyance.

Out for a driving lesson with Hank. We're going to grab breakfast somewhere along the way. See you later.

My head filled with visions of his burning up the clutch on Hank's very expensive automotive antique. I couldn't help but wonder how much fixing that would cost since I was reasonably sure I'd be the one footing the bill, and I wasn't thrilled at the prospect. The call that came in from Todd Hatcher a while later did nothing to improve my frame of mind.

"How are things?" he asked when I answered.

"Fine," I responded. It was one of Mel's raised eyebrow "fines," which means the exact opposite, but Todd didn't pick up on that.

"Well," he continued, "I'm still searching for any online sign of Lindsey Baylor between that initial arrest at age eighteen and her emergence as Caroline Richards late last year, but I'm coming up empty. No employment records. No tax filings. Her profile is still listed as available on several dating sites, but those didn't start until after her new ID came online. During all the intervening years, however, there were no postings of her on any social media. I've also been unable to locate any further interactions with law enforcement."

"Is it possible she left the country for that amount of time?" I asked.

"She couldn't have done so legally," Todd replied. "She doesn't have a passport. It's as though she vanished into thin air."

Scenarios where someone goes into hiding and emerges seven years later with a brand-new identity often suggest participation in some kind of illegal financial activity, most especially tax evasion. What exactly had Caroline been dodging?

"What the hell was she doing all that time?" I asked aloud.

"Beats me," Todd replied, "but if it was against the law, she was smart enough not to get caught. I was concerned and wanted you to be aware of that."

"Thanks," I said. "Appreciate it."

As I hung up, it occurred to me that I wasn't the only one who needed to be brought up to speed on the existence of that seven-year black hole in Caroline Richards's history. My concern was that she might well be surviving as some kind of serial scammer, and if poor besotted Jeremy was one of her victims, what were the chances she'd do the same thing to her newly found auntie during their reunion in Portland? Not ready to tackle the issue with Jeremy, I tried contacting Marisa Young, but my call went straight to voice-mail. I ended up leaving a bland message.

"It's me, checking in to see how things are going."

That was enough to let her know that more than two hundred fifty miles away, someone in Bellingham was watching and waiting to see how today's meeting would turn out.

As for Jeremy? Kyle had told me early on that it was likely his dad had reeled Caroline in by convincing her that he was in far better financial shape than he really was. So what happens when scammer number one discovers he or she is being scammed by scammer number two? Probably not a good outcome for either one of them. With that in mind, I decided to put the call to Jeremy on hold indefinitely in hopes that somehow Marisa would be able to suss out some information about Caroline's missing years.

Meanwhile, without my noticing, Mel had emerged from the bedroom. I had no idea she was there until she pressed the button, and the coffee machine ground into action.

"What's going on?" she asked.

Once she joined me in the living room, I gave her a brief over-view. She listened thoughtfully. When I finished, she took a sip of her coffee and asked, "How much time passed between the first appearance of Caroline's new identity and her hooking up with Jeremy?"

"I don't know," I replied. "It seems to have happened pretty quickly, a couple of months or so. Why?"

"If you're right about her being a scammer, she's most likely pulling the oldest trick in the book."

"What's that?" I asked.

"Getting one man to take responsibility for another man's child."

Wham, bam, thank you, ma'am!

"Why the hell didn't I think of that?" I demanded.

Mel favored me with a wry grin. "Maybe because you're a man?" she suggested. "Most guys fall for that trick hook, line, and sinker, especially ones like Jeremey who are under the mistaken impression that they're God's gift to women."

"But what should I do about it?" I asked.

"For right now, leave well enough alone," Mel advised. "If you try going into it now, it'll only make things worse. Once the baby arrives, there'll be plenty of time to suggest Jeremy might want to consider doing a paternity test. At that point, he'll have to live with the results one way or the other."

I thought about that for a moment before I spoke again. "Thanks," I said at last.

"Thanks for what?" Mel wanted to know.

"For keeping me from stepping in it any worse than I already have."

CHAPTER 33

Bellingham, Washington
Saturday, March 7, 2020

THAT'S ABOUT THE TIME KYLE CAME BREEZING INTO THE HOUSE.
He went straight to the fridge where he grabbed two sodas.

"How was the stick shift lesson?" I asked.

"It was great," he answered with a wide grin. "And that Shelby is amazing!" Then he headed for the door.

"Where are you going now?" Mel asked.

"Back to the garage," Kyle replied. "Hank went home to get his drums. He's going to bring them over here so we can try jamming together. Later." With that he ducked back out the door.

I was stunned. Three weeks earlier when Kyle had first shown up, Hank was the one who had voiced concern about the advisability of taking in a teenager. At the time, it hadn't occurred to me that in short order Kyle and Hank Mitchell would not only be on a first-name basis, they'd also be such good pals that they'd be playing drums together.

"I never saw that one coming," Mel murmured as the door slammed shut behind him.

"That makes two of us," I said.

That's when Mel's phone rang. She listened for a time before saying, "Okay. I'll be on the scene in twenty."

That sounded serious. "What's up?" I asked as she grabbed her coffee cup and headed for the bedroom.

"My guys just got an arrest warrant for George Pritchard," she told me. "It's bound to be a media firestorm, so I need to be on hand when they take him into custody."

While she headed out to attend to that unpleasant duty, I turned back to my iPad. An email from Yolanda told me that she had sent a message to an interviewee named Norma Adams regarding her son, Lawrence, age forty-three, who had died of an accidental drug overdose on May 16, 2018. It turned out that Norma herself had passed away only two months after doing that initial interview. The person who had responded to Yolanda's request for additional information was Norma's daughter, Janelle, who had been keeping tabs on her deceased mother's email account in case there were any lingering items that needed to be handled.

Before attempting to make contact with the daughter, I did the same thing I had done previously and read through the applicable case file. Lawrence, a decorated veteran of Desert Storm, had been found dead next to a dumpster in a Denny Regrade alleyway. His death had been ruled accidental, but throughout his mother's interview with Yolanda, Norma had insisted that her son had been murdered, and Ben Weston had flagged the file due to Norma's staunch insistence that her son was the victim of a homicide as opposed to an accidental death. Norma had admitted to Yolanda that Larry had been a homeless drug user, largely attributable to PTSD resulting from his military service. She also believed that he had been killed in the course of a robbery gone bad since his treasured collection of military medals had not been found with the body.

Since Janelle had expressed an interest in connecting with us, I was taken aback by her hostile response when I reached her by phone a little while later.

"Why the hell are you people going through all this crap again?" she demanded, once I identified myself. "Why can't you just give it a rest?"

I explained that we were looking into overdose deaths that had been mistakenly identified as suicides or accidents when they should have been investigated as homicides.

"Well, you're dead wrong on that score here," she responded. "My brother wasn't murdered. Larry Adams was a lying SOB who had my mother wrapped around his little finger. The part about his being homeless because of PTSD is a bunch of BS. He never saw a single day of combat duty. He ended up being dishonorably discharged after getting into a beef with his commanding officer during basic training. As for all his precious medals? They were stolen all right—from somebody else.

"Does the term 'stolen valor' mean anything to you? My brother could have written the book on that. I don't know how he ended up with all those medals, including the Purple Heart he liked to wave around, but he sure as hell didn't earn them. As for the drug paraphernalia found on his body? Mom insisted those were planted there by his killers to throw the investigation off track."

"So you have no quarrel with the accidental death ruling?"

"None whatsoever, but my mother was outraged. Finally, in hopes of shutting her up, I actually went downtown and spoke to the M.E. She told me there were indications of long-term intravenous drug use on his body, and that he had most likely run into a batch of something that had more of a kick to it than he expected. My understanding is that, when it comes to fentanyl dosages, there's a very small margin of error between living and dying."

"How did he support that kind of habit?" I asked.

"How do you think he supported it?" Janelle retorted. "My mother. I didn't know until after she died that she was virtually penniless. Her death was a suicide, by the way. She overdosed, too, on Ambien as opposed to fentanyl. Maybe somebody should be doing an interview with me about her death. I'd be only too happy to give them an earful. Larry was already gone at the time she died, but he's the one who killed her."

ONCE OFF THE phone with Janelle Adams, I sat for a long time lost in thought. The situation was eerily similar to Loren Gregson's. Both men had had loving mothers who refused to accept or even recognize their sons' shortcomings, and both had left behind sisters who were now doomed to carry far more than their fair share of the family's emotional burdens. It made me wonder about all those other fractured families out there.

Yolanda Aguirre's careful study was uncovering those wherever we looked. For King County, each death was just another hash mark in the ever-increasing numbers in their overdose column. My job was to identify the unknown serial killer who was lurking inside those indifferent statistics, but the depth of Yolanda's interviewing technique was also allowing me to see beyond the non-existent headlines and giving me an understanding of exactly how each of those individual deaths—so easily shrugged off by everybody else—was an all-consuming tragedy for the loved ones left behind.

Each was a pebble dropped into some family's existence that sent long-lasting ripples of sorrow and hurt in every direction. The overdose death of someone found next to a dumpster or in a back alleyway wasn't an attention grabber. Those kinds of deaths don't garner headlines or public attention. They also often fail to attract serious scrutiny from law enforcement.

And what had brought all this home to me? A caring old woman named Matilda Jackson trying to learn the truth about her grandson's death. In the process of doing that, she had given me something I had maybe lost track of in this overly virtual world—a healthy dose of basic human empathy. Because that's what I was feeling right that minute, not only for my particular overdose victims—the ones who had been murdered—but also for all those other affected people—the friends and relations who would spend the rest of their lives dealing with the absence of those who were gone.

Of course, grieving families had been there all along. I had met them time and again while working as a homicide investigator, but what I was seeing now, up close and personal, was how mushrooming drug overdose deaths were exponentially expanding their numbers.

I had just arrived at that uncomfortable conclusion when Mel came home. From the haggard expression on her face, I saw she wasn't in any better shape than I was.

She had gone to meet the arrest team wearing her full dress uniform, so the first thing she did was kick off her high heels and drop down onto the sofa beside me.

"How was it?" I asked.

"Awful."

"Let me guess, the wife and kids had no idea of what was coming."

Mel nodded. "That's right, not a clue. His wife, Alana, is utterly devastated. She didn't even know he'd been put on leave. As for the kids? The two boys are only five and seven. They're from a previous marriage, so although Pritchard is their stepfather, he's also the only father they've ever known. The poor kids were horrified when one of my officers put handcuffs on him, led him out of the house, and loaded him into the back of a patrol car. That's something I won't forget in a hurry."

"The media was there, I assume?"

"In full force," she replied, "and so was a band of hecklers. I have no idea how word got out about the impending arrest, but it did. Within minutes of our showing up at the house, a crowd gathered out on the street, calling him a dirty old man and a pervert as he was led to the patrol car."

"Which made things that much worse for the family."

"Exactly," Mel replied. "My department has several victim advocates on staff. I was tempted to send one of them over to talk to Alana. Fortunately she's from here originally. By the time we were ready to pack up and leave, her mother and sister had both arrived on the scene. I told them that if there was any way I could be of assistance, they should call me."

"And they probably will."

"I don't know what I should hope for," Mel said with a sigh. "If they call or if they don't, it'll be bad either way."

She stood up and collected her shoes. "I'm going to go change," she added. "Did you know Hank's still here?"

"I had no idea."

"His car's blocking the garage door, so I parked outside, but the racket coming from inside the garage sounded like machine-gun fire."

"That's the sound of two drummers drumming," I said mildly.

"I'll say."

She started for the bedroom, but she was still in the living room when Kyle popped his head in the front door.

"Hey, guys," he said. "Hank's about to head home, but he says Ellen was off today. She's made oxtail soup along with freshly baked bread to go with it. He wanted to know if we'd like to come over for dinner."

I had been in and out of the Mitchells' kitchen on occasion for a stray cup of coffee here and there, but never for an actual meal. And although Mel had been introduced to Ellen when she had paid visits to the call center, she had never set foot inside their home. As a consequence I was a little surprised when she replied to Kyle's question before I had a chance to open my mouth.

"Sure," she said. "What time?"

"Six thirty."

"Great," Mel said. "Tell him we'll be there with bells on."

"By the way," Kyle added, "he told me it's fine if we bring Sarah along. Mr. Bean misses her."

Mel is far more of a social butterfly than I am, but having just gone through that very public arrest scene, I was amazed that she had so readily agreed to go have dinner with people who were relative strangers. With that in mind, when she went into the bedroom to change clothes, I padded along after her.

"Are you sure you want to go to dinner tonight?" I asked.

"Why not?" she said. "I sure as hell don't want to cook. Do you?"

We both knew the answer to that question. Eating dinner with the Mitchells was a much better option all the way around.

CHAPTER 34

Bellingham, Washington
Saturday, March 7, 2020

THE FOUR OF US, THREE HUMANS AND ONE CANINE, ARRIVED AT Hank and Ellen Mitchell's house at 6:30 on the dot, having used our cell phone flashlights to illuminate the path up our steep driveway, along the shoulder of Bayside, and down the Mitchells' driveway. In the old days, I probably would have driven, but I'm more of a walker now.

Hank met us at the door. "Come in," he said heartily. "Ellen's attending to some last-minute details. Let me take your coats and Sarah's leash. Then I'll give you the nickel tour."

The place was illuminated as if in anticipation of a real estate open house. Every lamp was lit, including the massive chandelier hanging over a beautifully set live-edge dining room table.

Mel's and my furniture tends to be on the sleek side with leather-covered furniture and glass-topped tables. Clearly the Mitchells preferred a more homey look. In the living room space, upholstered chairs, a gigantic sofa, and antique wooden side tables were arranged around a massive river-rock fireplace. Sarah, not particularly interested in the decor, made straight for the Oriental rug in front of the blazing fire and settled down on that as if she owned the place.

Hank motioned to an empty spot to one side of the roaring fire. "That's where my drum set usually sits," he explained to Mel, "but today Kyle and I decided to leave it at your place. I hope you don't mind. We played with his band all afternoon. My arms are worn out, but I haven't had that much fun in years."

"What band?" I asked, puzzling over the idea that Kyle had already connected with a bunch of like-minded kids here in Bellingham.

"The Rockets," Kyle said, rolling his eyes. "From down in Ashland. Ricky's dad runs sound tech for the Shakespeare Festival. He signed up to be a beta tester on a new app that allows people to practice together online even though they're miles apart. It was great, and Hank's terrific!"

"A little out of practice," Hank admitted, "but for an old guy, I think I did okay."

Kyle grinned. "You did just fine," he agreed.

Looking around the house, it was apparent that once upon a time this part of it had been divided into three smaller rooms—dining room, living room, and kitchen. Open-concept living hadn't been a gleam in most interior designers' eyes back in the forties and fifties. Now, all intervening walls had been demolished, leaving behind an enormous living space that contained an upscale kitchen at the far end, a dining area in the middle, and a cozy seating area in front of the massive fireplace at the other end. Taken altogether, it was stunning.

Not wanting to disturb Ellen who was bustling around in the

kitchen, Hank led us in the opposite direction. Great care had been taken in bringing an old house with a midcentury modern footprint into a new era. As built, the house had contained four bedrooms and two baths. Now it had been pared down to only two bedrooms. One had been carved up to create three separate rooms—a powder room, a laundry room, and an immense walk-in closet that was now part of the master suite. In the master the original en suite and closet had been combined into a spalike bath. Of the two remaining bedrooms, one had been updated into a deluxe guest room complete with its own bath, while the last had morphed into Ellen's quilting studio.

When Hank had mentioned Ellen did quilting, I had envisioned something simple like the handmade quilt that had topped my single bed while I was growing up. It had consisted of alternating red and white squares inside a deep blue border. The quilt had been a gift from one of my mother's friends, and Mom called it my "Fourth of July quilt." Personally I had hated it, and it was one of the first items I ditched once I was on my own.

With that history in mind, when we walked into Ellen's quilting studio, I was amazed. The sewing machine alone was a sleek technical wonder that put my mother's old foot-pedal-propelled Singer to shame. The quilt that was currently in process wasn't made up of alternating squares. Instead, it was art, pure and simple. Alternating strips of pink, lavender, and yellow created a surprisingly realistic image of a tulip field, complete with a half-completed bright red barn currently in process in the foreground.

"This is gorgeous!" Mel exclaimed.

"It's actually a commission," Hank said proudly. "They're planning to raffle it off as a fundraiser during this year's Skagit Valley

Tulip Festival, which is coming up later in the spring. That means she's working on a bit of a deadline."

"How long has Ellen been quilting?" Mel asked.

"Long before the two of us met," Hank informed us. "When I asked her to marry me, that was her only condition—that she have a room of her own that was strictly for quilting. After a tough day at the call center, she says there's nothing like coming in here and working on a quilt for a quiet hour or so to unload the stress."

"Maybe I should consider taking up quilting," Mel said. After a short pause, she added with a laugh, "Then again, probably not. I'm not exactly the sewing type."

Considering the day she'd had, I didn't doubt she was stressed, but Mel didn't say a word about George Pritchard's arrest, and neither did I.

"That was me, too," Ellen supplied, appearing in the doorway behind us. "No interest in sewing whatsoever although my mother was a quilter for as long as I can remember. When Mom died, I inherited all her equipment. I meant to get rid of it, but somehow I couldn't bring myself to throw it all away.

"Thanks to Hank I now have equipment my mother never could have dreamed of. That top-of-the-line sewing machine is what makes it possible for me to create something as complex as this tulip field. My only regret is that I didn't take quilting up sooner while Mom was still alive. She would have loved doing it together."

"You're doing it now, and this one is amazing!" Mel declared. "Where do I buy raffle tickets and how much are they?"

"Ten bucks apiece," Ellen answered.

"Sign me up for twenty, then," Mel said. "Maybe I'll get lucky."

"If you'd like, I can drop the tickets by your office next week, but in the meantime, soup's on, and I do mean soup."

With that, we all trooped back to the dining room table. Like the quilt, Ellen's oxtail soup was a work of art. And being able to dip still-warm, homemade, buttered bread into that savory broth was heavenly. When Ellen asked if anyone wanted seconds, Kyle immediately raised his hand.

Dessert was a crème brûlée with a crust of burned sugar across the top. While we were enjoying that, the conversation somehow drifted back to quilting.

"You'd be surprised how many quilters are out there," Ellen said. "Two more girls from the What-Comm call center are taking it up, and when I worked at the call center down in Seattle, there were several there, too."

"Really," I said. "When I hear someone saying, '911. What is the nature of your emergency?,' I don't envision someone whose spare time would be devoted to making quilts."

Ellen laughed. "They do. In fact, one of the dispatchers in Seattle, Constance Herzog, is a nationally acclaimed quilter. She's won prizes all over the country. And she's been recognized for donating her work to domestic violence shelters so that when the women there move on to permanent housing, they'll have something tangible to take with them."

"Very commendable," Mel said. "Most of the time they come to shelters with nothing but the clothes on their backs."

"As far as Connie goes, I suspect there might be a bit of personal history involved," Ellen continued. "When she finished remodeling her studio, she held an open house, so several girls from the call center went. There was a framed picture hanging on one wall that looked like a mug shot, which was weird, so one of the girls asked about it. Connie said it was her dad and explained that was the only picture she had of him since her mother burned all the others."

"A mug shot?" Mel repeated. "Really? So did her father end up going to prison?"

"Nope," Ellen replied. "Whatever he was accused of doing, Connie said he got off."

By now I was all ears. Was this what we were looking for? Someone with a law enforcement connection, a personal interest in domestic violence issues, and possibly some personal experience with domestic violence? The burning of an ex's photos made that sound like a distinct possibility. And saying "he got off" was a far cry from saying "he didn't do it." The killer we were looking for seemed to target domestic violence perpetrators who had indeed gotten off. As far as I was concerned, that framed picture was unlikely to be a caring daughter's tribute to a beloved father, not by a long shot.

"We all talked about how weird it was afterward, but we decided that what a person does in the privacy of her own home was none of our business."

None of your business, maybe, I thought, *but it sure as hell sounds like mine!*

What I was feeling right then was that sense of euphoria that comes over you when you're working on a thousand-piece jigsaw puzzle and two pieces with nothing on them but clear blue sky suddenly click together perfectly. In this instance, my two separate puzzle pieces were Ron Wang's suggestion that our killer might be some kind of vigilante and Sandy Sechrest's revelation about how working with domestic violence victims while serving as a 911 dispatcher had motivated her to become a police officer. Maybe Constance Herzog had been pushed in the opposite direction.

At this point, she was still a 911 dispatcher who seemed to have a laserlike focus on domestic violence issues. So was it possible that this prizewinning Seattle quilter was also our serial killer?

There was nothing I wanted to do more right then than to race out of the house and get Todd Hatcher on the line, but you're not supposed to eat and run. So I minded my p's and q's and stayed put, all the while feeling as though I wanted to jump out of my skin. Finally, though, it was time to leave. As we gathered coats and jackets, inspiration struck and I turned back to Ellen.

"Is that other quilter's work anything like yours?" I asked.

"I suppose," Ellen said with a shrug. "She does landscapes, too."

"And if I wanted to see some of her quilts, how would I go about it?"

"Google the name Constance Herzog. You should be able to see what she currently has available online."

"Thanks," I said. "I'll do that. Mel's birthday is coming up. One of those might be just what the doctor ordered."

We finished thanking them for the lovely meal and headed out. Their front door had barely closed, when Mel turned on me.

"What the hell?" she demanded. "When have I ever mentioned wanting to own a quilt? Yes, I offered to buy raffle tickets, but I was only being polite."

Kyle and Sarah had gone on ahead. "I'll tell you later," I muttered under my breath, "but not right now."

CHAPTER 35

Bellingham, Washington
Sunday, March 8, 2020

THE NEXT DAY, KYLE TOOK CHARGE OF SUNDAY MORNING BREAK-
fast. We had bacon and waffles—not the kind that would have
required the use of a waffle iron, which we definitely don't own.
No, these were frozen ones Kyle had dragged home from his Costco
shopping trip—the kind that pops up out of a toaster, which we
do have. As for his Costco bacon cooked in the microwave? It was
perfectly crisp without a smidgeon of grease left on the stovetop.
It was beginning to dawn on me that having a teenager around
wasn't half bad.

AFTER GETTING HOME the night before and once Kyle had disappeared into his room, I had brought Mel into the picture and laid
out my plan. Cops can compel suspects to provide DNA samples

by obtaining the appropriate warrants. Private investigators can't request warrants, but, like the clown says in *The Little Engine That Could*—there's more than one way over the mountain to Yon. A handmade quilt would be covered with the quilter's touch DNA, and, in this case, my Visa card would take the place of a warrant.

"And you really think Constance Herzog is your killer?" Mel asked.

"I do," I said.

"And you're willing to buy a quilt to get a sample of her DNA to prove it?"

"Yup," I said. "It beats digging through her trash cans. If she actually made the quilt, skin cells, containing her DNA, should be all over it."

That sounded fine and dandy until we went online and studied Constance Herzog's inventory of available quilts. They were jaw-droppingly expensive. The one that caught Mel's eye contained a striking black-and-white silhouette of Seattle's skyline with the Space Needle front and center. It was a view that almost mirrored the one from the bedroom window of our old condo. The problem was it cost a cool two thousand bucks.

Mel started shaking her head. "You can't be serious," she said. "You're going to spend this much on a quilt on a hunch that the person who made it is your killer?"

"Go big or go home," I said. "Besides, what I'm really buying is the DNA."

With the decision made, I scrolled down to the "contact us" part of the web page and sent an email.

My wife's birthday is next week. She loves your Space Needle silhouette. Is that quilt still available? If so, would it be possible for me to purchase it and then drop by to pick it up rather than having it shipped? I'd be glad to drive down from Bellingham to get it as soon as possible.

Beau Beaumont

As I pressed send, I was somewhat leery about having used my real name for fear she might remember me from days past when I was with Seattle PD, but that couldn't be helped. I intended to pay for the purchase with my credit card, which would have my name on it, too. If she somehow made the connection to Scotty, I was fully prepared to pass him off as my beloved nephew.

Once that was done and since it was too late to call, I sent Todd an email asking him to do a complete background check on Constance Herzog and on her father, too, since I had reason to suspect that if she'd grown up in a family plagued by domestic violence, that might be the source of her intense interest in the same.

After sending both messages off into the ethers, I had crossed my fingers and Mel and I had gone to bed.

THERE WAS NO response to either of my emails when I got up on Sunday morning, and the same held true by the time we finished our Eggo breakfast. I was doing the Sunday crosswords when an email alert came in from Ron Peters, and it wasn't good news.

No luck on moving the needle on your cases. The powers that be in Homicide are concerned that if they reopen those three without having an actual named suspect, it'll unleash a flood of similar claims.

Sorry I couldn't do more right now, but keep me posted.

Ron

Disappointment must have shown on my face.

"What?" Mel asked.

I read Ron's email aloud.

"So what's the problem?" Mel asked. "If your suspicions about Constance Herzog are right, you're about to do exactly what they're asking—you'll be handing over a named suspect. Once you provide them with that along with her DNA and the physical evidence linking the three cases together, they won't have any choice. They'll have to reopen them if for no other reason than to mark them closed."

That's the thing about Mel. She manages to cut straight to the heart of the matter, as in, go ahead and solve them already! Now all I had to do was wait to hear back on my proposed purchase of a Constance Herzog original, but I'm not much good at sitting around waiting. In the old days I would have passed the time by belting down a shot or two of McNaughton's. Instead I took Sarah for a walk.

We were heading back to the barn when a call came in from Marisa Young. I answered with a question. "Where are you?"

"Back home in Fountain Hills," she said. "My flight from Portland was first thing this morning. I just got back from Sky Harbor and wanted to let you know what's going on."

"How was it?" I asked, more than half dreading the answer.

"It was amazing!" Marisa told me. "Absolutely amazing. I was sitting in the bar by the fireplace when she came into the room. I saw her stop and look around, and then she walked straight over to me. 'I know you,' she said. Then she reached into her bag and pulled out the teddy bear. 'You're the one who gave me this!'

"I couldn't believe that she still had it," Marisa continued. "And the fact that she recognized my face blew me away. She sat down, and we spent the next ten minutes crying. The people in the bar probably thought we were nuts, sitting there bawling like a pair of babies over a tattered, one-eared, one-eyed teddy bear. So thank you, Beau, for making that embarrassing crying jag possible."

It was not the answer I had been expecting.

"Did I ever mention that I spent fifteen years as a high school guidance counselor?" Marisa asked after a momentary pause.

"Not that I remember. Why?"

"Because," she replied, "that's a job that requires an ability to recognize the difference between someone who's telling the truth and someone who's lying. Given Serena's history, I was expecting that she'd try feeding me a bunch of bull, but she didn't. She told me about the night she woke up with someone pounding on the door and being rushed out of the house and into a car, and all the while she was holding on to her teddy bear.

"Over the years she kept asking her mother about what happened to the 'nice lady in that other house,' the one who gave her the teddy bear. Her mother claimed that Serena was mistaken and there wasn't any 'nice lady'—that she was the one who had given her Mindy."

Yup, I thought, *sounds like WITSEC all right.*

"They ended up living a tough life. Tricia worked the streets. From the time Serena was five or so, she remembers being left home alone at night with no supervision. At school there was a lot of bullying because she ate free lunches and wore clothing from Goodwill. And it was one of the kids at school who told her that her mother didn't have a real job—that she was a prostitute."

By then, Sarah and I were back inside the house. Since Mel was nowhere in sight, I guessed she was probably doing her Sunday stint in the soaking tub. As I shed my jacket, my face flushed with embarrassment over law enforcement's involvement in all this. Only a mindless, faceless government bureaucracy would think it would be a good safety measure to dump a young single mom on the opposite side of the country in a place where she had no friends or relations to offer support. I had been a homicide cop as opposed to a school guidance counselor, but I, too, could see this story had the ring of truth about it.

"It sounds terrible," I said at last.

"I'm sure it was," Marisa agreed, "and it got worse once Tricia started using drugs. A lot of the time the only food Serena had was what she got at school. On weekends, she went hungry except for what she could find dumpster diving behind fast-food restaurants. During those years, though, there were people who took pity on her and who would buy her an occasional meal or slip her a bit of cash now and then. Given the neighborhoods they lived in, some of those folks were pretty dodgy themselves, including a guy who made his living creating fake IDs, mostly for illegal immigrants."

"The one who created the Caroline Richards ID?" I asked.

"You've got it," Marisa agreed, "but you're getting ahead of the story, and it's almost like history repeating itself. Like her mother, Serena ran away at a very young age. When she was arrested for prostitution a couple of years later, her mom bailed her out of jail, but that was the last interaction between them. Serena never saw Tricia again. Instead, because of Serena's good looks, she moved to Seattle where she was able to sign on with an escort service, which eventually led to her meeting a guy who still, to this day, is a respected local businessman as well as a mover and shaker in King County politics. He was completely smitten by her and kept her as a side dish for a number of years, paying her rent and buying her groceries."

"Did she happen to mention a name?"

"Eventually. She conveniently left his name out of the story the first time around, but I managed to pry it out of her. He claimed he loved her and said that when his kids were older, he'd divorce his wife and marry Serena. She believed him, of course, but when she got tired of waiting, she decided that if she got pregnant, maybe she could speed up the timeline. That plan backfired big-time."

"Let me guess," I said. "Instead of marrying her, he kicked her out."

"That's right. It's also when she got in touch with one of her friends from the old days, the guy who provided her with a new identity. Then she went on dating sites looking for a possible daddy replacement, because she was afraid she wouldn't be any better at raising a child on her own than her mother had been. Even so, she didn't want to give up the baby and she didn't want the child to grow up without a father. That's the real reason she zeroed in on Jeremy. Apparently he looks a lot like her ex." Marisa paused and let out a long sigh before adding, "The whole thing is completely heartbreaking."

I couldn't have agreed more. Aloud I said, "Suspicions confirmed then. Jeremy isn't the father."

"No, he's not."

"But he's planning on marrying her. Does she even care about him?"

"Care about him?" Marisa said. "Yes. Love him? Probably not. She said she liked being around Kyle and his friends because they were so much closer to her own age. She told me she ended up making a pass at one of them, but Kyle saw what was going on. She was afraid he'd tell his father. Instead, he ran away and went to live with you. She says Jeremy has been so devastated at the idea of losing his family that she's worried he might become suicidal."

The idea of Jeremy possibly committing suicide gave me pause. Suicide is the kind of death that leaves families forever asking themselves where they went wrong and what could they have done to prevent it. But before I had a chance to say anything, Marisa charged on.

"So I made her a deal," she continued. "I told her she's welcome to come live with me. Between my divorce settlement and my inheritance, I'm in pretty good financial shape, but it's no free ride. There are a number of conditions she has to meet. Number one—she has to go home and tell Jeremy the truth about all this because, if she doesn't tell him, I will. Number two—she has to resume her original identity. I told her that her father died years ago. No one is looking for her anymore. That's all over and done with. She needs to go back to being Serena del Veccio. That way she'll have a real identity as opposed to a phony one. She'll be able to get a passport if she wants to, and she might even be able to travel."

"What's number three?" I asked.

"Once Jeremy knows the truth about her and the baby, if they decide they want to stay in a relationship, fine. If they call it quits, then she's welcome to come live with me, but as long as she's living under my roof, she has to go back to school. She has to get her GED and start taking college courses. I told her that I'm prepared to take her in and look after her and the baby until she's ready to be on her own, but if any of those conditions aren't met, we're done."

"It sounds like you made her a hell of a good offer," I said. "What did she say?"

"When she left the hotel in Portland last night, she said she was on her way home to Ashland to tell Jeremy. I told her to let me know what they decide. If she wants to come to Arizona, I'll fly her down. Jeremy gave her a car to use, but she doesn't have one of her own. I'm waiting for a call back, but so far she's maintaining radio silence."

Once Marisa stopped talking, it took a moment or two for me to respond. "Wow," I said finally. "This is all really generous of you."

"It's not generosity," she said. "It's called looking after family."

"But it's also looking after my family," I told her. "You may be giving Jeremy an opportunity to set things right with his wife and kids. So thank you for that."

"You don't need to thank me," Marisa said. "Your efforts on behalf of your family have given me the answers for mine that I've been seeking for years. I'm the one who should be thanking you, and if Serena decides to take herself out of the picture, maybe Jeremy's wife and kids will be able to forgive him."

"I'm not so sure about that," I replied. "Hooking up with Caroline Richards wasn't the first time Jeremy strayed off the marital path, and I'm not sure my daughter is willing to give him another chance."

"Well," Marisa said, "that'll be up to them then, won't it."

"Yes, it will," I agreed. "Let me know what happens."

"I'll be in touch first thing," she said, and that was the end of the phone call.

Right then Mel emerged from the bedroom wearing her plush bathrobe and with her wet hair wrapped in a towel.

"Who was that on the phone?" she asked. "And are you okay? You look a little off—like you've just had a shock of some kind."

"I've had a shock all right," I said, "and you're not going to believe it."

CHAPTER 36

Bellingham, Washington
Sunday, March 8, 2020

AFTER SHARING MARISA'S BOMBSHELL NEWS WITH MEL, MY next responsibility was passing it along to my client, who, in this case, paying customer or not, happened to be my grandson. When Kyle came in from another online jam session with the Rockets, Mel and I delivered the news together.

When we finished, Kyle's first question was, "Should I give Dad a call?"

"I wouldn't if I were you," Mel advised. "For one thing, we don't have any way of knowing if Caroline (Mel and I were still calling Serena Caroline at this point) kept her part of the bargain and told him what's really going on. If she didn't, you'd be stepping in it big-time. And if she did, by now your father knows that it was all an act on her part, and he's been played for a sucker. That would mean he'd be in a world of hurt. But don't forget, there's also a third possibility."

"What's that?" Kyle asked.

"Once everything's out in the open, they may end up deciding to stay together after all."

"Oh," Kyle said, "I never thought about that."

"No matter how this goes," Mel continued, "remember how you felt when all this came to light? You showed up here in Bellingham telling us that you needed some space. If I were in your dad's shoes right now, that's what I'd need, too—space and lots of it."

"Are you going to tell my mom and Kayla?" Kyle asked.

"No," I answered. "I'm telling you because you're my client. They're not. If they're going to hear about any of this, they need to hear it from your father rather than from me or from you."

"Do you think they'll ever get back together?"

I suppose that's the ultimate wish of every child of divorced parents, that somehow their mom and dad will magically put the past behind them and get back together.

"That'll be totally up to them," Mel advised Kyle. "Even with Caroline out of the picture—which may or may not be the case—there's no telling what your parents will do in the long run."

"And I have to live with whatever they decide?"

"Them's the breaks," Mel said. "That's how the world works. When it comes to parents getting divorced, their kids are always along for the ride."

When Mel spoke those words, once again I knew it was the voice of experience speaking, because she had survived her own parents' messy divorce. Kyle had no idea about any of that, but seemingly satisfied with what she'd told him, Kyle's next question was out of left field and totally in keeping with his being a teenager.

"What's for dinner?" he asked.

"Well," Mel replied, "when Gramps and I were working for Special Homicide, whenever we closed a case, we always went out to dinner that night to celebrate, and closing this case is definitely worth celebrating no matter what the fallout is. With the Covid shutdown coming, there's no telling when we'll be able to eat out again, so I vote we head over to Dos Padres in the Village."

Which is what we did. A couple of hours later we were at Fair-haven's favorite Mexican food joint. By then I had pretty well given up hope that Constance Herzog would contact me, but once we were back home and watching that evening's edition of *America's Funniest Videos*, she finally sent a reply.

Sorry it's taken so long to get back to you. Yes, the quilt in question is still available, and I'm sure your wife will love it. If you're still interested in purchasing it, please let me know.

I'm back at work starting tomorrow, and I'm on night shift this week. You could pick it up tomorrow afternoon around 2 P.M. if you like. FYI, I'd prefer your using a credit card rather than paying with cash or by check.

If that's a convenient time, please let me know and I'll send along my address information.

Yours sincerely,
Constance Herzog

"Got her," I said to Mel.
"Got who?" Kyle wanted to know.

He was definitely not the client on the Darius Jackson overdose case, so talking to Kyle about that one was off-limits.

"Constance Herzog, the lady in Seattle Ellen Mitchell was telling us about," I explained.

"The one who makes quilts?" Kyle asked.

I nodded. "Mel spotted one she likes on Constance's website. I'm going down to Seattle tomorrow afternoon to pick it up."

After another brief exchange of emails, the two o'clock appointment was confirmed, and I had the address of Constance's place on Evanston Avenue a few blocks north of Northgate Way. That's when a call came in from Todd Hatcher. Leaving Mel and Kyle to finish watching *America's Funniest Videos* in peace, I went into the other room to take the call.

"Boy, do you know how to pick 'em!" Todd said when I answered.

"What do you mean?"

"You asked me to look into someone named Constance Herzog, and she's a doozy!"

"How so?"

"For starters," he said, "when she was sixteen, she stabbed her father to death while he was in the process of assaulting her mother, Irene."

I was shocked, remembering that Constance Herzog had told Ellen Mitchell that her father hadn't gone to prison because he had gotten off, but that wasn't true. He hadn't been found innocent in a court of law. Instead, he'd been murdered!

"She stabbed him to death?" I asked. "Really?"

"Really," Todd replied. "I'm looking at a digitized copy of an article from the *Butte Mountain Gazette*, which went out of business in 2003. These days a teenager murdering her father in cold blood would be big news all over the country, but this happened back in

1982 before we ended up living in a 24/7 news cycle. I doubt the story had legs anywhere outside the state of Montana. But I have to hand it to her. She must have been operating on pure adrenaline at the time. She stabbed him once in the back with a butcher knife, but she did so with enough force that she severed his aorta. He died at the scene."

That's one way to become a successful serial killer, I thought to myself. *Start early.*

"So here's her basic bio," Todd continued. "She was born Constance Marie Landon in Butte, Montana, on November 18, 1966. Her parents were Frank and Irene Landon."

My heart skipped a beat. "Wait," I said. "I know that name. Hold on a second. Let me check something."

It took a few moments for me to scroll back through my notes and locate my interview with Harriet Bonham. In it she had told me plain as day that William Landon's older brother, Frank, had died of natural causes at the age of five in 1927. Now here he was dying again, due to a stab wound this time, in 1982. So that was how William Landon, the Brinks holdup man, had vanished from view. He had gone into hiding in Butte, Montana, by assuming his dead brother's name, but obviously he hadn't lived happily ever after.

"This explains a lot," I told Todd and gave him some of the background I'd been given by Harriet Bonham.

At that point, Todd continued. "Landon's sixteen-year-old daughter, unnamed in the article on account of her being a juvenile, was found at the scene still holding the bloodied knife. Neighbors had heard the commotion and summoned the authorities. The daughter confessed at the scene and was taken into custody. While Irene, the wife, was transported to a hospital for treatment of serious injuries, which included a concussion and deep bruising around her throat, the daughter was held in a juvenile facility for several days while the local authorities along with the coroner conducted their investigations. Once Landon's death was declared to be justifiable homicide, the daughter was released into her mother's custody."

"Is that when they moved to Seattle?" I asked.

"Property records indicate Irene Landon purchased a home on Evanston Avenue in the Northgate area in 1983. There's no mention of a mortgage, so she must have paid cash."

No doubt with some of her husband's stolen money, I thought. William had probably gone to work in the copper mines because he was worried that if he flashed too much money around, people might connect him to the Brinks robbery. Once he was dead, Irene must finally have felt free to spend some of it.

"How much did she pay?"

"At the time the assessed value was $55,000. It's worth a lot more than that now," Todd added. "The current assessed value is $750,000. Irene Landon died in 1997. Her daughter still lives in the residence."

"What else did you turn up?"

"Constance attended the University of Washington and graduated with a degree in Criminal Justice in 1988. She briefly enrolled in law school but dropped out in 1990 when she married Thomas Herzog. They divorced five years later with no indication of their having had any children."

I couldn't help myself. "What about him?" I asked. "Did the poor guy manage to make it out alive?"

Todd laughed. "According to what I'm finding, he's alive and well and living somewhere in the Phoenix area, a place called Sun City West."

"Glad to hear it," I said.

"Anyway," Todd continued, "Constance was out of the workforce for a number of years while she cared for her ailing mother. After her mother's passing, Constance hired on with Seattle's 911 call center as a dispatcher. Apparently she still works there, now in a supervisory capacity."

And using that position as a hunting ground for her victims, I thought.

"One more thing, Todd, were there any indications of other domestic violence incidents prior to Landon's stabbing?"

"Several," Todd replied. "I've only been hitting the high points here. I've created a folder with all applicable links, which I'm sending now. Anything else I can help you with?"

"Not at the moment," I said, "but you're in the process of helping me bring down a serial killer right now, so I owe you big. Are you ever going to send me a bill?"

"Let me ask you something," Todd said. "Are you billing anyone for your services on this case?"

"Well, no," I admitted. "I guess not."

"Then I'm not billing you, either," he said. "Let's just say we're both earning stars in our crowns."

CHAPTER 37

WHEN I PULLED UP IN FRONT OF CONSTANCE HERZOG'S RESI-
dence on Evanston Avenue North at two P.M. on the dot the next
day, I was surprised. If I had been asked to draw a picture of a
serial killer's home, this would have been it. The whole place was
surrounded by a twelve-foot-high laurel hedge. I suspected that
the massive root system involved probably played havoc with the
home's water and sewer lines, but those weren't my problem.

Almost invisible under a curtain of hanging branches was an
iron gate. A short person might be able to come and go through it
without having to bend over. Someone my size definitely couldn't.

As I stepped out of the Mercedes, I glanced up and down the
street, hoping to catch a glimpse of a derelict van, but no such
vehicle appeared. However, a bright red Prius was parked directly

in front of the house, and I quickly jotted down the license plate number.

One of the concrete fenceposts flanking the gate was equipped with what appeared to be one of those Ring doorbell contraptions. I was about to push the button when a disembodied voice inquired, "Mr. Beaumont?"

Obviously Constance had been keeping track of my arrival on a monitor of some kind.

"Yes."

"Hold on, I'll buzz you in. Please follow the sidewalk around to the left of the house. I'll meet you there. My studio is located out back."

The latch clicked. Bending over almost double, I pushed the gate open and stepped inside. The moment I did so, I understood the presence of that hedge. The yard was a mess—a massive jungle of weeds and tangled blackberry bushes—and the house itself was even worse. Once upon a time, it was probably one of those neat little bungalows that popped up all over after World War II. Now there was nothing neat about it. The wooden siding was pocked by layers of peeling paint. Cracks in the single-pane windows were covered by strips of yellowed packing tape. Rusty broken gutters dangled from their moorings on the edge of an aging roof whose cracked and broken shingles were topped by a collection of blue tarps.

The county assessor might be under the impression that the property was worth three-quarters of a million dollars, but this was clearly the answer to some ambitious developer's teardown dreams. As for the owner? It was obvious that Constance Herzog was someone who didn't give a tinker's damn what any of her neighbors thought about her lack of home and garden upkeep.

As directed, I headed to the left of the sagging front porch, following a cracked concrete walkway that led around to that side of the house. Someone had cut the blackberries back far enough that I could walk past them without snagging my clothing. My hostess, a short, heavyset woman with a headful of curly white hair, waited at the back corner of the dilapidated house.

"Good afternoon, Mr. Beaumont," she said with a welcoming smile. "I hope you didn't have any trouble finding the place."

"Nope," I said, "the GPS got me here without a hitch." I have to say Constance Herzog certainly didn't look like a serial killer. She had the appearance of a sweet little old lady who specialized in baking cookies for neighborhood kids and who went to church every Sunday come rain or come shine. What I noticed right off, however, was the Apple Watch on her left wrist.

The moment I saw her, Constance reminded me of Miss O'Connor, our guidance counselor back at Ballard High. She, too, had been short and stout. One day, she had barged into my homeroom class and grabbed Mark Bowen, our star linebacker, by the scruff of his neck. Even though she had to stand on her tiptoes to do it, she had muscled him out of the room. It turns out, Mark had spit a mouthful of chewing tobacco at a new girl arriving for her first day of school, and Miss O'Connor wasn't having any of it. Much to Mark's surprise, he was benched for the next three games.

This, of course, was a whole different kettle of fish. Constance Herzog's targets weren't simply missing playing in a few high school football games. They were missing the rest of their lives. Keeping that in mind, I put on the most charming face I could muster, one I hoped didn't scream cop.

"And the drive was fine," I added with a smile. "No snow, no ice, no rain. What could be better?"

"Sorry about the yard," she apologized. "It's a bit of a mess, but I'm about to unload the place, and the buyer's not interested in the house or the yard. The lot is big enough that he can put two houses where now there's only one. He's been pushing me to sell, but I'm holding out for a better offer. Come on. The studio is this way."

With that she led me around back and into a building that, long ago, must have been a two-car garage. Stepping inside, out of the desolation of the yard, was like walking into a whole new world. The interior of Constance's so-called studio seemed light and airy, but I was sure something evil was concealed behind all that brightness. Some sixth sense inside me recognized that this was a predator's den. As a sixteen-year-old child, Constance had made the decision to take a human life. That's a bell you can't unring, and although that first homicide may have been declared to be justified, the rest of them hadn't been.

I paused just inside the door to examine the interior. The space was lit with overhead pot lights. A quilting rack with an upscale sewing machine not unlike Ellen Mitchell's sat in the middle of the space directly under what I recognized to be a ceiling-mounted ductless AC and heating unit. A long drapery rod on one wall held several finished quilts, including the Seattle cityscape that was soon to be Mel's.

The other side of the room contained a tiny living area, complete with a kitchenette and a neatly made daybed. Most likely the two doors at the far end of the kitchenette led to both a bathroom facility as well as a closet. The back wall consisted of a series of cabinets and pantrylike doors, some of which probably held sewing supplies, but I couldn't help wondering if that was also where she kept her supply of fentanyl.

"Very nice," I said, after looking around the room. "You live here too?"

She nodded. "My mother didn't believe in doing preventative maintenance. She was also a hoarder. Once she was gone, fixing what was wrong with the house was way more expensive than redoing the garage. So that's what I did.

"Most of the time people prefer having their quilts shipped to them," Constance went on, "but since you were coming to pick this one up, I thought I'd leave it hanging so you could examine it for yourself before taking it home."

"Thanks," I said. "I appreciate the opportunity."

I walked over to the quilt and made a show of examining it on both sides, not that I had the foggiest idea of what I was looking for. After what I hoped passed for an acceptable amount of inspection time, I turned to her and nodded.

"This is perfect," I told her. "My wife is going to love it." Then I reached for my wallet. "Do I pay now or later?" I asked.

"Now is fine," she said. "But once we do that, if you don't mind, I'll need some help getting it into one of my shipping bags. I can do it myself, but it's a lot easier with four hands instead of two."

"Of course," I told her. "Happy to."

She ran my credit card past one of those little cell phone readers. Then I watched as she climbed up on a ladder to retrieve the quilt. After she removed the clips that had held it in place, the quilt came loose, and I caught it as it fell. And there, on the now bare wall the quilt had once covered, was a framed photograph. I knew instantly what I was seeing on the yellowing paper. It wasn't a mug shot at all. Instead, it was a framed, cut-down version of an old-fashioned Wanted poster of William Landon, the kind that would have been distributed in the aftermath of the armored car robbery back in the fifties. I allowed myself a quick glance, but that was all. I didn't want to be caught staring.

If Constance had had any idea I was onto her, I'm sure she would have taken pains to get rid of it long before I arrived, but that's arrogance for you. Serial killers often regard themselves as the smartest people in the room.

I gathered up the quilt, carried it over to the sewing table, and helped fold it. While doing so, we carried on a polite conversation. Constance wanted to know what I did for a living. I told her I was retired from selling real estate. Did my wife still work? No, she's retired, too. I wanted to keep everything understated and bland, without making her think I was there for anything other than my buying the quilt. What I was really doing was reveling in the idea that every time Constance Herzog touched the quilt, she was leaving behind a trail of epithelial skin cells that would soon turn into damning evidence. Once the quilt was loaded into a clear plastic bag, Constance sealed it shut with strips of packing tape. At that point I wanted to dance a jig. There's nothing better than tape—duct or packing—as a source of touch DNA and/or fingerprints.

Twenty minutes after my arrival, I wished my hostess a pleasant afternoon and left the studio, lugging the bag by the bottom so as not to disturb the places I knew for sure she had touched. The quilt weighed six pounds or so, but to my way of thinking I was carrying a ton of pure gold. Having already checked to be sure Gretchen Walther would be on duty, I got in my car and drove straight to the crime lab.

"What's this?" she asked when I placed the bag on the counter in front of her.

"It's a quilt that just cost me a cool two thousand bucks," I told her, "but if you can develop a female DNA profile off this and run it through CODIS, I'm willing to bet you'll get a match to the ones from the Darius Jackson case here in Seattle and from Jake Spaulding's over in Liberty Lake."

Gretchen shot me a scathing look. "Do I need to worry about a chain of evidence here?"

"No, you don't," I told her. "I bought the quilt fair and square and have a receipt signed by the lady herself to prove it. Will that work?"

I handed over the receipt. When she saw the amount, Gretchen's eyes widened. "You paid two thousand bucks for a single quilt?"

"No," I replied. "I paid two thousand bucks to legally obtain Constance Herzog's touch DNA. She threw in the quilt for free, and she's the one who handled all the packing tape. How long do you think this will take?"

"You're in a hurry then." It was a statement, not a question.

"Of course," I replied. "Should I hang around town or go back home to Bellingham?"

"It'll take however long it takes. Lucky for you, I'm something of a hotshot, so go ahead and hang around."

I did exactly that. And where did I go? Not to any of my old stomping grounds because they mostly don't exist anymore. Instead, I headed for the Homicide unit at Seattle PD.

CHAPTER 38

Seattle, Washington
Monday, March 9, 2020

NATURALLY, AS I WAITED FOR THE ELEVATOR AT SEATTLE PD
Headquarters, who should step off but my son, Scott—or Scotty, as he seemed to be known around there. I don't know which of us was more surprised. While working in the Tech unit, he had worn a regular uniform. Now I tried to get accustomed to him being dressed as a full-scale detective, all decked out in a suit and tie.

"I didn't know you were back in town," he said. "What's up?"

"I'm here to see Detective Sechrest."

"About that Liberty Lake case?" he asked. "Sandy told me about that."

"What about you?"

"I'm on my way to touch base with someone over at the courthouse."

He looked like he was in a hurry, but I held up my hand. "Wait," I said. "Before you go, have you heard back from your sister?"

Scott sighed and rolled his eyes. "I did," he responded. "I asked her how things were going."

"Let me guess. She told you everything was fine."

"Yup," he said, "like absolutely nothing out of the ordinary was going on. How did you know that's what she'd say?"

"Because she's my daughter," I told him. "She's more than slightly stubborn, and she hates like hell to admit she might have made a mistake."

"Like marrying Jeremy, for instance?" Scott asked sarcastically.

I didn't reply to that one.

"It annoys the hell out of me when she goes all big sister on me and treats me like I'm still a little kid who can't be trusted with anything important. I'm a grown-up now, for pity's sake—a cop even, not just her baby brother. Where does she get off?"

I didn't blame him for being pissed.

"Don't feel like you're the only one being left out of the loop," I told him. "Mel and I wouldn't know anything about what was happening, either, if Kyle hadn't told us."

That seemed to mollify him. He turned to go but then paused again. "How long will you be here?" he asked.

"Not sure," I answered. "I'm waiting for a call from the crime lab. Why?"

"I won't be at the courthouse long," he said. "If you're still here when I get back, how about we grab some dinner together, just the two of us?"

A chance to have dinner alone with my son? Are you kidding? That was even better than Kyle's asking for us to watch a movie

305

together. No way in hell was I going to pass on that offer no matter what time I headed home to Bellingham.

"Sure thing," I said, doing my best not to sound too enthusiastic. "Why not? I'll hang around upstairs until you get back."

Scott left then while I boarded the elevator and pushed floor number seven. The desk sergeant was on the phone, so I gave him a friendly wave as I passed by and made straight for Detective Sechrest's desk. She was there, but she was on the phone, too, so I took a seat and waited for her to finish.

"Scotty just left," she told me once the call ended.

"I know. We met up by the elevator in the lobby."

"What have you got for me?" she asked.

"A name and what I hope will turn out to be a ton of DNA evidence," I said, "but we'll have to wait and see how long it takes for Gretchen Walther at the crime lab to obtain a profile. In the meantime, I thought we should do some old-fashioned police work."

Obligingly, Sandy pulled out a notebook and a ballpoint pen. "Suspect's name?" she asked.

"Constance Herzog," I answered. "She's a longtime dispatcher at Seattle's 911 call center."

Sandy's pen stopped moving in midair. "A dispatcher from the call center?" she repeated in disbelief. "Are you kidding?"

"Not kidding at all, I'm sorry to say," I replied, "and not an ordinary dispatcher, either. She's a supervisor."

Sandy frowned. "Are you sure about this?"

"Reasonably so," I replied. "She's a quilter in her spare time, and I just forked over two thousand bucks to buy one of her quilts, which I dropped off at the crime lab on my way here."

"Hoping for touch DNA?" Sandy asked.

"Yup."

"Obviously you're willing to put your money where your mouth is on this," Sandy observed wryly. "So what else do you know about her?"

"For starters, at age sixteen she was arrested but never charged with killing her father. She stabbed him in the back with a butcher knife while he was in the process of assaulting her mother. Somehow the knife blade managed to slip past his ribs and hit his heart. He was pronounced dead at the scene. The death was ruled to be justifiable homicide."

"Is that why she chooses victims who are domestic violence offenders—because she's got daddy issues?"

"When we catch her, maybe we can ask her about that," I said. "And then there's the money. Remember those hundred-dollar bills found at all our crime scenes?"

Sandy nodded.

"Years before Constance's father met and married her mother, he lived in Cincinnati, Ohio, under his birth name of William Landon. While there, he was involved as the inside man in a Brinks armored car robbery. That happened in 1956. He left his coconspirators to take the heat, while he grabbed the money and ran. He settled in Butte, Montana, where, using the identity of his deceased older brother, Frank, he went to work in the copper mines. That's where he met and married Constance's mother. It's also where he was killed—in Butte. After his death, Constance and her mother moved to Seattle where they bought a house in the Northgate area without needing a mortgage."

"Purchased with money from the armored car robbery maybe?" Sandy asked.

"That's my guess, but not all of it by any means. Supposedly Landon got away with a cool four hundred thousand dollars."

"Unbelievable," Sandy muttered. "And all this background information came from where?"

"From a woman named Harriet Bonham who lives in Lexington, Kentucky. She had entered her DNA into GEDmatch in hopes of tracking down her mother's favorite cousin, someone she called the 'black sheep of her family.' I work with a volunteer cold case squad called The Last Chance. Our DNA expert ran the profile obtained from the Liberty Lake homicide through GEDmatch and got a hit."

"Do you happen to have Constance's address?" Sandy asked.

"I certainly do."

As I read off the address of the derelict house on Evanston, Sandy ditched her pen and notebook in favor of her computer keyboard.

"No known police activity reported at that address," she said a moment later.

"No surprises there," I said. "She lives alone in an accessory dwelling unit out back. The ADU doubles as her quilting studio. If someone wanted to rob the place, they'd have to use a machete to cut through the jungle of blackberry bushes. But a red Prius was parked out front. Here's the plate number."

More typing followed. "Okay," she said a moment later. "That vehicle is registered to Constance Marie Herzog. Is she married?"

"Used to be. Divorced."

"Let's hope," Sandy muttered. "With her for an ex, the poor guy could be dead, too."

That made me laugh.

"What's so funny?" Sandy asked.

"That was my first thought, too, but he's still alive and well and living somewhere near Phoenix."

"Okay," she said, "here's another vehicle registration. This one is for a 2007 Dodge Caravan."

"That makes sense. Witnesses reported that Darius Jackson was helping an old lady back to her van when he disappeared, so presumably she had one, but I didn't see a van parked anywhere near the residence when I was there earlier this afternoon."

"And when you bought that quilt from her, she had no idea you were actually investigating her?"

"Not as far as I know."

"And there's no chance that she'll run for the hills?"

"I doubt it. She set our meeting for two P.M. so she could make it to work this evening. She said she was working the night shift this week."

Sandy took a breath. "Okay," she said, "let's hope she didn't tumble to the idea that we're onto her. Buying that quilt was a brilliant way of getting a sample of her DNA, but it won't stand up in court. We'll need a search warrant for that."

"Obviously," I agreed.

Sandy stood up then. Thinking our visit was over, I started to get to my feet, too.

"No," she told me, "you sit tight. I'll be right back."

"Where are you going?" I asked.

"To have a chat with my captain," Sandy said. "I'm going to lay out everything you've just told me. If Gretchen gets a profile that matches up with that Liberty Lake case, we sure as hell had better reopen ours!"

While she was gone, I took the opportunity to call Mel and let her know what was up and that I had no idea what time I'd be getting home.

"Fair enough," she said. "Sarah's with me at work, and Kyle and I will be fine without you."

"Wait a minute," I objected. "I thought I was indispensable."

"Don't you wish," she replied. "So are you going to see Scotty and Cherisse while you're there?"

"I ran into him when I came to the department. We're going to grab some dinner together."

"Good," Mel said. "The two of you could use some father/son time."

I was sitting there twiddling my thumbs and thinking how different this squad room was from my old one back in the Public Safety Building when Detective Sechrest reappeared, grinning from ear to ear and giving me a thumbs-up from across the room.

"Got it," she said. "If the crime lab obtains a profile that matches the one from Liberty Lake, our cases will be reopened. A match will give us enough probable cause for the search warrants we need. I'll get those typed up so they'll be ready to go the moment we hear from the crime lab. What all should I ask for?"

"Go for her home, studio, and both vehicles along with all her electronic devices."

"Home and work computers?" Sandy asked.

"By all means," I answered. "And don't forget to include her Apple Watch. That appears on surveillance video from at least two of our crime scenes."

"If the warrants come through tonight, are you interested in doing a search warrant ride-along?"

Not wanting to be labeled a dirty old man, I managed to keep from jumping up and giving Detective Sandra Sechrest a hug around the neck. "Is the pope Catholic?" I replied.

She grinned back at me. "I'll be sure to bring along an extra vest."

Scott turned up then. "I'm seeing smiles all around," he said. "What's up?"

I gave him a brief rundown. "So where shall we eat?" he asked when I finished.

"How about the Metropolitan Grill?" I suggested. "That's nearby and the food should be good."

"Fine with me," Scott said.

THE RESTAURANT WAS only a few downhill blocks away, but without knowing exactly where we'd be heading afterward, Scott and I both drove our own vehicles there and utilized the valet parkers. A lot of the items on the restaurant's menu weren't available that night because the kitchen was trying to use up inventory before the inevitable pandemic axe fell. That was disappointing, but the truth is, we weren't much interested in the food. We were really there to talk, and talk we did.

It turned out that Scott and Cherisse were dealing with their own pandemic issues. Helene Madrigal, Cherisse's mom, lives in France. She's a widow who had come to the States for a short visit with the kids. Now, with all the uncertainty about international travel, Cherisse was reluctant to have her mother return home, knowing that once there, she might not be able to come back.

"We're trying to talk Helene into staying on with us until this Covid thing sorts itself out," Scott told me.

I like Helene, but having your mother-in-law hanging around for an indefinite period of time seemed like a bad call. I didn't say that out loud.

"She's really good with JonJon," Scott continued. "Cherisse really appreciates the help, especially with a baby coming."

That one almost got past me. "Wait a minute," I said. "Did you say 'baby'?"

Scott grinned. "I certainly did. We only found out a couple of weeks ago. We wanted the pregnancy to be a little further along before we told anyone, but that's the real reason we don't want Helene to leave. She might not be able to come help when the baby's born."

"Congrats," I said. "Do you know what it is?"

Scott grinned again. "Who cares? It's a baby, and you know us. We don't plan to find out what it is until we unwrap it."

Dinner was over and our waiter had just presented the bill when my phone rang. The caller was Gretchen Walther.

"You've got a hit!" she said. "The profile from the quilt matches up to that taken from both Jake Spaulding's crime scene and Darius Jackson's. I've already sent the results to Detective Byrd in Liberty Lake. Where else should they go?"

"To Detective Sandra Sechrest at Seattle PD and to Detective Boyce Miller at Kent PD. Tell him it's in regard to the Xavier Jesus Delgado homicide. The last time I saw Detective Sechrest, she was preparing to write up search warrant requests with the hope that we might be able to execute them tonight."

"We?" Scott repeated once the call ended. "What do you mean 'we'?"

"She said I could ride along if I wanted to."

"Then I'll go, too," Scott declared. "Let's get back to the department and figure out a game plan."

As we walked out of the restaurant, the other diners may not have noticed, but I was doing a close approximation of a happy dance. Not very dignified for a guy my age with two fake knees, but who cares? We were about to nail a serial killer!

CHAPTER 39

AS EXPECTED, REOPENING CLOSED CASES INSIDE SEATTLE PD
isn't a simple process. Bureaucracies are like that, and the larger
they are, the slower they move. The Kent case had been reopened,
but it had only circumstantial evidence. That meant that out of our
batch of cases, the only open one and our single avenue forward
was the Jake Spaulding homicide in Liberty Lake.

By the time Scott and I caught up with Detective Sechrest, she
had already swallowed her disappointment and pivoted to another
plan of action. Without questioning Scott's presence, she directed
us to the conference room.

"I've set up a Zoom call for half an hour from now. Detective
Byrd is working on getting a judge to sign off on her search warrant
requests. We may not have ours, but once she faxes hers over, we'll
be able to execute those. But she warned me in advance. The judge

over there has agreed to issue search warrants, but he doesn't feel we have enough to justify an arrest warrant at this time."

That was disappointing, but search warrants were a big improvement over no warrants at all.

Prior to that moment I'd never heard of a Zoom call, but live and learn. It wasn't actually a phone call at all since it was done via computers. Even so, it took the better part of half an hour to get everyone online and talking to one another. Once that finally happened, Detective Sechrest took charge.

"Since Mr. Beaumont here is the only one of us who has actually visited the suspect's residence . . ." she began.

"Call me Beau, please."

"Beau then," she agreed. "With that in mind, I think it's only fair to ask him how he suggests we go about approaching this."

Luckily I had already given some thought to the search process, and I took it from there.

"The house itself looks as though it's abandoned, but that doesn't mean it shouldn't be searched. Constance Herzog may have concealed evidence there. The ADU out back is where she actually resides. It's a quilting studio that doubles as a living space. That needs to be gone over with a fine-tooth comb. There's a framed picture on one wall of the ADU. It's of Constance Herzog's father. Be sure to take that into evidence because his involvement in a long-ago armored car robbery is likely the source of the hundred-dollar bills found at our various crime scenes.

"This afternoon I went to see her and purchased one of her quilts, which is what the crime lab used to develop her DNA profile. To gain access, I had to enter through a gate that comes equipped with an up-to-date security system. If we search her residence first, she'll no doubt be notified of our activity via one of her devices. Rather than give her time to start destroying evidence, I think we should execute the device warrant first, and we should do so at her workplace. Since that location happens to be Seattle's 911 communications center, it's bound to cause quite a stir, but that can't be helped."

"What next then?" Detective Byrd asked. "Her vehicles?"

"Correct," Sandy answered. "According to the Department of Licensing, she has two—a 2018 Prius and a 2007 Dodge Caravan. Here are the plate numbers." She read them off. "This afternoon when Beau went to the residence, the Prius was there but the minivan was not. That must be kept at an off-site location.

"Nine-one-one dispatchers work twelve-hour shifts, with the night shift going on duty at six P.M. According to my sources, she reported to duty on time and is still there. While Beau was at dinner, I took the liberty of having a patrol officer drive by the residence to see if the Prius was still parked outside. It wasn't, so presumably she drove that to work. I currently have uniforms checking all parking facilities close to the West Precinct. When the Prius is located, they have directions to place an AirTag on it. With search warrants only, we won't be able to take her into custody, but if she attempts to flee in that, or if she heads for wherever she keeps the minivan, we'll be able to follow her movements on my phone."

I'm old school. Back in the day the only way to follow a bad guy in a fleeing vehicle was to keep him in view. Using an AirTag wouldn't have occurred to me in a million years, and I gave Sandy Sechrest high marks on that score.

"What about weapons?" Detective Miller asked. During the Zoom call those were the first words out of his mouth.

"That's a big question mark," Sandy answered. "Constance Herzog isn't a registered firearms owner as far as the State of Washington is concerned, and she's never used a handgun in the course of her crimes, but that doesn't mean she doesn't have one. We must consider her to be armed and dangerous."

"What all are we looking for in the searches?" Scott asked, directing his question at me.

"Fentanyl and vape pens for starters," I said. "Some money, of course, specifically old hundred-dollar bills that predate the Treasury Department's inclusion of security strips."

After that a short silence fell over the room. Sandy glanced around. "Any other questions?" she asked.

"I'd be happy to join in on the search warrant team," Detective Miller offered. "Say the word, and I'll be there with bells on."

"Thanks, but no thanks," Sandy answered. "I asked the captain about that. He said that due to insurance liability constraints, only sworn Seattle PD officers can participate."

"Wait a minute," I objected. "I thought you said—"

She cut me off in midstream. "I know what I said. I promised you a ride-along, and I was wrong. The captain was adamant about that. Sorry."

Scott raised his hand. "What about me?" he asked. "Can I come?"

"You're in," she said. "And Ben Weston is planning on joining us, too, but for now Beau is out."

For the next several minutes, I sat there doing a slow burn. If I was hanging around town only to be sidelined at the last minute, what the hell was the point?

The Zoom meeting broke up a few minutes later. I told Scott that since my services weren't needed, I was going to head home. And that was my full intention, too. Sandy caught up with me before I boarded the elevator.

"Where do you think you're going?" she demanded.

"Home to Bellingham," I growled back at her. "Obviously I'm not needed here."

"You're not needed for executing the search warrants," she said, "and as I said earlier, I'm sorry about that. Orders are orders, but I've got another job for you."

"What kind of job?"

With that she held out her phone. It was turned on, and a closer inspection of the device revealed a map of downtown Seattle with a bright red dot sitting smack in the middle of the screen.

"What's that?" I asked.

"That's the AirTag attached to Constance Herzog's Prius," she said.

"Somebody found it?"

"Yes, they did, and he called to let me know so I could turn on the tracker. The Prius is parked on the second level of a parking garage at Ninth and Lenora, and I'm putting you on Prius-sitting duty. Since we don't have an arrest warrant, I'm afraid that once we execute the search at the communications center, she'll try to make a run for it. It'll be your job to keep track of her and let me know where she ends up."

With that, Sandy gave me her phone. That's when I noticed that a Post-it was attached to the back. On it were written the numbers 551980.

"What's this?" I asked.

"My birthday," she answered. "It's also my password. I'm what my dad called a Cinco de Mayo baby. The phone is fully charged, but if it happens to turn itself off, you'll be able to use the password to turn it back on. The moment that Prius moves out of its parking place, I want to know about it."

"If I have your phone, how do I call you?" I asked.

Sandy looked momentarily perplexed. "Call Scotty, then," she said finally. "I'll bet you have his number."

My slow burn vanished.

"Roger that," I said, stepping into the elevator and giving her a mock salute. "Happy searching."

CHAPTER 40

Seattle, Washington
Monday, March 9, 2020

SEATTLE'S 911 CALL CENTER IS LOCATED IN SEATTLE PD'S WEST Precinct. I have no idea why it's called that. It's not visibly "west" of anywhere, except maybe the I-5 corridor, and it's smack-dab in the middle of downtown Seattle at Eighth and Virginia.

Leaving Seattle PD Headquarters, I headed uptown. Denny Regrade Parking at Ninth and Leonora wasn't exactly inside the boundaries of what I consider to be the Regrade proper, but as with the West Precinct mentioned above, I'm not in charge of naming things. The parking facility was a low-rise, four-story affair that advertised an all-day rate of twenty bucks. It seemed to me that if someone was trying to scrape by on minimum wage in downtown Seattle, they wouldn't be able to afford parking, even at the eight-hour rate. It would take too big a chunk out of their paychecks.

J. A. JANCE

Hoping I wouldn't be stuck there for a full eight hours and expecting to pay the shorter hourly rate, I took a ticket and drove up to the second level where I quickly located Constance's parked Prius. Since traffic went both directions inside the garage, I knew that when it came time to exit, she'd have to go back the same way I had come. With that in mind, I parked in a vacant space five or six vehicles beyond the Prius.

I pushed the S 550's plush leather driver's seat back all the way, reclined it as far as it would go, and then pressed the button that heats the seat. After that I settled in for what I expected to be a long winter's wait. It may have been a number of years since I'd last done a stint of solo surveillance, but I'd still had the presence of mind to stop in the lobby and use the facilities before turning in my visitor's badge and leaving Seattle PD.

I remained disappointed that, after doing all the legwork on the Constance Herzog investigation, I had been aced out of participating in the execution of those hard-won search warrants. The payoff for me would have been seeing the shocked expression on Constance's supposedly cherubic features once she realized the jig was up.

But sitting in the parking garage, the worst part for me was not knowing what was going on. Had the warrants come through? Had the warrant team showed up at the call center yet, or were they still mired down in some kind of paperwork jungle at police head-quarters? For the briefest of moments I remembered the old, old days when I would have passed the time by pulling out a package of Marlboros and lighting up. But alas, those days are gone, too, right along with my reliance on McNaughton's.

Forty-six minutes into the wait, my phone rang. I hoped it would be Scott giving me an update. It wasn't. The caller turned out to be Kelly and she was pissed.

320

"What the hell?" she demanded.

"Why?" I asked. "What's going on?"

"Jeremy just called me in tears. He says Caroline told him that the baby isn't his. She's leaving him to go live somewhere in Arizona with her aunt, and he says it's all your fault. I thought I told you to stay out of our business—that I had things handled."

I was in no mood for being read the riot act by my daughter.

"You and Jeremy aren't the only people involved here," I reminded her. "Kyle is, too, and he's the one who asked me to look into the situation. If you think I'm going to apologize for that, you're dead wrong. And if getting to the bottom of it means having Caroline admit that the child she's carrying is someone's other than Jeremy's, wouldn't he be better off finding that out sooner than later, as in before he marries her rather than after?"

Kelly seemed dismayed when I growled back at her like that, but having her come after me because her cheating husband's girlfriend had taken off on him got on my last nerve.

"But Kyle . . ." she began.

"But Kyle nothing," I snapped. "There were red flags showing up in Jeremy and Caroline's household well before Kyle took off. In fact, they're the reason he did take off. That's why he came to Bellingham—to get away from what he considered to be a toxic situation."

"What red flags?" Kelly wanted to know.

"You'll have to ask him," I answered. "He told me about those in confidence. When I accepted his case, I did so as his private investigator, not as his grandfather. As far as I'm concerned, those red flags fall under the heading of client privilege. The same holds true for any information I uncovered about Caroline Richards. If Jeremy has discussed some of her history or issues with you, that's up to him, but telling you about them is not my responsibility. Neither is the fact that the child she's carrying isn't his."

That's the exact moment when I heard a car door slam shut somewhere on that level of the parking garage. I raised the seat far enough to see out and cracked open my window in time to hear a car engine turn over somewhere off to my left. Then a pair of backup lights came on. Moments later, I spotted the red Prius heading down the ramp that led to the exit. At that point I made no effort to hit the starter button. With Sandra Sechrest's AirTag hard at work I wouldn't need to keep Constance's vehicle in sight to follow its every move.

Holding Sandra's phone in my hand, I watched the red dot leave the garage and turn onto Lenora. That's when I heard Kelly say, "Dad, are you even listening to me?"

I wasn't. She had me dead to rights on that score.

"Kelly, I can't talk right now. I'll call you back later so we can finish this conversation, but now I have to go."

"Figures," she said and hung up.

By then the red dot on Sandra's phone was turning right onto Boren. That probably meant that Constance was headed for I-5, but I wouldn't be able to tell which direction until she turned either onto Howell or Olive—Howell to go south or Olive to go north. When she chose door number two, so did I.

Seattle's weather is nothing if not changeable. By the time I merged onto northbound I-5 it was raining hard enough that the spray thrown up by passing vehicles was almost blinding, even with the wipers running at full speed, but since the red dot was moving steadily ahead of me, I knew I was on the right track. I thought maybe Constance would turn off at Northgate. If the search warrant team was still at the call center, she might try to beat them to her house. But no, when she reached the Northgate exit, the red dot went straight past without slowing down, and I did the same.

Where the hell is she going? I wondered. *Is she making a run for the Canadian border?*

North of Seattle, she could have turned off toward the Edmonds Ferry Terminal, but she didn't. Instead, she stayed on I-5 as it passed Mountlake Terrace and curved around to the right, passing under the south end of Lynnwood. When the intersection with 405 also went by without incident, it seemed likely that she was opting for Canada. A quick check of the gas gauge told me I was down to less than a quarter of a tank—not enough to make it that far.

That's when Scotty called. "We're at the house and starting to process the ADU," he said. "Where are you?"

"I'm northbound on I-5 south of Everett," I told him. "If she heads for Canada, I'll have to stop for gas."

"Should we send another chase vehicle?" Scott asked.

"You could," I replied, "but I'm the only one with a tracker, re-member? I've got a quarter of a tank now. If it looks like I need to stop, I'll run up the flag."

And just that fast, on the outskirts of Everett, things began to go south as brake lights lit up all over the roadway ahead of me. Traffic slowed first to a crawl and then to a full stop. Clearly Constance had somehow dodged the backup because the red dot was still moving at a steady pace.

I inched along for another few minutes or so in what was now down to one lane of traffic before I finally reached the exit to State Route 526 where a box truck had zigged when it should have zagged, taking out another vehicle in the process. That one was up against a guardrail on the median while the truck lay on its side with wreckage blocking both the exit lane and the two right lanes of the freeway. The accident had occurred recently enough that I was able to thread my way past it before emergency responders arrived on the scene. At that point the red dot was still northbound on I-5. That's when Scott called again. "Where are you now?" he asked.

"In Everett," I said. "There was a traffic tie-up that slowed me down. Constance's Prius is still moving north. How are things on your end?"

"A search of the ADU turned up nothing," he said. "As for the house itself? The place looks like a hoarder's paradise. We're leaving a team of CSIs to deal with that. If there's any incriminating evidence to be found in addition to the devices, it's probably wherever she left the van, which is where she's most likely going. Sandy, Ben, and I are coming your way, and we're heading out now."

"There's a big accident in Everett," I warned him. "That's going to slow you down."

"Lights and sirens can move mountains," he replied. "Constance is a dangerous woman, and I don't want you coming up against her without backup."

"That makes two of us," I agreed.

Once I regained speed, I accelerated until I was going a good ten miles over the posted limit. Just as I seemed to be closing the distance between me and the red dot, I realized it was veering onto an exit ramp. I've driven this stretch of highway often enough that I know it by heart. I didn't need a road sign or a GPS to tell me it was Exit 206—the one that leads to Smokey Point on the right and the North Lakewood neighborhood on the left.

Smokey Point, Washington, isn't exactly a traveler's paradise, so why was she getting off there? Did she need gas, too? Was she stopping to get something to eat? Or had this been her destination all along? But then, rather than stopping at one of the businesses near the freeway exit, she continued eastbound on 172nd. I was aware that there's a small general aviation airport located a couple of miles north of that east/west thoroughfare. If Constance had a private plane lined up and waiting to take off, she might be able to make a clean getaway, especially since I had zero official standing in this jurisdiction and had no right to detain her.

When she drove past the road that leads to the airport without slowing down, I breathed a sigh of relief. But then, a quarter of a mile or so farther on, the moving dot turned right and came to a stop. Then, after a minute or so, it began moving again, southward this time, but at a much lower speed.

By then, I, too, had taken the Smokey Point exit and was proceeding east on 172nd, once again going well above the posted limit. Right about then I would have welcomed the flashing red lights of a traffic cop. I have a concealed carry permit, so I was armed, but when it comes to facing down a likely serial killer, having accidental backup from a passing patrol officer would be preferable to no backup at all.

I slowed as I approached the turnoff directly to the south of where the red dot had now come to rest. By then, businesses had thinned out. Since my stopping there might have attracted unwanted attention, I motored on past. As I did so, I noticed that the building in question was a YouStoreIt facility surrounded by a stout fence and with a closed gate barring the single lane entrance.

The idea of Constance having a storage unit—especially one located out of town—made total sense. Since the search team had found nothing of evidentiary value at her residence, it was probably all stored here, including, no doubt, the missing van itself.

I called Scott. "Where are you?"

"Lynnwood and heading north."

"Set your GPS for the YouStoreIt on 172nd in Smokey Point," I told him. "That's where she is. Let Sandy know she'll most likely need another search warrant to cover the storage unit. I'm guessing Constance is about to ditch the Prius and head out in the minivan. If she does that, the AirTag will be useless."

"I'll let her know," Scott said. "We'll be there soon. In the meantime, don't do anything stupid."

"Roger that," I replied.

Half a mile farther down the road, I made an illegal U-turn and headed back west. Scotty's advice was well taken, but . . . I may have been excluded from the search warrant team in Seattle, but Smokey Point is a hell of a long way outside Seattle's city limits, and I'd be damned if I was going to miss out on this one, too.

During my second pass of the storage facility, I paid close attention to the fence. Obviously the owner had serious concerns about possible thievery. The eight-foot-tall chain link was topped by a layer of rolled razor wire. The gate itself looked sturdy enough, but that was the facility's sole weak point, and that's what I targeted.

The entrance itself was one lane wide. There were signs posted on the gate, but I was too far away to read them. Since Constance had been able to let herself onto the grounds, I suspected that the entrance was equipped with some kind of keypad arrangement that allowed customers to come and go even when no employees were present.

Months earlier, I had been involved in a missing persons case in Alaska that had suddenly morphed into a homicide. With the perpetrator about to fly the coop in a private aircraft, my driver at the time, a memorable character named Twinkle Winkleman, had come to my rescue by smashing through an airport security gate in her aging International Travelall. Twink stopped the fleeing Cessna in a nose-to-nose standoff out on the tarmac.

Studying the gate, I came face-to-face with my own Twinkle Winkleman moment. If I parked my Mercedes directly parallel to the gate itself, Constance would be trapped. Her only way out of the facility would be blocked. She might be able to open the gate itself, but to get away, she'd have to go through or around my aging but beloved S 550.

Having decided on a strategy, I immediately put it into action. On my next pass, this time with headlights off, I turned into the storage facility's entrance. It took some backing and forthing to maneuver the Mercedes into place parallel with the gate. Once it was in position, I grabbed Sandy's phone and mine, too, and bailed. If Constance decided to try smashing her way through the barrier, I didn't want to be anywhere inside that vehicle.

Out of force of habit, I always carry a bulletproof vest in my trunk. I thought about grabbing it on my way past, but I was afraid the sound of the trunk opening and closing might attract unwanted attention. Besides, as far as I knew, Constance Herzog murdered people with drugs and knives. There had never been any hint of her using firearms.

It had stopped raining, but outside the vehicle it was bitingly cold. That morning when I left home, I hadn't anticipated being out in the weather for any length of time. Knowing I'd be riding in a heated vehicle and going in and out of heated buildings, I'd seen no need to bring along cold-weather gear. I was dressed like detectives should be—in a suit and tie—which was good for camouflage on a dark winter's night, but didn't do a damned thing to keep out the icy chill.

The area around the entrance gate was well lit, so I quickly moved out of the glow of that and huddled behind the welcome barrier of a stout wooden telephone pole half a block away. I had tucked in behind it and was breathing in the odor of creosote when my phone went off. The shrill sound cutting through the stillness startled me. Afraid Constance might have heard the noise, I answered in a hoarse whisper.

"What?"

"According to the GPS, we're fifteen minutes out. How are things?"

"All's quiet on the western front," I assured him. "I'll let you know if that changes."

I thought it best not to mention that my beloved Mercedes had suddenly been transformed into a sacrificial lamb. Call it a sin of omission. I wasn't exactly lying to my son, because things really were quiet at that very moment, but I had no idea how long they would stay that way. Once the call ended, I switched the ringers on both phones to silent and waited for something to happen, and nothing did—for the next interminable five minutes.

But then a light flashed on inside the facility. At the time I had been standing in the dark long enough for my eyes to readjust. I was able to make out that YouStoreIt consisted of one large multistory structure as well as four rows of single-story buildings, all of them separated by narrow strips of pavement.

The glowing headlights appeared to be located between the third and fourth set of low-lying buildings. I caught a slight bit of movement of the lights before they stopped again. With no traffic noise, I heard a car door open and close as clear as a bell. Seconds later another set of headlights joined the first. This time there was a tiny bit of movement on my AirTag monitor. The vehicle edged forward a few feet before turning abruptly to the left and then, only a few yards later, coming to a full stop. At that point the second set of headlights vanished.

That meant Constance was doing exactly what I had expected, ditching the Prius in the storage unit and taking the minivan on the road. In terms of my Mercedes, that wasn't good news since the van was a much larger vehicle and could do far more damage.

Gluing myself to the back of my sturdy phone pole, I waited, holding my breath, to see what would happen next. Moments later a pair of headlights emerged from between the buildings and came snaking toward the gate where the vehicle again came to a stop. The gate was built to swing open into the property. I'm not sure if Constance even realized the Mercedes was there until after the gate opened and the van was back in motion. At that point, she slammed on the brakes and laid on the horn. When nothing happened, she gave the horn another blast.

If I'd been in her situation on the wrong side of that makeshift barrier, I would have eased the van up to the rear of the parked vehicle and started pushing there. With the weight of the engine in the front, the center of gravity on most vehicles is slightly more than halfway between the front and back bumpers, causing the rear end to weigh a bit less than the front. Once I'd eased the parked car aside far enough for me to squeeze past, I'd be able to head for the hills.

That's what I was expecting, but it isn't what I got. Instead, Constance Herzog rolled down the minivan's driver's-side window and fired six shots one after another directly into the passenger side of my once beautiful Mercedes, shattering both the front and back windows in the process. So much for her not having a gun. And so much for my not doing anything stupid since my vest was still in the trunk. Even so, my immediate response was by the book.

329

I held up my phone, punched in Scott's number, and announced those words every cop dreads hearing: "Shots fired."

"What?" he demanded.

"You heard me," I muttered. "Shots fired. Send backup."

It wasn't exactly your standard father/son conversation, and Scott's response wasn't, either. "What's your location?"

"Outside the front entrance of YouStoreIt on the north side of 172nd Street in Smokey Point."

"Contacting the Snohomish County Sheriff's Office," he said and rang off.

I was worried Constance might have heard that exchange, although it seemed likely that the roar of those gunshots would have temporarily disrupted her hearing. All I could hope was that the telephone pole was still providing enough cover to keep her from knowing where I was.

For the better part of a minute, nothing happened. When the door of the minivan opened and she emerged, I could tell from the light inside the vehicle that she was still holding the handgun. That's when I realized that she had used that short interval to reload. She stood there for several seconds, swiveling her head from side to side as if trying to locate the owner of the parked car.

I had no idea how long it would take for reinforcements to arrive on the scene, so trusting my safety to that massive piece of Douglas fir, I attempted to engage her in conversation.

"It's over, Constance," I told her. "Put down your weapon and get on your knees."

She didn't do either. "That's not a cop car," she responded. "Who the hell are you?"

"I'm a private investigator," I said, "hired by the grandmother of one of your homicide victims, but I'm really working for all of them, Constance. And I'm going to take great pleasure in putting you away for the rest of your life."

"Like hell you are," she replied. Then, in what must have been a blind panic, she climbed into the minivan, shoved the gas pedal to the floor, and slammed into the passenger side of my poor Mercedes, striking it directly amidships. Although the vehicle hardly budged, the alarm went off letting anyone within hearing distance know that someone had just whacked the hell out of it. But did Constance quit then? She most certainly did not! Instead, she backed up a few yards, hit the gas, and slammed into it again.

In the meantime, I heard the welcome sound of approaching sirens wailing in the distance, but I stayed put behind my pole. Constance Herzog was still armed and dangerous, and it was a good thing she still had no idea where I was hiding.

Moments later a bevy of cop cars rolled up on the scene. Armed officers, some of them carrying Kevlar shields, began spilling out, but none of them were able to put a stop to the pathetic bleating of my stricken Mercedes. To do that, you need a key, and the key was still in my pocket.

I stayed right where I was, thanking my lucky stars Constance Herzog hadn't shot me. If she had and Scotty had found my vest still in the trunk, there would have been hell to pay. I might not have died from the gunshot wounds, but someone else would have taken me out, and it would have been a footrace to see who got to me first—Scott Beaumont or Melissa Soames.

My money is on the latter.

CHAPTER 41

Bellingham, Washington
Monday to Tuesday, March 9–10, 2020

WHAT HAPPENS AFTER THE ADRENALINE RUSH WEARS OFF IS LIKE stepping out of a hot shower into a cold one. With an immediate threat handled, time slows to a crawl.

I watched from afar as Snohomish County deputies ordered Constance to drop the gun and get on her knees. Then, without further protest from her, they put her in cuffs and walked her back to a waiting patrol car. Suddenly the missing arrest warrant from Liberty Lake no longer mattered. That night she was going to jail on charges of property damage and unlawfully discharging a firearm. By the time she got cut loose on those, she'd be facing something far more serious.

It wasn't until they had her in the back seat of the patrol car that I finally emerged from my hiding place into the glow of flashing red and blue lights surrounding the storage facility's entrance. As soon as Scotty spotted me, he sprinted over to me and grabbed me into a relieved hug.

"Thank God you're all right," he breathed. "When I saw all the bullet holes in your car, I thought you were a goner. What the hell happened?"

"I was afraid she was going to get away," I answered. "I figured blocking the gate with my car would slow her down long enough for you to get here, and it worked, but I sure as hell didn't expect her to come out with all guns blazing and plug it full of holes."

We walked together as far as the Mercedes where I was able to shut down the alarm. We were standing there examining the damage when Sandy Sechrest walked up to us with Ben Weston tagging along.

"Are you all right?" she asked.

"I am, thanks to my best friend over there, that telephone pole," I told her, pointing in that direction. "But if you hadn't gotten here when you did, and if she'd managed to figure out where I was, it wouldn't have ended well."

"When I sent you after her," Sandy said reprovingly, "I thought you'd keep tabs on her. I didn't expect you to go up against her single-handed."

"Believe me," I said, "I didn't, either."

"Well, take a look at this," she added, holding up what looked to be a briefcase. Handing it over to Ben, she clicked open the latch and raised the lid. What I saw staring back at me from inside were stacks of bound one-hundred-dollar bills.

"The money," I breathed.

"The money," Sandy agreed with a nod. "This was in her van.

Liberty Lake is faxing a search warrant for the storage unit here over to the Snohomish County Sheriff's Office. I have a feeling that whatever we didn't find at the residence is going to be here."

Those hundred-dollar bills were exactly the confirmation I'd been waiting for. "We got her, didn't we!"

"We sure as hell did," Sandy replied with a smile.

At that point the YouStoreIt manager showed up and called Sandy aside. A flatbed tow truck arrived next. Once crime-scene photos had been taken, the truck driver hauled my sorry-looking S 550 away to a body shop in Everett. As that was happening, another deputy approached me.

"If you don't mind, sir," he said, "I'll need to take you back to the station for an interview."

"Fine," I told him.

"Wait," Scott said. "How are you going to get home? Once you finish with the interview, either I can take you, or Ben can."

"No," I said. "You guys head back to Seattle and don't worry about me. I'll handle it. If need be, I can always rent a car."

The interview was no big deal, but it took time. Once that finished, it was three o'clock in the morning. Turns out renting cars in Everett, Washington, at that hour of the morning isn't an option, so a young deputy named Donald Davison was dispatched to take me home to Bellingham.

"There was some kind of big deal up in Smokey Point tonight," he commented as we pulled out of the parking lot. "Do you know what went on?"

No one had clued him in, so I did. "Your department, working in conjunction with Seattle PD, took down a serial killer."

"No way! A real serial killer?"

Did I mention Deputy Davison was young?

"Yes," I told him, "a real serial killer. We know of five victims so far but suspect there may be more out there."

"How did they catch him?" Donald asked.

"It's a her," I corrected. "A woman named Constance Herzog who looks for all the world like the sweetest little old lady you'd ever hope to meet, which is one of the reasons she got away with doing what she did for so long. Too bad for her, she made a couple of mistakes along the way, and we were finally able to connect those dots."

Deputy Davison was quiet for a time after that. Finally he asked, "Are you a cop, too?"

"Used to be," I said. "Now I'm a private investigator. My client is the grandmother of one of Constance's victims."

"A private investigator," he repeated. "Really? I always thought all they did was track down cheating spouses in divorce cases."

"I always thought so, too," I told him. "Turns out I was wrong."

Much earlier, I had called Mel to let her know what was going on. She had offered to drive down to get me, but I told her not to bother. That was back when I still believed the car rental option would work. But when Donald pulled into our driveway and let me out at a little past four, the lights in the house were still on. She threw the door open before I ever got as far as the back porch. Not only was Mel there to greet me, so was a tail-wagging Sarah.

"You shouldn't have waited up," I told Mel after we'd exchanged a kiss. "You won't be able to work on three hours' worth of sleep."

"I'm not going to," she replied. "I've called in sick. I'm staying home so you can give me a complete debrief."

"Fine," I said, "but that's going to have to wait until after I have a hot shower and a few hours of sleep."

I WAS DEAD to the world before my head hit the pillow. When I woke up, it was 11:15 A.M. on Tuesday. Mel had abandoned me, but I found Sarah snoozing on her doggie cushion on the floor next to my side of the bed. The two of us ambled into the living room together.

"It's about time," Mel said, greeting me without looking up from her computer. She may have been taking a sick day, but that didn't mean she wasn't working. "How are you feeling?"

"Like I'm not as young as I used to be," I replied, as I headed into the kitchen to press the coffee button. It wasn't until I was in the living room with my coffee that I got a good look at my wife's face and realized something was wrong.

"What's going on?" I asked.

Mel bit her lip, covered her mouth with her hand for a moment, and shook her head before answering. "George Pritchard committed suicide in his cell at the Whatcom County Jail last night," she replied. "He hung himself with a bedsheet. They found him this morning at six. I didn't think to ask that they place him on suicide watch, but I should have."

Sitting down beside her, I already knew that there was no right thing to say in that moment, but I had to say something.

"What happens in the jail isn't your problem."

"But it was my arrest," she argued. "I'm the one who initiated having my department take him into custody."

"Which, considering what he'd done, you were duty bound to do."

"What Pritchard did to his students was abhorrent," Mel continued as though I hadn't said a word. "He was charged with a crime, yes, but he hadn't been convicted. And the crimes he was accused of didn't add up to death penalty cases. What can I possibly say to his wife and kids?"

In all the years we'd been together, I had never seen Mel Soames so completely shattered, but once again I knew that any expression of sympathy from me would only make things worse.

"What you do," I said after a pause, "is put on your big girl panties and your dress uniform. Then you go to the family's home, knock on their door, and tell them how very sorry you are for their loss. Because the truth is, you are. They have lost a husband and father, and not just once, either. They've lost him in the flesh because he's dead, but they've also lost the person they always believed him to be. I'm not sure which of those two losses is worse."

Mel isn't one of those women who turns on the waterworks at the drop of a hat, but this time the floodgates opened. She leaned into my chest and sobbed as though her heart was broken and she'd never be able to stop. I was glad it was just the two of us there at the time and that she was at home instead of at work. If she'd had that kind of breakdown at the department, she never would have lived it down. All of the hard-earned respect she has won over the years would have evaporated.

At last, getting a grip on herself, Mel pulled away, wiped her eyes, and abruptly changed the subject. "I already talked to the insurance adjuster."

"What did he have to say?"

"She," Mel corrected. "She said that repairing the damage on the Mercedes will cost more than the car is worth. They're totaling it and sending over a rental for you to use until you can buy a replacement."

Following her lead, I left the Pritchard family's awful situation alone for the time being and focused on vehicular issues.

"So now I'm in the market for a new car?" I asked.

"Evidently," she said.

"But a new S 550 will cost a fortune," I objected.

"Then find a used one," Mel suggested. "That's what you did the last time."

For the next two hours I told her everything that had happened the day before, including the welcome fact that Scott and Cherisse were expecting a baby. During that time I heard intermittent email alerts coming in on my phone, but I ignored them. What Mel needed to do right then was talk about something that wasn't George Pritchard. And you'd better believe that when I told the story, I somehow failed to mention that I hadn't been wearing my bulletproof vest when all hell had broken loose.

Finally at three o'clock in the afternoon, Mel stood up. "All right," she said. "I think I'm ready. I'm going to go take a shower, get dressed, and go pay my respects to Alana Pritchard."

"Would you like me to come along?"

"Please," she said.

"Then I'd better get dressed, too."

While doing so, I couldn't help thinking about the similarity between what Caroline Richards had done to Kyle's friend Gabe and what George Pritchard had done to an unknown number of female victims. Both of them had committed sexual assaults. As far as I knew, Caroline had been a first-time offender while Pritchard was a habitual one. She was getting a second chance. Pritchard was dead.

WE WENT IN Mel's Interceptor. I rode shotgun, and Mel drove. At the Pritchard residence I sat in the living room with her and with

Pritchard's widow and sons as Mel said her piece. I wish some of the Doubting Thomas members of Mel's department had seen how she conducted herself that afternoon. The way she handled Alana Pritchard and her two shell-shocked kids was nothing short of masterful.

Alana and her boys were victims of her husband's wrongdoing every bit as much as the high school girls he had sexually assaulted, but that didn't mean they weren't shattered by his unexpected death. By the time we left the house forty-five minutes after our arrival, Alana had agreed that she would welcome a visit from one of Bellingham PD's victim advocates.

"Good work," I told Mel as we headed back to the house. "I think she really appreciated your visit."

"Thank you," Mel said. "And thank you for encouraging me to do it. I don't think I would have managed on my own."

"Yes, you would have," I assured her. "You're the one person I know who always does the right thing."

When we got back to the house, Kyle was home from what was likely his last day of in-person high school education. To my dismay, he looked almost as upset as Mel had been earlier.

"What's wrong?" I asked.

"It's my dad," he said. "I just got off the phone with him. He was bawling like a baby. He told me that Caroline has left him, and he begged me to come home so he won't be there all alone. I'm worried about him, Gramps. I've never heard him like that. He sounded desperate."

Gramps wasn't the one who delivered the comfort that time around. Mel did.

"Of course he's desperate," she said. "He's been played for a fool and had his heart broken to boot, but it's not your job to fix him,

Kyle. If you would rather go home than stay here, that's up to you. But even though Caroline is gone, don't assume that somehow you'll be able to wave a magic wand and get your folks back together. I'm pretty sure there were serious issues in their marriage long before Caroline showed up on the scene, and those aren't going to go away, either, not without some serious work and soul-searching on both their parts."

"What did you tell him?" I asked.

"I told him I'd think it over."

"You do that," I said, "but remember, this is a situation where you need to put yourself first. Don't let your father's mistakes, or your mother's, either, for that matter, impact your own future. They're supposed to be the grown-ups here, but they're not exactly acting like it."

"And you really don't mind either way?"

Mel and I both shook our heads. "Either way," I said.

At that moment I would have bet money that he'd end up knuckling under to his father, but somehow I managed to stifle saying anything more. My lobbying him in one direction was no more fair than his father's pulling him in the other.

All I could do was shut my mouth, and hope things would turn out all right. Obviously being a parent isn't easy, but sometimes being a grandparent isn't exactly a barrel of laughs, either.

WHEN I FINALLY had a chance to take a look at my email, the one from Scott was the first one I opened.

Hey, Dad, what a night! That storage unit was a treasure trove. We found an ice chest that functioned as Constance's killer toolbox—bags of fentanyl tablets, a mortar and pestle, needles, a box of latex gloves, and all kinds of vaping equipment.

We also found an envelope full of mug shots, twenty-three in all. Five of them we already know—Darius Jackson, Jake Spaulding, Xavier Delgado, Loren Gregson, and Raymond Loper. The others are from jurisdictions all over the Pacific Northwest. The ones Sandy has checked so far are all dead of fentanyl overdoses. As for the framed photo of her father? It was part of his old FBI Wanted poster.

For right now Seattle PD isn't releasing any information about the arrest. It's a CYA maneuver on their part, because too many of those other cases were originally ours. We've been asked not to notify any of the victims' family members until after the brass are ready to go public.

The part about the brass didn't surprise me in the least, but thinking about a total of twenty-three victims was mind-blowing. Constance Herzog wasn't just a serial killer, she was a serial killer on steroids. Operating from her brightly lit den of iniquity, she had escaped detection for years by hiding behind the facade of a harmless little old lady and garnering sympathy by pretending to be homeless. Her father's stolen hundred-dollar bills had been her calling cards, and her trophies were the collection of mug shots found in her van.

I thought about how Yolanda Aguirre's painstakingly conducted interviews had helped reveal the pattern and modus operandi that connected all the cases. But now there were eighteen additional families—grieving families—who may or may not have been interviewed and whose lost loved ones had never had a chance at justice being served. Maybe now it would be.

Finally, I went back to reading.

I wish you could have seen Constance's face when we walked
into the call center armed with our search warrants. She was
dumbfounded. She didn't have a clue that anyone was onto
her, but once she realized we didn't have an arrest warrant,
she took off. Thank God for you and that AirTag.

At this point she's still in the Snohomish County Jail, but
Liberty Lake's arrest warrant has come through. As soon as
she's released from Everett, she'll be transferred directly to
the Spokane County Jail to face charges in the death of Jake
Spaulding.

Ballistics have matched the gun she used last night to two
other drug-related homicides that took place years ago when
a war broke out between two competing networks of dealers.
The thinking is that Constance wasn't directly involved in any
of those, but bought the weapon on the street later for her
own protection. Why she went nuts and shot the hell out of
your car is anybody's guess. I think she had gotten away with
murder for so long that the thought of being caught sent her
into panic mode.

As for the money? It adds up to 86k. If we hadn't caught
her when we did, she would have been able to hide out and live
on that for a very long time.

In other words, good job, Dad! No, make that GREAT job!
But what's the word on your car?

Scotty

Of all the people in the conference room at the time, my son
was the only one who had understood how pissed I was at being

excluded from the search warrant team. And now he had done something about it by filling me in on the details. I hoped he hadn't sent the message on a work computer, because he could easily be fired for discussing an ongoing investigation with someone outside the department. But I wasn't going to breathe a word about it, and I knew he wouldn't, either. My response was suitably brief.

> Thanks for keeping me in the loop. As for the car? It's totaled, and I'll be shopping for a new one.
>
> Dad

For the rest of the day things were pretty quiet around our place. When it was time for dinner, Mel wasn't hungry. I settled for a peanut butter and jelly sandwich. Kyle rummaged around in the fridge and found the tail end of his package of bologna, so no one starved to death. Everybody went to bed early, but when I fell asleep, Mel was still tossing and turning.

CHAPTER 42

Bellingham, Washington
Wednesday to Thursday, March 11–12, 2020

I DON'T KNOW WHAT LIFE WAS LIKE IN ANYONE ELSE'S HOUSEHOLD on the first morning of "distance learning" in March of 2020. I can tell you it was hell at our place, and very little learning occurred.

A gloomy Mel, still agonizing over George Pritchard's suicide, left for work early, leaving Kyle and me to duke it out with something that was, to all intents and purposes, totally unworkable. The portal he was supposed to use went through endless cycles of downloading without ever letting us enter. Hours into the process we finally gained entry, but then in one class the video didn't work, and in another the sound didn't. At the end of the day, he had managed to be marked present in only a single class, but missing the others wasn't for lack of trying on our part.

When the official end of the school day finally put us out of our misery, Kyle went out to the garage to work off some of his frustration by beating the hell out of his drums. As for me? I took Sarah for a walk.

I had been so busy with the two cases that I had been neglecting Sarah. The good thing about Irish wolfhounds is that apparently they don't hold grudges. She was delighted when I took down the leash and asked if she wanted to go out.

As we strolled along—I wasn't up to doing a brisk pace—I couldn't help but think about Kyle. We had spent the day in the trenches together waging battle with the school district's unforgiving collection of technological screwups. I had enjoyed his wry humor every time our efforts were dealt another setback, but it wasn't until Sarah and I were out walking that I realized how much I liked the kid.

Ashland is far enough away that, although we'd been together for holidays and special occasions, I had never really known Kyle. Now I did, and I was seeing him not as a grandchild, but as a person, one nearing adulthood. He was likable and responsible. When faced with a family problem, he'd had brains enough to ask for help instead of simply grinning and bearing it.

But what bothered me that afternoon was the likelihood that Mel and I were about to lose him. As we walked along, I explained the situation to Sarah, not that she understood a word of it, but saying it out loud seemed to help.

"We've all enjoyed having Kyle around," I told her, "but he's going to be leaving us soon so he can go help his dad. We'll all miss him when he's gone, but he has to do what he has to do."

Because that's exactly who he is, I told myself, *someone who helps. He came here to help his friend Gabe, so why wouldn't he go back to Ashland to help his father?*

That's when Hank Mitchell and Mr. Bean showed up. Hank wanted to know how school had gone that day. I told him it was a

345

mess. I also thanked him again for dinner, but I didn't mention how having dinner with them had been the tipping point in bringing down a serial killer. I'd tell both him and Ellen about that eventually, but not until the brass at Seattle PD gave the go-ahead.

As we got close enough to our garage to hear Kyle banging away, Hank mentioned that Kyle had asked him to stop by on Saturday for another jam session, and that he was really looking forward to it.

Did I tell Hank Mitchell that Kyle would most likely be heading back to Ashland in the near future? No, I did not. I was already feeling blue at the prospect. In my opinion, misery does not like company.

THE SECOND DAY of distance learning was marginally better. Kyle managed to be marked present in three of his classes that day, and all the teachers involved felt obliged to assign homework. Since he was already working from home, that seemed more than slightly redundant, but I managed to keep my mouth shut on that topic.

Halfway through the day, Marisa Young called me from Fountain Hills. "Serena's here," she told me. "She flew in yesterday afternoon and brought her teddy bear with her. When I gave it to her all those years ago, I never dreamed that one day it would help bring her back to me. But after she got here, we had a come-to-Jesus conversation, and I laid down the law. Since her driver's license was fraudulently obtained, she's going to have to go through driver's training and have a valid license before I'll allow her to drive a car."

"I'll bet that was a tough pill to swallow," I put in.

"Yes, it was, but at this point, it's my way or the highway. To live with me, she has to be one hundred percent real. She spent today working with people in New Jersey to obtain her original birth certificate. No birth certificate means no driver's license, and that means no car."

Wow. Marisa Young may not have had any kids of her own, but she obviously had a solid handle on how to be a parent. There was part of me that wondered if the leopard could really change her spots. On the other hand, people do change—I'm a walking/talking example of that. But the thing is, the person involved has to want to change. Maybe Marisa's judicious use of carrots and sticks could make that happen.

"And then there's the baby," Marisa continued.

"What about the baby?"

"It turns out the father is Mr. Got Bucks. He owns several car dealerships in the Seattle area. He may not have wanted this baby, but that doesn't mean she isn't his."

"It's a girl?"

"Definitely a girl," Marisa answered. "I'm having my attorney draft a letter informing him that, pending a paternity test, he will be expected to pay child support. If he doesn't do so voluntarily, we're fully prepared to take him to court."

This all sounded good, but was Marisa tough enough to make it work in the long run?

"And what does . . . ?" Before I could finish my question, I paused long enough to get the name right. "And what does Serena del Veccio think of all this?"

"I think she's grateful," Marisa said. "I think she's tired of being Caroline Richards or whoever else she's been over the years. I think she's tired of lying. We've been in touch with someone inside the US Marshals Service. In their opinion, there's no longer any reason for her to remain in hiding. In fact, I think it's likely that once both Sal and his father were murdered, Serena and Tricia were no longer in danger. Too bad no one from the Marshals Service ever got around to letting them know."

"So how's Jeremy doing?" Marisa asked a moment later.

"Not well, apparently," I replied. "I think he's still somewhat bewildered. He's also alone and lonely and begging Kyle to come back home."

"Is he going to?" she asked.

"Beats me," I answered. "The jury's still out on that, but probably."

"Will you be sad to see him go?"

"Very."

After the call ended, I sat there for a while thinking about two different teddy bears—Serena del Veccio's and Benjamin Harrison Weston's. When Seattle's Teddy Bear Patrol first started and we were required to carry teddy bears in our patrol vehicles, I thought it was a goofy idea—right up until I needed one on the day Ben Weston's family was killed. Now, years later and as a result of the relationship that original teddy bear had started between a wiseass cop and a traumatized little boy, a serial killer was finally being brought to justice.

Who'd a thunk it?

CHAPTER 43

WHEN FRIDAY CAME AROUND THAT WEEK, MEL WAS BACK TO being her old self. That's what you have to do when you're a cop. You have to set your personal opinions aside and do your job. She called shortly after the nonexistent final bell sounded on distance learning for the week. Kyle was relieved, and so was I.

"Hey," she said. "Our favorite Thai place sent me an email saying they're switching over to takeout from now on. Do you want me to bring home dinner?"

I held the phone away from my face and relayed her question to Kyle.

"Absolutely!" he replied.

It was over dinner that the conversation finally turned to his father. I don't know if Kyle was aware of it, but as far as Mel and I were concerned, his looming departure had been the elephant in the room all week long.

"I've made up my mind about Dad," he said.

At that point the dinner table went completely silent.

"And?" Mel was the one who asked the question. For some reason, I couldn't quite make my voice work.

"It's not my fault that he can't keep his pants zipped," Kyle said. "Kayla and I talked it over. She said Mom's never been happier. I think she always knew Dad was fooling around on her, but she tried to hide it from everybody, including us. So Mom's not going back to Dad, and I'm not, either. If it's okay with you, that is."

"Fine with me," I managed, trying to play it cool.

"With me, too," Mel said.

At that point Kyle Cartwright favored both of us with one of his sly grins. "It's settled then," he said. "You're stuck with me for the duration, distance learning and all."

CHAPTER 44

Bellingham, Washington
Sunday to Monday, March 15–16, 2020

THERE'S A REASON MEDIA CONSULTANTS ADVISE POLITICAL
clients to break difficult stories on the weekends. Weekends are
regarded as slow news days, so that's when second- and third-string
newscasters and reporters are on duty. On Sundays in particular,
people are often caught up in family activities—going to church,
watching or participating in sports, and going on outings.

The only one of those that applied that Sunday in March of 2020
was the part about the second- and third-string newsies. People
everywhere else were on lockdown. Church services were canceled.
Bars and restaurants were closed. Everything fun and entertaining
had been blasted into pandemic oblivion for the foreseeable future.

So when Seattle Police Chief Nathan Palmer announced a live
news conference for noon on Sunday, hardly anyone showed up,

and that was the whole idea. By Monday the Constance Herzog story would literally be yesterday's news.

Since it appeared that the majority of her victims were from the Seattle area, Seattle PD and the King County Medical Examiner's Office were both about to take big hits, along with, unfortunately, blameless 911 operators everywhere.

Bellingham doesn't have its own TV stations. The news we see here is what's broadcast from Seattle. The guy reporting live on our TV screen that morning looked like he was barely out of junior high, but he did his best to brazen it out.

According to Chief Palmer, three of his homicide detectives, Sandra Sechrest, Benjamin Weston, and Scott Beaumont, had been given reason to believe that some overdose deaths that had been written off as either accidents or suicides were in fact unsolved homicides. Their investigation had led them to a 911 supervisor who had used her position to target victims she felt were habitual domestic violence offenders who had gone unpunished.

Through DNA evidence and recovered vape gun serial numbers, the female perpetrator had also been linked to a homicide that had occurred in Liberty Lake, Washington, and she was now in the Spokane County Jail where she was being held while awaiting trial on charges of second-degree homicide. She had been taken down during a shoot-out at a public storage facility in Smokey Point where she had gone in an attempt to flee the jurisdiction.

Ho hum! The way Chief Palmer related the story, it seemed boring as hell and hardly important enough to merit a live news conference. That was clearly our peewee league reporter's impression, too. He seemed at a loss as to what all the fuss was about.

Palmer didn't go into detail, nor did he pass along any names or numbers. He also didn't mention how reluctant his department had been to reopen any of their own cases. He didn't mention how Yolanda Aguirre's work with grieving family members had brought the cases together. He didn't mention Elena Moreno, her hardworking intern, who had gone through all those interviews carefully redacting the names. The only time he uttered the word *Beaumont* was in regard to Scotty, and that was fine with me. At this point in my life, I'm more than happy to fade into the background.

THE FOLLOWING MONDAY, driving the rented Cadillac Escalade that an insurance company representative had brought to the house on Saturday, I headed to Seattle to make the rounds and speak to the affected families. That's what homicide detectives do. They can't talk about cases while they're active, but once they're closed—once the investigation is over and before the prosecutors take charge—it's time to talk to the grieving wives and mothers and sisters and grandmothers, too.

Detective Sechrest went with me as the official representative of Seattle PD, but for most of the families, I was the individual they knew. We were there to provide closure, and maybe we did. Once Xavier Delgado's mother understood he hadn't committed suicide, maybe his sons would have their grandmother back. Our investigation had given Greta Halliday back her father's Elks ring and his iconic Chris-Craft in a bottle. As for Leann Loper? Although both her parents were still dead, only one of them had committed suicide. Would that lessen her burden? I hoped so.

I believe there's a Bible verse that says something about the first being last, and that was certainly the case here. Matilda Jackson had been the first of the family members I had spoken to, and she was the last one Sandy Sechrest and I visited that day. But Sandy was also the one person from Seattle PD who had encouraged Matilda to obtain Darius's autopsy report, which, ultimately, had ended up bringing me into the picture.

I had called ahead, letting Matilda and her sister, Margaret, know we were on our way. When we pulled up in front of the sisters' residence in Renton, it was less than a month after my initial visit, but in the interim the whole world had changed. Sandy and I were wearing surgical masks, and I was terrified that, although neither of us were exhibiting any kind of adverse symptoms, we might somehow be bringing a trace of that deadly killer called Covid into a home occupied by two elderly women, one of whom was already in ill health.

When we entered the bungalow's living room, all was mostly as before with Matilda seated in her recliner. The only difference was that her wheelchair had been banished to another room in order to make space for an additional guest.

"You got her!" Matilda said, before I had a chance to open my mouth.

"Who told you?"

"As soon as I saw that highfalutin police chief on TV yesterday, I told Margaret here, 'He's not going to say it out loud, but I know he's talking about my Darius's killer.' The next thing I had her do was dial up Benny Weston so I could ask him straight out. He's the one who said you did it."

"We all did it," I told her. "There were lots of people involved, including this one here. I know you spoke to her on the phone, but now I'd like to introduce you in person. This is Detective Sandra Sechrest."

"You're the one who said I should ask for a copy of the autopsy," Matilda said, beaming at Sandy. "Thank you for that."

Then Matilda turned back to me. "Mr. Police Chief didn't say, but how many people did that woman kill?"

Sandy was the one who answered. "We're still verifying the exact number, but it's probably more than twenty."

"How did she do it?"

"As a 911 operator she was able to access databases intended for law enforcement use only. That's how she located her targets. And she got away with it by fooling her victims into believing she was homeless."

"And she murdered people like Darius who offered to help her?"

"We believe so."

Matilda Jackson thought about that. "Well," she said finally, "she sounds like evil itself, but I hope someday I'll be able to forgive her. That's what you're supposed to do you know—forgive those who trespass against you. There'll be a trial, I suppose?"

"I'm sure," I replied, "but with all this pandemic business, I don't know how long it'll take for that to happen."

"I'm so old I may not live long enough to see it, but you've given me some peace of mind, Mr. Beaumont. Bless you for that. And bless you for that teddy bear, too."

Sandy Sechrest shot me a sidelong glance, but all I said to Matilda Jackson was a very sincere, two-word thank-you.

Sandy waited until we were back in the Escalade and I had fired up the engine before she asked the inevitable question. "What teddy bear?"

"That," I told her, "is a very long story."

ABOUT THE AUTHOR

J. A. JANCE is the *New York Times* bestselling author of more than sixty books. Born in South Dakota and raised in Bisbee, Arizona, she lives in the Seattle area with her husband and their two long-haired dachshunds, Mary and Jojo.